Cathi Unsworth is a ▨▨▨▨▨▨▨▨▨▨▨ lives and works in London. She ▨▨▨▨▨▨▨▨▨▨ry music weekly *Sounds* at the a▨▨▨▨▨▨▨▨▨▨ a writer and editor for many oth▨▨▨▨▨▨▨▨▨es since, including *Bizarre, Melody Maker, Mojo, Uncut, Volume* and *Deadline*.

Her first novel, *The Not Knowing*, was published by Serpent's Tail in 2005, followed the next year with the short story compendium *London Noir*, which she edited, and in 2007 with the punk noir novel *The Singer*. She has written and hosted a crime fiction radio show for Resonance FM, contributes features and reviews to the *Guardian, 3AM, Dazed & Confused* and performs regularly with the Tight Lip Group and the Sohemian Society. *Bad Penny Blues* is her third novel.

More at www.cathiunsworth.co.uk

Praise for *The Singer*

'A cracking page-turner that feels authentic, authoritative and evocative. And it's beautifully written. This is a bloody good book' Val McDermid

'Brilliantly paced, plotted and stylish crime novel from the hugely talented and highly original Cathi Unsworth' *Daily Mirror*

'If Cathi Unsworth's searing debut novel, *The Not Knowing*, was the perfect sound check, *The Singer* is the incredible show that everyone should be talking about…Gritty, raw with an authenticity that proves the author knows her stuff. Quite simply, Cathi Unsworth rocks' *Daily Record*

'[An] excellent slice of muso-noir…gripping' *Metro*

'This is not just essential reading, it's also the ultimate punk noir novel' *Bizarre*

The Not Knowing

'Those of us who mourn the loss of Derek Raymond and believe we will never see his like again have huge reason to celebrate...He is reincarnated in Cathi Unsworth...all the noir, the Black Novels we delighted in are restored to us in the guise of C. Unsworth...she has not only taken on his mantle but reinforced it with a freshness and vitality that makes you gasp in sheer amazement...I haven't been as excited by a new writer since I first read Ellroy or stumbled across the very first James Sallis...She is that good and better, that dark' Ken Bruen

'Brilliantly executed with haunting religious imagery, interesting minor characters, great rock 'n' roll references and a spectacular ending. *The Not Knowing* is a cool and clever debut. Sleep on it at your peril' *Diva*

'Unsworth worked for music magazine *Melody Maker* as well as *Bizarre*, and her knowledge and love of music, fashion and London pours out of the pages...a lovingly observed, well-rounded and well-crafted debut novel' *Barcelona Review*

'Hugely entertaining debut from a future star of gritty urban crime literature' *Mirror*

'Unsworth's debut ushers the reader into an early '90s twilight world of Ladbroke Grove bedsits, dingy magazine offices and seedy Camden pubs – a louche, lovingly evoked milieu...Unsworth has concocted a powerful story' *Time Out*

'Cathi Unsworth is the new cool...Unsworth ups the tempo by way of a dark, pacey plot and perceptively witty metaphors, making this near perfect debut very hip indeed' *Buzz*

'*The Not Knowing* is Unsworth's debut novel but it reads like the work of a seasoned veteran...mystery lovers everywhere, take note of Cathi Unsworth's name. I have a feeling she's going to be around for quite a long time' *www.bookslut.com*

BAD PENNY BLUES

Cathi Unsworth

CANCELLED

A complete catalogue record for this book can be
obtained from the British Library on request

The right of Cathi Unsworth to be identified as the author
of this work has been asserted by her in accordance with
the Copyright, Designs and Patents Act 1988

First published in 2009 by Serpent's Tail,
an imprint of Profile Books Ltd
3A Exmouth House
Pine Street
London EC1R 0JH

website: www.serpentstail.com

ISBN 978 1 84668678 8

Designed and typeset by folio at Neuadd Bwll, Llanwrtyd Wells

Printed and bound in Great Britain by Bookmarque Ltd,
Croydon, Surrey

10 9 8 7 6 5 4 3 2 1

For Mum and Dad

Consider the thought of re-incarnation as the ability to dissect the secret history inherent in our genetic coding and the multiple atrocities which have polluted our bloodlines.

Contemplate suffering as an acute oversensitivity to geography and the army of ghosts which litter the landscape, who have given their lives leeched of blood to the whimsy of brutarians who denigrate life by celebrating death.

Imagine that every stone, stairwell and street has absorbed the life, death and fear of everyone and everything that has come before you and your job is to give voice to this nightmare.

This is my murder.

Lydia Lunch, *This is My Murder*

We've kept an almost open mind
and things have wandered in
we've tolerated much
and gone deaf with the din
we've put up with the mess
the stains, the smell, the crowd
but now this thing that once was us
drags chains and wears a shroud

Shock Headed Peters, *Hate on Sight*

Prologue

I step out of the car and on to the kerb, the clack of steel-tipped stilettos on pavement. The sound sends a crackle into the still air of 1.10 a.m., like a radio has suddenly been turned on between stations; a hiss of interference and the distant sound of garbled voices speaking in foreign tongues. I look back into the window of the black Morris Ten. He is leaning across the seat, an earnest smile on a battered face, one front tooth chipped, dark hair greased back off a furrowed forehead.

Christ, he's eager, I think. And then a dark wave sweeps through me: resignation, boredom, something close to madness tapping on the corner of my skull. I know what it is, it's the feeling of being trapped. I want to get out of whatever it is I've got myself into but I don't know how, I'm caught up in a current that's taking me down.

He's saying something, but I can't make out what it is, the sound of the radio is coming in louder, a sudden burst of an orchestra tuning up.

But I hear myself talking back to him clearly, saying: 'Half-past three.'

This seems to please him. His grin deepens along with the lines on his forehead and he says something else, pointing at the side of the road. It's lost in the hiss of static, a sound like a toilet being flushed. Now he's leaning back into his seat, putting his hand on the gearstick, pulling away up the avenue, red tail lights under the trees, under the trees where nobody sees...

A sudden eerie note rises up around me, like a church organ maybe, but distorted, echoing around the trees and the empty road. I shiver involuntarily. It has been hot, stifling all day, and I've got on my new summer dress, but suddenly I feel a chill wind blowing up from nowhere. The dress that Baby bought me, I think, and the thinking of that name prickles out the aches in my body. The back of my neck and my right arm feel heavy, pain beating a dull tattoo through my blood like a finger running down a plastic comb. I become aware of a cold wetness in my knickers, a fresher pain down there too, a reminder of where the man in the car has just been, where too many other people have already been before. These thoughts run into my mind unbidden and I don't want them, memories swirl that need to be blotted out, lest those fingers start drumming louder on the side of my skull, the sparks of madness start to flare.

I'm standing on the corner of this long, wide avenue next to a tube station that's all shut up for the night. For some reason I can't read the lettering over the door, can only make out an Art Nouveau swirl of letters, but I feel like I know this place, I have been here at this time of night many times before. The station stares back at me through blank, empty windows. Squat and silent, it sits back on the pavement, detached, like whatever else is going on round here is surely none of its business.

I stroll past it, hearing the clack of my feet and the strange music, that distorted organ motif and the crackles of radiowaves, a sound like bubbles being blown under water. I turn around the corner, drawn towards it, and realise the music is coming from the building diagonally across the road from me. A high tower like a castle's keep made out of red brick, little tiny windows all the way up it but just one light on, one yellow light, right at the top. The spook symphony is coming from the window, getting louder and louder.

I suddenly think of a lighthouse, sweeping its beam across a dark and choppy sea. And the vision fills me with fear, like I have suddenly seen my death coming towards me, the light across the water, luring me to the rocks...

I turn away, catching my breath, clutching my handbag tighter. I realise that whatever plans I have made for this night are all going to fall through, that the boy I am expecting to meet here is not going to come. He was just using me like everyone else, I think, laughing at me, at how stupid I am, how easy.

I hurry away from the tower, back towards the tube and on to the avenue. I want to block the music from my head but it swims around me, laps at the corners of my brain and I can't think straight. The man in the Morris Ten, was he supposed to be coming back for me or was I just spinning him a line? I don't remember but I can't wait here, I don't want to be in this part of town, with another me waiting under every tree, yet I can't go home either, bad things lurk there too, more beatings, more fuckings, more petty humiliations. All the things I wanted flash through my mind: to be a mother, a wife, with a spotless kitchen in a nice house, an embroidery in a frame hanging over the fire saying Home Sweet Home, *a memory of my childhood and my sister Pat. All the things I will never be and never have and everything I tried not to think about, all coming down fast to the refrain of a ghostly keyboard requiem.*

Then suddenly, all the sounds disappear. Headlights are coming towards me up the avenue, a long dark car gliding slowly along, crawling beneath the trees, as if in slow motion. This is it, I realise, and somehow the knowledge sets me free of my anguished thoughts, fills me instead with the numbness of acceptance. This is the beam from the lighthouse, the lights across the water calling me home. I pat my hair, which is short and neat and recently cut, in the style of an actress I had admired. I smooth down the front of my blue-and-white summer dress. This is how I look on my last night on earth and

I step forwards towards my fate, lean into the window as it slowly winds itself down.

There are two people in there, but their faces are lost in the shadows.

I know that the nearest one is speaking to me but all I can hear is the hiss of radio interference. The music is starting up again but it no longer disturbs me, I'm numb and I know where I am going. My thoughts and my body are no longer mine. My hair and my dress are no longer mine. I get into the back of the car and it pulls away, in a U-turn across the avenue, picking up speed as it heads west, towards the lonely shore. A woman's voice says softly, sadly: 'Bobby...'

And I woke up, lurching forwards into a sitting position, drenched with cold sweat. I put my hands up to my head, feeling the fringe of my long blonde hair plastered to my forehead, desperate to make sure it was my hair and not hers. For a moment, between two worlds, I couldn't make out where she ended and I began, her thoughts and her memories had been so strong that they seemed as if they were my own. But they were so terrible, so alien, so shocking. Images of brutal couplings in the back seats of cars, underneath trees, in shabby rooms with other people watching, faces of old and ugly men, faces of black men, the certainty that I had a sister called Pat and most of all, that overwhelming sense of fear...

Fear and pain. God, she had hurt. I put my hand up to my shoulder where the worst of it had been. It wasn't tender at all. I hadn't slept on it badly, triggering the sensation. That had all been part of the dream too. Where had she come from, this woman with the short hair and the striped dress?

I was so disorientated that it took a few seconds to realise that the music, that weird music that had soundtracked this nightmare, hadn't disappeared with it.

It was coming through the wall next door. Those ghostly

keyboards and that radio tuning in and out of stations, it was actually real. The fear this phantom woman had felt coursed through my veins like quicksilver and I grabbed hold of Toby's arm, shaking him awake, gabbling: 'What's that noise, that horrible noise?'

He stumbled out of his own slumbers with a low groan, rolling towards me and propping himself up on his elbow.

'That noise, Toby, what is it?' My voice was shrill with panic.

'Uhhh,' he grunted, putting an arm around me, patting me gently on the leg as if to calm me down. He was never very good at waking up. 'That?' he said. 'Uhhh, sorry, I should have warned you about that. It's the boys next door. They say they're musicians and that, my dear, is what their music sounds like. Bloody horror show.'

He rolled across me and turned on the bedside light, his face suddenly illuminated by a comforting orange glow as a tired smile spread across his crumpled features. He looked so handsome with his hair all falling forwards in his eyes that I immediately calmed down. 'Come here,' he said, pulling me back down beside him. The night had been so hot we had kicked most of the covers off the bed, but like the woman in the dream, I suddenly felt cold.

'It's a horror show all right,' I said, nestling into the warmth of him. 'It gave me such a nightmare.'

'Oh Stella,' he said. 'I'm sorry. I really should have warned you, but I suppose I just got used to them and their odd little ways while I was still a gay bachelor myself.'

His words made me giggle. We had been married for only one week, spending what would have been our honeymoon if we'd had the money ostensibly redecorating, but not really getting very much further than where we were now. It didn't matter. We still had the rest of the summer to turn the basement of 22 Arundel Gardens from Toby's bachelor pad into the marital home of Mr and Mrs Reade.

'What time is it anyway?' he asked, looking over at the alarm clock. 'Ten past one! Horror show hours and all.'

It gave me a shudder, that did. Now I was awake and safe, the nightmare was beginning to fracture and dissolve, recede into the shadows. But one thing I could clearly remember was that I – or rather she – knew exactly what the time was.

Toby must have felt it because he cuddled me closer, found the edge of a blanket and covered me over with it.

'You cold?' he asked, and I let it go at that, not wanting to tell him what it really was in case he thought I'd gone a bit strange, mad even. It had been a horribly vivid dream, an insight into a world I didn't want to see again. And whatever had caused it – the music, the newness of my surroundings or just too much cheese before bedtime – I wanted to forget about it quickly. I resolved to banish the woman in the blue and white dress from my thoughts.

It was because of our honeymoon that I managed to do so; we were so engrossed in our own little world that we didn't bother to buy the papers in the week that followed, otherwise I might have read about the body of a woman that had been found by the river in Duke's Meadows, Chiswick, wearing a blue-and-white striped dress. It was a mercy, really, that I didn't. It would have shattered the idyll of the summer of 1959, the end of our first year at the Royal College of Art and the beginning of our marriage. There were so many things that we didn't know about each other then and ignorance was bliss.

Toby's kisses were warm on my eyelids as I finally fell asleep, the sound of a new world coming through the wall.

PART ONE

With This Kiss

1959

I

Roulette

Dawn crept stealthily over the Thames, the first shafts of sunlight stealing through the mist that clung to the grass, collected in the hollows at the base of the poplars, chestnuts and weeping willows that lined the banks of the river. Police Constable Pete Bradley watched golden beams glitter on the surface of the water and wound down his window to breathe in the new morning. At this time and this place, it didn't feel like he was in London at all.

The Thames Road between Hammersmith and Chiswick Bridges could almost remind him of home sometimes, and this was one of those occasions. The houses that backed on to the road here had long gardens full of honeysuckle and roses. There were piers for fisherman and wharves for sailing boats, little old pubs and ancient churches, almost like a perfect village green that had somehow managed to escape the pounding that the Luftwaffe had meted on the rest of the capital. The river wound its course around to his left, fringed on the other side by trees, not a building to be seen. The only other traffic on the road at this time of day was the milk carts and delivery vans, bringing today's headlines about the Mau Mau in Kenya and Liberace's libel victory into the newsagents, fresh bread and groceries to the shops.

For a second, Pete transposed the image of the Thames with that of the River Wharfe, saw in his mind the rolling limestone hills of his childhood and remembered the feeling of excitement that such a dawn would have inspired in his ten-year-old self. Fishing net and sandwiches wrapped in wax paper, his hand safe inside Dad's huge, rough paw, both of them singing 'Willow, Weep For Me' or 'Listen To The Mocking Bird', one of those old twenties songs he couldn't listen to now without an ache in his heart.

A loud snore from the back seat interrupted his reverie. Acting Sergeant Alf Brown lolled on the seat, his head back and his mouth open, revealing a gob full of fillings and a fat, greying tongue. Never a one for these night patrols, Alf was always conking out on the job. He lay in a slovenly repose, his waistline straining against the blue serge of his uniform, the sweet smell of whisky emanating every time he exhaled. Pete exchanged glances with Alan Corbishall, another young PC like him, who had drawn the short straw for the driving while Pete operated the radio. Alan rolled his eyes.

'At it again,' he said, 'the old soak.'

Pete shook his head. He'd not been in the force long, less than a year since he'd passed out from Hendon and he wasn't finding it exactly as he'd imagined. There were too many 'superiors' like Alf who seemed to have grown rotten with age, careless perhaps, or maybe just too jaded. They'd had their heyday in the fiery chaos of the Blitz and now, in these days of peace and austerity, they were burnt out from lack of drama and the sly profits of the black market. To hear them talk you wouldn't think that tons of bombs raining down on the city night after night was any kind of hardship or terror; on the contrary, living on the edge like that had given them a purpose that the dull 1950s singularly lacked. It had made them all into Dan Dare. Now, it seemed, they could only reclaim that spirit of derring-do from the bottom of a bottle.

Pete had applied to become an aid to CID, the first step towards becoming a detective, wanting something to stretch his mind more than the plodding routine of the beat bobby would allow. He knew he had to start at the beginning, with the drunks and the domestics and the petty thieves, but even so, he wanted to be doing something of real use. He knew he had it in him. He'd got this far after all.

The young copper stuck his head out of the window, inhaled the smells of river and dew and divined the start of another hot day. It was ten past five by his wristwatch and they were approaching Barnes Railway Bridge, where the landscape subtly altered: the rather grand houses of Mortlake sat stoutly on the other side of the river, while on this side, buildings had given way to the green expanse of Duke's Meadow.

Or 'Gobbler's Gulch' as Alf referred to it. A piece of common ground where, under cover of darkness, illicit trysts took place in the back seats of motorcars – frustrated young lovers, cheating spouses, brasses and their johns getting sweaty under the shady trees. Alf never tired of delving into his stock of dirty jokes about it when he was actually compos mentis. But in the first light of dawn it was empty and its rolling banks looked pretty inviting, a good place to stretch out and enjoy a picnic.

'*Willow, weep for me…*' Pete could hear the words of that song in his head again, as he caught sight of one such sturdy old specimen. As his eyes travelled slowly down its gnarly branches to the trunk, the smile left his face.

Something was there. An odd shape. Something not right.

'Slow down a minute,' he said to Alan. 'What d'you reckon that is over there?'

At first it looked like a collection of bags had been dumped under the tree, blue and white bags. But not quite…

Alan put his foot on the brake and peered over.

'I can't quite make it out, Pete. D'you want to take a look?'

'Aye,' Pete opened his door. 'It's probably nowt, but just in case.'

It was the strangest sensation, as if an unseen force was propelling him out of his seat and towards the riverbank, out through that fresh new morning that had only seconds of its stillness and innocence left to give him. The hairs prickled on the back of his neck. A flash of Dad walking in front of him, fishing rod over his shoulder; the feelings of a ten-year-old boy on a bright summer day; knowing with the certainty of a ticking clock that those feelings were about to run out, would be lost forever the instant he got close enough to those blue and white bags to work out what they were.

What she was.

It was a woman, a tiny woman. In a blue-and-white dress that had been torn savagely open, ripped right down to her waist, exposing her breasts. She was lying with her feet towards the river, her head turned towards the right, with her legs slightly crossed and her left arm extended as if it had been trying to grasp something. Pete pulled up short for a second and the world stilled, the twittering of birds and distant hum of the city all blanked out, as if he were standing in the middle of an invisible cocoon. He knew for certain she was dead and more than that, she'd been murdered.

This is it then, he thought. This was the reason he had joined the force, to do something better with his life than toil and die down pit. But even as he thought it, he had another realisation and it was one that would never leave him:

But I've got here too late. I can't help her now.

Carefully, he knelt down on the grass beside her. Poor little lass looked like a broken doll. The skin on her face was waxy white and devoid of any make-up, her short dark hair wet with dew, her brown eyes wide open, staring into infinity. He tried to read the expression, remembering the books he'd read about Victorian detectives and their conviction that you could catch the image of the murderer in the lens of the victim's eye. Bloody rubbish that were, he thought, but still, he wanted to have some kind of communion with her, some kind of insight into what it was that she saw, who it was that had done this to her. But there was no expression left. Her eyes were glazed. Her mouth was open too, but not slack. Her jaw was set hard, she had been gasping for her last breath. Looking down, he saw the scratches on her neck and her collarbone. Of course, he thought, she's been strangled.

Her skirts were bunched up around her waist, revealing a white slip. Pete looked down her bare legs to her dirty, shoeless feet. He fought the urge to close her eyes for her and stood up stiffly instead, remembering his duty not to touch a thing but to recall all the details, to look for anything that didn't make sense. Well, the shoes being gone for a start. And a handbag? He cast his eyes around the grass. If she'd had one, it wasn't here now.

'Clever bugger, eh?' he said aloud.

He heard a shout and looked back towards the car. Crumpled, bleary Alf was hurrying towards him, his eyes as red as his face, eager to reassert his authority.

'Get on the radio,' Pete called. 'We've got a dead body here.'

Of course, as soon as they had called the station it was no longer their case. Top brass from the Criminal Investigation Department were dispatched and while they waited for them all to arrive, Alf and Alan stood guard at the scene, making Pete stay in the car, on the radio. He watched as a series of cars and vans pulled up, disgorging a posse of sergeants and aids who hurried to take charge of the situation, set up a tarpaulin across the scene for the pathologist to do his work away from prying eyes.

A tall, stern-looking man in a tan gabardine mac and a trilby emerged from a black Rover and walked briskly towards Alf, taking a notebook out of his pocket. His seniority was made plain by the way Alf contorted himself, puffing out his chest but wiping a nervous hand across his forehead as he talked, shifting his weight from foot to foot. After a few moments, the man in the mac closed his notebook, gave a brief nod and began walking in Pete's direction.

He had a clipped moustache and grey-green eyes, not without a trace of humour in them, Pete thought, despite the severity of his face. All the same, he got out of the car sharpish and stood with his back ramrod straight.

'PC Bradley?' The man had the voice of an officer as well as the bearing. 'DI Bell, CID. I gather you were the one who found the body?'

'Yes sir.'

'So what can you tell me?'

'Well.' Pete felt a bead of sweat trickle down his forehead. It wasn't just that the day was hot again already, but that this was a man who wouldn't suffer fools like Alf, who would demand that the facts were relayed to him clear and precise.

'I noticed her as we were driving down the road here, I was looking towards the river and I could see her dress, although I wasn't quite sure what it was at first. It didn't look right, somehow, so I thought I'd stop and take a look. I got out the car, and I reckon I'd be about fifteen yards away from her when I realised I was looking at a body. When I got up close I saw a young-looking woman, about twenty, twenty-two, short brown curly hair and brown eyes, in a blue-and-white striped summer dress, lying with her feet towards the river. The front of her dress had been ripped open and her torso was bare. She wasn't wearing a brassiere, or any stockings or shoes and there was no sign of a handbag neither. I knelt down beside her and saw red marks on her neck and collarbone, scratches like, and from the way her mouth was open and her eyes were bulging, I would expect she had been strangled.'

DI Bell nodded, pen poised in mid-air over his notebook. 'I see,' he said. 'And what do you make of that then?'

Pete had been going over the details in his mind ever since, searching for the clues that would give the killer away, the peculiarities they would be able to use to catch him. Only this was the first time he had seen a murdered woman and he had to put that shock and pity behind him and concentrate, like the pathologist would, on what those peculiarities were.

'Two things that strike me as odd,' he offered, hoping that he wasn't about to make an ass of himself in front of this much older, more experienced man. 'One, the fact that she wasn't wearing any shoes and her feet were dirty. I don't think she was killed where she lay, I think she was dragged here after and left.'

Even as he said it he didn't know quite why he'd had this sudden conviction, the words had just come to him and now they had spilled out in the open, he wondered if he was fantasising, overstepping the mark.

But Bell's expression said otherwise. A spark went off in those grey-green eyes.

'Interesting,' he said. 'And what was the second thing?'

'She wasn't wearing any make-up,' said Pete. 'None at all. She had her best dress on but no paint on her face. What woman goes out like that?'

Bell's eyes narrowed. 'Good point, Constable. So you think our killer did a bit of a clean-up job, so to speak?'

Pete felt himself flush.

'It does sound daft…' he began.

'Not at all,' said Bell. 'You've been very observant.' He snapped his notebook shut. 'Good day, Constable Bradley.'

As he stalked away towards the murder scene, Pete saw the

scowl on Alf's face. He realised that he hadn't mentioned his superior officer to DI Bell at all and wondered if there would be consequences. The adrenalin drained out of him. Suddenly, he felt bone tired.

They spent the beginning of their next shift stopping embarrassed couples from parking their cars in Duke's Meadow and asking them questions instead. Of course, it was futile. Given the nature of their night's assignments, they didn't want their details taking down and nobody would admit to being in the vicinity on the night of 16 June 1959. But the landlord of the pub directly across the river, The Ship in Mortlake, had something to offer. About five to midnight he'd seen the headlights of a car on the other side of the river. Almost as soon as he clocked them, the lights had gone off and he'd heard a piercing scream, a woman's scream that suddenly stopped, as if 'choked off'.

He was sure of the time, the landlord was. He'd looked at the clock as soon as it had happened.

More information circulated. Two nights before, in Ranleigh Gardens, Chiswick, a good-looking model had been attacked on her way home by a fair-haired man who jumped out of a doorway and tried to strangle her. She had bitten him hard enough for him to drop her and run off. Could the two crimes be connected?

Then the pathologist's report came in. The girl had been manually strangled, fingers on the side of her neck, thumbs on the windpipe, until she was dead. Abrasions on her back suggested she had been hauled over the front seat of a motor car, and marks on her heels that she had been dragged across the ground to the foot of the tree. She was dead no later than 2 a.m. And just before she'd died, she'd had sex.

She couldn't be identified by her fingerprints. If the state of her body had revealed her profession as the oldest one in the world, she hadn't any convictions for it. They didn't have the victim's identity for thirty-six hours, until her face went in the papers and the girl she had shared a flat with in Holloway came forward.

The dead woman was a prostitute, Roberta Clarke, who preferred to be called Bobby. She had worked with her room-mate, Maureen Knowles, up in Finsbury Park, down Bayswater Road and around Notting Hill. Bobby had a false name that she used sometimes, Ellie Driver, but that wasn't on any records either, suggesting that maybe she'd not been on the game for long. She had only just turned twenty-one – the key hadn't opened the door very far for poor Bobby.

Once they had her identity, they found out a lot of other things too. But for Pete, following events as closely as he could from his lowly foot soldier position, that was when the details blurred and contradicted themselves, when the timeline shifted and the things of which he was certain could no longer be put into any logical order.

The last person to have seen Bobby alive was a self-described handyman from Stamford Hill called Harvey Webb, who claimed to have dropped her off at Holland Park tube at ten past one in the morning.

One hour and ten minutes after the landlord was certain he had heard the scream.

He'd made arrangements to pick her up again at half past three, but the only person waiting for him then was a copper, who'd brought him in for questioning – the area was a well-known pick-up spot. Once Bobby had been discovered, Harvey was brought back in and questioned hard, but in the end, they'd let him go. He had a witness at a coffee stand who'd seen him between 1 and 2 a.m., and stains on Bobby's dress from where she appeared to have wet herself with fright on a leather seat didn't match the upholstery of Harvey's Morris Ten.

Bobby's boyfriend, a West Indian boxer called Algy 'Baby' Ferrier, also had an alibi. He had been at a club in Westbourne Park Road called The Blue Parrot during the crucial time frame. It was shady deeds in Dark Town: Baby existed in the semi-legitimate milieu of late night speakeasies that proliferated around Ladbroke Grove, where he always had a spaced-out looking white woman in tow, providing him with his readies no doubt. He was bent all right, but there was nothing that could be done to put him in the frame for this one, much as some would have wished it. Talk about Bobby got more lewd when it was revealed she had been consorting with a coloured man. In the minds of many, the tart had got what she deserved.

But Pete couldn't think of her that way. He could only think of the crushed body on the riverbank, so tiny and alone in the perfect dawn of the day she'd never see. He read the accounts of her life and then looked between the lines of them. Bobby Clarke hadn't known much happiness. She'd been deserted at regular intervals throughout her childhood, first by her fortune-hunting father, then by her mother. Her paternal grandmother had brought her up, along with her sister Patricia, and they were joined from time to time by their errant father and the latest in his line of new brides and accompanying half-sisters. Always sisters. Her father, it seemed, singled Bobby out as the biggest disappointment to him, constantly berating her for her appearance and habits. Stifled in a Victorian house full of women and no honourable men, no wonder she'd wanted to run off to London and then not had the first clue how to look after herself.

It was the mother, down from Cheltenham with her second husband, who came to claim the body. Mr Clarke had made himself absent; no doubt the shame was too much for him.

Other stories added more layers of conflict to the events of the night itself. Screams had been heard in Holland Park at 12.30 a.m., neighbours had seen a man grabbing a woman by the throat in a beige shooting wagon, but nobody had intervened. That was the trouble with that neighbourhood, it was a dangerous place to mind anybody's business but your own, so the witnesses said. The beige car surfaced again, driving at speed from Chiswick Bridge at 1.15 a.m. But then so did a yellow Ford, a yellow and black Ford Consul and a big black car, possibly a Daimler.

The days turned into weeks and the story dropped off the front pages. Pete got reassigned to day patrol, probably at the behest of Alf, who had been increasingly brusque towards him since that morning with DI Bell. Pete didn't mind. He had been accepted as an aid and would be transferred shortly to begin his new job in a different part of London. He wondered if Bell had something to do with that, too, perhaps the strange events of that morning had set the wheels of fate in motion. Or perhaps he was just being fanciful.

Just before he left Chiswick, he heard the strangest thing. He'd taken to ending his week's shift by treating himself to a few pints of brown in The George, a big, red brick pub opposite the station on Chiswick High Road. He didn't have much of a social life in London, still thought of himself as an outsider, but this move to days had given him one new friend at least.

It was a Friday night, before his first weekend leave for six weeks, and he was in there with the older Sergeant he'd been recently assigned to, Dai Jones. A tough, bald Welshman, Dai was the polar opposite of Alf: a man who was scrupulously clean and possessed of a fierce intelligence, someone that you could really learn from. More than that, Dai's background was not unlike Pete's own. He'd worked down the pits as a young man, before the war had delivered him, as he'd put it, up from the earth and on to the sea. They could relate to each other and enjoyed each other's company, both on the beat and out of work hours. Dai was so clever, Pete often wondered why he had never been promoted beyond Sergeant.

'Be my bad temper,' Dai would reflect, without any bitterness. 'I have been known to blow my top from time to time. Doesn't do you no favours with them starched shirts upstairs, but what do they know about real work, eh? I told too many people to bugger off in my time, that's my problem, but the thing is, I was always right. That's what they don't like, see. That's what you got to be careful of if you want to go right to the top.'

They were in the saloon bar, propped up against the counter that way, Dai said, you could always keep one ear to the loose talk that might be blowing in the wind and one eye on the rest of the room. He was never really off-duty, even midway through one of his war stories, when his dark eyes began to glitter. A man Pete had never seen before was coming over.

'Evening Dai,' he said. A man in his mid-twenties, thin and with sandy hair that he'd tried to plaster down but still had bits sticking up at the back, a loose tie around a flushed red neck and a baggy, threadbare suit.

'Evening Francis.' Dai put his pint down on the counter, wiped the foam from his top lip. 'What you doing so far from home?'

'Oh, you know. Like to keep an eye on the old patch.' The sandy man grinned and scratched his head, sending more unruly locks springing upwards. 'See what's going down out here in the sticks.'

'Dah.' Dai grimaced. 'Be your work brought you over won't it? You want to stick your nose into one of ours, is it?'

'Can I get you another?' He ignored the jibe and looked over at Pete. 'Or am I interrupting something vital? Telling you how he sunk the *Bismarck*, is he?'

Pete tried to suppress a smile as Dai feigned outrage.

'Can't you remember anything I told you? It wasn't the *Bismarck*,

it was a bloody U-boat, May the 9th, 1941. You see,' he nodded to
Pete, 'it just goes in one ear and out the other. I hope you're going
to make a better student than this one. Pete Bradley, this is Francis
Bream. He used to be my batman down here until somehow he
got himself a promotion and they shipped him out to West End
Central with all the other spivs and gangsters.'

Laughing, Pete leaned over and took the other man's hand.
With his scruffy hair and pencil moustache, Francis Bream did
have a touch of the spiv about him.

'Call me Frank,' the fellow said. 'And don't pay too much
attention to this old seadog's stories. Now can I get you both a
drink?'

They accepted, but Dai still retained his aura of suspicion.

'Now then,' he said, lifting his fresh pint and examining the
cloudy brown liquid as if it might contain twigs. 'What they really
got you down here for?'

'I told you.' Bream shook his head. 'I'm just looking in on me
old company. Nothing ever happens around here anyway, does it?
Oh, apart from that tart they found by the river…'

'Oh, so that's it, is it?' Dai said. 'Well, you're in luck, boyo. It was
Pete here that found her.'

'Oh.' Bream raised his eyebrows. 'Was it really? Must have given
you quite a shock, her sitting there like that.'

Pete frowned. 'What do you mean sitting there?'

'That's where she was, wasn't it, sitting up against a tree looking
out at the river?' Bream looked at him quizzically. 'She can't have
looked all that dead from a distance.'

'No, you've got it wrong,' said Pete. 'She wasn't sitting. She was
lying on the ground by the side of the tree. Flat on her back, she
were. That's why I couldn't quite make her out, why I went over for
a better look.'

Bream shook his head. 'Strange,' he said. 'That's not what I heard. I had a mate came down there from CID, swears he saw her plain as day, sitting up against the tree. Said that was why it looked so eerie, from the back it just looked like she was sunbathing, you'd never guess something was wrong.'

He fixed Pete earnestly with bloodshot green eyes.

'You pissed, Francis?' asked Dai. 'He knows what he saw. How many people do you know go sunbathing at five o'clock in the morning? Someone's pulling your leg, old son.'

'No.' Bream shook his head earnestly, hair bobbing up and down like straw in a bird's nest. 'Mac was definitely there, and it really spooked him. He's one of those dead straight ice-creams he is, not the type to make things up. Maybe the pathologist moved her.'

Dai snorted. 'Now you really are talking daft. Alec Jobson was the pathologist on that one. Twenty years in the service he's been, when would you ever catch him pulling a stunt like that? I'm telling you Francis, you listen to that canteen chatter too much. It's all Chinese whispers, that's all.'

'Well.' Bream considered. 'I believe you.' He nodded at Pete. 'But I believe my mate Mac, too. Someone must have moved her, maybe one of the other coppers...'

'If you say so, sunshine.' Dai shook his head and swiftly made to turn the conversation in another direction. He was obviously embarrassed that this old colleague of his was talking this way, making no sense and appearing to be half cut as well. Bream let the subject drop, finished his drink and then ambled away.

They watched him pick up his coat and hat from the rack by the door. His lightweight mac was crumpled, like he'd slept in it. There was something irrefutably seedy about him, Pete thought, but he didn't take the man for a liar or someone who'd deliberately stir things up. He wondered if someone really had moved the body, someone with a bad sense of humour.

'Do you really think...' he began.

'No I don't,' Dai cut him short. 'You don't want to pay any attention to Francis Bream. Bloody dreamer he is.' He turned back to the bar, pulled out his wallet from his breast pocket. 'Bloody bad penny,' he added under his breath, too quietly for Pete to hear.

2

Dream Lover

I awoke to the sound of children laughing and screaming in the communal gardens outside. Streams of sunlight fanned above the sagging curtains that struggled to cover the French doors at the end of our bedroom, spilling weird shapes across the lumps of furniture below. Not for the first time, I thought, those curtains will have to go.

Toby was still sleeping beside me, his face looking so innocent and childlike in sleep that I felt a great warm rush of love coil around me. I stared at him, content and happy, luxuriating in the knowledge that he was mine, all mine. Then the memory of the night before pushed into my consciousness like an unwelcome guest, bringing with it the faint traces of a headache clinging to my temples. For a second, it took me back to another time and another place, a murky, formless memory from early childhood of waking up with the exact same feeling, in the nursery of my grandparents' house, in the time of the Blitz. It was a feeling I wanted to swat away.

I slipped out of bed, shrugged on a Chinese silk dressing gown lying over the chair by our bed, a beautiful, embroidered work of art that I had bought on the Portobello Road for pennies. I reminded myself that I was here now, far from Bloxwich and all the bad times.

The room was a mess, the remains of last night's meal and an empty bottle of wine on the floor, furniture from the rest of the house all crammed in a huddle in front of the French doors, along with stacks of canvases and Toby's easels. We were painting the flat room by room, saving this one for last. Last night we had all but completed the big front room that would be our sitting room cum dining room and it occurred to me that both the headache and the nightmare could well have been exacerbated by paint fumes.

I gathered up the crockery on to a tray and slunk out of the messy bedroom and into the hall, where it was cool and quiet. Our flat was cut off from the rest of the rented rooms in the house by a heavy door at the top of the stairs. Down here was a little kitchenette, a bathroom and the wonderful front room, all of it ours to do with exactly as we pleased.

The kitchenette, where I went to now, was my least favourite room. It was pokey, without a window and only an ancient ceiling fan to extract the aromas of some of the exotic cooking we had been trying out on our little two-ring stove. There was a tiny sink, above which a cranky old heater dished out hot water in fits and spurts, and next to that, a pantry we had made from an old cupboard with a printed curtain tacked over the front of it. We kept the icebox under the sink in the bathroom, the coldest room.

On top of the stove, last night's pans sat crusted with the incriminating remains of vegetable curry and rice. Shaking my head, I put the tray down on the draining board and then moved them into the sink, pouring a little detergent in each and then timidly turning on the tap.

I stood well back as it belched and gurgled into action, spurting a jet of boiling water into the curry pan, pausing for a second to make vomiting noises, then steadying itself into a more reasonable flow. When I had filled both pans, I turned the tap back off with a tea towel over my hand. The exertion had already left it red hot.

In the cupboard on the wall I found a jar of aspirins, filled a glass from the more reliable cold water tap and drank them down. I would have a quick bath while the pans soaked, I thought, then I'd see about breakfast.

The electricity meter was in the hall, and we kept a jug full of pennies beside it to keep it fed. Another bargain from Portobello, it was a Spanish water pitcher with a gay painting of a cockerel on the side that I liked to think was one of Picasso's. It wasn't, of course, but there was a sizeable Spanish community around here, displaced from Gibraltar during the war, who sold plenty of crockery like this, along with delicious olives, *jamon* and cheese on the market stalls. Like the West Indians, who had started to come over at the beginning of the decade, they gave this ramshackle place a colour and vibrancy all of its own.

It was so different from the digs in glum Earl's Court that I had taken when I first moved down here. The houses here were similar to those, early Victorian stucco turned almost black with dirt and soot, carved into guesthouses and cheap rooms to accommodate as many transients as possible. But there was an aura of dank melancholy that hung over the rooftops like a shroud there. It was full of pubs catering to a steady trade of dispossessed alcoholics, ancient prostitutes and hobbling war veterans with hollow, staring eyes. Here it was far, far different. A secret world where every doorway was hiding a new intrigue and different types of music pumped under every floorboard, from American jazz to Jamaican ska to Irish rebel songs.

Of course, a lot of people said that it was a dangerous area. Last summer there had been a full-scale riot, started by racialist Teddy boys from Notting Dale. It had gone on for days, and even now the Fascists were still trying to stir up trouble. Oswald Mosley was out canvassing for the local elections, hateful slogans were daubed on the walls and a coloured man called Kelso Cochrane had been stabbed to death on the railway bridge in Westbourne Park only a month ago. But things hadn't turned out the way Mosley wanted. Instead the residents had bandied together to follow Cochrane's funeral cortège down Ladbroke Grove, over a thousand of them, black and white. The world was changing and it really felt like here was where that change would begin. As far as I could see, it was the only place for an artist to be.

Now that I had completed my first year at the Royal, I could consider myself an artist, and I couldn't resist wandering back to the front room as my bath filled up to view the proof. It had been Toby's idea that one of the geometric designs I had been working on should become a mural at the far end of the room. *The Point of No Return*, he called it, it was black and white lines disappearing into circles and over false horizons, something I'd worked out doing technical drawing at school and had been playing about with ever since. I'd even utilised it to make screenprinted scarves and shopping bags, some of which I'd sold to admirers who had seen me wearing my own. I was studying General Art and Design, but Toby reckoned I could easily branch out into fashion if I wanted.

Toby had added his own signature to our mural, something that came directly from his work. A big, red circle in the top right corner, a little trail of smaller ones in the bottom left. These were his 'notes', for Toby, the Fine Artist, was developing his own style of painting, based on the strange jazz records by Roland Kirk and Charles Mingus that he bought from an even stranger couple of guys who had their own record shop on Ledbury Road.

I had found that music difficult to get into at first, but after a while, it made sense. The records were atmospheres, filmic dreams, suggesting the shapes of stories and letting you fill in the pictures in your head. Or in Toby's case, across many canvases, where the notes became blurs and blobs of colour and light, as if he were capturing sound. One of the guys from the jazz shop had told Toby about a couple of his friends who were running a gallery out of a semi-derelict house nearby and he was hoping to have his first exhibition there soon.

I studied our mural delightedly, feet sticking to the paint-splattered dustsheets on the floor. It had really turned out better than I had ever hoped.

Just like the rest of my life.

It was only just over a year ago that the letter from the Royal had come, promising me the chance of a future far away from the tall chimneys and dull canals of the Black Country. A moment of bittersweet joy, for it was my Pa who had so wanted me to follow my muse all the way, not to give in to the conformity of what the rest of the world expected. Pa, who had spent his own teenage years in the bloody trenches of Normandy. He would have been so proud of that letter.

But Pa was five years gone by the time it arrived, a victim of a horrible disease called Ankylosing spondylitis, which caused his spine to curve forward until he was bent in half, humiliating and deforming him before it led to the kidney failure that eventually killed him. But even with all the pain that he went through and the foreknowledge that he was going to die, he never stopped encouraging me, never stopped being my gentle, funny, loving Pa.

'The most important thing in life,' he told me, 'is never to grow up.'

After he passed, life became gradually more unbearable. Ma was struck more by terror than by grief, the terror of being without a husband, an emptiness that I could in no way compensate for. Both my maternal grandparents followed Pa into the grave shortly afterwards, leaving the pair of us still more bereft and alienated from each other. It pushed me into my studies. I took my A-levels in Art, English and TD, and at the same time attended night classes at the local art school for an Ordinary National Diploma, building up the portfolio that would get me into the Royal, mixing with the students in our one coffee shop afterwards, stretching out my 9 p.m. curfew to its limits.

Then Ma came home with another man. A fat, red-faced man called Dennis, whom she had met in church, of all places. A man like that never should have been anywhere near our church. I was deeply suspicious of him and my last year at home had been one of exquisite torture that only the letter had relieved.

But, I reflected as I lowered myself into the now full bath, in a way, it had been our mothers that had bonded Toby and me. Strained maternal relations was one of the things we had in common, that had turned our relationship serious.

I met Toby at the Freshers' Ball, thanks to the only other girl on my course, a short, vivacious northerner called Jackie whom I also shared digs with in Earl's Court. Jackie had done her foundation course in York, along with a serious-looking beatnik called George, who was now in Toby's class at the Royal. We ended up sharing a table that night and the party carried on throughout the rest of term. Together we had explored all the delights of London, from the jazz clubs in the bomb sites of Tottenham Court Road to the Angry Young Men at the Royal Court in the King's Road. Then, just after Christmas, Toby had proposed.

We waited until I turned twenty-one before we married at Chelsea Town Hall, with Jackie and George as witnesses. Afterwards we drank champagne and ate steaks in Au Père de Nico's, nearby on the King's Road. Then I gathered up my belongings from Earl's Court and decamped to Ladbroke Grove.

I had sent Ma a postcard from my 'honeymoon', a picture of a red London bus. I didn't know if she'd received it yet, or if she would even care when she did. There was not a lot she could do about it now.

I stepped out of the bath on to the new, black-and-white lino we had laid down a few days previously. The bathroom was the first room we'd done, the easiest one. The white paint sparkled off the walls through the frosted glass window. Our whole idea for the flat was to make it fairly austere with just a few eye-catching pieces in each room, the mural being the pulling point of the front room. In here, it was a big Rococo mirror we had hung above the sink, which looked somehow ridiculous and imaginative at the same time.

I wrapped one of the big, fluffy white towels we had got from Woolworths around me. The headache had gone, replaced with nothing worse than hunger pains. I thought of fresh bread from the bakery, fresh oranges from the market to squeeze for juice, the prospect of finding more treasure on the stalls and of Toby's exhibition. I let my memories gurgle away like the water down the plughole and got ready to get on with the day.

3

Mean Streak

'The old men who are supposed to be in charge of this country have sat back and watched a crisis develop without lifting so much as a finger. While they live it up in Hampstead, Highgate, the Cotswolds and Bournemouth, ordinary, working-class, white Britons are forced to live next door to people who are used to an entirely different way of life. You know what I'm talking about, don't you?'

A cheer rose up from the throng surrounding the flatbed truck on the corner of Ladbroke Grove and Lancaster Road. The speaker was an unprepossessing man, short and slight, dressed in an immaculate double-breasted grey suit, a starched shirt and tie, with a severe haircut that accentuated his high widow's peak.

Yet the words that he'd been casting across the assembly at the street corner, a turnout of working men from the coal and coke yard in their blackened shirtsleeves, drinkers lured over from the Kensington Park Hotel across the way, housewives in their headscarves and the Teddy boys who acted as stewards, were evincing a rapid transformation.

'Carnivals in the street!' he raged, the words filling his meagre frame with an electrifying fury. His audience, captivated now, boomed back their approval.

'Jungle rhythms pounding out at all hours of the day and night! Free sex and lots of it!'

Pete stood under the streetlight on the opposite corner to the ranting man, just outside the KPH. Through the open door of the saloon bar, he could see a handful of men drinking in quiet determination to ignore the hullabaloo on the street outside. From the length of time he'd been in Notting Hill – two months now, as an aid – he knew that most of the regulars at this pub cum B & B were Irish. Mosley's Unionists had been playing hard for their support, recalling his condemnation of the black and tans in the twenties, when the then youthful firebrand Labour MP had been the only politician to rail about the injustices in Ireland in Parliament. But despite his diligent doorstep visits, his incessant, snake-charmer repartee, there was a hardcore here defiantly turning a deaf ear. Like the drinkers in the KPH. Among them sat a huge black West Indian, with the build of a boxer and a look of cold fury in his eyes as he stared straight ahead of him, a vein pumping on his temple, slowly cracking the knuckles of each hand over and over again.

Pete had wanted to experience something beyond the mundane beat of Chiswick and now he had got it. The streets around Ladbroke Grove were like a frontier town in the Wild West, roughly divided into three territories. To his right, down Lancaster Road and up to Latimer Road was the area known as Notting Dale and it was from the little rows of cottages there that most of these Teddy boys sprang. To his left, on the other side of Portobello Road, were the roads owned by the Polish landlord Peter Rachman, whose houses overflowed with West Indians. Down the middle of Rachman's lands, joining Ladbroke Grove to Royal Oak, ran Westbourne Park Road. To its north, the immense coal and coke yard sprawled down the side of the Grand Union canal, to the south a warren of streets inhabited by the Irish.

There were other immigrant communities here – Spanish, Indians, a smattering of Portuguese and a subculture of writers and artists drawn by the cheap rents and shady, shifting atmosphere of the place. But the Teds, the West Indians and the Irish, there were your fighters. To Pete's wide eyes it seemed that on every corner, at every hour of the day and night, there was a brawl taking place. Be it Teds jibing at the equally dandified young coloured men, or a posse of drunks supporting each other while they took turns to vomit into the gutter, all the men here hunted in packs with the women screeching on their encouragement from the sidelines.

Tonight's BUP rally was another way of exploiting these tensions. Oswald Mosley was an old man now, sixty-three, the firebrand of the Left turned disgraced Fascist who'd spent the war in prison, washed-up, Pete would have thought, to everyone's ears but his own. But the lieutenant who was working up the crowd for him now obviously thought different. Thought he had tapped into something here.

During the riots last summer, a lot of Pete's new colleagues had told him, it wasn't just Teddy boys stirring things up. There'd been others amongst them, older faces, posher accents urging the violence on. Two of Mosley's sons went about dressed like Teds themselves, he'd seen pictures of them in the *Daily Mirror*, dandies playing at thugs.

As he scanned the faces in the crowd, Pete wondered if there were any *agents provocateurs* here amongst them. Wondered if this mob needed any more stoking before the fuse was lit and things turned ugly. He was well aware of the powerful effects that a good speaker could have on those who already had rebellion pumping through their veins; he had seen the shop stewards at work outside the pit back home. But this meeting was for a different end to the justice those men had demanded for the miners. This was a corrupt and evil gathering. His skin prickled in the heat of the late summer evening. In the civvies he now wore to blend in with the crowd, he missed the feel of the baton on his belt for the first time since coming out of uniform.

There were a couple of beat bobbies from F Division that had drifted over as the rally began and now stood further down the pavement on his side of Lancaster Road, feigning a calm interest, chatting to a group of men who had taken their pint glasses outside to watch. But Pete could see they were as alert for trouble as he was. His job as an aid was hardly different from theirs, he was sent to patrol the streets looking for opportunist criminals as well as getting a feel for the neighbourhood and recognising the persistent sources of trouble. The problem was keeping track of them all, there were so many rackets going on in the Grove.

'And what do I say to these immigrants?' the orator continued his tirade. 'I say look, my friends, you have beautiful warm islands with clear blue skies and warm, warm seas where you can swim. You have wonderful golden beaches. Go back and dance on them, not on our staircases at night.'

In the lounge bar of the KPH, a white man put his hand on the shoulder of the West Indian boxer, who looked up at him and shook his head, then spat on the floor.

'Yeah,' bellowed a thickset Ted standing yards in front of Pete, his chest puffed out and his hands deep in his pockets. 'Send 'em all home!'

His companion, an acne-riddled beanstalk in an oversized mauve drape coat laughed hard and added a familiar taunt: 'Lassie for dogs, Kitty Kat for wogs!'

They didn't sound like the offspring of a Knight and a Mitford deb.

Pete shifted uneasily from his left foot to his right. One of the beat bobbies had come forwards a bit, to the edge of the crowd, while the other stayed where he was, keeping his back. Another couple appeared around the corner of Westbourne Park Grove and the big old Elgin pub there, a villainous dive where Mosley did a lot of his canvassing. If any more of them turned up, Pete realised, the thieves around the rest of the Grove would have a field day. Maybe it was time he moved along himself.

Still a new face on this patch, he wasn't supposed to give himself away as a copper until the moment he made an arrest. He'd been deliberately keeping his profile low, getting himself acquainted with the clientele of the pubs that demarked the unseen boundaries of the territory. The KPH had been this evening's first port of call and he had intended to work his way via the Elgin up to Portobello, where trouble of a differing kind from Mosley's rabble-rousing had been anticipated.

In a few hours, at midnight tonight, a new law came into effect that was poised to have dramatic impact on the nefarious business of this neighbourhood. The Street Offences Act would make it a crime for a prostitute to loiter or solicit in a street or public place, including all those shady little mews and unlit passageways that bisected the streets and squares around here.

The places Bobby Clarke had known.

It wasn't just because the area offered more scope for his brain than Chiswick that Pete had asked for a transfer to Notting Hill nick, although this was what he told himself and the divisional chief at the interview. The Chief Superintendent at Hammersmith had viewed his request with one eyebrow raised but let him go anyway. They needed men who were keen for this kind of work.

Pete was still haunted by Bobby, and her killer, who was still at large. At the inquest, just two days ago, DI Bell's summation to the coroner's jury had been an echo of the words Pete spoke to him on the riverbank: 'My impression is that she was not strangled where the body was found, but it looks as if the crime was committed elsewhere.' Despite a nationwide appeal and a fine-tooth comb search for her bag and shoes, they had come no further than that.

Now Pete had seen for himself the spot where Harvey Webb had set her down that night on Holland Park Avenue, where the girls all waited under the tall plane trees. It was just five minutes' walk from his base at the top of Ladbroke Grove. He'd hung around the coffee stand by Holland Park tube station and spoken to a few of them. Some had made him as a copper straight off and refused to pass the time of day, but there were a couple of girls, younger ones, who hadn't minded admitting that the crime had really spooked them, that they had taken new precautions since then. Many had taken to working in pairs, so that one could take down the number plate of any car her friend got into, just in case she never came back. Between them, they had tried to finger a likely candidate for the murderer from the pool of knowledge they had of the men that used this part of town on a regular basis. But as one girl had told him:

'There's so many queers out there, how can you really tell? But, if you ask me it's the ones who don't act queer you have to be more careful of. The ones who act respectable...'

The place he'd really wanted to go was The Blue Parrot Club, the place where Bobby's boyfriend the boxer hung out. The clientele there was almost exclusively West Indian, well-known to the West London drug squad and, so Pete had been told, the only white faces that frequented it were young men who came down there to score and Swedish au pairs looking to get lucky with the rude boys. He was going to have to be careful about making an appearance there without being immediately fingered as a narc. So he'd been taking his time, frequenting the other cafés and restaurants where the colour mix was easier: Totobag's Café on Blenheim Crescent, where the writers and jazzers came to listen to the amiable owner's Jamaican records; and the Safari Tent on Westbourne Park Road, where would-be-Harry-Belafonte Johnny Millington held court in a white tuxedo. Pete had two subjects he could talk about with ease in such places: boxing and jazz, both passions his father handed down. They were subjects that went down well in Ladbroke Grove.

But it didn't look like he would have the chance to use either to buy a little information tonight. For, stuck on the crossroads between Mosley's rally and Portobello's toms, between wanting to see how this piece of street theatre played out or what this distraction could be helping to shield, Pete's night was about to take another turn.

Just as Mosley's warm-up man announced his main act, a little fellow came out of the KPH lounge bar on wide bandy legs. His dress was shabby – a moth-eaten tweed jacket above a pair of black trousers worn at half-mast, shiny with age and shyness of laundry. He pulled a flat cap down over his crinkly brown hair and broad, heavily lined face, eyes like two dark little almonds taking a rapid shufti of the scene around him, thin mouth working on the end of a matchstick.

Pete felt a prickling sensation down the back of his neck. Here was a face he'd seen in the rogue's gallery at the station; Gypsy George O'Hanrahan, who despite his down-at-heel appearance apparently made very good money stealing to order and earned his soubriquet not just from his tinker roots but because he had a magical ability never to get caught with his palm full of silver.

Facts logged at the back of Pete's mind suddenly whirred into the forefront. George hadn't been seen around for a while. He was a rootless character who didn't like to spend too much time in one patch, lest his habits became predictable. Messages could be left for him at certain pubs, it was said, yet the landlords of his preferred hostelries all seemed to suffer from collective amnesia whenever his name was mentioned.

No one here wanted to stay on the right side of the law.

Gypsy George stood within touching distance of Pete, but if he smelt Old Bill he gave nothing away. Instead, he rocked on his heels for a moment, took a lungful of air, as relaxed as a country squire gazing fondly across his acres at sunset. Pete followed the direction of his stare to the far side of Lancaster Road, where one of the Teddy boys was standing at a distance from the rest.

He could have sworn he saw the Teddy boy nod.

Then George stepped down off the kerb and barrelled his way briskly up the Grove, just as Oswald Mosely took the loudhailer in his hand and began his poisoned seduction.

'Good people of Labroke Grove,' he began. 'I come here to tell it to you as it is. To call a spade a spade...'

But his words dissolved into the air around him as if they had never been spoken. Pete was in that quiet zone again, his blood buzzing through his veins, an instinct that urged him to leave this place for the bobbies to deal with and find out instead where the little man was going. He waited just a heartbeat, eyes fixed to the cap on the top of George's head, and then followed in the direction of the setting sun.

4

What Do You Want

Henekeys was heaving by seven o'clock, the dregs of the day turning into night as Toby and I walked with our new friend up Portobello Road. The market traders were packing up and the shoppers had all blown their wages; now it seemed that everyone was drawn towards the old ginhouse on the corner of Westbourne Grove and Portobello Road. A beacon for the thirsty, all painted white with beckoning windows revealing the old wood and glass interior, glowing warmly orange from within.

Clustered around the square bar at the saloon in the front, the stallholders in their aprons drank gin from the day's takings and old men in cloth caps sat quietly, gumming roll-ups and staring blankly across the rims of their mild and bitters. In the back, amid the potted palms, wickerwork chairs and old photographs, was a much younger and livelier crowd, talking loudly and smoking furiously over their glasses of Chianti and G & Ts.

The young man we had met in the jazz shop late that afternoon was taking us to meet his partner-in-crime. Chris Hawtry bore a faint resemblance to Vincent van Gogh, with red hair and a neat little beard clipped in the exact fashion of the Dutchman's. On his top half he wore an artist's smock and red paisley cravat that served to heighten the illusion, but the rolled-up-at-the-cuff blue jeans and heavy duty workman's boots that went underneath rather smashed it. It was a bizarre combination of art and rock 'n' roll but on him it looked perfectly natural. And despite his somewhat fearsome countenance, Chris's soft, considered voice revealed a thoughtful intelligence.

We had only known him for a couple of hours but already knew that he was quietly but firmly anti-establishment. He had been one of the Aldermaston marchers, part of a generation convinced that the world could end at any second at the whim of a bunch of powerful and senile old men. On that point, I agreed with him completely.

Chris had studied fine art, but dropped out when he found his coursework no match for his ideals. He had made his way to Portobello Road instead, supporting himself by buying and selling antiques, something he said he had a knack for, 'knowing the deep and enduring sentimentality of the British people for anything that reminds them of a time they've never lived through'. A bric-a-brac stall on the market had led to his meeting and sharing a house with another disillusioned young artist, this time a refugee from St Martin's, and together they planned their revenge on the establishment. Opening a gallery was just the first step. They intended to make a real name for themselves by opposing everything that was considered tasteful and fashionable.

'This love for the French Expressionists, it's that same sentimentality at work,' he had opined, leaning against the Blue Note section, a copy of Art Blakey and the Jazz Messengers' *Moanin'* in his hand. 'It can't last. This is a Cold War now and the feel will become more brutal, more like the German Impressionists, I think...'

'Like John Bratby,' Toby agreed. 'Look how well he's doing. Although I'm going down another route myself, much more inspired by what you've got in your hand than anything that's hanging in a gallery right now. Did you know Art Blakey put out an album called *Theory of Art*? That's kind of where I got my inspiration from.'

'Indeed?' Chris looked from the record sleeve to Toby and raised his eyebrows.

'Jazz,' Toby warmed to his theme, 'is a landscape in the head. The notes are the colours, the rhythms shape, the form. There's a lot of anger in jazz and that to me is where the new energy is coming from. Not from old Europe, from black America.'

'You have a very good point there.' Chris looked impressed. 'The arts should feed into each other like that. You'll have to come and meet my partner, David. He'll like you a lot, I think.' He checked his wristwatch. 'He'll probably be taking his constitutional to Henekeys right now, if you'd like to join me?'

Through the throng of Henekeys' drinkers I could see a couple of guys we knew from the Royal, handsome upstarts surrounded by serious-looking and very beautiful young girls who hung on their every pronouncement. Underneath a potted palm with his head in a book, oblivious to his surroundings, sat the author Colin Wilson, who had delivered a lecture to us at college last term on the New Existentialism. He looked pretty mild for the *enfant terrible* of English letters, lost in a saggy black polo-neck sweater, his blond fringe falling over his thick, black-rimmed spectacles. Probably the frowning beat girls that flocked around the Royal students didn't even realise who he was. I know I wouldn't have if I hadn't encountered him before.

Chris's friend sat in the far right-hand corner, next to the jukebox and an armchair in which a fat ginger tom slept as peacefully as Wilson was reading. Hidden under a cloud of thick black curly hair I could just make out a chin and a wide mouth, but his eyes were hidden behind a pair of sunglasses and the rest of him was swathed in black to complete the shadowy effect. There was a girl sitting next to him, of about my own age, with waves of long blonde hair and an upturned nose, dressed in red gingham like Brigitte Bardot. I saw her eyes travel up to the screenprint scarf I was wearing and widen slightly with approval.

'David,' said Chris, 'I thought I'd find you here. I've just met these two very interesting young people, Toby and Stella Reade. Toby's looking to exhibit his work, and I think you will enjoy his ideas.' Chris's blue eyes sparkled as he spoke.

It was funny how he called us 'young people', I thought, he must only have been four or five years older than us at most.

'Hey hepcats.' The creature with the black hair got to his feet, slowly uncoiling like a cobra coming out of a basket to a full height of around six foot two. He plucked the cigarette that was caught between the folds of his hair out of his mouth and put it into the ashtray, wiped his hand on his black leather trousers and offered it to Toby. 'I'm Dave Dilworth and this,' he opened a wide palm towards the girl, 'is the lovely Jenny.'

She looked up at us with shrewd blue eyes rimmed in darkest kohl. She had a lemonade and a packet of Gitanes on the table in front of her, an aura about her so sophisticated as to be vaguely intimidating.

'I love your scarf,' she said to me and gave a disarming smile.

'Thank you,' I said, 'I made it myself.'

'Far out!' she exclaimed, her perfect diction rendering the slang slightly comical. 'Then you must make me one too! I'll pay you for it. Don't you think she looks great, Dil? So unlike the rest of the herd.'

'Crazy.' Her hairy companion nodded, folding himself back down into his seat and reaching for his fag. On every finger he had a thick, silver ring, some of them engraved with intricate patterns, and round his neck was an Egyptian Eye of Ra on a thick silver chain. I had never seen anyone like him in my life – half gypsy, half leather boy. How could I possibly look different compared to him?

'I keep telling her,' said Toby, putting his hand on my shoulder as I sat down next to Jenny, 'she has a genius for design. I can just see her setting up her own boutique.'

'Really?' Jenny's eyes flashed with interest.

'What can I get you?' asked Chris.

The men all wanted cask ale, this pub was noted for it. I went for their cider, it had been a hot day and I was thirsty. Jenny declined any alcohol, sticking to her lemonade and the pungent-smelling French cigarettes.

'So what about you, Toby?' Dave asked when that had all been taken care of. 'Where you at?'

His way of speaking was similar to Jenny's, like they'd both taken an overdose of Jack Kerouac. Only Dave's deep, laconic Londoner's voice was more adept at handling the beat idioms than Jenny's prim diction. It sounded quite natural coming from him.

'Well, as I was telling Chris, jazz is my metier.' Toby leaned forwards, fixing the sunglasses with his piercing blue eyes. 'John Coltrane, Art Blakey, Roland Kirk, Miles and Mingus. Most of all Mingus, I get such a keen sense of place from him. I mean, I've never actually been to the fishmarket on San Francisco Bay, but he's taken me there; I've seen the fog rolling in over Alcatraz, the seagulls up there in the sky, the paddle steamers passing by. What I try to do is tap into that, bring the landscape to the canvas the way he puts it into the music; that soulfulness, that energy.'

Dave nodded, his lips curling into a smile. 'Outta sight, dad. You got good taste,' he said.

'Yes,' said Chris, 'it's right that the best art forms should suggest new ideas to each other, don't you think David? Toby was saying earlier, that's where the real energy's coming from, black America. God knows they have enough to be angry about.'

'Yeah, well we threw a few dustbins into the riot last summer didn't we Chris?' Dave said. 'Smashed a few of Mosley's runts before we had to run like hell from the Old Bill. It's a point of family pride for me; my old man and his old man fought the Blackshirts in Cable Street. Can't believe he's still coming round here. Can't believe the people still fall for it. They should have kept him locked up 'til he rotted, bleedin' old bastard. But sorry, I digress. Tell me more about this work of yours, Toby, it really fries my wig.'

Toby continued to elaborate on his theme, Chris and Dave butting in all the time with thoughts of their own. Once you got used to their unusual, contrasting mannerisms, they were great company; Chris precise and prescient, soaking up everything Toby said and immediately contextualising it; Dave wandering off into far-fetched ideas of his own then pulling himself up with another pithy remark. Gradually I stopped thinking that they were in any way unusual, just that they were men with great minds that I wanted very much to be friends with.

Jenny didn't join in with them, she looked mildly bored and after a while started to engage me in another conversation.

'Did you see that programme about life on Mars?' she asked me. 'They think that life as we know it is just starting up there, that there's some kind of primitive moss oxygenating the atmosphere, because moss can survive in the extreme cold. That's what our scientists think anyway. The Russians think it's a dead planet, they've been studying Juno, which is right next to Mars, and it's wobbling on its axis. They reckon it could be a kind of synthetic satellite like the ones they've made, ejected by the Martians millions of years ago. What do you think about that then? Were there really little green men or just a lot of old moss?'

'I haven't given it much thought,' I admitted, thinking how strange she was. She reminded me of a bright little girl trying to impress the grown-ups in that strident way children have when they know they're being ignored. 'We don't have a television set.

We've been spending all our spare money doing up our flat. We've only just got married, you see.'

Jenny's eyes flicked down to the rings on my left hand, the square, silver engagement ring with the dark blue sapphire that we'd found in an antique shop in Kensington when we got engaged and the plain, platinum ring I'd chosen for our wedding.

'You're quite young to be getting hitched,' she considered. 'You must be awfully in love.'

'Yes, well, we are,' I said. 'How about you? Have you been with Dave for long?'

Her blue eyes rolled over to him and lingered there a while, then she took another drag on her cigarette and looked back at me. 'Not long,' she said, 'a couple of months, I suppose. I met him at St Martin's, but he dropped out so he could live like a hobo with Chris.'

'Oh really?' I said. 'We're both at the Royal. What are you studying?'

'All kinds of things,' Jenny said, 'that come under the loose banner of art.' She gave a little laugh and tossed back her mane of hair. She really did look like Brigitte Bardot.

'Originally, I wanted to design record sleeves,' she said, 'but now I've seen that scarf of yours I'm starting to get interested in fashion.'

'Well thank you,' I said, feeling out of my depth. 'So do you have any plans to get married, you and Dave?'

Jenny laughed, blowing out a stream of smoke. 'Dil thinks that love is just the gimmick that makes sex respectable,' she narrowed her eyes, 'and I'm inclined to agree. But,' she tilted her head to one side, examining both myself and Toby at length, 'I must say, you two make a good advert for it.'

I was lost for words at this, but Jenny was clearly just getting started. She looked down into my wicker basket, where amongst the day's food shopping were a couple of books I'd picked up cheap;

Sartre's *Iron in the Soul* and Zola's *Germinal*. Spotting them, she lifted them out and began to examine them.

'Wow,' she said, 'you're a deep thinker too. I think I'm going to like you Stella. I think we're going to be great friends.'

She flashed me that disarming smile again and raised her glass to me, clinked it against my own.

'Salut!' she said with a perfect French accent. 'Here's to new friends.'

Toby was clearly thinking the same thing. 'Do you mind if the chaps here come back to the flat and take a look at the canvases?' he said. 'I know we're in a bit of a mess, with all the dustsheets and that, but…'

'We've seen a lot worse,' Dave finished for him. 'You ought to see the state of our drum.'

'Of course I don't mind,' I said. I didn't want anything to stand in the way of Toby getting his first exhibition, especially now I had met the curators.

'Oh are we going over to your pad now?' Jenny said. 'Cool. I can't wait to see if it's as stylish as you are, Stella.'

She got up and arranged herself in the mirror above where she had been seated. Her wickerwork bag was much nicer than mine: square, with a little catch on the lid and the same red gingham lining as her dress, I noticed, when she opened it to retrieve a white angora bolero to go over the top of her bare shoulders. She had on cork-soled wedges and when she stood up she was a good four inches taller than me in my flat ballet pumps.

It wasn't far to walk to Arundel Gardens from Henekeys. The boys bought a couple more bottles of beer and cider to take with us while Jenny stared at her reflection in the mirror, adding another layer of powder to her already perfect face. Then they set off together in a bunch, leaving me to dawdle behind with Jenny, who walked at the same languorous, self-contained pace as she applied her make-up. For the length of Westbourne Grove, Kensington Park Road and finally Arundel Gardens, all the men that passed us stared and whistled at her. She merely rolled her eyes and pronounced: 'How very *dreary*.'

Back at the flat, Toby had already begun moving the canvases from a stack in our bedroom out to the front room, which by now was at least dry. Dave, who had opened some beers with his penknife and found glasses from the kitchenette, was using a tea chest in the front room as an impromptu bar. Chris was rifling through the albums we had out by the Dansette, the selection we had been painting to.

Jenny followed me into the room and stopped dead in front of the mural.

'Wow!' she exclaimed. 'Out of sight!' She looked over at Dave. 'If this is what his work is like, then man, you've got to have him.'

'Actually,' Toby came into the room behind a pile of canvases, 'that mural was Stella's design. It's the same idea as that scarf you were admiring.'

'Of course!' said Jenny, and narrowed her eyes thoughtfully. 'Well, well, well…'

Chris put the needle down on *The John Barry Sound* and I set about trying to be as helpful as possible. I brought through some chairs from the bedroom, and the easel to rest the canvases on, found some glass ashtrays for the smokers to use. Then, after making sure everyone had all they needed, I excused myself to go to the bathroom.

My face in the mirror was red and shiny. I'd put my hair up into a French pleat and little tendrils had escaped to form curls around my cheeks, making me look about ten years old. I splashed some cold water on to my face, dabbed on a bit of powder, touched up my lipstick and ran a comb through my fringe. I had begun to feel very gauche compared to Jenny.

When I stepped out into the hallway the bedroom light was on and the door was open, which was strange, because I thought I had closed it after I'd taken all the chairs and the easel out of there. I had no wish for the others to see the mess we were currently living in, nor all of our private things.

I put my head around the door. Jenny was standing in the middle of the room, nosing her way through a box of books. She smiled when she saw me.

'I couldn't resist taking a peek,' she said. 'You really are quite the little bookworm aren't you?'

I felt myself go red again. 'Look, do you mind?' I said. 'I'd rather you didn't come in here. That's why I kept the door shut. We've only just moved in and...' My words died in my throat as I saw her eyes suddenly well up with tears.

'I'm sorry,' she said, dropping the book she had been holding. 'I should have realised.' Then she took a hanky from the pocket in her skirt and started sobbing into it. 'I always do stupid things like this,' she went on, 'no wonder I never have any real friends. Nobody likes me and it's all my own fault.'

'Look,' I said, feeling guilty now, 'it doesn't matter. It's just such a mess in here, what with the decorating and everything, I didn't want you to see the place looking like this. I'm not angry with you, honestly.'

She looked beautiful even in the midst of her tears, not even smudging her kohl, her face just shining luminescently. She stumbled over to me and gave me a fulsome hug. 'Oh thank you Stella,' she said.

'Look, why don't you just step into the bathroom there and sort yourself out and I'll make you something to drink,' I said, pulling away from her grasp.

She stood there just staring at me, her eyes completely blank.

'What do you want, Jenny, a cup of tea? I'm sorry I don't have any lemonade.'

I realised I was speaking to her as if she were a child. But it seemed to bring her back to herself.

'I'd love a cup of tea,' she said. 'With just a little milk and one sugar.'

'All right then, I'll get that for you. I'll see you back in the lounge,' I said.

I realised my hands were shaking as I poured the boiling water into the pot. Jenny had completely unnerved me.

Thankfully, everyone was still having a high old time in the lounge. Chris and Dave had looked through Toby's best canvases and offered him space to show five of them alongside their own work at their opening exhibition, which would be held in a month's time. We could begin taking it over to their place in Vernon Yard as soon as was convenient, to see where we wanted to hang them.

'This is all very fortuitous,' said Chris, pouring me a glass of cider without being asked. 'Toby's work was just what we needed to forward our agenda. You'll see exactly what I mean when you've looked at what David and I are going to exhibit.'

'Yeah man,' agreed Dave, 'we're gonna hit the squares right between the eyes. This is the start of the over-the-counter revolution.'

'Wonderful,' I said, wondering what he was talking about.

I put Jenny's cup of tea down on the chest. She was taking her time in the bathroom. 'Here,' said Dave, peering behind me. He had taken his sunglasses off to look at Toby's paintings, using them like an Alice band to hold back his hair. He had dark brown, almost black eyes, and high cheekbones over a full, sensual mouth. It was a wonder he kept a face like that hidden. 'Where's that girl gone? I thought she was with you?'

'Oh, she just had to powder her nose,' I said, feeling a tremor of guilt again.

'That'll be Jenny,' he said with a wry smile, his gaze still on the door beyond me.

She emerged a few moments later, looking fresh as a daisy, took the cup of tea gratefully and sipped it demurely, sitting herself down on the floor by the Dansette, her expression now completely beatific.

Dave went and sat down next to her, talking to her quietly and earnestly, stroking her long blonde hair. I ignored what they were saying, drifting to the other side of the room with Toby and Chris. But it didn't surprise me when, ten minutes later, Dave was making their excuses.

'Jenny's beat,' he said, 'we're gonna make tracks. Thanks for the night, man.' He shook Toby by the hand, then took my own and gave a funny little bow. 'It's a real pleasure to meet some fellow travellers. This is the start of something, man, this is kismet. I'll check you cats soon.'

'Yes thank you,' said Jenny, 'it's been a scream.'

She sounded sincere when she said it, and she smiled at me, but her eyes were still curiously empty.

Toby showed them upstairs while Chris lingered, looking vaguely uncomfortable.

'You don't mind if I don't go straight off do you?' he asked, once they were out of earshot. 'Only I can tell when those two need some time to themselves.'

'Of course not,' I said. 'I can see what you mean.'

'Yes,' he said, frowning and stroking his beard. 'She's a funny girl, is Jenny…'

Then he gave a little laugh and shook his head. 'Still, who am I to talk about that, my entire family think I belong in Bedlam. So what about this geometry of yours then Stella, where do you see it taking you next?'

I realised Chris didn't want to share any more personal thoughts with someone he'd only just met and this made me like him all the more. So I started to tell him about my plans for making 3-D blocks that could be arranged like a big jigsaw to any number of solutions, all of them designed to present an optical illusion. Soon Toby had come back down to join us and we spent the next couple of hours in happy discussion about the possibilities of art.

It was getting on for midnight, the alcohol long gone and several pots of tea later before Chris looked at his watch and decided that he really should be going.

'Well, please do come across to the house any time you like. You've got the address, Toby, it's 4 Vernon Yard, just down the Portobello from Henekeys, tucked away on the left there.'

Toby saw him out, while I began clearing up the debris of our impromptu party, wondering if I should say anything about Jenny's strange little fit. I was in the kitchenette washing up the cups and glasses when he came back down, shaking his head in mild disbelief. 'What a day. What a night! Can you believe it?'

'Of course,' I said, wiping my hands on a tea towel. 'When you're married to a genius, you just expect this kind of thing to happen all the time.'

He pulled me into an embrace. 'You're brilliant, darling. Thanks for being so good about having people back when we're in such a state here.'

'It got you an exhibition,' I said, 'that's all that counts. But they really were nice people, Chris and Dave, even if I don't entirely understand what Dave is talking about half the time. I'm glad we met them.'

I looked up at his grinning face. He looked down at mine,

searching my eyes for what I hadn't said. 'What about Jenny?' he asked. 'Was she all right? I never really got chance to talk to her.'

'She was weird,' I said. 'Just after I came out of the toilet, I caught her in our bedroom, going through a box of books.'

'Really?' He frowned. 'Do you think she was trying to steal something?'

'I don't know,' I said. 'I don't see why she should want to do that, she looked pretty well-heeled to me. What could we possibly have that she couldn't get for herself?'

Toby laughed. 'Happiness?'

He was right, I hadn't thought of that. All that stuff about love being a gimmick. Maybe she was just put out that for all her glamour, Dave wouldn't commit to her.

'Anyway, that's enough about her.' Toby grinned at me wickedly. 'I haven't seen enough of you this evening. I propose that we get straight to bed.'

So we did.

5

Smoke Gets in Your Eyes

Gypsy George walked up the Grove in the same unhurried manner as he had left the KPH, rolling along on his bandy legs with hands stuffed in his pockets. Outside the Elgin, he stopped in front of a couple of little tykes who were sitting on the steps, a girl and a boy who couldn't have been more than four or five, drawing patterns in the dust with a stick and swinging their grubby legs with boredom, waiting for their parents to eventually stagger out. George leant down to them and started fiddling behind his left ear, saying something to them that Pete couldn't quite catch. He saw their eyes widen with wonder as George suddenly produced a little yellow bird from underneath his hat.

Pete was pretty perplexed by this too, having seen the hat go on. He tried to work out whereabouts on his person the thief could have disguised such a thing and it was only when George sat it on his finger and made out that it was talking that he realised the bird was actually stuffed and not really alive.

The little girl stared up at him dumbstruck, while the boy, who looked to be the youngest of the pair, reached up with tiny fingers. George smiled and put the bird up to the youngster's ear, making some more funny talk, before his other hand reached into his pocket and he produced for each of them a penny. In the flicker of an eye, the bird had disappeared, not that either of the children noticed, so amazed were they by their sudden windfall. George ruffled the boy's hair, smiling fondly, then stood up and pushed open the door to the public bar.

Pete was surprised by this spontaneous act of benevolence, but at least he had the wit about him not to barge straight in after the generous gypsy. For, as George disappeared into one door, the Teddy boy who had nodded to him earlier came out of the back of the saloon, which opened on to Westbourne Park Road.

Pete stayed exactly where he was, slowly took out his packet of Player's and lit one up, never taking his eyes off the Ted, who made a sudden left and disappeared into the Mews behind the pub. He counted to ten and sure enough, George followed, out the back door and round the same corner.

The Mews doubled back on to Ladbroke Grove, so it seemed safe to bet that, when they had finished discussing their business, George would come back out of it. It was all Pete could hope for, there was no way of following them and staying unobserved. He stayed close to the wall of the pub, smoking his fag down until it almost burnt his fingers, writing out a description of the Ted in his mind, the surest way to commit his image to memory that he knew.

Five foot eleven, slim build, fair hair with a slight wave to it, blue eyes, wearing a black-and-white chequered sports jacket, black drainpipe trousers and black winklepicker shoes. A very wide face with a slightly hooked nose, probably in his late teens or early twenties, broad shoulders and a slightly knock-kneed walk...

Pete's luck was in. After only a few more minutes, George reappeared, alone, and began barrelling his way towards Portobello Road, picking up a surprising show of speed as he did so. He went right on the corner of Kensington Park Road just as a radio car hurtled past, siren on, swinging left. Pete instinctively pulled back but George paid it no mind, continuing on his way without so much as turning his head. On the corner of Blenheim Crescent he weaved left and disappeared into another hostelry of dubious repute, Finches.

Pete crossed to the other side of the road to consider his options. Like The Elgin, Finches was on the corner of two roads and he wondered if George would simply travel through this one too. In the gathering dusk, he took advantage of the further shade provided by the awnings on the shop opposite and stayed where he could see both exits. His mind was racing and so was his heart.

The windows of Finches were made of thick, bottle glass, so that apart from a diffuse yellow glow, you couldn't make out what was going on in there, just the way the local villains liked it. Pete knew that this was another joint favoured by the white working class, although some of the braver – or tougher – West Indians had begun using it lately. Dressed as he was, in his shabbiest old tweed suit, with similarly battered trilby pulled down over his brow, Pete could have passed himself off amongst them, yet he preferred to stay where he was. If George was up to something, he didn't need a pub fight or a surly local starting something to get in the way of himself and his quarry.

Yet stay still on Portobello Road for long enough and trouble would surely find you. It hadn't been five minutes before Pete heard a voice beside him, soft and low.

'You looking for something mister?'

She was probably in her late teens, but like all the toms, looked older. Harsh make-up covering premature lines and a helmet of hair bleached an ugly orange. A summer dress revealing an elevated cleavage, along with several purple bruises along her neck, clumsily covered with smears of what looked like toothpaste.

'Looking for a good time?'

One of her front teeth was missing and her eyes were glazed, wreathed in purple shadows that clashed nastily with the thick blue paint on her eyelids.

'No,' said Pete, turning his eyes back to the pub, 'and you won't be having much of one if you stop out here much longer.'

'What you on about?' Her voice clanged into a harsh whine.

Pete slowly raised his right arm and took a lengthy gander at his wristwatch.

'In just under four hours' time,' he said, 'I could have you nicked for talking to me like that. So be a good lass and hop it.'

The girl recoiled. 'You're a bogey ain't you?' she screeched. 'I should have smelt it!'

Pete continued to stare at the pub, praying that Gypsy George didn't choose this of all moments to take his leave. Girls around here didn't tend to just do what they were told. Not when they could have a fight about it instead.

'What d'you want to pick on me for?' the brass continued. 'I ain't doing nothing wrong.'

Pete pushed his hat back on his head, turned and stared at her hard.

'Do you want me to just nick you now?' he asked quietly. 'It'd be no bother. Though I doubt your boyfriend would be very pleased with you.' He looked pointedly down at her bruised neck. 'Any more than he already is, like.'

Her mouth opened and closed like a landed fish while her eyes blazed with an elemental hatred. It made her look ten times better than her previous, soporific glaze.

'Get on with you, love,' Pete continued, suppressing a smile. 'Don't waste my time and I won't waste yours.'

'You talk funny, mister. You must be a queer!' was all she had to say to that, but at least she pushed herself off and up the road and just as well she did. Gypsy George was already halfway down

Blenheim Crescent, a little toolbag in his right hand, when Pete turned his head again.

A jolt of excitement propelled him up the pavement after him. His luck was holding, the girl had unwittingly provided him with some cover – if Gypsy George had noticed him at all it had probably looked like he was engaged in a lovers' tiff. Still, his heart stayed in his mouth as he dogged the little man through the darkening streets, fully aware that the sleight of hand George had demonstrated to the kids outside the pub was probably the least of his devious talents.

It was a fairly twisting path that George took too: back across the Grove and up to Elgin Crescent, threading through Rosemead Road on to Lansdowne Crescent, to the very top of the hill, where the most imposing of the white stucco mansions sprawled out among their parks and gardens, providing every opportunity for the thief to get lost under a hedge or over a crumbling wall. It was very beautiful up here, and Pete had often wondered how these buildings would have looked before the war, before the paintwork had turned grey and brambles and nettles had overrun the gardens. Wondered if they would ever get restored to their former glory, or just go on quietly crumbling into dust.

But there was no time for thoughts like that now; only the desperate need to keep George within his sights.

Round the back of the crescent, two terraces converged, backing on to a wide, communal garden. A wrought-iron fence backed by a high privet hedge and the overhanging boughs of trees shielded the park from prying eyes. Gypsy George stopped. He slowly turned his head around, sniffing the air like a hound picking up a scent, and Pete only just had time to duck down behind a row of overflowing dustbins at the side of a driveway. The stench of decaying vegetables assailed his nostrils along with a sudden fear that George had sensed his tail all along and was waiting until the last moment to deceive him into giving the game away.

For when he raised his head again, the little thief had melted into the dusk. Pete's heart hammered in his chest. He crouched forwards, peering out from behind the bins. George had gone neither to the left nor the right, it seemed he had just vanished, using the same Romany magic that had fashioned a bird out of thin air.

Don't be daft, Pete chided himself. Stay calm and look harder.

Through a tiny gap in the privet hedge, he thought he saw the merest flicker of movement. Of course, he thought, little bugger's gone straight through it. Cautiously, he stole towards the last place he'd seen George standing, wondering if that tool bag he'd been toting had contained some kind of bolt-cutters. But when he got up close, the railings were all intact. He pushed against them to make sure, noting at the same time that there was nowhere near a big enough gap in the hedge even for an illusionist such as George to slip through so quickly. His brow furrowed and he stepped sideways, trying to see another way through the obstacle, when an overhanging branch knocked his trilby askew. Pete looked up sharply. There, wrapped around the lower bough of the nearest tree, was a length of rope.

It wasn't magic, but a breathtaking combination of agility and speed. By the time Pete had caught hold of the end of the rope and pulled himself up to the crook of the branch, George was long gone.

Pete steadied himself against the gnarled bark of the tree, breathing hard. He looked out across the gardens, trying to catch another flicker of motion. But George had timed this well, the darkness was folding her cloak around them rapidly, and all Pete could make out were the outlines of hedges and walls where people's gardens backed on to the communal park, and the clusters of trees, black shapes diffusing into the grey of coming night. A solitary blackbird sounded out a last frantic burst of song and then everything went still.

Pete crouched down, holding on to the rope for balance. He scanned around the back of the houses, waiting for something to change, some tiny sign to point his way. All he could hear was his own breath. They may only have been three streets away from Notting Hill nick itself, but up here, shielded by the tall houses from the noise of the main road, they might as well have been in the middle of the country.

Then he saw a pinprick of light, flashing for a second out of the top floor window of one of the mid-terrace houses. Without another thought, he swung off the tree, sliding down the rope and dropping on to the grass below with a dull thud. Keeping the house fixed in his line of vision, he began to run.

He slowed as he reached the garden wall and ducked down low, running his fingers along the brickwork, feeling his way to the gate. Peering through the wooden slats, he could see that the French doors at the back of the house had been left slightly ajar. He crouched back down beside the wall, at the side of the gate, trying not even to breathe and praying that the thumping of his heart wouldn't give the game away.

The minutes stretched out in elastic time in the still cool of the garden. Pete's ears strained for the tiniest of sounds above the gentle murmur of the breeze through the grass and the occasional yowl of a cat. He felt like all his senses were heightening, ready for the chase, the hairs rising on the back of his neck.

There was the tiniest of clicks as the backdoor closed and a padding of footsteps, soft-soled shoes hardly making a sound. The moment that the gate opened and the shape of George appeared on the other side, Pete launched himself straight at him in a perfect rugby tackle, bringing the thief crashing to the ground. A startled gasp rose from George's throat but he had been taken too unawares to put up much of a fight with a man twice his size and weight, pumped full of adrenalin, who had him flat on his back with his arms held tight behind him within seconds.

'George O'Hanrahan,' Pete said, 'I am arresting you for suspected breaking and entering. You do not have to say anything but what you do say may be taken down and used in evidence against you.' George twisted and squirmed underneath him, uttering oaths in a language the copper couldn't understand. He was a strong man and had Pete not had the advantage of surprise he doubted he could have subdued George so successfully. But he kept his whole weight down on the thief's back until George had thrashed out all his rage, then resignedly fell silent.

Still sitting on top of him, Pete reached for the toolbag George had dropped and pulled it open, expecting to find jewellery or candlesticks, something that was obviously valuable. Instead, by the light of the torch he fished from his pocket, he made out only two well-stuffed brown envelopes and a canister of film.

Underneath him, George grunted ill humour.

'Not what you were expecting there, bogey?' he said. He started to laugh, breaking into a hacking cough.

Well no, it wasn't, but George was still a wanted man.

'Jaysus man, can you get offa me?' he implored. 'You're killing me here.'

'All in good time,' said Pete. 'Soon as I work out how I'm going to get you out of here.'

This was a problem he hadn't thought about when he'd dived out of the tree, but there was no way they were going to go back the way they'd come. They were locked inside a private garden without a key, so there was really only one thing for it. 'All right O'Hanrahan.' Pete hauled his quarry to his feet, still keeping his right arm firmly in a lock. He could have used a pair of handcuffs but there were only a few sets at the station and senior detectives took priority. 'You'll have to show me how you get in and out of these places so easy. Let's leave by the front door, shall we?'

Pete was just steering him back through the French doors and into the house, George still twisting and squirming in his grasp, when the lights came on and a loud, upper class voice sounded out.

'Stop right where you are!'

An elderly butler, his white hair sticking up from the crown of his head, stood brandishing a brass poker on the threshold of the most opulent kitchen Pete had ever set eyes on. It was like something from a stately home, with a huge range and copper pans hanging down from the ceiling, over an immense oak table on which a block of chopping knives sat ominously. For a second, Pete and the butler stared at each other in mutual surprise, a moment that George immediately took advantage of, kicking Pete as hard as he could in the shin and trying to swivel round past him to freedom.

'Ooof!' The pain was sharp and he tottered backwards, George pushing at him like a bullock. Luckily, the butler was more ferocious than his advancing years suggested. 'Stop thief!' he yelled, charging them with his poker aloft. Pete saw the glint of the yellow metal flash before his eyes, coming down hard across the side of George's head. The little man's eyes rolled back in his head and he dropped to the floor, out cold.

'Got you!' the butler yelled, raising his poker arm again to strike a second time. Pete dodged out of his reach, putting his palms up as he did.

'Steady,' he said, 'I'm a police officer.'

'What?' The butler's eyes were red-rimmed and there was a strong smell of whisky on his breath. Pete reached for his warrant card while there was still time.

'PC Peter Bradley, 215, I'm an aid to CID at Notting Hill station,' he said, sticking it right under the old man's nose. 'See for yourself, sir.'

'Well,' said the butler in exasperation, 'what are you doing in my kitchen?'

'Catching this one,' said Pete, nodding towards George's slumped figure, 'on his way out.'

It turned out that the old boy was the retainer of Lord Douglas Somerset, who was out at the theatre and not expected back until after midnight. He'd not heard George breaking in because he'd fallen asleep listening to the radio in his quarters downstairs, helped no doubt by that little nightcap or two he'd taken after his Lordship gave him permission to retire. Once he had calmed down, the poor old dear was mortified that he'd let the family honour down in such a way. He'd been in the service of the Somersets since he was Lord Douglas's father's batman in South Africa. Pete felt sorry for him as he explained all, leaning against a chair, wiping his forehead with a handkerchief, the poker now discarded on the table.

'You've no reason to chide yourself, sir,' he said, poking at George's prone form with his foot. 'This one's a master criminal. He's been on our list for years; this is the first time he's ever been caught in the act. You should be proud of yourself.'

While George was still unconscious, they called the station to summon a helping hand. The butler tried to remember which playhouse his lordship was attending to no avail; in the end he left a message for Somerset at his club in Mayfair, where he was bound to decant himself after the show. Pete left him to check over the house with one of the beat bobbies who rolled up in the radio car, while he and the other dropped the dazed thief back on to his feet and carted him off. George continued to slur and curse all the way to the nick, but upon crossing the threshold, grew grimly silent.

The booking sergeant looked up as Pete marched George through the front door of the nick, an expression of delight on his face.

'Well, well, well,' he said, 'if it isn't the gypsy king himself! Bet you didn't see this coming in your crystal ball, did you old son?'

George said nothing, just stared at the man with cold hatred in his black eyes, a red weal throbbing on his left temple.

It must have been pretty humiliating for him.

'Check every inch of the bugger,' Pete said, as he handed him over. 'I've seen him pull things out of thin air once already tonight. For all I know he's got a Gainsborough stashed down the back of his drawers.'

CID were all over George and the contents of his toolbag the moment he was whisked off to the cells. Pete gave what he hoped was a thorough debriefing of the night's events to his Sergeant, Derek Cooper, stressing that, in his opinion, they should be searching the Grove for George's Teddy boy accomplice. There had been a few troublemakers hauled off from the Mosley sideshow earlier, but none of the yobs in the cells matched this one's appearance. Then, midway through their conversation, Cooper was called out to speak to someone and when he returned, his expression had changed from active interest to a perplexed frown.

'That Teddy boy you said you saw talking to the suspect, can you run through his description for me again?' he asked.

Pete did so.

'Well that is peculiar,' said Cooper, tapping his pen against the top of the desk. 'We've just had a young man come in who's a perfect match. Only,' he leaned forwards, a questioning look in his eyes, 'this one says he's Lord Douglas Somerset's son.'

6

It's Only Make Believe

It took me longer than I thought it would to put the finishing touches to the costumes for the opening night. I must have been sat in our back garden for six hours solidly, stitching on sequins and ribbons to turn two ballet leotards into showgirls' catsuits. It was intricate, repetitive and boring work. But it was just what I needed that day.

A letter from Ma had come in the morning post. She was as unhappy with my wedding as I had been with hers. She couldn't know how closely the two events were entwined.

Dennis and Ma had been married back in January, at the Bloxwich registry office. It had been a day of black skies and heavy snow, an omen perhaps, of what she was letting herself in for. A meal in the pub afterwards with my aunts and uncles and a smattering of friends from church, roast beef and hard potatoes. I couldn't get a single thing down me. The memory of Pa was so strong I could almost see him there, as he was before the illness, wearing his beret on the side of his head and his pipe in the corner of his mouth, watching with horror at what his Mary was doing.

It was the thought of Pa that had propelled me towards the public telephone by the toilets in that dim and dusty pub. Just before I had left, I had confessed to Toby my impending dread about the nuptials. He told me to call him if I needed picking up from the station. Thank God, I managed to get through to him.

Back at Euston, I alighted on the concourse feeling more alone than ever. As soon as I saw him striding towards me, a look of tender concern in his big blue eyes, the tears wouldn't stop. He took me back to Earl's Court in his little grey Wolseley, made me cocoa and let me sob it all out of my system. That night we exchanged our family histories, or at least, the stories of our parents.

Toby always tried his best to hide it, but his family were proper rich. The reason he had a whole basement to himself in Arundel Gardens was that it belonged to a property owned by his family. The rest of the floors were split into flats and rented out, but Toby had persuaded his father to let him have this space for himself when he came back from National Service to start college. Things had become so unbearable for him at home he couldn't contemplate returning. His father understood that much at least.

General Arthur St John Reade was a career soldier who had distinguished himself in Africa during the war. By comparison to the society of Desert Rats, he found London hard to tolerate and spent all his leave ensconced in his club in deepest Mayfair. Toby said he had always been a distant figure, idly patting him on the head at Christmas and then moving off, leaving behind an impression as thin as a trail of cigar smoke. His mother, Pearl, had been a successful stage actress before he was born and had married for money rather than love. Disappointed by the way things turned out, left alone and bored in their huge house in Putney, she had let Toby be brought up by his nanny while she pursued her lost muse through the bottom of a gin bottle and a succession of affairs with younger men.

Just before he left to do National Service, he had found his mother in bed with his best friend from school.

'We're not going to be like that are we, Stella?' he had asked, his eyes red-rimmed, as the clock ticked towards 4 a.m. 'Selfish idiots getting married for what we can get out of it.'

'No.' I grasped his hand in my own. 'No we're not.'

That wasn't how Ma had seen it. All afternoon, I had sat and stitched sequins for her every word of recrimination, the shrill, hurt hysteria that had emanated from those pale lavender pages, along with the lingering smell of her perfume.

It was only when the light began to fade into dusk that I realised that I must already be late. I was supposed to be meeting Toby at Vernon Yard at eight, to put the finishing touches to everything. I looked up from my work and blinked rapidly. All that concentrating had made me go almost cross-eyed, an affliction I had suffered from as a child. Lights had come on around the square, mothers calling their children in for bed beyond our garden gate, the birds warbling their evensong. The world took a while to come into focus.

Once it did, I packed up and locked up quickly, throwing everything into my sewing basket, including the last batch of leaflets that we'd yet to hand out, to drop into Henekeys on the way. I must have been thinking ahead of my feet, running down our front steps and turning without looking, as I collided headlong with a man who was about to go up the steps of the house next door.

'Steady there, love.' He grabbed hold of my shoulders, saving me from bouncing straight off him and on to the pavement. He was a thick, solid bear of a man, easily over six foot, but his voice seemed oddly delicate by comparison.

I looked up, startled. He was smiling back, a nice, easy smile on a slightly battered face, with a wonky nose and a scar running through his left eyebrow, which had been cleanly shaved and carefully groomed. His thick black hair was cut into a sharp, Italian style, as was the dark blue fabric of the suit he was wearing.

'Are you OK?' he asked, letting go of me. He smelt strongly of aftershave and soap.

'Y-yes, thanks,' I stammered, knowing that my face had gone bright red. 'I'm so sorry, I was in such a hurry I didn't look where I was going.'

'Well, no harm done,' he said, looking down at my basket and the twinkling sequins within. 'I say, that looks nice. What is it?'

'Oh, just some costumes,' I said, 'for an exhibition my husband's putting on. They've taken me ages, which is why I was late, they're so fiddly these little sequins.'

I had no idea why I was telling him this.

'An exhibition?' he said. 'How exciting. What is it, art, theatre…?'

'Modern art,' I replied. 'It opens tomorrow, just around the corner in Vernon Yard. Perhaps you'd like to come?'

I fumbled about trying to find him a leaflet without getting myself speared on the needles and pins that were still sticking out at all angles from the unfinished outfits.

'I hope you don't mind me asking,' he said, 'but you came from next door, didn't you? Are you Toby's new wife? I mean,' he gave a self-conscious chuckle, 'not that he had an old one…'

'Yes,' I said, having extracted what I was searching for. 'Are you a friend of his?'

'Well not really ducks, but we did get to know him quite well last summer. We had a few garden parties and seeing as he was a neighbour we invited him out of politeness. We didn't want to disturb him when he could have been having fun, you know. Lovely young man he is. I'm Leonard Jacobson, by the way, but my friends call me Lenny – I live in the next basement down from you with my friend, James Myers.'

'Stella Reade,' I said, offering him the leaflet and then my hand. 'Pleased to meet you, Lenny.'

'AGOG,' Lenny read, 'What's that all about then?'

'It's Toby and another two local artists, Chris Hawtry and Dave Dilworth,' I said. 'They've got kind of similar ideas, a bit of Abstract Classicism and Cubism, but they needed one thing to link it all together.'

'I bet they did.' Lenny nodded solemnly and I wondered if he understood what I was saying.

'So they used an idea from the Situationists and named themselves after the giants Gog and Magog. The ancient guardians of London.' I felt a bit foolish as I didn't properly understand where this idea of Dave's had come from, but Lenny's expression suddenly got more enthusiastic.

'Ooh I know, like at the Lord Mayor's Show,' he said and this time it was my turn to smile through my incomprehension. 'Very nice. Well ducks, I better not hold you up no more, but I'll tell James and I'm sure he'd love to come. It was nice to run into you,' he squeezed my arm, 'and we'll see you tomorrow. Ta ta now love, and give our best to Toby.'

It was only as I reached the corner of Kensington Park Road that I suddenly made the connection. Lenny and James lived next door to us on the right-hand side. That meant that it was them who were making that weird music on that night of the dream...

The memory made me shiver involuntarily but I pushed the feeling aside. I thought Lenny had been lovely and surely his friend would be too. By the time I had reached Vernon Yard, I could only think about what was to come on opening night.

Dave stood at the doorway, grinning. A shiny black top hat was pushed down over his curls, a red ringmaster's tailcoat around his shoulders. He brandished a megaphone in his hand and his dark eyes glittered.

'Roll up, roll up,' his voice took on an electronic drone as he lifted the contraption to his lips, 'for the greatest show on earth.

It's the new art of the future folks, made by our proletarian hands for the delectation of your upper crust eyeballs. Scenes to dazzle and amaze! Sights that can even make you think! We've used more ink here than on the tattooed lady's torso, more sets of brains than the two-headed lamb. You've never seen anything like it, ladies and gennelmen, step right this way. You'll be amazed! You'll be astounded! You'll be AGOG!'

We had strung Chinese lanterns across the tiny mews and, on the cobbles below, a line of people snaked down towards Portobello Road. The spectacle had been planned down to its finest details, which was why Jenny and I were now standing in our showgirl outfits, yellow and blue plumes of feathers rising from the jewelled tiaras on our heads, fishnet tights and tap-dance shoes and the longest false eyelashes over our electric blue eyes. We were holding trays full of cava for the guests to take when at last El Diablo Dilworth allowed his impatient audience through the door.

Between us, in the entrance hall, stood a large, stuffed tiger. It stared ahead with glassy eyes as the ringmaster finally stood aside, an expression that was at odds with those on the faces of our guests.

What greeted them was a room like something from *Alice in Wonderland*. Distorting mirrors lined the walls, fairylights twinkled among them, illuminating posters for the circus and all manner of strange, spotted, striped and large-fanged beasts, including the two-headed sheep. Dave had managed to borrow the lot from a friend he had made, a dealer in the Red Lion arcade named Cedric, who had once been in the circus and now made a living out of taxidermy. It was a fortuitous friendship, for nothing could have encapsulated better Chris's theories of the British. All the vaudeville of yesteryear was here for them to gawp at – all the better to throw the artists' own work into stark relief.

They had to turn right through the hallway into the first of two rooms, which would once have been the stables part of the mews house. Chris and Dave had ripped out everything from them, whitewashed the walls and polished up the cobbled floors, so that there was a big, clean space in which to hang the work, at odds with the cramped confines of the circus hallway.

In the front room were Chris's huge cityscapes, rendered in Cubist-influenced geometry and dark shades of black, blue and grey, punctuated by cool yellow and mauve. Somehow they seemed at once ancient and modern; the smoked ruins of the Blitz turned into fairytale landscapes, surrounded by the weird Futurism of the emerging new buildings. His more figurative studies of people – an old man sat in a drab café eking out a cup of tea; women out shopping on Portobello standing on the corner for a gossip – seemed to segue nicely into Toby's jazz stylings.

The last thing they would see, in the room beyond, was Dave's work. This was far angrier and seemed to go beyond art and into a kind of on-the-street reportage. Unlike Chris and Toby, who suggested how you might feel about their images, Dave confronted you with his. He was an avid photographer and had amassed vast collages of local life, including some scenes from the race riots, Mosley's rallies and the racialist graffiti painted on the walls, which were juxtaposed with photos taken in mushroom clubs, of people dancing, singing and laughing.

Out of these images came paintings of policemen with their batons flying, Mosley raising his arm in a Hitler salute and coloured men crouched down and cowering, under slogans such as 'Know your rights', 'Declaration of Human Rights' and a newspaper headline from the *Kensington Post* saying, *Will good intentions pave the road to Notting Hell?*

They were all rendered in thick black, grey and red oils and looked really harsh. But among them were smaller paintings of the dancing, laughing people, in yellows, browns, oranges that seemed to fill up the room with light. Dave positioned his photos and newspaper cuttings amongst them, giving a running commentary on the two lives of Ladbroke Grove.

It wasn't long before the place was heaving with all sorts of people, from art college buddies to newspaper reporters, lecturers, beatniks, and bohemians of all stripes. Jenny and I spent most of the evening running up and down the stairs to what she had accurately described as the hobo kitchen, where the bottles of cava lay in a sink full of water and a rapidly diminishing block of ice.

'So much for us,' she said, popping the cork on another bottle. 'We're just glorified scullery maids in these stupid outfits. That's all our contribution to this bloody prole art struggle amounts to.'

I held up a tray of empty glasses and watched her pour the bubbles in, pouting like she was screen-testing for Roger Vadim. Her figure was so va-va-voom it made me feel like an underdeveloped child.

'But still,' I said, 'it's pretty exciting isn't it? I mean, the amount of people who've turned up...'

Jenny wrinkled her nose.

'I suppose it rather is,' she conceded. 'I had no idea Dil knew *so* many different kinds of creatures and some of them look seriously rich. Ringmaster is right, isn't it? He's got them all right where he wants them.'

I had spent a lot of time with Jenny in the run up to the exhibition. As Jackie had gone off to fruit-pick her way around France for the summer, she was the only female company I'd had and I'd started to get used to her idiosyncratic ways. She never made further mention of her *faux pas* in my bedroom. Instead she seemed to be constantly bestowing on me gifts of perfume, make-up and silk scarves, as well as making good her promise of buying my screenprint designs for far more money than they were worth.

She was so determined we were going to be the best of friends that it was starting to seem like we were.

'But you wait,' she said, finishing off the bottle, ''til we open our shop. We'll have them waiting on us for a change then. See how they like it.'

The idea that had been budding on the night we first met had now turned into something of an obsession for Jenny. I let her get on with thinking it, knowing that it could never become a reality. After all, we were back at college in another few weeks, when would we ever have the time or the money to open a shop?

'Yes,' I joined in with the game, 'and there'll be none of this fake champagne then either. It will be Moët & Chandon all the way.'

'Exactly.' She tossed her feathered head imperiously and led the way back downstairs.

Fed up with lingering in the hallway, we wove our way through the throng, past the lions and tigers and into the gallery, so we could take all the action in. Jenny gave me a wink and ducked into Dave's room with her tray, while I circulated in the front, offering fresh glasses and trying to work out who was who amongst the chattering mob.

I saw Toby, talking to a couple of men bearing cameras and notebooks, and my heart skipped a beat. They were the press, they had to be. Chris, in another corner, was talking to a man in a thirties suit and horn-rimmed spectacles and a black-clad aesthete with the pale eyes of a Russian soldier. Other artists, I reckoned. There was a woman who looked like a dowager duchess in fox furs, examining the paintings through a pince-nez, probably a collector and hopefully as well-heeled as she appeared. There was a plethora of young men attended by serious-looking women in turtle necks and slacks, all making earnest comments about what they were seeing and how it was affecting them. Fellow students, probably penniless. The conversation roiled around me like waves.

I felt a hand on my arm.

'This is brilliant, ducks, I can't believe it. Your Toby's a genius – and I love the little circus on the way in.'

It was my next-door neighbour Lenny, all spruced up to the nines, this time in emerald green.

'You look fab in all your feathers.' He leant over my tray and gave me a peck on the cheek. 'I can see all that hard work paid off.'

'Thanks Lenny.' I offered him one of my few remaining glasses of cava. 'Isn't James with you?' I was both curious and apprehensive about meeting the man responsible for making all those weird sounds. Toby had explained to me that it was James who made the music and went looking for bands to produce. Lenny had a straight job at the bank that probably paid their rent.

'He's just gone through there.' Lenny nodded towards Dave's room. 'I'll introduce you when he comes back. He's been having a hard time with his work recently, poor love, this is just what he needs to get out of the house and mingle. With some people who have a few ideas of their own for a change.' He took a sip of the drink, arching his black eyebrows as he did.

'Hmmm, let's see if I know anyone here.' He scanned the room, eyes narrowing, then moved in closer to me and said in a low whisper, 'See her there?' He nodded towards an Amazonian blonde wearing what looked suspiciously like genuine Christian Dior and smoking a cigarette in an ebony holder. 'That's Winston Churchill's daughter that is. She likes to slum it round here, you know. She's a fan of' – he raised his eyebrows – '*dark meat*. Quite a few of them like that, as you probably know. Can't say I blame them. It's better than all that stiff upper lip they're used to. Stiff upper lip and loose drawers, dear.'

I suppressed a giggle and indicated the dowager duchess. 'What about her?'

'Lady Millicent Maybury,' he said, 'notorious lesbian.' He caught the look on my face and chuckled. 'Honestly dear, you can't get a member of the upper class who isn't kinky. You want to be careful of who you're hanging out with. Oh look, here comes your Toby.'

'Lenny,' said my husband, reaching over to shake hands, 'how excellent to see you. It's been a while hasn't it?'

'Too long, Toby, too long. But I can see you've been doing all right for yourself,' said Lenny, winking at me. 'And an exhibition, too. No wonder we haven't seen you.'

'Were they journalists you were just talking to?' I asked.

'Yeah,' Toby's face was alight with excitement, '*Kensington Post*. They're going to run a review in their art section this Friday. And not only that, I've had two other galleries asking me to come in and see them and I think I might even have made a sale with that old lady there in the fox furs.'

'You deserve a drink,' I said, looking down at my tray so as to avoid Lenny's eye and therefore a fit of giggles. 'Only, I see there's none left. Hang on a minute, I'll go and see if there's any more upstairs.'

'Ain't she lovely?' I heard Lenny say as I moved towards the door.

I clattered up the stairs and came to a halt at the kitchen door.

There was a little old couple sitting at the kitchen table. Not the sort of the dowager duchess or all the rich people that Lenny had pointed out, but a sweet old man with a walking stick between his legs and a tiny little lady in her best navy blue suit and hat. Normal-looking people. The last kind you would have expected to find here.

The man looked up as I entered. He was about sixty, I would have guessed, wearing a battered pea-jacket over a pair of cords that had seen better days, a peaked cap on top of a wide, round face that looked oddly like a weather-beaten baby's. A totally innocent pair of blue eyes and a crinkly, gap-toothed smile. He fished his walking stick out to one side and lent on it to hoist himself to his feet, a motion that gave me a sudden pang, a memory of Pa.

'Hello,' he said in a gentle rumble, traces of a country accent. 'Is that Jenny?'

'No, I'm Stella,' I said, 'Toby's wife.'

He looked puzzled so I added: 'One of the other artists downstairs.'

'Oh, I see,' he said, the smile returning to his face. 'Well I'm Cedric, and this is my wife Mya. David said we could sit up here. I hope you don't mind, but it's a bit crowded for us down there.'

He offered me his hand and it closed around mine, big, warm and rough. There was an infinite air of gentleness about him and at once I realised who he must be, the man who was so good with animals.

'Cedric,' I said, 'you're the one who lent Dave all the circus things?'

''As right, girl.' His smile deepened. 'He's all right is David. Got an old head on young shoulders, he have. He reckon I'll have a whole new lot a customers after they seen this show. I hope he's right.'

'Oh, how nice to meet you.' Impulsively, I sat down opposite them. 'And you too, of course,' I said to Mya.

Mya smiled sweetly. She looked like a little bird. There was something that felt familiar about her.

'Those are all the memories of our youth down there, dear,' she said. 'We met at Billy Bolton's circus, Cedric and I, on Bournemouth seafront in the spring of 1923.'

Cedric shuffled back down into the seat next to his wife and took her hand, smiling at her as if they had only just met. All of a sudden I felt tears prick at the back of my eyelids. It was because he reminded me of Pa, I supposed. Or maybe it was because they were still so obviously in love. I said a silent prayer that Toby and I would still be like that in another thirty-six years.

'He was a lion tamer, did you know?' Mya continued. 'He was twenty-four when we met but already a hardened veteran. The Lion Boy they called him.'

''As right.' Cedric nodded. 'England's youngest lion tamer I were. Only ten year old when I run away to join the circus. They tried to put me in an orphanage, but I weren't having none of that. Got to be with my animals, I have.'

'Gentle as lambs they were with him,' Mya agreed. 'The most ferocious lion, the biggest tiger, you couldn't imagine it dear, but they were like pussycats to Cedric.'

'So those ones downstairs,' I realised, 'are your old circus companions?'

''As right,' said Cedric, ''As why I learned how to do the taxidermy, so I wouldn't ha' to leave them behind. And 'as seen me all right since we retired from all that. 'As how I earn my living these days. Always with my animals.'

'Anyway dear,' Mya put her hand on top of mine, 'you'd better get on, don't let us old folks slow you down.'

The strangest feeling came over me when she touched me. A rush of disjointed memories, but memories that were like dreams, images coming in rapid succession. Grandma's bedroom, air raid sirens, fire. Pa's funeral, church, the organ playing 'Abide With Me'. A dark avenue of trees and the noise of a toilet flushing. All of a sudden I felt faint.

'Oh my dear,' I heard her say and it sounded like it was coming from a long way away. She lifted her hand up and put her fingertips together, then began moving them over each other as if she were trying to count quickly.

Just like Grandma used to do, my own voice said in my head.

'It's all right, it's all right,' Mya said to me. 'Come back Stella, it's all right.'

I looked up at her and the room seemed a bit too bright, as if I'd just woken up from a dream.

'It's all right,' she repeated. I blinked.

'Oh, there you are, Stella.' Another voice behind me. Sharp, with an edge of practised boredom underlining it. Jenny.

'Sorry.' I turned round, still feeling as if tendrils of sleep were curling around me and I had to shake myself free from their grasp.

'Toby said you'd gone to get more drinks, but you've been gone for half an hour.'

'Have I?' I touched my forehead. It was hot, and the tiara was digging into me, something I had only just realised. As soon as I did, my temples started throbbing. Half an hour? I could have sworn I had only been here for five minutes.

'I'm sorry,' I said, 'I've just been talking to Cedric and Mya here. Do you know them? They lent Dave the circus things.'

Jenny looked at me as if I was gabbling.

'It's all our fault, dear,' said Mya. 'We've been diverting her with our old circus tales I'm afraid. Nothing that you would be interested in, I'm sure.'

'Indeed,' said Jenny, reaching the last bottle of cava out of the sink and popping its cork. She placed it on my discarded tray and put it down in front of me.

'There you are, Stella,' she said, 'the rich and about-to-be-famous are waiting.'

Mya looked up at her then back at me. 'You get on now dear and don't worry. You'll know where to find me when you need me.'

I still felt disorientated as I walked down the stairs after Jenny.

'I think this tiara is starting to give me a migraine,' I said, trying to explain to myself more than to her why I was feeling this way. But Jenny didn't seem to hear it.

'It's bad enough Dave hanging out with those boring old squares,' she said, 'without you getting caught up with them, too. I know they've been *sooo* helpful, but really. They creep me out. Especially her. Apparently she was a fortune teller, what a load of crystal balls.' Jenny shuddered.

'Anyway,' she went on, 'you won't believe what Dil's up to now. A room full of bread-heads all bursting to give him their cash and he's talking to some bug-eyed monster who says he's a record producer. That's what he really wants, you know, to be a bloody pop star. This is all such a joke to him, Stella, no matter what he says.'

'Oh,' I started to say, 'that'll be my next…'

'Just take a look for yourself,' she said, virtually pushing me through the hallway and into the throng downstairs.

7

Midnight Shift

Pete looked through the window in the door of Interview Room 3. It was him all right, still wearing that checked sports jacket and the ridiculous shoes, too long in the limb to be comfortable in the hard wooden chair he was hunched over, too much on his mind to sit still. He scraped his hand through his greasy pompadour as he spoke to the constable opposite him, his left foot jigging under the table, eyes darting up and down and around the room.

'Well,' Cooper scratched his chin thoughtfully, 'that'll make life interesting. Right then, let's introduce ourselves shall we?'

He pushed the door open. Sports Jacket was still in mid-flow and the constable with him looked up, relieved.

'Thank you, Constable, we'll take over now.' Cooper smiled, projecting orderly benevolence in Sports Jacket's direction. 'Detective Sergeant Cooper,' he said, 'and this is PC Bradley. Now you are Earl Somerset, is that correct, sir?'

The young man shot to his feet, still pushing his hair back from his forehead, his eyes like spinning plates.

'Giles Somerset, please call me Giles.' He extended his hand, fretfully shaking with both of them, his palm slippery with sweat. Absent-mindedly, he wiped it on his trousers before sitting back down. 'Look, officer, can you tell me what's going on? I got home to find old Dodson at his smelling salts with a policeman saying the place has been burgled and no one can get hold of Father. I get here and no one will answer my questions, then I'm put in a cell as if I'm the one under suspicion. Is this normally the way you do things?'

'This isn't a cell, sir,' said Cooper, 'it's an interview room. We've brought you in here to keep things private. You don't want the world and his wife to be hearing what you've been saying at the front desk now do you?'

Giles Somerset grimaced. 'I see. Well, I suppose I appreciate that,' he said.

'Now then,' Cooper continued, 'we've apprehended the fellow caught breaking into your father's house and everything he was attempting to make off with. Once my CID lads have finished searching the miscreant, we'll begin questioning him. But just for background, do you mind if we ask you a few questions pertaining to your father's house and business?'

Pete saw a number of emotions pass over the young man's face as Cooper spoke, almost as if he was reading his thoughts. Shock, fear and then a sly kind of cunning settled across his features as he lounged back on his uncomfortable seat.

'No, not at all,' he said, spreading his fingers out on the desk in front of him. For a moment he seemed to be studying his nails, then he looked up, those round blue eyes attempting a choirboy's look of innocence.

'What do you need to know?'

'Your father's background sir, I believe he's a peer of the realm?'

'That's right,' Somerset said. 'Though he's on his summer recess now, which is probably why you can't find him. He tends to spend as many of his evenings at St James as possible.'

'That's his club, is it sir?'

'That's right. It's so discreet you practically vanish when you go through the door. Perfect for people like Father who don't like to be disturbed.'

'He's a military man I believe?'

'Yes.' Somerset's eyes swept the floor. 'Royal Fusiliers. Goes back centuries, our family and that regiment, all the way back to Monmouth's Rebellion, if you really want to know. Even old Dodson's a relic from South Africa, as he no doubt told you.'

Pete traded glances with Cooper, wondering if they were thinking the same thing. Old Somerset sounded like he was a fellow to be proud of but his son's tone was dull, verging on disgusted.

'Are you his only son, sir?' Cooper asked.

'No, I'm just the last one he was capable of. The others all followed in Father's footsteps and won honours fighting Jerry. I'm afraid I was still in my cot at the time. Look, how is this helping you anyway? Shouldn't you be quizzing that blasted burglar instead of me?'

'We're coming to that,' said Cooper, rearranging his tie, a signal for Pete to take over.

Sensing an opening in Somerset's agitation, Pete went in obtuse. 'Are you an admirer of Oswald Mosley, sir?' he asked, keeping his tone mild.

Somerset recoiled, a feint of disgust mixed with anger and a glimpse of genuine fear.

'Mosley?' he said and coughed. 'That traitor? That fascist? What on earth do you ask me that for?'

'Well.' Pete leaned forward, still keeping the smile on his face. 'It's just that I could have sworn I saw you at his rally earlier this evening. On Lancaster Road, round about seven thirty?'

'You must be mistaken.' Somerset tried to regain his composure, but his foot had started jiggling up and down again, beads of sweat broke out on his forehead.

'That's a very distinctive jacket you've got on,' said Pete.

'These jackets are all the rage.' Somerset's tone turned scornful. 'Not that I'd expect a plod like you to know it. Besides, I've been at a friend's all evening, in Kensington. A friend,' he smiled grimly, 'who will be able to vouch for me if you're going to carry on with this ridiculous line.'

'Well, that's nice to know,' said Pete. 'Because just before I set eyes on this fellow who looked just like you, I had decided to follow a notorious criminal I spotted coming out of the Kensington Park Hotel. You won't believe what happened next. This recidivist gentleman had a conversation with your lookalike, round the back of the Elgin public house. He then went on to collect a toolbag, amble up the hill and casually break into your father's house. How do you credit that, eh, sir?'

Somerset's face turned a chalky white. 'Look,' he finally said. 'I told you. I was in Kensington all evening. I can prove it.'

'Right, if we could just have the details of the person you were with, we'll get a conformation on that,' Cooper said. 'Then if you don't mind waiting a few minutes more, we'll be right back with you. I'm sure you appreciate we have to do everything by the book.'

Hatred blazed in Somerset's eyes as he spat out a name and number. On the other side of the door, Cooper handed the information to Pete.

'I think you're right, he's in on it, the devious little sod. You follow this up, I need to know what CID have got, then we'll continue our little conversation. Dugdale,' he called to the constable who had previously been attending to Somerset and was now loitering further down the corridor smoking and staring at the ceiling, 'get back here smart and stand guard of this one. Don't let anyone else in here besides myself and PC Bradley.'

Pete hoofed it back to his desk, the rest of the room a chaotic babble, the result of George's collar and the Teds in the cells downstairs. Officers worked the phones chainsmoking, slammed in and out of the neighbouring CID office and bashed away at their typewriters, letting out whoops and expletives as they did so.

He put one hand over his ear as the operator put him through to the number Somerset had given, KENSINGTON 4242. The address was a mansion on Melbury Road. Pete tried to picture it as the phone rang. Corner of Holland Park; very grand, very secluded.

'Minton residence,' came a voice on the other end of the line.

'Good evening sir, may I speak with Miss Jennifer Minton?'

'I'm not sure if Miss Minton is at home, I'm afraid. May I ask who is calling?'

Pete smiled. 'Certainly, sir, this is PC Bradley at Notting Hill Police Station.'

He heard the intake of breath. 'Just one moment, sir, I'll see if I can find her for you.'

'Thank you,' said Pete, his smile deepening as he caught sight of another aid, Dick Willcox, threading his way through the desks towards him, brandishing the evening paper.

'Pete,' he said, dropping the rolled-up linen down on his desk, 'page 28 when you've got a minute. That tip I was telling you about.' He winked and about-turned, hurrying back across the floor.

'Hello,' said a female voice on the other end of the receiver. 'This is Jennifer Minton. What do you want?'

She sounded bored and annoyed in equal measure. Pete pictured a female mirror image of the man in the interview room downstairs.

'Sorry to disturb you Miss Minton,' Pete laid the Yorkshire on thick and slow, 'I've got a young fellow here who's just come home to find his house has been burgled. It's been a nasty shock for him, as you can imagine, and he's still rather upset about it all. He says that he's been with you this evening and I just need to confirm that that is the case. I don't like to have to do this, but it is routine.'

'Are you sure you're a policeman?' the voice came back. 'Only you haven't told me his name.' There was a pause that he didn't rush to fill.

'I take it you mean Giles?' she said.

'That's right,' Pete said, thinking, damn, she obviously wasn't the mirror of Somerset; she was smarter than that.

'Yes,' she said, sounding more annoyed than bored now. 'Giles came for supper at six o'clock, probably left about an hour ago. Is that everything you need to know?'

'Yes, thank you Miss Minton,' said Pete, 'you've been very helpful.'

Helpful to lover boy, he thought, as he put the receiver down. He knew his eyes hadn't deceived him. Somerset must have set his alibi up before his meet with Gypsy George, or maybe Miss Minton had thought it up for him. The lad himself didn't seem capable of such foresight, whereas she sounded sharper than one of those cut-throat razors the Teds downstairs were so fond of gouging each other with.

Cursing this turn of events he reached for the paper Willcox had left, turned to page 28. There, on a scrap of paper, was written:

Filth. Cine film and two envelopes of prints and negs.

Pete's mind turned in a somersault. Willcox had been an aid slightly longer than he had and they'd often paired up on patrols where they'd developed a nice rapport. Willcox's passion for racing was matched by Pete's for boxing so any time they wanted to trade information that was supposedly off limits to them, they'd pretend it was their latest tip and pass it across, hidden in the sports pages. Willcox had obviously hung around CID long enough to get wind of George's haul.

What kind of filth? Pete wondered as he ripped the paper into shreds over the dregs of a cup of tea left on his desk, then tossed the sodden mess in the bin, the image of Bobby Clarke's dead body floating unbidden into his mind's eye.

Whose filth? He hurried out of the room, through the desks and the chaos and back along the corridor, down the stairs to the interview rooms. Father's or son's? Was the son blackmailing the father or did he need George to liberate something his father had on him? And would Cooper divulge any of this to him or would he now want to continue the interview alone?

Cooper was outside the door of Interview Room 3, pacing, one of the bulging envelopes in his left hand, cigarette smoked down to the filter in his right. For a man who usually exuded unflappable calm, he was beginning to look pretty frayed at the edges.

'Bradley,' he said, dropping the butt down on the floor and stamping on it. 'What did she say?'

'What he said she would. He was with her from six o'clock 'til ten o'clock.'

'I see.' Cooper grimaced. 'Well…'

'Derek Cooper, me old darlin'!' a voice boomed down the corridor.

Their heads snapped round. Striding towards them was a huge, thickset man with black hair plastered back over a bulging forehead, a red sweaty face bearing the grin of a satisfied carnivore. He wore a well-cut black suit, white shirt and what looked like a regimental tie, which went with the Sergeant Major's bearing and bark. Loitering slightly behind him was a man in a scruffy mac and sticking up sandy hair.

'Oh Christ,' said Cooper.

Pete honed in on the sandy man, heard Dai Jones's voice in his head. *They shipped him out to West End Central with all the other spivs and gangsters.*

Francis Bream. If he recognised Pete, he didn't show any signs of it.

The big man drew level and in one swipe lifted the envelope from Cooper's hands.

'You won't be needing this, me old son,' he said, eyeball-to-eyeball with the other man. 'You've done a sound job so far, but now Uncle Harry's taking over.'

Cooper's face flushed. 'On whose orders?' he asked, a tremor in his voice.

'Only Scotland Yard's finest.' The big man's smile deepened to the point where Pete could imagine him biting Cooper's head clean off. 'The orders of DI Reginald Bell.'

Behind him, Bream's eyes darted around, not stopping on Pete's for a second.

'That means our light-fingered Romany friend, too. He's coming with us, back to the bright lights of the West, where his presence is long overdue. I've got something very special lined up for O'Hanrahan, don't you worry.'

He clapped Cooper round the back, nearly pitching him over. The DS recoiled, coughing, humiliated.

'Frankie boy.' The big man turned to his comrade. 'Get in there and deal with young Somerset, I'll be helping myself to our friend George. Derek me old beauty, if you could just show me the way.'

Bream's eyes finally met Pete's, but there was no visible recognition. He merely smiled and shrugged, then opened the door of the interview room.

'This way,' said Cooper.

The big man gave a theatrical bow and Pete made to move aside.

'You're the arresting officer aren't you?' he said, locking in with eyes as dark as Gypsy George's. 'Peter Bradley, is that right son?'

'Sir.' Pete returned the stare.

'Detective Sergeant Harold Wesker. But my friends call me Harry. Good work old son, that is one devious bastard you got bang to rights this evening. You obviously have the bollocks required to make a proper policeman,' he said, looking across at Cooper as if that wasn't a quality he shared. 'I won't forget your name. Now quick march, Derek, the gypsy king requires my presence.'

Towards dawn, when Pete was finally typing up his report, Dick Willcox sidled up to his desk again.

'Dick,' Pete said. 'Tell us something. Who the bloody hell is DS Harold Wesker when he's at home?'

Dick glanced backwards to make sure no one was listening. 'Harry Wesker? Alternatively known as The Bastard. He's West End Central's top man on vice, which is why he took over the show here as soon as he got wind of it. Got your number did he?'

Pete nodded. 'Afraid so.'

'Well, look out Pete. He used to run undercover ops with the SAS during the war and his nickname stems from his unsubtle but ultimately successful interview methods. He really is the biggest bastard in the Met.'

'Aye,' said Pete, rubbing sleep from his eyes. 'That's what I were afraid of.'

8

Lonely Boy

'Do you know something?' said Lenny, standing back from the tailor's dummy. 'I think you could do this for a living. You've got the eye.'

It was only a simple shift dress. But the black-and-white pattern silk-screened on to it, along with swinging line from armpit to the hem, turned it into something quite startling. In theory, it was an exercise in 3-D Art that was part of my coursework. But really, it was a kind of test I'd done on myself, to see if I really did have a flair for dress design.

'Well thank you,' I said, feeling a rush of pride. 'I couldn't have done it without you.'

'It's a pleasure dear, it really is.' There was a wisp of sadness in his voice.

I had found Lenny sitting disconsolately on his doorstep one evening not long after the AGOG party, staring up the road and smoking, the pile of butts at his feet suggesting he had been there for some time. Toby was staying late at college that night, so I invited my neighbour in to share supper and whatever was troubling him. As he picked his way through his omelette, Lenny explained that James had got himself a new job in north London, where he could build his own studios and run his own label. It was a live-in arrangement, so he had moved out that day, and though

Lenny tried to sound pleased about the opportunities it presented for his friend, it didn't seem as if they had parted on the best of terms.

I hadn't actually got to meet James on the night of the party and I couldn't tell Lenny why I was glad about that. Just as I couldn't explain to Toby the real reason that I had to leave shortly after Jenny had propelled me downstairs, excusing myself instead with the line I had given her, that I had a migraine and needed to lie down in a darkened room.

Well, it was half true.

I kept to myself what had happened with Mya. It was all too uncomfortably similar to the night of my dream, to long-buried memories of my Grandma's house and all the other things I thought I had left behind. So I couldn't help feeling relieved at Lenny's news – no more late-night musical horror shows. Which I guiltily masked in a show of sympathy, telling him that he was welcome to come round any time he wanted.

We had become pretty close since then, and during our conversations he had revealed that he had originally apprenticed as a tailor before he worked in the bank. Lenny seemed wistful when he talked about those days, which gave me the idea to see if we could turn my Op Art into a dress.

Jackie was studying Textiles as part of her course, so I got her to sneak us into the department one night and show us how to set up a silk screen. I couldn't tell which Lenny was more delighted with: the magic of the pattern appearing on the cloth or Jackie herself. Seeing them together was like watching a reverse mirror image – he with his bruiser's demeanour softened by silk shirts and little, elfin Jackie with her cropped hair and jeans. They had got on so well I was hoping that something more might come of it.

'I can't wait for Jackie to see it.' I gave him a sideways glance. 'I wonder what she'll think.'

'She'll love it.' Lenny's gaze remained firmly upon the creation as I spoke, then he turned to me and smiled. 'It was a bit of a team effort wasn't it? Now you should get someone gorgeous to model it for you and see if you can get any orders.'

'Hmmm,' I said, thinking, I know the very person. But I hadn't seen Jenny since the party either. She'd apparently rowed with Dave towards the end of the night and flounced off in a huff, no one had seen her since. I wondered if it was worth trying to get in touch with her and asking her to wear it for my end of term show, or whether I should just leave well enough alone.

'It all makes me realise, I should be doing something to sort my life out,' Lenny said. 'All that old claut of James that's still cluttering my place up, I need to get rid of it.' He shook his head. 'It's obvious he isn't going to come back for it. I might as well sell the lot and have a fresh start.'

'Well,' I said. 'If you need a hand, we'd be happy to help.'

'Claut' was an understatement. Inside Lenny's flat you could hardly move for boxes, cables, an old piano and all manner of amplifiers and broken musical instruments. Piles of music papers covered every surface and his shelves heaved under a weight of books. A thin layer of dust covered it all.

No wonder he never wanted to go home.

Toby had hired a van so they could take all the music gear down to Soho to sell, while Jackie and I were going to sift through the rest, separating what Lenny might be able to flog from what to just chuck. Getting everything out took a whole morning and sorting through the piles of decaying papers a good part of the afternoon. We collapsed on the settee that had been hidden for so long at around four o'clock, clutching much-needed cups of tea.

'What a palaver,' said Jackie, peeling off her grimy rubber gloves and rubbing at her hair. 'I'm sweating like a pig here.'

'Can you believe they used to live like this?' I said. Once the boys had loaded up and we'd been able to see what was actually Lenny's, more troubling aspects of the room had come into view. Like the various holes in the wall, caused, Lenny had said, by James's fondness for hurling things around when he had a temper tantrum.

'No,' Jackie replied. 'But I tell you what, I'm glad I never had the pleasure of making this James's acquaintance. He sounds like an overgrown toddler to me.'

She drained her cup and stood up, surveying the bookshelves.

'And all of this still to go,' she said. 'Will it never end?'

She dragged over a cardboard box and we started on the shelves. We found a lot of magazines with Buddy Holly on the cover. Some sheet music for his songs. Then:

'What's this?'

Jackie held up a cloth drawstring pouch, which she proceeded to open up and peer in. 'Some sort of cards in here. They don't look much like playing cards.'

'Let's see,' I said, swallowing. My throat had suddenly gone dry.

'Flamin' heck!' Jackie exclaimed. 'Take a look at this.' She passed me a black leather bundle, held together with string.

The hairs prickled all down the back of my neck. It was a Bible. Or it had been. The leather cover was intact, but the contents appeared to be held together only by the tight binding. Protruding from the middle of the book was a mortise key, around which all the pages had curled up and ripped, as if in a frenzy someone had spun the key in circles inside it. But how they would have the strength to do such a thing...

We stood, staring at it for a few silent minutes.

'Jackie,' I said as quietly and steadily as I could. 'Bring it over to the sink.'

She looked up sharply.

'Why? What for?'

'Just do it,' I said. 'Drop it in the sink.'

Looking worried now, she did as she was told and as she did, I pulled open the window. I said a silent prayer as I turned on the cold water. As soon as it hit the covers of the desecrated book, the key shot out of the pages, bouncing off the back of the sink.

'Jesus!' Jackie recoiled.

'Put your hands under the tap.' I said. 'Let it wash off you too.'

'Stella.' I had never heard Jackie sound the slightest bit ruffled, ever, before. But now she seemed on the verge of hysteria. 'What the bloody hell's going on?'

'It's OK, you'll be fine now,' I said, hoping I was right. 'You can take your hands out, just shake them dry, don't use the towel. Right.' I went back into the front room to find a rubbish sack. 'Let's get rid of it, get it out of the house. No, wait,' I stopped, realising what else would be there and where I would find them. I located the cards and the board and added them to my refuse collection. Then I marched outside and lifted the dustbin lid, hurled the bag in and slammed the lid back down on it.

No wonder I'd had that dream, I thought as I marched back inside. No bloody wonder. And what else has he been letting into this house…

I stopped my train of thought when I saw Jackie's face.

'Jackie,' I said, reaching out to take her hands, which were still wet and trembling. Jackie had been brought up a strict Catholic, taught by nuns. However much we fancied ourselves as modern, emancipated women living in a world of our own making, far away from all of what they taught us when we were children, you couldn't escape from it that easily. It was dragging her back to see the Bible defaced, the way what I had been brought up with was dragging me back.

'Jackie, I've never told anyone else this, not even Toby,' I said. 'Please don't think that I'm mad. But I was brought up a Spiritualist. My grandma was a medium and my grandpa was a faith healer. Even Ma has got the gift. But everything they did, they did for good, please believe me, they were devout Christians in their way. And they rammed it down my throat never to mess around with things like this.'

'Things,' Jackie croaked, her eyes starting to well up, 'like what?'

'The ouija board, tarot cards, all that bloody nonsense I've just chucked out.'

'I think I need to sit down,' said Jackie.

'Good idea,' I said. 'I'll make us some more tea.'

'Aye,' she said. 'Put five sugars in mine.'

By the time the kettle had boiled she had composed herself again. I sat down next to her, put my arm around her shoulders.

'Why did we have to wash it?' she asked as I handed her her tea.

'To stop anything...' I caught myself from saying 'else', 'bad from coming through.'

'Oh,' said Jackie, 'I see.' She took a thoughtful sip and stared ahead of her, pondering what to say next. 'It's a funny thing. The way I were brought up, Spiritualism is the same thing as witchcraft.' She shot me a sideways look and the first signs of a grin flickered around her mouth. 'I should have you burnt at the stake.'

'That's why,' I said, 'I don't want anyone to know. It's not as if I intend to follow in Grandma's footsteps or anything. In fact, I'd like nothing more to do with it myself.'

'Aye, well. The thing is,' Jackie continued, locking her eyes with mine, 'I'd have to burn myself and all.'

'What do you mean?'

'Well, Stella.' She gave a little grimace. 'You've told me your secret so I'll tell you mine and you can see if you think I'm mad or need to be burnt at stake an' all.'

I frowned. I couldn't imagine what she was talking about. She laughed as if she could read my mind.

'You are a love, Stella. I know you've been trying really hard to set me up with Lenny and I do appreciate your efforts, don't get me wrong.'

'Well,' I started, 'I hope this hasn't put me off him. I'm sure it's got nothing to do with Lenny and everything to do with that revolting James.'

Jackie laughed softly. 'No, love, it's not put me off him. You don't see it do you? There's nothing that could have put me on him in first place. I'm a lesbian, Stella. Lenny's homosexual. That's what we have in common, that's why we get on so well. It's our common language, the language we don't want straight folks to hear. I know you imagined that Lenny and James were just palling up like bachelors do, but they were actually more like man and wife...as today has so clearly demonstrated.'

'Oh my.' I felt myself blush to the roots, seized by a mortifying embarrassment. I'd been in London over a year now, at art college for God's sake, how could I have been so naïve? So much for being a modern, emancipated woman.

'Oh, Jackie. I'm so sorry.'

'What, that I'm a lesbian?'

The words hung in the air and there was a challenge in her eyes. I suppose she had been expecting me to recoil from her, just as I had feared her reaction to my revelation. But I couldn't see her any differently. Jackie was the first woman I had ever got on so well with, nothing could change that. Besides, whatever else had been weird about my childhood, I had never been brought up to hate anyone.

'No, that I was so stupid that I didn't realise,' I said. 'I think I'm such a woman of the world and here I am, as provincial as they come. I don't think there were any lesbians in Bloxwich, though.'

'None in Pocklington neither,' she said. 'So you don't hate me then?'

'Of course not Jackie.'

We fell into a hug, trying not to cry, and stayed there for a few minutes, saying what didn't need words. Then the front door slammed and we both jumped.

'Everything OK?' Toby's voice sounded from the hallway. 'We've managed to get rid of our lot, how about you?'

'Well,' I said, looking from Jackie to Lenny as he came through the door, 'we found something rather unpleasant, so we've thrown it away. I'm sure it was James and not you who was messing around with the ouija board.'

Lenny's jaw dropped open. 'Oh my God,' he said. 'Not his Buddy Holly things. Oh dear me, I had no idea they were still here.'

Toby just stood there, scratching his head.

'Buddy Holly things?' He sounded vaguely amused. 'What do you mean, old man?'

'Oh these stupid things that James started getting involved with,' Lenny said. 'I knew it would all end in tears. I told him.'

He sank down on the settee, looking like he was about to cry.

'It was this band James started working with about two summers ago, Jimmy Saint and the Sinners they were called.' He shook his head. 'He was a sinner all right, that Jimmy. He was into all these weird things, these *séances*.' He said the word as if it was dirty enough in its own right. 'He convinced James that he could talk to the spirit world and James has always been fascinated by the supernatural. He was brought up in the country you know, the Forest of Dean. I think they still burn witches out there.' He gave a shudder. 'I told him I didn't want no part of it. I said, James dear, I'm a Jew, and we don't mess around with drek like that. I made him some sandwiches to entertain his friends with and left them to get on with it. When I got back the next day, James was full of how they tied the Bible up and asked the spirits to give them a sign and then the key started spinning and tore up all the pages. All the rest of the band wet their knickers with fright, but James just loved it. It proved to him that there was something there,' Lenny waved his hands, 'on the other side.'

'My God.' Jackie shook her head.

'That's incredible.' Toby looked like he was thoroughly enjoying this tale. 'Could he have been some kind of magician, this Jimmy, you know, sleight of hand and all that?'

'I don't know,' said Lenny. 'He might have been, I suppose, except it got worse after that, something happened that there's no way I can explain. God, I don't even know if I should be telling you this.'

'Oh go on,' Toby urged. 'You can't stop now.'

'Well, then they did a full-blown séance. James, Jimmy and this other feller, Mark, who was supposed to be an experienced spirit guide. They sat in a row, all holding hands, James on one side, Jimmy in the middle and this Mark at the other end, writing down what the spirits told them. Well, according to James, as soon as they began, the lights started flickering on and off and then the table started shaking, but Mark just kept on writing. Suddenly the overhead light went really bright and the bulb shattered over their heads. When they looked at what Mark had been writing, it said' – Lenny's voice started to waver – 'it said, *Buddy Holly is going to die, in a plane, on February the 3rd.*'

Toby frowned. 'Oh,' he said, not quite so amused now. 'And when did he die again? It was early this year, wasn't it?'

'Well, this is the thing.' Lenny looked round at all of us. 'They did the séance in January of '58, when Buddy was just about to come over. James sent him a message telling him not to get on a plane on that day, he was so convinced it was going to happen. But it didn't. Not that time anyway. It was exactly a year later when Buddy did get killed in a plane crash. February the 3rd, 1959.'

'My God,' said Toby quietly. 'So there was something in it after all?'

'Yes.' Lenny reached for his handkerchief from his jacket pocket and dabbed delicately at his eyes. Jackie stared at me, shaking her head.

'That's when things started to go bad between us,' Lenny went on. 'James was devastated when Buddy died and I think he held it against me that I'd never approved of his séances, he didn't think I was being sympathetic enough. He'd started taking lots of these diet pills and staying up all night to make records. I actually think he was going quite mad with it all. But I had no idea that he'd kept all this stuff here. After everything that happened, I would have thought he would have thrown it away, got shot of it. To think it's been sitting here, all these months...'

'Yes, well.' I got to my feet, trying to bite down on the agitation within. 'It's gone now. Try not to think about it any more.'

Lenny looked up at me with bloodshot eyes. 'Yes dear,' he said. 'Thank you. You did me a mitzvah.'

I looked back at him, hoping I had done us all one.

9

Learning the Game

It wasn't his usual reading matter. He felt embarrassed taking it down off the shelf each week and it gave him a headache to wade through the contents. But *Tatler & Bystander* was gradually providing Pete with a goldmine of information on the circles of society he would otherwise be hard pressed to penetrate. Picture after picture of chinless wonders, debs and dowagers preening their way through the season. Clinking crystal glasses with politicians, ambassadors, film stars, sportsmen and singers in a seemingly endless succession of race meetings, shooting parties, hunt balls and charity galas. In amongst them, two recurring faces: Jennifer Minton and Giles Somerset.

In the days after the Gypsy George arrest, Pete had waited on tenterhooks to be summoned to give his evidence. Days turned into weeks and no word was forthcoming. He tried to make discreet enquiries but Derek Cooper stonewalled him. Dick Willcox came up with a probable scenario: Lord Somerset refused to press charges, Harold Wesker was sent in to bury the whole thing while taking care of George on outstanding charges – a couple of identity parades and the thief went straight to Pentonville. A wanted criminal behind bars, a prominent peer protected, everybody's happy.

Except Pete. His rage vacillated from hot to cold, but he hadn't forgotten what Dai Jones had taught him: '*It doesn't do to show too much initiative, sunshine.'* He kept his mouth shut and let the society magazine become his icepack. It was the start of another file to keep under the floorboards in his one-room digs at the station house in Hammersmith; along with the one that contained all the information he had on Bobby Clarke. Two senior policemen keeping the chills coming as he clipped out pictures and wrote up notes in the grey hours between shifts when he couldn't sleep. Wesker got the glory for putting Gypsy George away but there was a man behind him, wasn't there? Wesker had said it himself. DI Bell.

Bell and The Bastard. It didn't seem possible.

In the hours he was working, he pushed it all to the back of his mind, got on with the endless dirty business of Ladbroke Grove. It seemed that the more familiar the streets and their inhabitants became to him, the more there was to learn. The place threw up surprises like it threw up mushroom clubs, the dance parties the West Indians held in the basements round Powis Square, which had the ability to fade back into the night as quickly as they'd flared the moment that 999 was called.

There was a mindset here that you had to accept in order to get on with it, one that had at first seemed totally alien to Pete. But, as the months passed, he began to see the twisted logic of it. The people here were dirt poor – the Irish and the coloureds were only there, after all, to do the jobs that no one else wanted – but they put all their passion into their leisure hours: the fighting, the thieving, the whoring, the parties. They looked to themselves and wanted nobody's help. Which was why, when he once tried to get into an ambulance with an Irishman with a razor slash to his face that had virtually severed his lip, the man pushed his way past and leapt on to a passing bus. Or how it could be that a man who had been glassed by a woman at a party would be buying the same hellcat a drink a day later. You couldn't impose your own notions on to anyone here, as Oswald Mosley found out when he was beaten into last place in the local elections in October.

Poverty and rage also led to the steady stream of murders F Division had to deal with, for which there was no apparent logic at all. They were sordid and desperate affairs, not the sort of thing that would ever make the national papers. Pete had one man die on him in the aftermath of a pub fight, his jugular severed by a carving knife outside the Elgin, leaking out his life over the pavement, in bloody seconds. But despite the amount of weaponry carried around by the citizens of the Grove, that was an anomaly.

Usually, the victims were women and usually the murderers were their husbands…or their pimps. There were more prostitutes in the Royal Borough of Kensington than anywhere else in West London. But whichever way they were beholden to a man, the end result was the same – drunken, jealous rows that left broken necks and ruptured organs, contrite, sobbing perpetrators and hollow-eyed, shocked children in their wake. Routine human misery, older officers would call it. Nothing so shocking as the Christie murders that many of them had worked on a few years back, but nothing Pete could entirely get used to either. These women had only had brief, messy and painful lives and their violent passing bequeathed an ominously similar fate to those they had left behind.

Another generation of little Bobby Clarkes, with no one to clear their dirty laundry up for them.

Although, as Pete had discovered, they weren't without their champions amongst the smooth, clean, smiling faces that beamed out of the *Tatler & Bystander* each week. Some people had ideas for their betterment, big ideas, which could lead them out of squalor and into a bright new world. People like the architect Alex Minton, Jennifer's celebrated father, who even now was bidding for a plan to turn the slums and bomb sites of W10 into a soaring concrete city in the sky, according to this article Pete was reading.

Minton smiled out of the page with his perfect teeth, immaculate suit and Dean Martin haircut. He was sharing a drink with an equally smooth looking Tory MP, one of Macmillan's Eton in-laws, and his birdlike little wife. Young Jennifer was not in sight, but that was hardly surprising. The last time her father had a building erected in London, in the spring of 1958, she'd gone on a march to protest against how ugly it was.

Pete had found the details of that out from the newspaper archive in the library. Jennifer's good looks had landed her a big splash in the *Daily Mail*. She explained how she and her fellow St Martin's School of Art students were disgusted that the post-war rebuilding effort had come to such a pass, and the fact that her own father was inflicting such eyesores on the nation had only spurred her on to lead the parade of duffel-coated beatniks to make their views felt. Clearly smitten, the journalist concurred with her.

The other papers were quite keen on this story too. It was in the *Daily Telegraph* that Pete had found the picture that included Giles Somerset marching along and waving his banner outside a building site in Hornton Street, Kensington. NO MORE UGLY it read. Seemed that he was an art student too, best place for him, as he was clearly illiterate. Yet again, Somerset came up short compared to his blonde-haired lady friend, who had clearly mastered the class on how to embarrass your father publicly a long time before his own pathetic attempts came to nowt.

A knock on the door cut through Pete's brooding.

'Who is it?' It was a constant source of pain to him that they didn't allow locks on the doors in the station house. Anyone would think they were a lot of children in here, not grown men who had been in the army and then passed a rigorous load of exams to earn the privilege of a uniform.

'Dickie Willcox, secret agent,' came the reply.

'Come in.' Pete closed the magazine and rolled himself up off the bed. Dick strode in, looking dapper, his best suit cleanly pressed and Brylcreem in his hair.

'You're not reading that toff's mag again are you?' His eyes missed nothing. 'I don't know Pete, look at you, sitting here in your string vest reading about High Society.'

Pete gave a rueful smile. 'What are you all dolled up for anyway?' He brushed biscuit crumbs off his chest.

'Oh don't tell me you've forgotten?' Dick looked mortified. 'It's the dance tonight. With the nurses from the hospital.'

'Oh.' Pete vaguely remembered Dick enthusing at the prospect at some point in the not so distant past. It was a fairly regular affair, at the social club downstairs, bringing together the two most abundant sources of bachelors and spinsters in West London. He had so far managed to avoid it, not fancying himself as the type who could impress a sophisticated London nurse in such loaded social conditions.

'Come on, Pete, you've still got time to spruce yourself up. It don't start for another half hour.' Dick sat himself down on the end of Pete's iron bed, picked up the crumpled magazine.

'Don't you ever stop working?' he asked. 'Give yourself time to relax?'

Pete looked at himself in the shaving mirror above his sink. His skin was sallow from a long run of night duty and there were the beginnings of bags under his eyes. His hair – which grew in unruly curls if he didn't have it razored off every two weeks – was starting to sprout out at all angles.

'I can't remember,' he said. Tentatively, wondering if he should give in and make a night of it, Pete picked up his shaving brush.

'Well I'll tell you what.' Dick watched his friend slowly work up a lather from his block of soap. 'You won't get out of this place unless you find yourself a wife. And I don't want to have to come up here to meet my old mate the sad old bachelor Bradley in another fifteen years' time…'

Pete picked up his razor. 'I suppose you've got a point,' he conceded. Policemen were not allowed their own properties unless they were married and he certainly didn't want to be stuck in this cell without a lock forever.

'They're a decent lot of birds that come here,' Dick enthused. 'Plenty to choose from. Not quite Marilyn Monroe, mind, but there's a couple that come close to Diana Dors, if you squint at them in a certain light. Or, there's plenty of those Maureen O'Hara types, if you fancy one of them Irish colleens. They ain't stupid neither. That's what I like about 'em. You gotta have brains to be a nurse. I don't really mind what colour their hair is but I couldn't bear a bird that didn't have brains. Imagine having to talk about Cliff Richard or Tommy Steele the whole time. Cor, dear me no.'

'Me neither,' Pete agreed. 'Although I'd take Lana Turner over any of your Marilyns. I prefer a bit of mystery to mine.' He tried to sound like a man of the world, never mind that the only women that he'd really spoken to over the past year were the prostitutes on his beat. And there was seldom any mystery to them.

'She might even take you,' Dick considered, 'if you put some decent strides on and smarten yourself up. Chuck a bit of aftershave on after that, will you? You'd be quite a catch if you gave yourself the chance. Like that Albert Finney you are, one of them Angry Young Men. The birds all go for that, you know.'

Pete only had one suit that met with Dick's approval. Unfortunately, it was his funeral suit, but Dick didn't reckon that mattered, said it was a step up from the baggy tweeds that Pete preferred. He demonstrated how to do up a tie so that it went in a smart thin line, and even went back to his own room to fetch some Brylcreem to tame Pete's unruly locks. Pete had never had such a fuss made over his appearance in all his life. Made him feel like a bloody girl, he said, as they finally made their way downstairs.

'I know what you mean,' Dick quipped. 'I feel like a girl myself. And tonight we might just strike it lucky…'

There was a jazz band playing on the stage at the back of the hall, some kind of twenties revivalists they looked with white tuxedos, dickie bow ties and plastered down hair. The singer was a tall, effeminate type, singing 'A Nightingale Sang in Berkeley Square' in falsetto, clear-cut vowels. There were a few couples waltzing around the dancefloor, but mainly, at this early stage of the evening, the two factions sat at tables facing each other across the great divide. Dick strode across to the bar, nodding at friends, taking in the scenery with an easy smile. Pete followed warily in his wake. As they waited for their drinks, Dick tapped his foot along to the band.

'You like that, do you?' asked Pete doubtfully.

'The Temperance Seven? Yeah, they're great. They've done a few of these dances here, I think they're local chaps, something to do with the art college scene. Great fun.' Dick passed a pint of ale over. 'I thought you liked jazz?' he said.

Pete took a sip. 'Aye,' he said. 'That's right.'

His heavy frown just made his companion laugh.

'Come on old son, lighten up. Here, I can already see a couple of birds looking over. I told you you'd be a hit in that suit, you grim Northern bugger. Makes you look even more dark and Satanic than you did before.'

To Pete's surprise, Dick was actually right. Although his friend did most of the talking, leading the way into conversations with his easy charm and knack for small talk, it seemed to be Pete who they all looked at with hopeful eyes, asking polite questions which he did his best to answer without appearing too gruff or monosyballic.

After a while, Dick persuaded the Diana Dors blonde he had his eye on to take to the floor, while the band played an annoyingly chirpy version of 'Let's Call The Whole Thing Off'. Pete watched how they moved together. Tall and lithe, Dick had as much ease and grace on the dancefloor as he did in conversation; the pair of them affected their own take on the Charleston, laughing through every moment. Pete wondered if he would ever feel so at ease, so carefree as that.

'Excuse me,' came a voice beside him. 'Do you have a light, please?'

Pete turned. An elegant young woman had taken the empty seat beside him. Not quite Lana Turner, although her opening gambit struck a chord of amusement. She was very tall, very slim, her honey blonde hair cut short and neat with just the hint of a bouffant at the back. Her wide face was handsome, rather than pretty, but honest and strong and there was a look of purpose, challenge even, in her clever blue eyes, which exactly matched her soft wool pullover.

'Certainly.' Pete fumbled inside his jacket pocket, hoping to God that somehow he did look like Humphrey Bogart or Albert Finney or someone like that. Because for the first time in what seemed like an age, he felt an overwhelming surge of attraction.

'Thank you,' she said, looking up at him through the smoke. Most of the women he'd been talking to all night were Irish, as Dick had predicted, or native Londoners. This one had something else to her voice, a rural burr, that added to her air of intrigue.

'What's your name?' she continued, her eyes sparkling. But not with nervousness, like the others who'd tried to engage Pete in conversation all evening. With a sense of mischief instead. She crossed her long legs. She was wearing cream slacks, wide at the cuff, but they didn't disguise how shapely she was underneath. She was different to every other woman in the room, with their rigid hairdos and strappy gowns, far more stylish and far more at home with herself.

'Pete,' he said, 'Pete Bradley.' He cracked a smile to match hers, a genuine one, and offered her his hand. Around the table, the other women traded scowls.

'I'm Joan,' she said. 'Joan Wyles.'

Suddenly, Pete could see the end to his lonely room in Hammersmith.

10

Please Don't Touch

Against the greyness of the December day, they were a sudden splash of colour. They came bouncing down the steps of a townhouse on Kensington Park Road, luminous orbs spilling out on to the pavement. As the oranges rolled towards me down the hill, I instinctively reached down to try and catch them.

It was a bit of a fiasco – there were so many of them and they were moving fast, bouncing off my feet – and without a bag to put them in they were quite difficult to keep hold of. But once I had corralled them, fishing one out of the gutter and another from under the railings of the gardens, I looked up to see who had dropped them.

She was standing on the top of the steps with one hand on her open mouth, the other limply hanging on to a broken string bag. Huddled inside an ancient fur coat and hat, she looked like a little bird that had puffed out all its plumage but was still losing the battle against the icy chill of the wind. My heart jumped when I realised who it was.

Mya.

'My dear girl,' she said and her face crinkled into a delighted smile as I trudged up the steps towards her. 'How very kind of you. This silly bag has broken and I don't know what I would have done if I had lost them. It's getting so hard for me to bend down these days and my poor husband's gone down with a terrible cold, he needs all the vitamin C he can get. Would you mind just helping me get them inside?'

I wondered if she recognised me. I had, after all, been wearing a ridiculous outfit the last time I had met her, and today, hidden under a duffel coat, a beret and one of Toby's old school scarves, I scarcely looked like the same person.

I followed her into a hallway, where the diffuse light straining through the grimy window over the door cast a dull pallor and the air smelt of mothballs, damp and dust. A staircase stretched up into the gloom ahead of us.

'This way,' she said, turning around to smile at me again. 'If you would be so kind.'

The stairs were difficult for her, I could see. Her thin hand gripped the banister with whitening knuckles as she hauled herself up each one, her breath steadily becoming more laboured as she did so. A wave of sympathy washed over the anxiety I had at first felt about running into her. Now I was just glad that I had stopped to help an old lady in need.

'Here we are,' she said, catching her breath outside the doorway of the first floor flat. She produced a bunch of keys from her crocodile handbag and began working her way down a series of locks.

'I'm afraid our landlord isn't the most reasonable man,' she said. 'We've had to put on a couple that he doesn't have the copies for. Thankfully we were registered as sitting tenants before the Conservatives got back in. Ah, now, here we are. Cedric, dear,' her voice trilled, reedy and high, 'I'm home.'

Her hallway was just as I would have imagined it to be. Pots of aspidistras, an elephant's foot umbrella stand, a brass coat rack and a big, full-length mirror at the end of it. Aside from the framed circus posters and the stuffed lion, it was just like stepping into my grandparents' house.

'Are you all right, girl?' I heard her husband's voice from the next room.

'Yes, dear, but I had a bit of an accident with your oranges, the bag broke and they tried to escape. Luckily, this lovely girl was here to help me. We'll just put them away and I'll be straight through.' She turned back to me. 'If you don't mind just leaving them in the kitchen for me, I'll let you get on your way.'

Her eyes were bright and kind but I still couldn't detect any hint of recognition in them. I followed her through to a small kitchen and deposited the errant oranges in a china fruitbowl on the sideboard. Then she led me back out into the hallway.

'Well, dear,' she said, opening her front door. 'Thank you again, that was very kind of you – many's the person who would have walked straight by. You won't mind if I don't come back down the stairs with you?'

'Of course not,' I said, strangely disappointed now that she hadn't asked me to stay for a cup of tea. But she was right; I had been in a hurry just before the oranges stopped me. I was headed to the bus stop to get the 52 into Kensington and put the finishing touches to my end of term show.

'Now then.' She opened her handbag and I was about to protest, thinking she was going to give me some kind of reward money. But she extracted a small card, which she pressed into the palm of my hand. 'Take this,' she said, 'and if there's anything I can ever do for you in return, this is where to find me.' Her hand closed over mine for a moment before I stepped out into the gloom of the landing.

'Goodbye, dear,' she said, closing the door.

I ran back across the road to the bus stop, wondering whether she had recognised me or not. The 52 was pulling in and I only just had time to jump on board and find myself a seat, absent-mindedly putting Mya's card into my bag. I promptly forgot all about it.

●

'By heck.' Jackie's eyebrows shot up and her eyes widened. An expression of grudging admiration filtered through her down-turned mouth to curl back her top upper lip.

We had reached the last night of our end of term exhibition, an extravaganza over three floors of the Fine Art annexe in Exhibition Road which had been attracting a steady stream of viewers all week. Toby and his fellow Fine Artists were on the top floor; Graphics, Fashion and Textiles took over the second; and us General Art and Design bods got the bottom rung to ourselves. It was the Thursday before Christmas and events had turned distinctly festive since the GAD boys had put the contents of their cocktail cabinets together to produce some dubious-looking punch for the guests and gone around sticking sprigs of holly and mistletoe in inappropriate places over people's work.

As the only girls in the room, Jackie and I had spent much longer than our peers carefully setting up our work to be viewed to its full advantage. We had canvases and collages galore, but it was our special projects that had really made us stand out.

I had my jigsaw blocks and my dress. Jackie had the Cubist curtain print designs that she'd made in Textiles and a fantastic piece of stained glass. I had shied from the option of learning that arcane art, but when I saw what she'd come back with, I wished that I hadn't. She had made her most brilliant piece in indigo, turquoise and amber, a woman reclining in a bath, with all the colours of the beach and sea running through it. People had been stopping dead in front of it all evening.

But now the gaze of the room followed Jackie's.

'Oh my Lord,' I said, swivelling my own eyes in the same direction.

Jenny had been reinstated at Vernon Yard by the next time Toby and I had visited, sitting on a pile of Chinese silk cushions at Dave's feet, smoking languidly and looking more bored than ever. It was not long after the incident at Lenny's and Toby was still so full of what had gone on that day that he'd instantly launched into a full dramatisation of the Buddy Holly séance. Wishing that he hadn't, I told the others how helpful Lenny had been with my dress. As soon as those words left my lips, the lights had come back on in Jenny's eyes.

'She's got some brass neck,' Jackie said, shaking her head. The two of them had only met for the first time that day and I wasn't sure if they were going to get on.

Jenny came sashaying towards us, with dark black eyes and stark white lips, her hair dramatically cut into a bob. Now I could really see why Lenny had been so enthusiastic about my eye for the cut. As Jenny moved, the lines on the dress became a dazzling optical illusion, as if they themselves were dancing in front of your eyes, moving in waves, pouring in and out of the black hole printed on her left shoulder.

Jenny's face lit up with a triumphant smile. 'You see,' she said, stopping in front of us to pirouette round full circle. 'I *told* you you could be a dress designer, Stella.'

'Ain't it gorgeous?' Lenny stood behind her, beaming like a proud father.

Jenny looked down through her false eyelashes at Jackie, amusement playing across her face. 'I mean,' she said, 'how could anyone resist?'

Jackie grunted. 'You scrub up a treat, love,' she said and turned back to her exhibit with a shrug, started talking to somebody else.

Jenny laughed, turned her gaze back to me. 'You wait, Stella,' she said. 'They'll all come running.'

She was right, too. Shortly after Jenny's grand entrance, I got a tap on the shoulder.

'Excuse me.' It was a woman in an elegantly cut black suit. 'Are you the designer of this dress?'

It turned out she was a buyer from Dickens & Jones who was looking for new talent. She thought my dress was highly original and gave me her card, promising that she could set up a meeting as soon as was convenient. The moment I had finished talking to her, someone else came up and asked me if it was possible to buy the dress off Jenny's back. Several others followed suit. By the end of the evening I had a fistful of business cards in my hands.

'Do you think we can get back in here in the holidays,' I whispered to Jackie as another debutante furnished me with her phone number and an idea of an acceptable price for the dress that made my head swim. 'To use the screen printers?'

'I dare say,' Jackie replied. 'I think I've made an impression on the old fruit that taught us. I'm the only one that listens to his stories about Les Ballets Russe, that's got to be worth the keys to his lock-up.'

'Because,' I said, pulling Lenny into a conspiratorial huddle, 'the way things are going tonight, we have the makings of a nice little business sideline.'

'I told you,' said Lenny.

I looked over to where Jenny was engaging a severe-looking woman with a tight black bun and red lipstick in conversation. 'She was right,' I admitted. 'She is the best advert I could have had for it.'

'I know.' Lenny cocked his head to one side, regarding her. 'I bet that's not just any old Kensington fossil she's chatting up over there. That's probably the editor of *Vogue*.'

'Aye,' Jackie nodded, 'she's got ambition, I'll give her that.'

'Three shops, twelve buyers,' I counted the cards out in the pub round the corner afterwards, 'and the fashion editor of the *Daily Mail*.' Lenny had almost been right about the lady with the black bun. I guessed Jenny's family moved in such circles. Her father, Chris had told me, was some sort of architect.

'Sixteen squares all wanting to be hip.' Jenny sat on a barstool leaning against the counter. She had changed back out of the dress into an all-black combination of polo-neck, ski pants and long boots. With her new hairstyle she looked stunningly Modernist, commanding the drunken gazes of just about every male student who had crowded into the tiny snug bar. 'That's just the tip of the iceberg,' she continued, blowing smoke from a black Sobranie. 'There'll be scores more wanting the look, you'll see.'

'You've done brilliantly, darling.' Toby squeezed my waist and I almost dropped all my precious cards into the grate. I was sitting on his knee on a chair by the fire where it was beginning to get hellishly hot, but there were so many of us rammed into this little back room we were lucky not to be standing.

I went to put them back in the zip compartment of my handbag and realised there was another card already in there. I lifted it out and examined it.

The Christian-Spiritualist Greater World Association, it read, *3 Lansdowne Road, London W11. Mrs M Matherson, Readings and Consultations, call* KENSINGTON *7080…*

It was Mya's card. I quickly shoved it back inside my bag, hoping Toby hadn't noticed what I was fiddling around with. Of course I had known what she was and why she was interested in me, I just didn't want to acknowledge it, didn't want to get involved. But now this stuff seemed to be following me around…

'What's all the fuss about a frock?' A voice cut through my sudden paranoia. Toby had brought his new friends Bernard Baring and Terence Singer up to the pub with him. A couple of fellows I had pegged as students at the AGOG party, who, despite being in the year below us, were already starting to make names for themselves.

It was Baring who spoke and his voice had just enough of an edge to it to make me look up sharply. He had a hooked nose and pale eyes, scruffy, shoulder-length hair and a fraying grey pullover. He looked as mean as he sounded.

'A frock!' Jenny shot back at him. 'I should say not. It's a work of art. Op Art. You know about that, don't you?'

Baring's expression changed as he looked at her, his brow furrowed.

'Don't I know you from somewhere?' he said.

Jenny narrowed her eyes as she exhaled smoke.

'I don't think so,' she said icily.

'I'm sure I do…' he began.

Jenny stubbed her cigarette out. 'And I'm sure you don't,' she said.

Baring shook his head, a slight colour rising in his cheeks, and returned his stare to me. 'Well, well done dear,' he said, lifting his gaze over my head towards Toby. 'She must be very clever, your wife.'

'She certainly is,' Toby agreed, taking it as a compliment. 'At this rate we'll have no problems raising the rent for a studio next year.'

'Oh,' said Baring, 'a studio. Did you hear that Terry?' He nudged Singer in the ribs. Singer, who was more than half cut, smiled soporifically as he leant against the fireplace.

'Oh yes.' Toby grinned at him, oblivious to how envious Baring sounded. 'Bring on the 1960s,' he said. 'The fifties have gone on long enough. We're all going to make our mark on the new decade.'

I saw Jenny roll her eyes and glance at her watch.

Toby was in his cups himself, carried away with end of term fever. Aware that the euphoria of the sixteen cards was draining out of me faster than any amount of restorative alcohol was going in, I wondered how hard it would be to get him out of here.

Respite came through the door in a blast of cold air and a long black coat.

'Greetings, hepcats,' said Dave. 'Who wants to come to a party?'

'At last.' Jenny slid off her stool and wound her way towards him, trailing her coat and bag behind her. 'It was getting awfully dreary here, wasn't it Stella?'

'Yes,' I looked at Baring, 'it was.'

But Baring was staring at Dave now, with something like awe in his eyes.

'Well then, ladies and gents, your chariot awaits…'

'What?' Toby swivelled round. 'Dilworth, my man! Did you just mention a party?'

With a huge sense of relief we made our escape from the over-heated pub. There wasn't room in Dave's old station wagon for more passengers so we left Baring and Singer on the pavement, the former scowling, the latter trying to flag down a cab while reeling around a lamp post.

'God, what a pair!' Jenny said as we started away.

'Good men, both of them.' Toby was much more drunk than I'd realised, a big, silly smile plastered all over his face. 'Hope they manage to catch a cab.'

I exchanged glances with Jenny in the rear-view mirror.

'Here.' Toby rummaged in his breast pocket and pulled out the bottle of brandy that had obviously been sustaining him throughout the day. 'Who wants a nip? I say, I can't wait to get to this party, where did you say it was again?'

'Ledbury Road,' Dave was smiling now, 'cat I knew from St Martin's. He's just built a spaceship out of plastic coffee cups and his rich missus thought he should throw a party to celebrate. A *launch* party…'

We all started laughing at that, driving through the park, which was hung with Christmas lights.

'Prepare for blast off!' shouted Toby. '1960, here we come!'

PART TWO

Night of the Vampire

1963

11

The Night Has a Thousand Eyes

'En-ery! 'En-ery! 'En-ery!

Thirty-five thousand pairs of lungs bellowed out his name. The tiers of Wembley Stadium echoed the impact of thirty-five thousand pairs of stamping feet, thirty-five thousand pairs of clapping hands, a sound so dense and electrifying it felt like thunder roaring around the auditorium. The energy of the masses all focused on one man. A man to be a hero in a world that had turned, a world that had changed, into Tuesday 13 June 1963: a time of defecting spies and defective politicians, Kim Philby gone into the Moscow cold, John Profumo roasted over the Westminster coals, eight days gone from office.

'En-ery! 'En-ery! 'En-ery!

The anniversary of the Battle of Waterloo, but which Empire would fall tonight? A young American in the White House, riots in the Deep South and down below, the twenty-one-year-old Kentuckian challenger was stepping through the ropes. On his head was a cardboard crown, on his back a red robe bearing the words: THE GREATEST. The world had turned and the world had changed. All the mighty din of the crowd, all the anger and rage directed at him for his insolence, for calling his opponent a bum, a tramp and a cripple, just rolled straight off his perfect, gleaming brown skin. Cassius Clay just couldn't stop smiling.

'En-ery! 'En-ery! 'En-ery!

Eight years older and twenty pounds lighter, Henry Cooper entered opposite, his expression set, as grim as granite. He didn't have to play to the crowd, every one of those thirty-five thousand hearts was beating just for him: our 'Enery, the Pride of England. Pete felt all his hairs stand on end as he watched him, a strange feeling inside him tearing him back to the past, to memories of his father, a man like Henry Cooper who stood up straight and stoic against all the abuse you could hurl at him, who would use actions, not words, to prove his strength and courage. He wished his dad could be with him now.

Pete had never been ringside at such a fight as this in all his life and was pretty sure that if he lived to be a hundred he would never see the like of it again. He'd had special favours bestowed on him to get these seats, so close to the ropes he could see Liz Taylor's diamonds glittering in the front row. And for the first time in over a year, he wouldn't have to feign any of his emotions with the company he'd been keeping. Tonight, they were all on the same side.

The British Empire heavyweight champ had a record of twenty-seven wins, his last defeat way back in December '61. Had a left hook on him that could floor an ox and everyone was depending on him to deploy it and see off this unbeaten upstart with his big, loud mouth. Cassius Clay had been lording it up in the back pages of every newspaper for weeks, posing for pictures down the dogs and in the clubs, predicting that by round five, 'Enery would be history. He had provided some distraction from disgraced Tory ministers with their call girls and their lies; that trail of carnage that led back to Ladbroke Grove and the recently deceased Peter Rachman. But Pete didn't work that beat any more.

'En-ery! 'En-ery! 'En-ery!

Aptly named referee Tommy Little stood between the two men as they faced off from their corners, bouncing up and down on impatient feet, shadow-punching the air. Out of his cape, Clay's physique was perfect, his muscles round and burnished mahogany, everything in proper proportion. Cooper was leaner, stringier, a post-war, post-ration-book diet no match for what you could get in the land of plenty. For Clay, this fight meant a chance to get to his real goal, a shot at Sonny Liston and the world heavyweight crown. But for Cooper and everyone calling out his name, this was a rare occasion to prove to the world that Britain still had men who could fight clean.

So when the man standing next to him nudged Pete in the ribs, bellowing out Henry's name, he smiled straight back at Detective Constable Ronald Grigson. Then he nodded to the man next to him, DC Francis Bream, and let his gaze finish up, for just a second or two, on the red face of DS Harold Wesker, which was turned towards the ring. Then he joined his voice to the rest of them as the bell sounded and the two men sprang across the ring towards each other.

Cooper had his dander up all right, he went straight into his opponent, ducking Clay's right with confidence, trying to lure his opponent in to his own left, get him on to the ropes. He was all out aggressive which was unlike him, and it seemed to unsettle the cocky Clay, who had doubtless figured he'd done half his job already in the pages of the linens. Within seconds Cooper had him in a clinch, brought up that lethal left under Clay's armpit, got him on the nose, it looked like.

'Take that you brown bastard!' Wesker bellowed, spittle flying out of his mouth, vein on his forehead like a pulsing worm wriggling across his red skin.

'He's got 'im.' Grigson jabbed Pete in the side again, pointing towards the ring, where Clay had broken free of Cooper's embrace, spitting blood, phlegm and outrage. Little's arm came down between them for a second and then Cooper was straight back in, out to do as much damage as quickly as he could.

'I knew our noble 'Enery could 'ave him.' Grigson's face was more grimace than smile, but as Pete had learned, that was his happy look and talking bollocks was all part of the parcel that came with it. Grigson didn't like to hear any voice other than his own, apart from Wesker's that was. They were a right comedy duo they were, especially when they were down the cells, practising some moves of their own on whoever had been unlucky enough to fall into their clutches that day.

Pete kept his smile in place and his eyes on the action. Cooper ducked under another barrage of punches, got his hands up around Clay's shoulders a second time, pushed him back on to the ropes. Got a few more punches in before the bell rang, the sound of the crowd enough to take Clay's head off for him. This first round was the Englishman's, no question, and Pete was right with him, admiring the quiet dignity couching his fury, the way he'd turned ice into fire.

'Mebbe he should have kept his trap shut,' Pete shouted back at Grigson. 'He's got 'im going now.' Grigson nodded, his sneer deepening as Clay remonstrated with the ref, the jeers raining down on him as he did so.

The bell sounded for round two and instantly, it was different. Maybe Clay had absorbed all the words, turning them to fuel, spitting back the pure power he had within him. Maybe all the noise was just so much grist for his mill, a force he could feed off. But this time it was he who ducked the other's punches easily, he who looked both calm and deadly, searching for the blind spot that would open Cooper up to him.

He barely seemed to touch the ground as round and around

Cooper he wove, flicking out blows that connected, opening up a gash above Cooper's left eye. Found the weakness, the thin skin, the blood that came too easily. Howls and screams around Pete now, as Cooper pushed Clay back on the ropes, trying to sink the left, only hitting air.

'Hit him 'Enry, belt the fucker!' Grigson erupted. 'Kill him!'

But Clay was almost mocking Cooper now, opening his arms as if to say, 'This all you got?' The bell sounded, round two all Clay's.

Grigson threw his Woodbine to the floor, stamped on it angrily. Pushed past Bream – still with the sticking-up hair, just less of it these days, pink and ginger freckled skin showing through his crown – to stand at Wesker's side. The Bastard's Apprentice, with his matching dark suit and dark hair, two square-shaped heads shining with hair grease and perspiration. Looked like Wesker was sweating more than Cooper right now, mopping his forehead with a large white handkerchief.

Now he had spent so much time with them, Pete knew why Bream kept such a low profile and his yap shut, it was the only way of getting by with these two and not becoming the Bastard Brothers' constant target practice. Well, perhaps, not the only way. He had had to take a different tack himself, after all.

After two years as an aid, Pete had taken his detective's exams. His pass mark came back high. He had commendations from his superiors, his standing enhanced by his marriage to Joan in the summer of 1960, a married man always goes further, as his best man Dai Jones had often told him. Joan had been a revelation to Pete. Dick Willcox was right about the intelligence of nurses, and Joan displayed a streak of independence that endeared her to him still more.

They'd set up home in Oxford Gardens, one of the quieter streets off Ladbroke Grove, a two-bedroom garden flat in a big terraced house – with promotion came a pay rise on top of the police housing allowance and Joan was insistent on buying, putting down some roots in the Wild West. Though she'd given up working after they married, she filled her days with better things than just knitting and cooking, although she was skilled at the both of them. Joan helped out with all the charity work a policeman's wife could manage, took charge of the social functions, got involved with the church and the youth club. Charmed them all, the way she had charmed his ma, when he had first taken her back up to Yorkshire to meet what was left of his family. He was that proud of her he couldn't think how he had ever managed to live without her.

But of course, with every ray of sunshine came a black cloud chasing along behind.

Pete wasn't surprised to receive an offer of a transfer to West End Central to work with Harold Wesker. It was like he'd been expecting it. The bad feeling that fate had placed a finger on his shoulder the night he apprehended Gypsy George and first encountered The Bastard had never really gone away.

The bell sounded in the ring below and Clay was straight into Cooper's corner, jabbing, circling, working his mouth along with his limbs. With every passing second he looked bigger, stronger than the flailing champ. With the cut above his eye leaking more blood and the sweat flying from his forehead, Cooper couldn't seem to pull his sense of purpose back, he looked lost in the middle of this ring where only minutes ago he had looked so strong. Pete felt it in his guts, like it was him who was taking the pounding, all bleeding and disorientated, shouted louder in the desperate hope that his voice could somehow give the other man wings.

'En-ery! 'En-ery! 'En-ery!

Cooper put his head down, butted Clay back into the ropes, gave himself a few more seconds before the ref broke them apart and then the American was back in his face, outmanoeuvring his every jab, ducking around him, smiling, taunting. Slowing his pace down but still rocking on his hips from side to side, like there was music in his head he was moving to, some secret Kentucky hot jazz soundtrack.

This was almost too painful to watch. Cooper just couldn't keep up with him, kept falling into a clinch like a drunken man. Pete's insides twisted again as Clay's chopping right found that cut once more, opened up Cooper's eye then proceeded to just dance around in front of him, doing that thing again with his arms, until the round came to a merciful end. Pete sucked his breath again as the air filled with jeers, looked across at Bream, who caught his eye and shook his head.

He was an enigma, was Bream. Whatever did, or didn't, go on inside that pointy head of his had been the biggest mystery of West End Central as far as Pete was concerned. It had taken him ages to work out why Wesker wanted him around when there were plenty more like Grigson who were more suited to their kind of work.

'That's not right,' Pete said to him, as trainer and seconds bustled around the injured Cooper, trying to fix that cut as best they could. 'Way he's taunting him, like.'

'No,' Bream agreed, opening a pack of Player's and offering one. 'But 'Enry ain't finished yet. He's just slow to anger, that's all. You'll see.'

'Right.' Pete lit the cigarette, wondering. The enigma of Bream was down to such insights as this one just offered, opinions that came from a lifetime of doing what Bream did best. Watching. Waiting. Reading the signs. He could see why Dai had once had high hopes for him. When Bream made a pronouncement, however unlikely it sounded, he was usually spot on.

Even so, round four began in the same ponderous fashion, Cooper loping after the light-footed Clay as if he were wading through treacle.

'He's just messing about now.' Pete shook his head.

'He predicted round five, didn't he?' Bream reminded him. 'He's waiting for that.'

For long seconds they stood in the centre of the ring, boxing at thin air. Then Cooper started to move towards the corner where he'd got Clay off his guard the first time.

'See,' said Bream, 'he's rallying.'

It didn't look much like it to Pete. Clay ducked through Cooper's embrace, danced him back to the middle, where he seemed happiest, then pushed the Englishman back to the ropes. Cooper shook his head and kept coming. Clay started throwing longer punches, Cooper evaded and pulled him back in, reaching out for a body shot. Bream was nodding his head, clenching his fists, the crowd picking up the chant once more.

'En-ery! 'En-ery! 'En-ery!

Down below, the two men locked together, heads down, caught in a slow dance, their eyes burning into each other. There was no taunting or idle mockery now, this was a battle for supremacy dredged up from the deepest, darkest part within themselves they could muster, retina to retina, fist to fist. When they came out of it, Cooper's left paw whizzed past Clay's head by millimetres. Clay threw a roundhouse right and Cooper ducked, luring his opponent back into that same corner again, this time looking like a man with a purpose, this time finding what it was on the end of his left wrist, 'Enery's 'Ammer connecting with Clay's jaw so hard it was almost like those cartoons where you see the stars whirling round people's heads and Clay was down, down on to the ropes, dropping on to the canvas, a look of stunned amazement on his face.

'Well I...' Pete began but his voice was lost in the roar of the Wembley crowd, the thirty-five thousand now back on their feet, counting:

'One...two...three...four...'

And then the bell sounded and there was chaos, screaming, as

Clay hauled himself back to his feet and weaved over to his corner, propped up by his trainer, his eyes wide with shock.

'No!' Bream was beside himself now. 'Saved by the bleeding…'

A huddle of figures enclosed Clay, slapping at his legs and calling over the referee, who joined them and then moved across to speak to a steward from the ringside. But it was virtually impossible, from where Pete was standing at any rate, to see what was going on behind the wall of tracksuits that surrounded Clay. Bream clearly had a better view.

'Now look!' he was pointing furiously into the mêlée. 'He's give him some snap. I saw that ref! That's out of order! Ref! Ref!'

Elation turned rapidly into outrage as the seconds ticked on, stretching out in that way they did when you were waiting to pounce on a villain, time turning to elastic, stretching out like nerves ready to break.

'Come on ref!' Pete heard himself yell. He could hardly contain the feelings that rushed inside himself now, the frustration and rage he normally buried so deep. 'Get on with it man!'

At last the bell sounded and both men were back on their feet, pitching towards each other as if to rip out the other's throat. Cooper wanted Clay back in that corner, back under the 'Ammer, but again, once bitten, Clay was twice the fury he had been before. If time had been suspended for the previous minute, now it seemed to be speeding up as the American fired a volley of short, rapid punches to Cooper's head. The wound over the Englishman's left eye began to spurt blood like a burst main.

Bream put his hands up to his own head as if it were he who was injured, sank to his knees in anguish. Next to him, Grigson and Wesker continued to hurl abuse at Clay, still not giving up as the blood covered Cooper's face and neck, rained down upon his chest, blinding him. Pete felt his own clenched fists drop down to his sides as the ref stepped in between the two men, put his hand on Henry's shoulder. Felt desolation hit as courageous Henry, so near and yet so bloody far, smiled in resignation and shook his head, walked back to his corner, still so full of dignity that Pete could feel the tears prick at the back of his eyeballs. Cooper merging with Dad once more, Dad buried under the cave-in, brave and strong and stoic no more, crushed under a hundred tons of Yorkshire earth.

So this was the way it was going to be. This was the way it was always going to be. Pete shut his eyes, blocking out all the sound and the fury around him, pushing the tears back down, deep down, taking his own courage from that moment of darkness.

When he opened them again, Clay's hands were in the air and his face was cracked into the widest grin, his skin was shining not just with the sweat but with the glory, like the light was all pouring out of him.

'Chancy coon bastard!' screamed Grigson, waving his fist but looking as if he was about to burst into tears, too. Wesker put a comforting arm around his shoulder, muttered something in his ear. Bream remained crumpled up on the floor, his head in his hands, rocking on his toes. All around them, people wore looks of shock and despair as they shuffled out of the stands and back down the aisles; the stuffing was all knocked out of them too.

This is just going to make it easier, thought Pete, to do what I have to do.

He knelt down beside Bream. 'Come on, Frank,' he said. 'You can't sit there all night.'

Bream's unruly hair bobbed up and down. 'I wish I could,' he said from the depths of his armpits. Then he gave a huge sigh and unfurled himself, staggered back on to his feet and looked at Pete dolefully through watery green eyes.

'Try not to take it so personal,' said Pete, knowing that he was talking to himself, too.

'I don't see how,' said Bream. 'I put a whole week's salary on 'Enry.'

Wesker's huge paw came down on his shoulder, almost knocking him down again. 'Frankie, me old sweetheart, there's an old army saying that's always served me well: from the pits of despair comes fortitude. 'Sides, you won't need money where we're going.'

'I'm going to bed,' said Bream, shaking his head. 'I can't take no more tonight, Harry.'

'No you're not,' said Wesker, propelling him forwards. 'Not beddy, Frankie, Teddy. He's expecting us. It'd be rude to let him down.'

The other two detectives walked in step behind them, but in his heart, Pete had detached himself once more, the sides were different again and would stay that way. Saying nothing, he moved from the scene of the defeat of one British champion towards the nightclub of another, back to the place that Wesker liked the best. The bright lights of Soho.

12

I Saw Her Standing There

'What is it about your style that young people really go for, do you think?'

The young woman asked the question with a sharpened pencil poised above her shorthand pad. She was the fashion reporter from *What's On in London* who was putting together a feature on the 'Carnaby Street Village' and had come knocking on our door as we were in the process of moving in.

'I think,' said Jackie, leaning back in her chair, 'it's because your mother wouldn't like it. I mean, when I was growing up, I had to go to church every Sunday in a dress my mum made, that was exactly like the one she had on.' She shook her head. 'Like a miniature of her. I hated it. I've never so much as worn a skirt since I left home. And you know, this is 1963. We just don't want to be like that any more.'

The reporter's hand flew across her notebook as she took it all down.

'And do you think,' she looked up at me, 'that because of your husband's popularity and the fact your designs are worn by fashionable people like Jenny Minton, that it gives you a cachet other designers don't have?'

I looked at her in her twinset and pencil skirt, neat blonde chignon and bright blue eyes. A lot of girls who looked like her were following my husband around these days.

'Oh undoubtedly,' Jackie answered for me. 'You could say that we owe it all to Jenny. She modelled the first dress we ever made, at a show at the Royal Academy at the end of 1959. We got so many orders for copies that it changed what we were doing from messing about with fashion and textiles into the start of a business.'

She fixed our pretty inquisitor with her most charming smile. 'But in those days, Jenny was just one of our mates from Henekeys who looked a lot better in a frock than we did. Or,' she shot me a wink, 'I should say, a lot better than I would. Our Stella's always been a class act. That's why Toby had the nous to marry her.'

'I see.' The journalist snapped her little notebook shut. 'Well, I'd better not take up any more of your time, I can see how busy you are. Thank you so much for speaking to me, I'm sure this will be a great addition to the piece.'

'It's a pleasure,' Jackie said and we all stood up, walked back downstairs with her through the half-fitted shop to the front door.

'Like I said,' Jackie unlocked it for her, 'we'll be open for business Saturday after next, if you want to stop by. Come and have a vol-au-vent.'

The journalist's smile never dimmed, she shook our hands and snapped away smartly on her stilettos, disappearing around the corner into Marshall Street.

'Do you think everybody will ask about that?' I asked, watching her go.

'What?' said Jackie. 'Jenny or Toby?'

'I was thinking Toby,' I said, 'and his popularity. But I suppose I mean both of them. That was what she was implying, wasn't it? That people are only interested in us because of them.'

'Well,' said Jackie, 'I doubt she'll be the last.'

'I suppose it is quite surreal,' I considered. 'That we were just art students and now...'

And now it was July 1963 and all Toby's predictions about this decade seemed to have come true. My husband was now a famous artist who had had big exhibitions and documentaries made about him. He'd made so much money since he hooked up with the entrepreneurial Pat Innes, whose gallery in Mayfair had become the hub of the Pop Art world, that we had been able to move out of Arundel Gardens into a three-storey house in Powis Terrace.

Meanwhile, I seemed to have been caught up in the momentum of something else entirely. Those sixteen cards had grown into a cottage industry between Jackie, Lenny and me, taking over from our studies at the Royal when we left. When orders became too much for us to manage, Lenny had gone down to the wholesalers in the East End, found a factory that would make up our designs. With his rag trade patter and business acumen, and our ever-expanding client list, we had gradually managed to build up enough capital to stop making ranges for other shops and open one of our own.

So here we were on Marlborough Court, a little square connecting Carnaby Street, Marshall Street and Ganton Street. The cheapest rent in central London, despite being only a couple of streets away from Mayfair. Although it was only a couple of streets away from Soho, too, and definitely erred on the seedier side of the West End. But round the corner on Carnaby Street, a couple of guys were putting in clothes shops and there was definitely something floating in the air that our *What's On* journalist had caught a whiff of.

'And now we're not Jackie and Stella Student,' my friend finished my sentence for me. 'We're Brockett & Reade, designers. But we've done it off our own bat whatever folk like her say – and don't you ever forget it.'

I followed her back upstairs, to where we were trying to get our office into shape. It was still in a state of chaos, clothes hanging on rails, boxes of wool stockings, samples for boots, filing cabinets and our trusty mannequins.

'Maybe,' said Jackie, 'we should have introduced her to the real Jenny…'

One of the dummies had pins sticking out of its head like a voodoo dolly. This was the one that she called 'Jenny'. Jackie enjoyed the fact that it sat in the middle of a load of posters and store cards depicting Miss Minton in our designs and that she was blissfully unaware of its status.

It was now about two years since Jenny had shocked us all by upping sticks and moving to Italy with a very louche black jazz singer, precisely a week after she first met him. Nobody could have been quite so stunned as Dave, who had been unaware at the time that they'd even split up.

She wanted to find herself, she'd told me, do some painting, explore *la dolce vita*. She certainly seemed to have been doing the latter, rapidly ditching her jazzer for a series of Italian lovers and even appearing in a couple of new-wave films, which was what had piqued the journalist's interest. Although none of her parts had been very big, Jenny illuminated the screen. Not just because she was so beautiful that the camera loved her, but that strange blankness about her could be filled up convincingly with a part, a brief foray into someone else's world.

Still, her loyalty to our enterprise remained steadfast. She always insisted on modelling our latest range for us and was due back to do just that for our opening day.

Jackie looked at her watch. 'It's five to six. Do you think we can call it a day for now, start early tomorrow?'

'I don't mind if you push off,' I said. 'But I think I'll carry on for another hour or so. Toby's not back 'til tomorrow and I'm in no rush to get home.'

'Are you sure?'

'Course,' I said. 'What you up to, anything nice?'

Jackie wiggled her eyebrows. 'I'm going up the King's Road for a drink,' she said. 'Just catching up on the gossip, but you never know...'

Jackie, like Lenny, didn't seem to have anyone steady, although I still thought it would be easy for anyone as naïve as I had been to mistake the pair of them for a married couple. They spent most of their time together gossiping and bickering and soon it would be a full-time job – Lenny was working out his notice at the bank to join us here.

'Well,' I said, 'you have a good time, you've earned it, kid.'

I listened to her clatter downstairs and out of the door, into the bright summer night, whistling as she went. Once she had gone, it felt for a moment as if she had taken all the brightness and happiness out of the room with her. But it was just a cloud passing across the sun, I told myself, as I opened up another cardboard box.

The journalist's words had irked me, though. Jackie might think otherwise but I still wasn't sure whether our success was entirely down to our talents or to the rich and influential contacts Jenny had consistently sent our way. Would it have been so easy for us without them, I wondered. Would I even be doing this now, if it wasn't for Jenny?

The only way to chase those thoughts away was to immerse myself in the tasks of rearranging furniture and finding drawers for this, that and the other. Until it got so late that I had to turn the light on.

'Gosh,' I said to the mannequins. 'It's nine o'clock already. I suppose I should be heading home.'

Even though it would be to an empty house. Toby was in Edinburgh, at the opening of a Young Contemporaries exhibition with Bernard Baring. Unfortunately, Toby's college friend had never gone away, he had become just as famous and followed him around like a bad smell. Another reason why it had been easier for me to throw myself into this fashion lark was to fill in the holes of Toby's regular absences, to avoid having to spend time in the company of this particular friend. Baring's attitude towards me had got worse; he was always condescending, sniping. Yet Toby never seemed to notice.

I stood for a moment in the courtyard, wondering which way was best to go home. My growling stomach suggested I should visit the late night grocers, so I walked down Marshall Street and turned left on to Broadwick Street, towards the jumble of streets that formed the parallel universe of Soho. Streets full of French patisseries and Italian coffee shops, jazz clubs and cheap restaurants that made a gay front for the world that lurked beneath. The narrow alleys populated by tuppenny Marilyns and ha'penny Liz Taylors, standing on their doorsteps with make-up plastered over their unsmiling visages like armour-plating. Men in camel-hair coats and hats pulled down low, smoking and spitting on the pavement. People you didn't want to make eye-contact with.

Soho was thronging, people spilling out of pubs and cafés, dressed in their best for the theatre or a show. I headed down Wardour Street, had almost reached Old Compton Street when a familiar voice called my name. Coming across Meard Street there was Chris, one arm wrapped around a sheaf of cardboard folders, the other waving at me.

'I thought it was you,' he said. 'How the devil are you, Stella, it's been much too long hasn't it? You look marvellous, I must say.'

'Thank you,' I said, a sudden wave of emotion rolling over me. Chris looked exactly the same as he always had, a white shirt open at the collar and rolled-up blue jeans, a bashed-up old pair of boots and his smile still circled by a goatee. We had hardly seen him or Dave since we moved to Powis Terrace and I realised how much I had missed them.

'What are you up to these days?' I said, trying to mask a wobble in my voice with a smile. I nodded at his folders. 'And what are all these?'

'Ah,' he said. 'The reason you haven't seen very much of me lately, I'm afraid. Something I've got involved with, a bit more important than our art struggle, I rather think.' He raised his free arm and looked at his wristwatch. 'Would you have time for a coffee? I'd love to explain it all to you. And find out what it is that's keeping you out alone in Soho.'

'I tell you what,' I said. 'If you don't mind me just getting a few things from the shop first, I'd love to.'

We ended up in a long, narrow, Italian coffee shop on the top end of Greek Street. Chris went to the counter for a couple of espressos, while I minded the bags and folders. I would have preferred to sit near the door, as it was a warm night, but he insisted on sitting at the back of the café, right next to the gurgling Gaggia machine.

'I'm probably being paranoid,' he said, bringing the cups to the table and settling himself down. 'But you never know if walls have ears around here and I've been working on something that's pretty sensitive.'

'Oh?' My spoon of sugar paused over my cup.

'Yes,' he said, leaning across the table. 'I've been working for the National Council For Civil Liberties for the past eight months.'

'What's that?' I asked, stirring the sugar into my drink.

'We attempt to get justice for people who've been wrongfully convicted.' Chris's eyes danced the way they had always done when he had something exciting to tell you. 'People who've gone to jail for things they didn't do.'

'Really?' I was showing my ignorance now. 'The police actually do such things?'

Chris shook his head. 'You'd be surprised. I've been talking to people who've had long sentences handed down and yet they've done nothing, have no previous convictions, just the word of a policeman against them. At the moment, the Home Secretary won't even take a look at their cases, so we have to build up more evidence. But without us, these people would have no hope at all, that's why this work really matters.'

'My word,' I said. I had always known Chris was a bit of an activist – and the terrifying events in Cuba last October had certainly been enough to get him and several thousand others back into supporting CND – but this was a major commitment.

'It started off voluntary,' he went on, 'then a permanent position came up and I was in too deep to turn it down. I've been doing a lot of interviews and I think soon we will have enough to challenge the court. It's quite incredible, but a number of people – and I mean a large number, the last chap I spoke to just now was the eleventh person we've heard about – seem to have been put away by one detective over the past year, all on fabricated evidence.'

I was stunned. Not just by what Chris was telling me, though I found that shocking enough. But also because he was unwittingly connecting with the thoughts that had been disturbing me all evening, ever since that journalist opened her mouth. Had my life gone in the right direction since we left college? Or had I missed something along the way?

'Thing is,' Chris continued, 'the officer in question works out of West End Central so that's why I've got to be careful of what I say and how loud I say it.'

'Of course,' I nodded. 'Gosh, Chris. You *are* doing something more important than the art struggle aren't you? It makes what I'm doing all seem rather superficial.'

'Not at all.' He shook his head. 'We've all got to play to our strengths. The thing is, I actually like doing this more than trying to be an artist. Don't get me wrong, I had a lot of fun with David and I think we did achieve something, but it does all pale compared to people's lives and liberty. I can do something about it, so I do. But it must be a similar thing for you, Stella?' He smiled encouragingly. 'I mean, you started out wanting to do fine art and here you are, about to open a clothes shop, you must be doing what you enjoy the most, too?'

'Yeah,' I said, feeling little pricks behind my eyelids again. 'Yeah, you're right. It's funny how we all get swept along doing different things, isn't it?'

As I spoke, a song came on the jukebox. It was James's latest protégé, a boy with bleached hair, singing a song about Eddie Cochran – another tragic rocker, taken before his time. James must have been at his ouija board again.

'How is Dave, by the way?' I asked, trying to ignore the reverb-heavy lament. 'I haven't seen him for ages.'

Before he could answer there was a screeching commotion from the front of the café. A very stout, unpleasant-looking middle-aged woman in a shabby purple suit with a fox fur collar was having a row with a younger girl, in an even more grubby-looking mustard-coloured dress.

'I told you, you silly tart,' the older woman snarled, revealing a set of yellow teeth smeared in red lipstick. 'I ain't got your quid.' She grabbed hold of the girl's chin and sunk her painted talons in as hard as she could – I could see the pain register in her victim's bewildered brown eyes. 'And there won't be no bleedin' quid unless you lay off the gin and get to work. Now go on, get out of it.' With that, she spun the other woman around, stuck a pointed toe up her backside and literally booted her out of the door.

People sitting around the purple woman started to laugh, clapping her on the back as if she had just done something really funny. I was waiting for the owner to sling her out, but he continued mopping the top of the counter with a dishcloth, blind, deaf and dumb to the whole incident.

'Did you see that?' I asked Chris, wondering if my eyes had actually been deceiving me.

He shook his head as if he were more than used to such behaviour.

'It's always fun and games around here isn't it?' he said, and his eyes drifted from the women to the clock above the counter. He must have realised he was running late, as he started stacking all his files together again in a purposeful way. 'Anyway, Stella,' he said. 'I'm sure I've held you up here long enough. Are you walking to the tube?'

'Yes,' I said, gathering up all my bags and getting to my feet. After that performance, I had no desire to sit around here any longer.

Chris walked me through Soho Square and up to Tottenham Court Road tube. 'I'll leave you here if you don't mind,' he said as we approached the entrance.

'Oh?' I frowned. 'Don't you live in Vernon Yard any more?'

'Technically, yes,' he said. 'But I spend more time at the office these days. I can get a bus from here up to Camden Town. That's where I've got to go.' He leaned forward and kissed me on the cheek.

'It was really good to see you Stella. Give my love to Toby, won't you? Oh and David, yes, I forgot to say, he's been working with that old neighbour of yours, James, was it? He's made a record, a very weird thing, but that's what he's into nowadays. Music apparently being more accessible to the masses than art.' He raised his eyebrows. 'Anyway, I'd better dash, I think I can see my bus on the horizon. Bye now Stella, take care of yourself.'

'Bye,' I muttered, watching him weave his way through the traffic towards the bus stop on the opposite corner. I had a strange feeling I had missed an opportunity as Chris disappeared into the crowd, and I wished I could call him back, but what could I say? I couldn't even admit my thoughts properly to myself. With a painful feeling in my chest, I walked down the tube steps, went back to my big, empty house.

13

Ring of Fire

Pete stopped for a moment to rub his eyes; he was starting to lose focus. The grandfather clock behind him, steadily ticking the night away, began to whirr, the prelude to its quarterly chimes. But quarter past what was it now?

He had begun to type up his report at eight o'clock, after they'd had tea. Some time after that, Joan had kissed him on the forehead and told him she was going to bed. The overflowing ashtray to his left indicated that this had been some hours ago now.

Pete turned in his chair. Quarter past two it was. Still he wasn't through the half of it.

He ran his hands through his hair, tried to get his thoughts in order.

His work in Soho was almost done. The black car had come for him just before the Cooper–Clay fight, to deliver the tickets and more. It was time to get everything together, he was told. The National Council For Civil Liberties had been petitioning the Home Secretary on exactly the same matter that he was investigating.

The first time the black car had come was in May 1962. Pete had been on his way to see the Chief Superintendent, to turn down the offer to transfer to West End Central. He had worked out exactly what he was going to say, how he was flattered but felt he could do more for the community here in Notting Hill, where he had put down roots, where he knew the villains and had an effective system of snouts. He was worried that this might not sound like enough, but he was going to stand firm anyway. It might be dirty work in Ladbroke Grove but at least his fellow officers knew how to handle it. Not like the gangsters and spivs in Soho. He had no desire to get mixed up in any of that.

He had been on the crest of the hill, five minutes away from the station, when a black Rover parked on the side of the road in Lansdowne Crescent sounded its horn. Pete had looked over to see a man getting out of the driver's seat, beckoning him over. He thought it was going to be somebody lost, asking for directions.

'Peter Bradley?' the man said instead. 'Detective Constable?'

Pete frowned. He didn't recognise the man although he didn't have the sort of face that you would remember, he was as sober and purposeful as his grey flannel suit. The car had tinted windows and as the fact registered, he took a step backwards, ready to take flight. A villain could look as sober and purposeful as the next man, all the better for him if he did, and getting revenge on someone who had put you or your associates away only streets from the nick would be the kind of stunt that could make you a legend.

'Don't be alarmed, sir,' said the grey man quickly, fishing into his breast pocket, 'here's my warrant card.' He flicked it open before Pete could catch his breath.

DS Paul Rouse, it read. It wasn't a name Pete was familiar with either. He looked up, a question forming in his eyes that the other man answered before he could speak.

'If you don't mind,' DS Rouse said, 'there's someone here wants a word with you.' He opened the rear door of the car and there inside was a face Pete hadn't seen for a long time. DI Reginald Bell pointed to the empty seat next to him.

'I won't keep you long,' he said, making a show of studying his wristwatch. 'I see you are thirty minutes early for your chat with

the Chief Superintendent, that gives us twenty to ourselves. I'll
have you back here in good time, I assure you.'

Pete's throat went dry, cold chills running down his spine. Bell
and The Bastard. Now he was going to find out.

'I remember you from Chiswick,' said Bell as the door closed
behind Pete. 'Roberta Clarke.' He fixed him with those grey-green
eyes, hard and sharp as flints. 'You impressed me then, Bradley.
You were much more on the ball than that burnt-out wreck of a
sergeant. So I've been keeping an eye on you.'

The motor of the car started up and Pete felt it pull away on to
Ladbroke Grove, turning right at the junction.

'I believe you did your National Service with the First Battalion
of the Coldstream Guards,' the Detective Inspector went on.

'Yes sir.' Pete hardly knew what to say, so kept it cautious,
deferential, assuming it would all be explained to him in Bell's
good time.

'That was my regiment during the war,' said Bell. 'A small
company of men whom God hath made instruments of Great
Things.'

'Yes sir.' Pete held eye contact with the other man, wondering if
this meant that he had served at Dunkirk, where the regiment had
received honours for bravery.

'And though poor, yet honest as ever corrupt Nature produced
into the world,' Bell continued, 'by the no dishonourable name of
Coldstreamers.'

'Thomas Gumble,' Pete dredged back from memory. '1671.'

Pete saw that same sparkle come into Bell's eyes that he had
seen on the riverbank in Chiswick.

'That's right, Detective Constable. You joined the Metropolitan
Police after your duty was completed, applied to become a detective
as soon as you could, with results we all know about. Your Chief
Superintendent says you are a man of integrity, that you have a

superb arrest rate and a way of turning a villain's ear. But the most important thing he has to say is that you work best by yourself.'

'I suppose so sir,' said Pete, feeling a little bolder now. 'Why, what's this all about?'

'I will explain,' said Bell. 'But indulge me in one notion first. I believe you are about to go and tell your Chief Super that you have no desire to transfer to West End Central and work with DS Harold Wesker. This is not because you don't fancy the work, but because you have met Wesker and you don't much fancy working for him.'

Pete felt his stomach flip. He tried not to blink, said: 'Yes sir, those are my feelings entirely, although I beg your pardon but I don't see how you can know.'

'You've met the man,' said Bell. 'For an honourable Coldstreamer, that is enough.' He raised his hand and pinched the top of his nose, screwed up his eyes for a moment as if he was in pain. 'Detective Sergeant Harold Wesker was a very brave man himself, during the war,' he said, looking back at Pete. 'He was parachuted into Italy with eight other men from the Special Air Service and he was the only one to survive. He was captured by the enemy, tortured and sentenced to death. But he managed to escape by dressing up as a char lady, joined a group of partisans and fought his way through the country, blowing up as much of the infrastructure as he could on his way. He was awarded the Military Medal here and a Resistance Award for bravery in France. When he came to the police in 1951 his record showed him to be fearless, energetic and inventive and initially he was a superb policeman. However…'

Bell winced again, looked out of the window.

'Something went wrong with him when he transferred to West End Central. It sometimes happens when a man is working too closely within areas of organised crime. I am beginning to develop a theory that it has got something to do with the blasted streets of Soho itself…'

He stopped himself, shook his head and looked back at Pete.

'Bradley,' he said, 'what I am going to ask you to do will require more than bravery, it will require the utmost integrity, which may be the only thing you can rely on when you are forced to go behind the backs of your fellow officers and risk everything that comes with that. But I believe you have the qualities I need and I believe you will go in to see your Chief Superintendent, in fifteen minutes' time, and tell him that you are ready to face the fresh challenge of a transfer.'

Quarter of an hour later, Pete was dropped back on the corner of Lansdowne Crescent, feeling a mixture of elation and ice-cold fear.

'*Nulli secundus*, Bradley,' the DI said as he closed the car door.

Pete read back through the densely typed pages, wondering whether those fine qualities Bell had talked about had served him well at all. The trouble was, since he'd been part of West End Central, Wesker's behaviour had become so bizarre that even incidents Pete knew he had witnessed with his own two eyes read back like utter fantasy.

Only at the beginning had any of it made a certain kind of sense.

Wesker had courted a reputation with the press as the man who was cleaning up Soho. He liked the linen drapers and the linens liked him back – he was just the kind of tough guy they wanted to scourge society's sinners; a bona fide war hero with a jocular way with words to spice up their yarns.

The way Wesker told it, the streets that ran between the murky borders of Tottenham Court Road, Regent Street, Shaftesbury Avenue and Warren Street were a nest of dire villainy, the product of an organised crime wave as pernicious as in Al Capone's Chicago. Only the toughest police officers – himself and Grigson mainly, but with a youthful army of aids for Uncle Harry to train – stood between the honest public and utter anarchy. As part of his act, Wesker naturally had to maintain an intimate relationship with all of the moody gaffs that were run on his patch.

Pete's induction to Wesker's beat had been a heady tour of pool halls, amusement arcades, bookies, speakeasies, spielers, strip clubs, clip joints, jazz dives, late night eateries and public houses that catered for very specific parts of the trade. In some ways it was very similar to Ladbroke Grove, but somehow in these older streets lurked a darker sense of corruption, a historical weight of venality and violence. Generations of criminal families had organised these streets to their own business needs. The more atonal modern jazz plied in basement rooms by some of the best musicians Pete had ever seen was the perfect soundtrack to frenetic, discordant Soho. The good-time Jamaican ska of the mushroom clubs in Powis Square would have seemed too carefree here.

Pete and Bell had worked on a persona for him to hide behind, a further mask to slip over the face he strove to keep impassive, the disguise within the disguise. It was based on the drill sergeant who had taught Pete how to box in the army and the playing of the part had helped a lot. As had his boxing credentials. Bell already knew Pete had been his regiment's middleweight champion and how that would play in Wesker's macho world; Wesker himself was a former champion amateur boxer. The constant supply of fight tickets, supposedly from one of Pete's snouts in the Grove, but really courtesy of Bell himself, maintained that insider illusion.

Every day, Pete filed away his real feelings into a separate compartment in his head while the logical part of his brain set to work deducing Wesker's angles. It seemed to boil down to a vested interest in a couple of nightspots owned by a certain villain called Sampson Marks.

Marks was an unpleasant-looking man with a face like a hatchet, which he was at pains to detract from with the finest tailored suits, an abundance of gold and diamond jewellery and a cloud of musky cologne. He was a descendant of the firms that ran Soho in the days of Billy Hills and Jack Spot, who had first made good in the East End and then come looking for a whiff of West One glamour. He had even once been involved in an enterprise that included Peter Rachman, a restaurant in Mayfair, but had managed to slide out of that just before Profumo made the name too hot to handle. Now his business was concentrated between a strip club in Old Compton Street and a much more salubrious venture, a supper club that attracted the cream of the entertainment world and was, to all intents and purposes, owned by the ex-boxer Teddy Hills.

Teddy. The World Light Heavyweight Champion of 1949, an amiable bear of a man who had since forged a successful career in light entertainment, unable, like many of his kind, to keep away from the bright lights when his career in the ring dimmed. Teddy who was always out front with the punters while other men made use of his office, in all probability blissfully unaware of what they were really doing there. Or so Pete hoped. Thanks to Wesker, Pete had spent a lot of time in Teddy's club and his liking for the former pugilist went beyond the admiration that lingered from his boyhood into what seemed like a genuine friendship.

But it wasn't Teddy's club where the trouble had begun. It was Le Continental, the faux-Parisian revue of strippers run out of Marks's Old Compton Street premises. Five people had been arrested over the course of five days in September 1962 for attempting to extort monies from Marks with violence. The press saw it as another victory for Wesker, a bullet to the heart of organised crime.

Pete hadn't been in on the first two arrests, but he had seen the suspects in the cells with bloody noses and missing teeth. Grigson and one of his protégés had brought them in. An Italian called Alfredo Togneri and his neighbour Alec Chesterfield, both twenty-two. The charge sheet said they had been in possession of offensive weapons – Togneri a flick-knife and Chesterfield an iron bar – which they had used to intimidate Marks on the steps of Le Continental.

In the CID office, Wesker was on the phone. Standing in the doorway, Pete caught the end of the conversation while the other man's back was turned.

'...what's done is done, darling, at least we got one of the bastard's known associates,' he was saying. His jacket hung on the back of a chair, his shirt was open at the neck and there was blood on his cuffs. 'As for the other slag, well, that's what we in the army call getting caught in the crossfire.' He laughed. 'But don't sweat, me old sweetheart. I'll drop by Shaftesbury Avenue tomorrow and see if I can't pick something up.'

The next day a mechanic named Sidney Hillman, who worked on Shaftesbury Avenue, joined the ranks of the accused. Pete found out more about him while he and Bream were dispatched to look for another member of the gang, a Greek called Theo Georgios. Bream had been in on a few more meetings than Pete. While they sniffed out the Greek on Berwick Street, he provided running commentary on the arrest of the mechanic.

'It's a long-standing thing between Hillman and Marks,' Bream informed him, 'come out of some angst over a scrubber, wouldn't you know it. One of the girls worked down the club. Hillman come after him with an axe, apparently. Marks dropped the charges, probably on account of the bird, you know how soft-hearted he can be.'

Bream said this with no apparent irony.

But it was Marks whose nickname was 'The Chopper', for the methods he used to keep his women in line, so the legend went.

'So what the guv reckons is that Hillman put this gang together to try and get his revenge. Once we've got the rest of them, we'll get the story straight. Oh, hang about.' Bream's hair seemed to bristle like antennae as his eye caught a group of people coming out of a doorway of a bookies just ahead of them. 'Here comes our bubble.'

Georgios had a girl on each arm, he was flush from the 1.30 at Kempton Park and about to take them both out for dinner. He didn't come quietly but Wesker had parked the van around the corner so it wasn't too far for Pete to drag the screaming Greek, while Bream tried his best to hold off the harpies, who rushed to his defence. Once inside, Pete felt the man suddenly freeze when he came eyeball-to-eyeball with The Bastard.

'Mr Wesker,' he said. 'Please, I can explain.'

Wesker smiled, teeth glinting, patting his truncheon across the palm of his hand. 'I'm sure you can, me old darling. But first, I want to take a look at that motor of yours.'

'Motor?' Georgios looked perplexed.

'White Ford Anglia,' Bream read out of his notebook, 'registration number PAR 147.'

Georgios looked from Bream to Wesker. 'Why?' was all he said.

Wesker found a detonator in the White Ford Anglia, which had recently been serviced by Hillman's Motors of Shaftesbury Avenue. But that still wasn't the end of the matter. On the night of the 26th of September, Grigson arrested another man outside Le Continental. Ernie Fletcher was identified by Marks as part of the gang who had been threatening him on the night of the 21st, who had fled when Togneri and Chesterfield had been nabbed.

The whole mob had been up at the Old Bailey on 6 December 1962. Marks had testified, alongside one of his girls, how all five had waged a sustained campaign of intimidation against him in the weeks leading up to their arrests. Wesker stood up tall in the dock as he confirmed the array of weapons that had been found, exuding a stentorian sense of gravity as he spoke. The jury didn't take long to convict. Hollow-eyed Togneri was sent down for seven years, Hillman and Georgio for five, Chesterfield for three and Fletcher for fifteen months.

Long sentences for men with no previous convictions.

Pete didn't know what the Civil Liberties people had that he didn't, but he had worked long and hard trying to establish how Hillman could have put this gang together. Togneri and Chesterfield were neighbours. Togneri was friends with Hillman, but Chesterfield was adamant he didn't know the mechanic. Georgios had his car serviced at Hillman's garage but beyond that they were not known to socialise together. And the only thing that connected Fletcher was that he and Georgios had once had an argument in the street and threatened each other with the police. From his reaction in the van, Georgios obviously had had previous run-ins with Wesker – but whatever it was that he was about to explain to him had nothing to do with what he was ultimately charged with.

The only thing that Pete felt certain of was that Hillman was the man Marks and Wesker really wanted. The key to it was probably the girl Hillman and Marks had fought over, one Gladys Small. But she didn't work for Marks any more, her name was phoney and she had no fixed abode. Whoever she was, she had just disappeared into the Soho night.

Pete's brain ached. The clock told him it was a quarter to three now.

There were still another seven names to go through.

14

You'll Never Walk Alone

'Well, well, well. If it ain't the little Welsh rabbit.'

I look up and the room swims in and out of focus, the lights from the candles on each of the little tables making golden ribbons in front of my eyes. From out of the darkness a pair of cold grey eyes bearing down on me, the face behind the voice, the voice that I hoped never to hear again.

I see him in his black suit and his white shirt and his black tie, the light dancing round him like a halo, only he wouldn't wear a halo, not him, not The Chopper. Scars on my arms from him, scars on my legs, on my back, on my belly, on my backside. Two years old but suddenly they hurt afresh, throbbing out a flesh warning that brings the room back into focus, the lights falling away, the sounds of music and chatter replacing them.

'That's all you ever do is rabbit, ain't it girl?'

He kneels down so his face is level with mine and I can see those long lines down the side of his mouth, deep as scars, his face the same shape as the tool of his trade, a hatchet with a haircut, pasty white skin with pockmarks and blackheads and those eyes, those cold, cold eyes.

'What d'you want?' I hear myself say, my skin prickling with fear like a million tiny little electric shocks, telling me: Get out of the room, get out of the room…

He waves a finger in my face.

'See, there you go again, Welshie, all facking mouth – ain't you ever gonna learn to keep it schtum?'

I shrink away, avert my gaze to the empty glass in front of me, smeared with lipstick and grubby fingerprints. My discomfort makes him laugh, makes him lean in closer so I can smell his breath, tobacco and whisky over rotten teeth. He whispers in my ear.

'You're on the skids, ain't you Welshie? Big Tits Beryl's given you the boot I hear.'

My mind shrinks and crawls. Big Tits Beryl: coat hanger in her beefy hand, thrashing the arse off me after I did something wrong...something with the lorry drivers...something I don't want to remember. Rubbing it better afterwards with baby oil, saying she was being lenient on me, doesn't want me to look like damaged goods or I won't be able to go out and earn for her, but it was for my own good. Rubbing it in greedily, hot fingers searching out the places her steel whip never reached, rubbing and rubbing, hot and red, fear and disgust rising up in me.

I pick up the empty glass; think about smashing it into his face, adding to the scars there. Remember the chopper and put it down again.

Get out of the room, get out of the room...

'Ain't no one paying for any more of that mother's ruin?'

He's changed his tone now, talking softer, more conciliatory, but still with that underscore of menace between us, white sparks dancing in the air.

'I could have a job for you if you want it.' He stretches out that finger again, traces a line along my jaw. 'Looks to me like you need it, girl. You ain't no Lily of the Valleys no more.' His grip tightens on my face, fingers sharp into my skin, he turns my head around to face him, bores into me with those cold, empty eyes.

'But you'll do,' his mouth twisted into a sneer, his breath curdling the air, 'for this little scene.'

'I don't...' I begin but a wave of applause drowns out my words, people around me getting to their feet, applauding whatever it was that we were in here to see. If only I could remember where was here and what this was...

The Chopper's hand under my elbow now, dragging me out of my seat, unsteady on my feet, the lights blurring and sliding now as he propels me away from the crowd, from the people and the noise, down a back set of stairs, some secret place that he has access to, always the secret places with The Chopper, down and down the staircase, music ringing tinny, distorted through the walls, out into the Soho night.

I know this is Soho but I can't remember how, have I been here before, this back yard with cobbles, this dark space between the bright lights? It feels familiar, and yet...

There's a black car waiting there, a long black car.

The black car. Oh God, oh Jesus, I know what this car is for, what those two figures in the front seat want with me, those men, their faces lost in the darkness.

I try to pull from The Chopper's grasp, but his hands are firm, digging into my elbows. Bruises blooming under his grip, I can feel them, and my feet slip on the cobbles, my worn-down heels that I never had the money to get mended sliding backwards. The Chopper hauls me over, curses dropping from his crooked lips, leans across to the man in the passenger seat.

'This'll do for you,' he says. 'Got enough gin in it to withstand most anything. Likes it rough anyway, silly little slag.'

He opens the back door, bundles me in, says something else to the man in the passenger seat, something I can't hear.

Here comes the candle to light you to bed.

The seats are smooth, made of leather, it smells of cologne in here, clean and expensive, but I don't feel safe, not at all. There is a wooden partition between the men and me so that I can't see them, the windows are tinted so I can't see out either. The engine starts up and the car begins to move, not a car, no, a coffin on wheels. I reach for the door handle on the left side, there is nothing there.

I turn to my right. She is sitting there in her blue-and-white striped summer dress, her brown hair cut in the style of an actress she had favoured, something not right about the tilt of her neck. I watch with horror as she puts up a hand to push her head back up and looks at me, her eyes filled with pity, and as she does a strange music begins to play, sounds like it's coming from a radio, like the music on the stairs it is tinny and distorted but I can hear a man laugh and a woman scream.

I look at her ruined face and I start to think of all the times I cracked my heels on the Whitechapel Road earning brass for Beryl, all the dirty lorries and shabby cars and none of them so terrifying as this, this sleek, purring coffin taking me out of this world and into the next, a song I once heard in a coffee bar playing out my funeral march, mocking me. I look down at the stained skirt of my mustard-coloured dress and I remember what my ma said to me before she died, how I had to wait 'til I got married and then I could have a string of pearls as long as the sidings in Barry, but never take money from a man, no, never take money from a man, and I called myself Smart, but I was never smart. I should have listened to my ma but now it's too late, The Chopper's got his revenge on me, no peace in the valley for me. The Chopper has found me and come back for me and put me here in this coffin where I can't escape and soon it will be the earth, the cold, cold earth and I will lie there, my mouth open in a scream until the flesh falls away and there's nothing left, no funeral, no chapel, no 'Abide With Me' sung

*like a beautiful wave of peace by the men from down the mines.
Just nothing: a long, loud, screaming nothing.*

I sat up in bed, a silent scream stuck in my throat, staring into the
blackness, wondering where the hell I was and what the hell I had
become. Only when I had realised that what I was looking at was
just a sliver of orange from the streetlamp coming through the
curtains in my room in Powis Terrace did I realise that I wasn't the
girl in the mustard-coloured dress.

And that the noise I could hear was not the sound of a car
taking me to my own funeral, just the dull thump of bass from
someone playing a record in the house next door.

I threw back the covers and slid out of bed, cold sweat sticking
my nightie to my legs. Went into the bathroom and turned on the
light, stared at my chalk-white face in the mirror above the sink.

It was me looking back. Not the girl in the mustard dress from
the café in Soho a few hours before. Not the girl in the blue-and-
white striped dress come back from my nightmares of 1959…Or
was I Alice, staring through the looking glass? Everything in the
room seemed too white, too big, too bright. The porcelain under
my fingers as cold as a mortuary slab.

Then my stomach heaved.

*'Anarchists in leather jackets looking for aggro, bearded Communists
in donkey jackets, Ban-the-Bombers, wild-eyed girls with straggly
black hair, blue-jeaned Teddy boys and joyriding Beatniks…'*

Two weeks later, I stood in the middle of a packed tube, trying
to read the paper while holding on to the overhead strap, swaying
uncomfortably against my fellow passengers. I was due at the shop
to meet Jenny, for her fittings for the opening. I hadn't anticipated
sharing the carriage with this lot.

But the night before, there had been a riot in Trafalgar Square, a protest against the visit of King Paul and Queen Frederika of Greece. Two thousand people tried to get down the Mall. I'd never heard of such violence on a march before.

'As traffic came to a standstill, police helmets clattered across pavements, fists flew and prancing police horses bowled over crowds,' I read. 'Some rioters, waving banners that read Down With The Nazi Queen, fought off bobbies from the top of a doubledecker bus. A few youths who made it to the Mall were stopped by flying tackles.'

I thought of Chris, sitting in the café, the night I saw the girl in the mustard dress and then had that terrible dream about her.

'It does all pale compared to people's lives and liberty.'

The focus of the protesters' rage was the assassination of the left-wing Greek MP Gregoris Lambrakis. One of the leading figures in the anti-nuclear movement, he had been run over by a lorry and killed after delivering a speech at a pacifist rally in Thessaloniki. No one was in any doubt that Greek government agents were responsible – even Harold Wilson had boycotted the state banquet.

'Central London today,' I read on, 'becomes virtually a "police state". Some 5,000 uniformed and Special Branch men will be taking over the area...'

'What you reading that for?'

I looked up, saw a wide, ruddy face, a dense brown beard and a pair of beady brown eyes boring into me through bottle-thick specs.

'I'm trying to understand what this is all about,' I said.

'Understand?' he said. 'There ain't nothing in that paper that's gonna make you understand, love. They ain't gonna tell you the truth are they?'

It was gone rush hour, so there were no pinstriped suits to

defend the honour of the Establishment, only a scattering of middle-aged matrons who reacted to his words with a mass shifting of tweedy bottoms on seats, and tourists clutching their children close. Everyone else on the train appeared to be with him.

'You ain't stupid, are you?' he said, softening his tone. 'I bet you don't want nuclear missiles on our doorstep neither, do you?'

'No,' I said, 'no I don't.'

'And you don't want Nazis sipping tea in Buck House.'

I shook my head, holding his gaze.

'But they,' he took the newspaper out of my hand and folded it in half. 'They don't care what you think. Our interests are not their interests. They want us to know our place and stay in it, so they can carry on with their business of making money and screwing us over. But we don't have to take it. We can make a difference. Show them...'

The train shuddered to a halt at Bond Street station. The anarchists, communists and beatniks made for the opening doors. But those beady eyes remained fixed on mine, a messianic flame burning in their depths.

'You could get off here and join us,' he said. 'Or you can carry on with your nose in a paper, understanding nothing.'

He was so different from Chris, I thought, even though they would probably both be on the same side. I didn't doubt what he said was true, but I didn't like to be spoken to like a child. I thought he was one of those people who enjoyed going on demos just for the fighting and the chance to be self-righteous about it.

'Come on Rob,' one of his companions put a hand on his shoulder. 'It's out here for Claridge's.'

'Yeah,' he said, 'I know.' He looked back at me. 'You coming?' he said.

'*People's lives and liberty...*'

'No,' I said.

He smiled, a sardonic curl of his top lip. 'You don't want to know, do you? Well,' he handed me back my paper. 'Sweet dreams then, darlin'. Just remember, when they finally come for you, there won't be no one left to defend you.'

His words were still echoing in my mind as I put the key into the shop door on Marlborough Court.

It was eerily quiet in our corner of the West End, no sign of the police state in our little courtyard. The radio played innocuous pop songs as Jackie and I worked away, putting the finishing touches to our shop floor, deciding which outfits we wanted Jenny to wear.

Our model arrived at midday, radiating the Tuscan sunshine that had given her skin a honey-coloured glow. Even her basic outfit of black shirt, white slacks and black ballet shoes looked effortlessly sophisticated.

'Got through the barricades all right?' asked Jackie as she let her in.

'What do you mean?' Jenny frowned.

'There's supposed to be five thousand coppers out there and a load of angry peaceniks,' Jackie said. 'Stella met some of them on the tube, we thought there was going to be another riot. Only we've not heard a squeak of it here.'

Jenny shrugged. 'Me neither. I got off at Great Portland Street and walked from there, I didn't see anything going on. In fact, I thought it seemed rather like a ghost town, I wondered where everybody was.'

'Outside Claridge's, according to my anarchist,' I said.

'Well, let them get on with it.' Jenny dismissed the subject as her eyes travelled round the room. 'You have been busy haven't you?' she said. 'This looks superb…'

We had all the fittings in the shop painted dazzling white, had the floor tiled in huge squares of black and white and worked my old jigsaw blocks in around the place to add a splash of colour. Shiny chrome rails and porthole mirrors to distort the perspective. It was supposed to be like being inside one of my Op Art paintings.

'So how's it going for you?' I asked. 'Any more films in the offing?'

'Maybe.' She shrugged. 'I'm not really pursuing it, I'm just enjoying myself painting, seeing what comes. Now what have you got for me to try on? Come on, I'm dying to get stuck in.'

I was halfway through pinning her into a dress when the phone rang. Jackie went to get it and came back frowning.

'Jenny, it's someone called Dodson,' she said. 'He said it's urgent.'

Jenny looked at me with wide eyes. 'Oh God,' she said. 'I wonder what that can mean?'

So did I. I had never heard of someone called Dodson before.

'Excuse me,' she said and ran up the stairs to take the call.

'Sounded like an old fella,' Jackie whispered behind her departing back, 'a very nervous old fella and all. What the heck is she up to now?'

A few minutes later, Jenny stood at the top of the stairs, her face ashen, her pupils wide.

'I've got to go,' she said, clutching on to the banister with whitening knuckles. 'I'm really sorry, but my brother's just been arrested, I've got to get him out of there.'

Jackie and I turned to look at each other, our own faces reflecting Jenny's shock.

We never knew she had a brother.

15

Flash! Bang! Wallop!

They met late at night, on the bomb site bordering the canal that had just been cleared for construction, under the cover of cranes and concrete mixers. Once a notorious slum housing successive waves of immigrants since the turn of the century, now this place was to be rebuilt into 'civic housing' for the poor, designed and overseen by the recently honoured architect, Sir Alex Minton.

Pete wondered if Minton knew anything about the people he was planning to send to live up in the concrete tower block proposed for the site. That ninety-five per cent of the men who lived round here had criminal records; that police had to patrol the streets four deep of a weekend; that a family of fourteen would probably fit into the same space as Sir Alex's own lavatory. He couldn't shake the image of a rat's nest in the sky, everyone crawling over each other. His own head was crawling too, from lack of sleep and the contents of his report, events he could hardly keep up with and write down in detail at the same time. He would be back on duty again in six hours.

'You've been working hard, Bradley.' Bell's eyes registered appreciation as he took Pete's thick folder from him.

'It's all there, sir,' said Pete. 'Though whether you can believe it is another matter.'

Besides the Togneri racket gang, there were four more cases in that ream of paper, works of Harold Wesker's personal fiction.

First there had been the shopkeeper, Horace Golding, charged with receiving stolen lighters. Pete had seen Wesker plant them on the unfortunate man. Golding had tried to stand up for himself but in the end, his lawyers had made him plead guilty and he'd served nine months for it. Golding had got out of jail only three weeks ago. If anyone had gone straight to Civil Liberties, Pete reckoned, it was him.

Then there was the bookie, Nobby Clarke, accused of blowing up one of his firm's offices with a detonator Wesker had found in his car – exactly the same kind of device as Georgios had been nicked for. Clarke and his mate Iain Woods, who had the misfortune to be in the car with him at the time, were arrested by Wesker in the early hours of the 24th of April. Both pleaded not guilty but went down anyway, on the strength of Wesker's testimony.

Events got steadily worse. Wesker arrested four men at the Establishment Club in May, for threatening the doorman. Two of them were deaf and dumb and had been using sign language. Of the four, only one of them had any previous. Wally Green had done three stretches for burglary, receiving stolen goods and armed robbery. But his companions were a grocer, an electrical engineer and a company director – hardly the type you'd expect to find carrying around the flick-knives, razors and iron bars that Wesker and Grigson had produced for their charge sheets.

Then, when four friends of Green's came to Marylebone Magistrates' to make bail for him, Wesker had the lot of them nicked for 'attempting to pervert the course of justice' – again by using sign language. So that made eight people currently awaiting trial, four of whom were physically disabled.

The whole thing beggared belief.

Except...Nobby Clarke used to knock about at Teddy Hills's

club. Pete had seen him there a few times; he had a notorious head of red curly hair. Clarke's friend, Iain Woods, had form as a fence, same as Green; and Clarke, Woods and Green all socialised at the same pubs and club. Discounting the 'crossfire' of apparently respectable businessmen caught up in all of this, all roads seemed to lead back to Teddy's.

He had put all this into his report. Whether Bell would let him follow up on it was another matter.

The DI's eyes moved rapidly down the pages as he worked his way through the pile. Pete rubbed the back of his head, where his hair was starting to sprout a thick mass of curls. Three weeks late for the barber he was. Maybe he could fit in a trim before he had to report back to work, but that would mean only four hours' sleep...

'Bradley.' Bell's voice cut through Pete's thoughts. 'I can see you have done a thorough job here and I don't want to keep you any longer than necessary.' He tapped the window between themselves and the driver.

'Would you drive us to Oxford Gardens, please?' he said.

'Thank you sir.' Pete was grateful for the lift, even though it was only a ten-minute walk.

Bell closed the cardboard folder, scratched his moustache as the car crunched across the rubble and up on to the Goldborne Road, staring out of the blackened windows into the sulphurous glow of the street lights and the figures that flitted past.

'I'll have you back here as soon as this is dealt with,' he said. 'You'll be transferred before anything happens to Wesker, hopefully it'll stop you catching any flak. It could be days, rather than weeks, so prepare yourself.'

Pete followed Bell's gaze. A woman stood on the corner of the Portobello Road and Goldborne Road, underneath the lamp post there. From the length of her skirt and the low cut of her blouse, there was no mistaking what she was doing hanging around. As they passed her by, she leaned her head backwards, dragging on a cigarette like it was the only thing sustaining her, eyes closed to the deadbeat world around her. Pete had an inkling of how she was feeling.

'Thank you sir,' said Pete as the car drew up at the end of his road.

'Bradley,' the DI said. 'My advice to you now is to put in for your detective sergeant's exams. I know you'll make a better fist of that than Harold bloody Wesker.'

Bell's face set into grim lines as he spoke the last sentence.

As he walked up his drive, Pete could see floating shapes out of the corners of his eyes, the phantoms that followed him when he'd not had enough sleep, the beginnings of hallucination. He tried not to think about any of it as he made his way into the darkened house.

'Out! Out! Out! Out!'

The line of police outside Claridge's was three men deep, a thick blue snake twitching backwards and forwards, ready to encircle the advancing protesters with their banners and their beards, draw them in and strike. Flanked by men on horses and strategically placed plain-clothes, the body of the beast stretched around the corners of Brook Street and Davies Street, blocking off the entrance to the hotel on both sides. A clash of the red, white and blue with the black, brown and grey, the CND signs waving above the Union Flag, the shouts for Queen and country drowned out by laments for a dead Greek MP.

'Lambrakis! Lambrakis!'

'Down with the Nazi Queen!'

Six hours later and the meeting with Bell seemed like a distant dream, part of the hallucination of the night world of the Grove, as here in Mayfair, the air thronged with the sound of stamping feet and clanging horseshoes, the oceanic roar of the mob.

The Bastard Squad was positioned around the back of the protest, to anticipate trouble before it arrived or mount a vanguard attack. Wesker was desperate to be in the thick of it. Smacking his fist against his palm, cracking his knuckles, imagining he was breaking the heads of those that had dared to criticise a queen, his Queen, the woman he had fought his way through Italy for. Long-haired nonces and deviants, bastards the lot of them, they were all going to get it, he had briefed his team before they left the station in their wagon, one of a brace of them now parked at the hotel's rear.

'Don't hold back lads,' he had said, a vein pumping on his forehead, sweat prickling his brow. 'They're all traitorous scum and if it were up to your Uncle Harry, I'd court martial the fucking lot of 'em.' Grigson at his side smiled evilly, nostrils flared to savour the bouquet of chaos in the air, ready for more aggro than these protesters could possibly have dreamed of.

Pete and Bream stood back from them as always, lurking in doorways, watching, waiting for the fuse to ignite. It didn't take long. A lanky young man with a long blond fringe broke away from the back of the protesters and started to walk towards Brooks Mews, looking around him as if searching for something. In his hand was a paper banner that read: *Lambrakis* RIP.

Pete frowned. There was something familiar about the lad, but he didn't have time to work it out, just saw Wesker walk towards him, gesturing at Grigson to follow, before a sudden rush of people came round the corner to join the back of the marchers. Another wave of Ban-The-Bombers piled into the throng, about twenty of them, all with their weird beards and corduroys, badges and banners. Their leader was a stout, bearded fellow in a donkey jacket, wielding a megaphone. When he shouted into it: 'No Nazis here!' they all responded: 'Out! Out! Out!'

Pete exchanged a glance and a nod with Bream, moved out of his doorway and into the midst of them. He was thankful he'd not had time for his appointment at the barber's now, at least his messy hair and his naturally saggy jacket let him blend in with the students. Let him get closer to Wesker. Through a sea of hair and arms he caught sight of him, holding up the blond lad's paper banner and shouting something at him, saw Grigson calling over a couple of beat bobbies. There was a flash of indignation in the young man's eyes before the handcuffs came out and fear replaced it, and it was that look that sent Pete's mind spiralling back to Ladbroke Grove nick in the summer of 1959, that same look, only with a greased-up Teddy boy quiff instead of a floppy fringe, a black-and-white checked sports jacket instead of a tonic suit.

Wesker was nicking Giles Somerset, hauling him off by his collar while Grigson and the uniforms pushed everyone else out of their way. Somerset's eyes were wide and he was pleading nine to the dozen. Wesker was enjoying every second of the lad's distress.

The crowd surged from behind him and Pete felt himself pressed forwards; he went with the flow to avoid falling over, pushed up against the protester with the megaphone, the smell of sweat and adrenalin in his nostrils. The man put out a hand and laid it on Pete's arm to steady him.

'All right there, mate?' the protester said, brown eyes magnified through his thick specs as they ran up and down the length of Pete, rapidly sizing him up and turning hostile.

'Here lads,' the protester shouted to his companions, 'something smells bad around here. I reckon it's filth.'

'Don't be so hasty…' Pete began, but the other man didn't give him the time to finish his sentence. He pushed his megaphone into someone else's hands and lunged straight at Pete. From the flicker in his eyes, Pete saw it coming and ducked his head out of the way, catching hold of the other man's arm and trying to twist it behind his back, only there were bodies everywhere, pressing and barging into them. A woman started screaming and her screams were joined by the shrill of a siren, the wagon containing Wesker and his prey coming past the back of them. Pete struggled to stay upright while the protester flailed under his grip and his friends grabbed hold of Pete's arms, trying to prise him off. He felt kicks to his ankles and his shins as he instinctively moved backwards, dragging the protester with him, and then suddenly there was Bream beside him, pushing arms off him, a couple of bobbies bringing up the rear, wading in with truncheons raised.

Pete felt like his arms were about to be pulled out of their sockets as he dragged the man out of the fray, his ears ringing with noise; elbows, hands and feet everywhere, hair in his mouth. The protester had stopped struggling now, made himself a dead weight that Pete had literally to haul on to the pavement. The bobbies moved in quickly, surrounding them, kneeling on the man's chest as Pete intoned the words of arrest.

'Nazi scum!' the man shouted, then spat straight into Pete's face. His glasses had come off in the scrum and his face was purple with rage. For one second Pete felt his arm swing backwards, his hand balled into a fist. Then he caught himself, fought it back down, white light crackling across his temples as he shook his head to clear it, reached for his handkerchief instead to wipe the mucus off his face. He would not be like Wesker. He would not be like Grigson.

It took three uniforms to get the protester back on his feet and push him towards the wagons. Pete put his hands on his knees and caught his breath as he started back into the mêlée, where Bream and a bobby were pulling out another couple of weird beards, twisting and shouting in their grasp. He could feel blood running down his shins but the pain hadn't kicked in yet, his adrenalin was pumping too fast. He straightened up, went back in to Bream's aid. Got the other two into the wagon with their leader, and they screamed their way back to West End Central.

•

More screaming in the cells, the place fit to burst, a clanging cacophony of boots and metal doors, cries of pain and howls of rage. In the detention room, the three protesters slumped on to chairs, silent now, their ringleader radiating resentment, the other two more like fear. Pete's arrest was one Robert Parry, twenty-seven, of Ellerslie Road, Shepherd's Bush, who gave his occupation as a librarian. The other two were Stephen Fairchild, twenty-two, and Graham Dixon, also twenty-two, students at the LSE. Pete had Parry booked for assaulting an officer, Fairchild and Dixon for affray. On the table in front of them were the contents of their pockets – cigarettes, matches, leaflets about Lambrakis and CND, library cards, keys, loose change. Bream taking it all down, the Front Officer elsewhere, up to his eyeballs in prisoners. The bruises on Pete's legs were starting to throb.

A face appeared at the door.

'Well, well, well. What have we here then?'

Wesker walked into the room, surveyed the trio with a look of amusement.

'Sir.' Bream passed him the charge sheets. Wesker's smile deepened as he took it all in. He handed the clipboard back, honed in on Parry, leaned over the desk, smiling that bloodhound's smile.

'Assaulting an officer?' he said. 'Oh dearie me.'

Parry glowered back.

'Who are you?' he said, giving Wesker the same strafing look he'd earlier employed on Pete.

'I'm the Chief Super,' said Wesker. 'Your worst fucking nightmare, son.'

Pete shifted his weight from one throbbing leg to the other, tried to keep his expression blank. He had never heard Wesker promote himself like this before, wondered what was coming next.

Parry laughed. 'You ain't nothing,' he said, 'but a Nazi tool of the state.'

Beside him, Fairchild and Dixon looked set to wet their pants.

Wesker's smile deepened and he leaned forward across the desk until he was practically nose to nose with Parry. 'I fought fucking Nazis when you were in short trousers, you horrible piece of scum,' he said softly. 'That is a very grave insult you have just levelled at me.'

Wesker drew back slowly, putting his hand into his pocket.

'An insult that's worth,' he said, drawing his hand back out, 'about two years.'

Even Parry flinched as Wesker slammed down a piece of brick on the table in front of him.

'And look!' the DS went on, producing another piece and slamming it in front of Fairchild. 'One for you! Oh and...' He went for the opposite pocket now. 'One for you too!' Dixon almost fell off his chair.

'A present from your Uncle Harry!'

'Sir,' Bream began. 'They're already bang to rights. You don't need...'

'Don't need?' Wesker looked at him as if he were mad. 'I've got every bloody need. No long-haired nonce calls me a Nazi and gets away with it. That's why,' he stomped over to Parry again, picked up the brick he'd placed in front of him and slammed it down again for emphasis, 'the biggest piece goes to the biggest boy!'

Wesker put all his weight behind his right arm, so that when his fist connected with Parry's jaw there was a crack as loud as a gunshot. Parry screamed, spitting teeth and blood, falling sideways on to Fairchild with the momentum of the blow.

'Please!' Dixon leapt out of his own seat, put up his hands. 'Stop it!'

'Stop it?' Wesker roared. 'I ain't even started yet!'

Dixon cowered back into his chair, Parry lolled over Fairchild, who looked like he was about to faint. Wesker stared at Bream with wild, bloodshot eyes. 'Add them to the charge sheets,' he said, looking down at the pieces of brick. 'Then get them down the cells,' he said, turning to Pete. 'Out of my fucking sight.'

Parry's moans filled the air behind the slamming door. Pete looked at Bream, then at the prisoners, then back at Bream again. The other man shook his head.

'What a bleedin' carve up,' said Bream, picking up his pen.

16

Charade

'Brother?' Jackie and I said in unison.

Jenny stared back at us as if she didn't know where she was, then closed her eyes, slapping her palm to her forehead.

'I don't mean...I mean a family friend, an old family friend, I call him my brother because...Oh God, never mind that. He's in West End Central Police station, he just got his one phone call, they arrested him outside Claridge's and they've beaten him up, they've charged him with possessing an offensive weapon, a piece of brick, I mean,' she broke off her rapid-fire ramblings with a snort of a laugh, 'for God's sake, Giles isn't capable, he's never been capable. What the hell was he doing getting involved in things like this again without me? He can't do anything for himself!'

She sank down on to the top step, one hand still clutching the banister, the other over her face.

Jackie looked at me. 'I've got a half bottle of brandy in my desk,' she said. 'I reckon she needs it.'

I nodded. The pair of us climbed up the stairs and helped her to her feet, manoeuvred her over to a chair in the office. Jackie fetched her secret stash while I held Jenny's hand, trying to soothe her into making some sense.

'Oh God,' she kept saying, over and over. 'What am I going to do? Oh God, oh God, oh God...'

'Here.' Jackie shoved a mug under her nose. 'Get this down you.'

Jenny looked at her with a glazed expression. She took the mug and drank, spluttered as she did so, then winced and said: 'Ugh, God, it's horrible.'

But it seemed to do the trick.

Jackie took the mug back off her. 'Now talk normal, woman,' she said. 'Tell us from the beginning, what's this all about, then we'll try to help you.'

Jenny looked from Jackie to me, gripping my hand so hard the nails started to dig in.

'P-please,' she said, 'if I tell you girls this, you can't tell anyone else, you mustn't. Not Toby, not Lenny, no one else can know. Promise me?' No longer empty, her eyes now blazed with a ferocious intensity.

'It's all right Jenny,' said Jackie, showing a surprising softness, reaching out and stroking Jenny's hair. 'Your secrets are safe here, we promise.'

Tears started to form as Jenny spoke. 'Giles, he's...He's a boy that I've known since I was little. His mother and my mother were friends, are friends, we played together since before we could walk. I always looked after him, he was such a dimwit even then; so trusting he would have gone off with the first person to offer him a lollipop.' Her voice quavered but she tried to hide it behind a smile and carried on.

'Giles has a tendency to...get involved with people he shouldn't,' she said. 'Extremists of some form or other. It doesn't matter to him what side of the fence they're on, he just gets completely carried away. It's all a big rebellion against his dad and believe me, I can understand that.' Her voice grew bitter.

'But really,' she said, 'he should have grown out of it by now, for God's sake, his old man is practically senile, there's not much he can do to shock him any more. Anyway.' She shut her eyes again, gave a deep sigh and continued.

'I know this is going to sound terribly corrupt, but Daddy dearest does have a certain amount of influence in high places and if I could call him he would get Giles out of jail like that.' She snapped her fingers. 'The trouble is, since I went to Italy, I haven't had any contact with my parents at all. I don't think.' Her voice broke again and more tears fell. 'I just can't go back to them now. I've come too far. But I can't just leave Giles either, he's such a terrible fool and Christ knows what they've done to him. Oh God, what am I going to do?'

I felt something inside myself connect with Jenny. I knew plenty about estrangement and how it played on your mind. Apart from the stiff, formal Christmas and birthday cards we exchanged, it had been five years since I'd seen my ma.

'Did you say he was at West End Central?' I asked, suddenly realising that I did know exactly what to do about this.

'Yes,' she said.

'Right, well, I think I know who we should call. I bumped into Chris Hawtry in Soho a couple of weeks ago, completely out of the blue.' I wanted to make her feel quite sure that I was not suggesting any involvement with Dave. 'Turns out he's been working for Civil Liberties, helping people who've been wrongfully arrested, and some of them were by police at West End Central. I'm pretty sure that he'll know what to do.'

'Really?' She stared at me. 'But that's brilliant. How do we get hold of him?'

I extricated my hand from her grasp and went over to the desk with the phone and the directory on it.

'I expect that they're in here,' I said.

'Well, I say,' said Jackie. 'That's a turn up for the books.'

I didn't ask whether she meant Jenny's revelations or Chris's new vocation. I was just thankful to find the National Council For Civil Liberties listed in the book. Even more so when I managed to get put straight through to Chris – by some miracle, he wasn't up to his neck in anarchists already. Jenny told him a version of the story that left out all the personal details, just that a good friend of hers had been arrested on the protest and then had an offensive weapon planted on him at the police station.

As she talked to him, the colour started coming back to her face and her posture grew slowly more relaxed. Chris really did have a vocation for this sort of work, I could see it right before my eyes. When she put the phone down she was almost smiling.

'He said he's going to appoint a solicitor right away,' she told us, 'and then go to the police station to try and find out what's going on. He's going to call me back as soon as he knows anything.' She caught sight of her own reflection in the mirror and automatically started patting down her hair.

'I can't thank you enough for this,' she said, still staring at her reflection. 'Would it be OK if I called Dodson back now, just to let him know not to worry?'

'Course,' said Jackie. 'Help yourself. Come on Stel, let's leave her to it.'

Downstairs, Jackie went straight over to the radio and turned up the volume. 'Bloody hell, what a can of worms!' she said. 'Old family friend.' She shook her head. 'Have you ever seen her get so worked up about anything before?'

'No,' I said, 'and who is this Dodson person anyway?'

Jackie pushed a box of boots across the floor and started ripping the packing tape off, making as much noise with it as she possibly could.

'Probably a butler,' she said, 'they never have Christian names do they? These upper crust families, the way they carry on.' She started taking the boots out in pairs, flicking off the wood shavings that they'd been laid in. 'I could have just rung Daddy and got him out of jail like that,' she carried on, imitating Jenny's accent. 'I mean, what the hell are us little people supposed to make of that? And is Chris going to get her a free solicitor now, when she's got money coming out of her eyeballs?'

'Who is her dad anyway?' I asked, crouching down to help her, dimly recalling an old conversation with Chris. 'Some sort of architect, isn't he?'

Jackie gave a low whistle. 'Her dad,' she said, 'is *Sir* Alex Minton. The bloke that's rebuilding half of West London, putting up a load of tower blocks right on your doorstep. He's one of the richest bastards in England, so I suppose she must have risked a lot, running off to Italy like that. I wonder if he disowned her.'

'What…' I began, but a creak on the stairs cut me short.

'Right,' said Jackie loudly, 'I reckon we should put some of these in the window,' she stood up, 'and the rest of them over…Oh, all right, Jenny. Is everything OK now?'

Jenny nodded. 'Thank you so much for everything,' she said. 'You really don't know how much it means to me.' She stood there looking forlorn, her eyes sweeping across the floor, clearly unable to decide what to do next.

'So,' I said gently. 'Do you want to carry on with the fitting, or would you feel better coming back tomorrow or something? We don't mind, do we, Jackie?'

'No,' said Jackie, 'we've plenty to keep ourselves busy with here. You do what you like love, whatever you think's best.'

'Oh, but of course I want to stay here,' Jenny said, 'I'll do the fittings and then I could help you arrange the things, whatever you want. I mean, Chris said he's going to call back here later didn't he? I'd rather keep busy until he does. Keep my mind off things.'

'Of course that's all right,' I said. 'So, er,' I looked over to Jackie, 'shall we carry on where we left off?'

'I tell you what,' said Jackie, 'why don't you put kettle on first?'

'Yes,' said Jenny, nodding. 'Tea. How very British, Jackie.' The ghost of a smile played around her lips. 'That's exactly what we need.'

Chris arrived on our doorstep at a quarter to five, another bunch of folders under his arm. 'Hello Stella. Amazing place you have here,' he said. 'The rest of the West End is in total chaos, but you're so tucked away you'd never even know.'

'Is it really that awful?'

'I've never seen anything like it,' he said, shaking his head. 'Anyway, I've just been at the police station and seeing as I was in the vicinity, it seemed easier to drop by than call. Jenny is still here, isn't she?'

'Yes,' I said, 'come in, please.'

'Hello everyone,' said Chris, 'sorry to barge in on you like this, but I've got some news for Jenny and I thought it best that I dropped round to talk to you rather than making you come all the way over to Camden. There is rather a lot to discuss and I hate to appear rude, but it does have to be confidential.'

'That's very good of you Chris,' said Jackie. 'Would you like to go upstairs to the office?'

The minute they had disappeared, Jackie reached into her jacket pocket and pulled out the remains of her bottle of brandy.

'Here,' she said, offering it over. 'I think we could both do with something a bit stronger than bloody tea now.'

'You can say that again,' I said.

17

How Do You Do It?

Pete knocked back his pint, bitter down his throat to match the memories of the day's events still swirling through his head. Plonked the empty glass back down on the back bar of Teddy's club and turned to Bream.

'Another?' he said.

'Keep 'em coming,' Bream nodded.

Pete watched the brown liquid pour down the side of the fresh pint glass. Saw again Giles Somerset cringing in the corner of his cell, black eye and torn jacket, crying as he rocked himself back and forth. Saw the dark, accusing eyes of the man he had been put in with, remembered his own shock as he recognised him as the former West Indian batsman Kingsley Puttnam, sitting there with his front teeth knocked out. Asking Wesker what Puttman was there for, receiving the reply: 'Fuck him – I ain't got time for that coon now, I'm too damn busy.' Watching Wesker's eyes turn narrow, knowing that he'd gone too far, alerted Wesker to some discrepancy in his character that he should care about the state of a prisoner, especially a coloured prisoner.

Wesker calling him in just as he was about to finish his shift, giving him a bollocking – Robert Parry was not Robert Parry at all, his real name was Stefan Kirk, a regular little red activist who Special Branch had under obs. Wondering if Pete was really up to this job or if a few days on the front line were getting too much for him, was he folding under fire, going soft? Grigson standing outside Wesker's door as he left, cracking his knuckles and smiling that evil smile.

Bream waiting by the front door, suggesting a drink at Teddy's and Pete calling Joan to tell her he'd not be back for a few hours yet, hearing the disappointment in her voice and hating himself for it, but needing that drink and needing to be at Teddy's.

For behind it all, behind all those broken teeth and iron bars, those dodgy detonators and pieces of brick, he could see one face: the hatchet mug of Sampson Marks. If this was going to be his last night at West End Central then it had to be one last dance at Teddy's, one last vat of bitter for the road.

'Pete,' said a kindly voice at his elbow. He turned to see Teddy himself, a gap-toothed smile on his battered face, black, curly hair falling over his formidable brow. He wore a Savile Row suit in pale grey, with a purple shirt unbuttoned at the neck, revealing a black fuzz of chest hair. Teddy didn't look entirely comfortable in his get-up, as if even the finest stitched cloth in all of England couldn't quite contain his huge shoulders and thick arms and at any moment the seams would rip open. But his manner was genial. 'Bad day at the office?' he enquired.

Pete couldn't help but smile. 'You could say that, aye,' he replied.

'I've been trying to keep up with it all on the news.' Teddy shook his head. 'Down with the Nazi Queen, what a bleeding disgrace. You can have those drinks on me.' He nodded over to the barman who put two fresh pints down on the counter. 'You deserve it, putting up with animals like that. Harry not with you tonight then?'

'Not so far as I know.' Pete feigned indifference, passed Bream his pint. 'It's just me and Frank, drowning our sorrows.'

'Well.' Teddy raised his own cut-glass tumbler of whisky and clinked glasses with them. 'God bless you for it.'

There was a round of applause from the audience as the crooner on the stage finished his act, and Teddy put his glass down on the bar to join in.

'Did you catch much of Simon's act?' he asked Pete. Pete wondered for a second what he was talking about, then realised it was the man on the stage he was referring to. Pete hadn't paid him any attention at all, but he didn't want to seem rude.

''Fraid not, no,' he said. 'We've not been here long.'

'Shame,' said Teddy. 'If it was a normal night you could have brought your wife to see him. I'm sure she's a fan. Mrs Wesker certainly is.'

Pete craned his neck to try and make out who the figure in the pale pink suit taking his bows actually was. The name Simon didn't ring any bells and the music couldn't have been worth hearing, otherwise he would have noticed it.

'Do you want to come back and say hello?' Teddy went on. 'Maybe get an autograph for Mrs Bradley? He's a good pal of mine, Simon, I'll introduce you.'

Pete considered the offer. Maybe Joan did like Simon Whoever He Was. Then his signature would be a good peace offering when he eventually did get home. And maybe this was going to be his last night as a valued customer at Teddy's so he'd better make the most of it.

'Cor, I wouldn't mind,' Bream said before Pete could reply. 'Me old ma's dead sweet on Simon Fitzgerald, she's got all his records, framed photos on the wall, you name it. If I could get his autograph for her I reckon I'd get Sunday lunch every day for a month and all me laundry done with no moaning for once.'

'Good,' Teddy laughed, 'follow me then, lads.'

Simon Fitzgerald looked almost comically like a miniature

version of Teddy, with the same dark gypsy looks and wide, lopsided smile. The pale pink lounge suit made him look smaller still and sadly out of date. Simon was a crooner in the style of Bing Crosby – the mothers might all still love him, but in 1963 he was a man out of time. Which maybe accounted for his uncomfortable, nervous demeanour.

When they got backstage, he had a showgirl on each arm and was midway down a bottle of Bell's, holding court to an audience of middle-aged men, their wives in pink satin and permanent waves and a gaggle of tuxedoed musicians. In the middle of the room was a long table with a white cloth over it, laid out with fruit bowls, champagne buckets and ice trays full of beer, two enormous vases of flowers and a selection of garish-looking finger food, salmon mousse, cheese and pineapple sticks, avocados and vol-au-vents.

In the corner, a shifty-looking fat man with a greasy comb-over was deep in conversation with Sampson Marks, fat, bejewelled fingers holding a handkerchief to his brow, piggy eyes using the mirrored walls to subtly keep tabs on everyone in the room. His corrupt corpulence reminded Pete of his old Sergeant, Alf Brown – no doubt he was Fitzgerald's manager. Some of the middle-aged patrons, he slowly realised, were actors and actresses, light entertainment types you'd see on the telly. Fitzgerald was putting on a show for them and they were laughing and nodding appreciatively. But the singer looked strained, his eyes flicking towards the door and then down at his wristwatch every few seconds. When he saw Teddy he visibly brightened.

'Oh Teddy, darling, how did it sound out there?' He extracted himself from the showgirls and rushed forwards to greet his friend. His accent was Scouse with a camp twang and he moved with a mincing gait. Funny, thought Pete, how both Fitzgerald and Wesker liked calling other men 'darling'.

'Wonderful, Si, as always.' Teddy clasped him in a bear hug. 'You always know how to play the crowd just right.'

'Ooh,' said Fitzgerald in an undertone, 'but I was sick with nerves beforehand. It never gets better, Teddy, no matter how many times.'

'You're a natural, Si, a star, you don't have to worry about a thing,' Teddy reassured him. 'Now here's a couple of friends of mine I'd like to introduce you to, Pete Bradley and Frank Bream. They work with Big Harry, you know.'

'Ooh,' Fitzgerald said again, regarding the pair of them with glittering eyes. Slightly the worse for wear, Bream stumbled as he walked forward, offering his hand.

'Mr Fitzgerald,' he said, 'it's such a pleasure to meet you. Teddy's right; that was a terrific gig. I wondered if you wouldn't mind,' he fished around in his jacket pocket for his notebook, 'signing an autograph for me old ma. Shirley's the name,' he went on, pressing both notebook and a fountain pen into Fitzgerald's hand. 'Shirley Bream, that's B-R-E-A-M...' He grinned, breathing toxic fumes over the singer, who wrote his signature down quickly and passed the book back, looking over uneasily at Teddy.

'Harry Wesker, you say?' he said to him.

'That's right.' Bream stared at the signature, a beatific smile spreading over his face. 'Uncle Harry. He talks highly of you, Simon.'

Fitzgerald looked somewhat pained.

'That's right,' Teddy encouraged. 'Mrs Wesker is a big fan of yours, remember? Dolores?'

'Oh yes, of course.' Fitzgerald's smile was entirely false. He turned quickly to Pete.

'Lovely to meet you,' he said, offering a limp hand. 'Any friend of Harry's...'

Pete cringed at the other man's clammy touch. There was

something really repellent about him that went beyond the faux-sophisticated patter and the girlish shade of his suit. But Pete had no intention of upsetting Teddy, or Bream, who was just reaching an interesting, loose-lipped stage of drunkenness. He also had Joan to think of.

'I don't suppose you'd mind doing the same for my wife?' he asked, proffering his own notebook. 'I would have liked to have brought her with me tonight, but we were on duty 'til late, dealing with a riot.'

'Of course.' Fitzgerald smiled politely and signed his name. 'You must have had a terrible time with all those awful beardy Bolsheviks – do you need something to drink?' He indicated the table as he handed the notebook back. 'Champagne, beer, spirits – it's all there. Help yourselves, please.'

There was a ring of desperation in the last three words and Pete took the hint, ushering Bream forwards with him. Clocked Fitzgerald putting his hand on Teddy's sleeve and moving him out of earshot, talking quickly but inaudibly.

'Look at that,' said Bream, still staring at the autograph as if he was having problems focusing on it. Bream had been taking nips out of his hip flask all day; mixing them with a rapid succession of pints had pushed him over the ledge of intoxication. He had obviously found the events of the day too much to handle too; the incident with the bricks undermined his usual cautious defences, otherwise he wouldn't have spoken out of turn in front of the prisoners the way he did.

'Me ma's gonna love that.' He lifted it up to his lips and kissed the page. 'You beauty,' he said. 'This is gonna buy me a lot of favours.'

'You should be in a jazz band, Frank,' said Pete, fishing a bottle of pale ale out of one of the ice buckets and wiping it on a linen napkin.

'Why's that?'

'You can improv better than Louis Armstrong. Terrific gig indeed. We never saw five minutes of it.'

Bream laughed. 'Well,' he said. 'You have to flatter these sensitive types.'

Pete let the ambiguity of this last sentence run through his mind and put the napkin back down. The pink and green food was congealing on the table, a film of sweat breaking out over the top of it. A bloody waste it was too, adding to the underlying feeling of claustrophobia and fake bonhomie that rang around the room and down the edge of Pete's nerves like the shrill laughter of the women. He couldn't see a bottle opener anywhere so he prised the top off with his teeth, a trick he'd learned in the army. Bream stared up at him admiringly.

'Get that down you.' Pete passed it over to him and picked another bottle out of the water.

'How d'you do that?' Bream asked.

'It's a knack,' said Pete, watching Sampson Marks and the fat man in the mirror. He bit off the second lid and spat it into an ashtray, saw the manager pass Marks an envelope that he quickly palmed into his jacket pocket.

'You're a man of many talents, Pete.' Bream wiped foam off his moustache with his sleeve. 'Talking of which, take a butcher's at that,' he said, nodding his head in the direction of Simon Fitzgerald, still talking nineteen to the dozen to Teddy, but now with one hand resting proprietorially over a showgirl's sequinned buttocks. 'If my ma only knew what a sweetheart her Simon really is.' He looked back at his autograph one more time before finally putting it away. 'Just as well she doesn't, eh?'

'What do you mean?'

Bream leaned closer, lowered his voice to a whisper. 'He's a twister that Simon. Kinky. You know. Makes out like he's a real family man, with his pipe and slippers and his loving wife at home, but once he's off the leash there's no stopping him. I bet you a monkey he'll be leaving here in the company of both those two darlings.'

'Really?' Pete watched as the other showgirl moved back in, bringing the bottle of whisky to replenish Fitzgerald's glass. The girl at his side winked at her as she did it, twirling the stem of her champagne glass coyly, resting her hand on Fitzgerald's other arm. 'I was beginning to wonder if his bread wasn't buttered on the other side, like.'

'He does come on like a bit of an iron hoof, granted,' nodded Bream. 'But don't be fooled. I've heard some funny stuff about him in my time.'

'What like?'

'Parties,' said Bream, swaying slightly. 'Orgies. There's a certain scene that caters for, shall we say, bizarre tastes. Ropes and whips and whatnot. Mainly it's toffs that set it up, which is why you never hear about it. Only they can't always be that choosy about what girls they can get to do that kind of thing, and you know how toms can talk.'

Bream belched. 'I nicked this piece one time for running a house of ill-repute,' he went on. 'Big Tits Beryl they called her. I still see her around sometimes in Soho, only she's a lot more discreet with her business these days. I give her a packet of fags and she started telling me some tall tales, dropping some names, hoping I would let her off with a caution, which in the end,' he put his empty bottle down on the table and fished around in the ice bucket for another one, 'I did. But he was one of the names she mentioned. Simon Fitzgerald. She didn't like him much. Reckoned he could get a bit rough with a girl when he'd had a few. Had a reputation for it.'

Bream finally got purchase on another bottle, started waving it around in the air.

'Let me,' said Pete, taking it off him, not wanting him to lose his train of thought with the effort it would take to get the lid off.

'Ah, yeah, thanks Pete. So you see, he ain't all that he seems to be, old smoothie Simon. I reckon it's something to do with him being so short – you know what I mean. It's always the littlest ones that fight the hardest ain't it, got the most to prove? Now Teddy, on the other hand, is a big man and she couldn't say nothing but good about him.'

'Teddy?' Pete didn't like to think of him being involved in anything like that.

'Yeah, Teddy's a real gent, apparently. Doesn't play away from home much, but when he does, he knows how to treat a lady.' Bream waggled his eyebrows. 'Even if she is just a lady of the night. He don't have nothing to prove.'

'Right.' Pete took a swig of his drink to hide his own discomfort, attempted to join some dots in his head between prostitutes, madams, showbiz stars and toffs. Rewinding Giles Somerset, held overnight in his cell. Gypsy George and his bag of filth. *Parties. Bizarre tastes.* Why didn't Wesker recognise Somerset when he had come straight to Notting Hill nick to save him the last time?

'*Frankie boy.*' He saw Wesker again in his mind's eye, outside the interview room, tucking the envelope of evidence under his armpit. '*Get in there and deal with young Somerset, I'll be helping myself to our friend George. Derek me old beauty, if you could just show me the way...*'

Cold chills started prickling down Pete's spine.

'Lucky bastard is what I say,' Bream burbled on, 'two of them. I wouldn't mind...'

Bream had been at his side just about all day, maybe he didn't see who it was Wesker had nicked. But still, why hadn't anyone come to the young earl's rescue this time? And why hadn't Wesker let him go when he found out who he was? Had he really gone so mad that it no longer registered?

'...pair of Bristols like that, it's enough to make your eyes water...'

'Gents.' Sampson Marks appeared at Bream's shoulder. His lips formed a thin line that hardly moved as he spoke, a cigarette dangling between, smoke drifting up. His eyes, just as narrow, moved coldly towards Pete.

'Looking a bit the worse for wear tonight, Frankie boy,' he said, putting a hand on Bream's shoulder, keeping his gaze levelled on Pete. 'I heard you was in the wars today,' the left side of his mouth curled slightly upwards, 'bit of trouble with all that long-haired scum.'

'Here Sam.' Bream's eyes slowly focused in on Marks. 'Got any more showgirls going spare? I don't half fancy some crumpet.'

Marks laughed, a hollow bark that never reached his slits of eyes. 'I don't think you're in any fit state for crumpet, Frankie. I think it might be time for bed and cocoa instead.' He slowly removed his cigarette from his mouth and blew a plume of smoke into Pete's face. 'Don't you?' he asked.

'Aye,' said Pete, staring back, knowing now that Wesker had sussed him, that he'd passed his doubts along to the person who really ran this club and Christ knows what else besides.

'Aw.' Bream slumped, like a disappointed child. But he must have caught something in the tone of Marks's voice, because he offered no resistance, spread out his arms, palms up. 'Well, I suppose, if you say so, Sam.'

'I'll call you a cab.' Marks was still looking at Pete.

'Don't go to any trouble,' said Pete, 'I can see him home all right.'

'See that you do,' said Marks. 'I don't want him bothering my girls when he gets in this state. I've cleared up after him too many times before.'

'What's that Sam?' said Bream.

'I'll see you to the door,' said Marks. 'Make sure you're headed in the right direction.'

'There's no need,' said Pete. 'We know the way.'

'I'm not sure that you do,' said Marks.

'Wh-what's this all about?' Bream looked confused now. 'I haven't offended anyone have I?'

'No, Frankie.' Marks began to steer him towards the door. 'I'm just making sure that your friend here takes care of you properly.'

Pete followed behind them as Marks propelled Bream down a set of stairs that led directly down from the backstage. Wondered every step of the way whether Marks was about to pull out a shiv, or an iron bar, or a gun. Felt his blood hammering through his head, fists clenching and unclenching, eyes locked on Marks's hands and what he did with them. When they came to the bottom of the stairs there was a fire door. Pete swallowed hard as Marks pushed it open. Would there be a reception committee waiting for him on the other side of it?

But it was just the car park behind the club, a cobbled yard with a couple of motors parked there. Nice motors. A Rover and a Jag.

'You'll be OK will you Frankie?' Marks was coming on all concerned now, putting his arm around Bream's shoulder. 'I should use that cab firm down Goslett Passage there, seeing as your good friend won't let me call you one on the house.'

'Yeah.' Bream was even more unsteady on his feet as the night air hit him. 'Yeah, that's fine, thanks Sam. What time is it?'

'It's past your bedtime is what it is.'

'Yeah,' said Bream, wandering over to the wall, undoing his flies and urinating like a carthorse down the brickwork. 'You say so, Sam.'

Marks turned back to look at Pete. 'You look after him,' he said. 'The man's a friend of mine. But you ain't.' His voice dropped into a low hiss. 'I don't want to see your face around here no more, *Cunt*stable Bradley. You get me?'

Pete smiled, the blood pumping a familiar tattoo now, the song it used to sing to him before he stepped into the ring, the same refrain that always came when he knew he was about to grab a villain and the villain just couldn't see it coming. 'Gladys Small,' he said, 'she ever turn up again, did she?'

For a second he saw a muscle twitch under Marks's left eye. The question caught him unawares.

'I don't know what you're talking about,' he said.

Their eyes locked and the world turned, an eternity spun through a cobbled yard at the back of a nightclub in Soho, an empty forever reflected back in the black of Marks's eyes.

'Cor, I needed that.' Bream came staggering back, zipping up his flies, bowling into Pete and breaking the spell. 'Right then, are we off?'

'Aye,' said Pete. 'That we are. Good night Mr Marks, thank you for all your gracious hospitality. I'll be sure and return the compliment to you one day.'

Marks said nothing, just spat on the ground.

Bream started singing 'Show Me The Way To Go Home'. Kept it up all the way back to the station house where he still lived, almost kissed Pete goodbye as he slithered out of the door. When Pete got back to Oxford Gardens there was a car parked at the end of his drive. Its headlights came on just as the taxi drove away.

Pete felt the bruises on his legs pulsing. Every bone in his body ached. He stood at the end of his drive, wanting only to crawl next to Joan and fall asleep for a thousand years.

But instead he walked towards the car, to DI Bell sitting inside. They all knew.

18

It's My Party

'Now then,' said Lenny, 'you can open your eyes. What do you think?'

I blinked. Laid out in front of us on a scarlet tablecloth was a cake in the shape of the letters B & R, zebra-striped in black-and-white icing. Surrounding it were plates of red cupcakes and sandwiches cut into neat triangles, bowls of black olives and red cherries and a line of champagne buckets full of fizz. A pyramid of clean glasses gleamed in the sunlight that poured through the window, free of its shutters for the first time since we arrived at Marlborough Court.

'It all matches,' said Jackie. 'Lenny, you're a genius.'

'Well I wouldn't say that. But I do know an awful lot of Jewish mommas who are good at these things.' Lenny winked and reached for a bottle. 'And now, I think we should have a little snifter to wet this baby's head before the hordes descend.'

Pop went the cork, and the fizzing of the bubbles as they slid down the glass matched the effervescence pumping through my veins. Now that we had actually got everything ready, the way it all looked was such an achievement that I couldn't feel anything but happy and proud. That I was doing the right thing with my life, after all.

'Cheers my darlings.' Lenny handed us a glass each and we clinked them together.

Jackie gave a whoop of delight. 'We did it!' she cried. 'We really did it!'

'Yes,' I said, my eyes rolling round the room; the clothes on their chrome rails, spaced neatly apart; the brand new black fibreglass mannequins displaying hipster trousers and Op Art shirts, a triangular shift dress with a target motif; the jigsaw blocks forming little stairways around it all. 'We really did, you know.'

Jackie put her arms around me and bounced me around in a celebration dance.

'Aw,' said Lenny. 'Ain't you sweet? Well my dears, here's to a raging success.' He took another sip of champagne, picked an imaginary speck of dust off his purple suit and adjusted his cufflinks.

'And I can't tell you how good it felt to finally hand in my cards at the bank. Oops!' The doorbell cut through his reverie, 'that'll be our top model.'

'Morning.' Jenny padded in, wearing her usual off-duty get-up of black slacks, shirt and pumps. Her hair and make-up, though, looked as if she'd come fresh from the beauty parlour, her manicured nails the same shade of barest pink as her frosted lips. The dark eyeshadow, liquid liner and false eyelashes were heavier than usual – the effect was dramatic, but was it hiding the ravages of a couple of sleepless nights?

'Do you want to join us for a glass?' asked Lenny, lifting up the bottle.

She smiled wanly. 'No thanks,' she said. 'But I'd love a coffee if you possibly could?'

'Of course, dear, of course. I won't be a sec.' Lenny clattered off upstairs.

'Everything OK?' asked Jackie.

Jenny nodded. 'We got him bail yesterday at the Magistrates' court, thank God. Well, thanks to Chris, actually. The solicitor really knew what he was doing; I don't think they expected that. He's had Giles's clothes taken off for scientific examination, to prove that he wasn't carrying that brick around with him, and do you know what?'

We shook our heads solemnly.

'He had to hire an independent analyst, because if he hadn't, the same policeman that arrested Giles would have been able to take them to their lab. Can you believe how corrupt that is?'

Jackie whistled.

'Was it the same policeman Chris was already investigating?' I asked.

Jenny nodded. 'Harold Wesker his name is. He's an utter bastard. In fact, that's what his nickname is, The Bastard – and he's proud of it.'

'Here we are ducks,' Lenny came back down the stairs and Jenny put a finger to her lips before turning round to take the mug from him.

'Thanks Lenny, you're the most,' she told him.

'Your hubby will be joining us today, won't he?' Lenny asked me. I nodded.

'Hmmm,' Lenny attempted to look nonchalant, 'is he bringing that Pat with him, by any chance?'

I smiled. Pat Innes tended to have that effect on people. He was dazzlingly handsome, tall and thin with jet black hair and violet eyes, always immaculately suited with a waistcoat and dandy striped shirt. He was some sort of Irish aristocracy, although you wouldn't guess from his highly mannered voice. But his eyes and his hair, his whole posture, seemed so much more fluid than the stiff English types you normally saw inhabiting that style of tailoring.

I had seen both men and women falling over themselves to catch his eye. But according to Toby, Lenny had a better chance than most.

'Yes, they'll both be here around three,' I said.

'Great,' said Lenny, his eyes lighting up.

'Well,' said Jenny, 'before we get too cosy, I should really get dressed. Stella, would you mind giving me a hand?'

Her tone was quite sharp, but inside the dressing room she turned to me with glassy eyes.

'Oh Stella,' she whispered. 'You should have seen what those bastards did to my…Giles. They beat him up. Punched him in the head, ripped his clothes, treated him like an animal. You should have seen his face.' She clutched hold of my lapels, bowed her head, shaking. I put my arm around her, trying clumsily to console her.

'Sorry.' She lifted her head; went over to the mirror and delicately adjusted her eyeliner with her finger. 'I'm making a right mess of myself, aren't I, and that's all you want on your opening day.' She reached into her bag for a tissue. 'I won't let you down today, Stella, honestly. It was just…just so bloody awful and unfair.'

'I know, I'm sorry too.' I put my hand on her shoulder. 'It was terrible what happened to your friend. I'm really glad that Chris could help you so much, thank God I ran into him.'

'I know.' She grabbed my hand and squeezed it hard, smiled at me in the mirror. 'He was a total hero and so were you. Now let's get on with the show, I don't want anyone else to see me looking like this.'

Only minutes after we stepped back out of the dressing room, Jenny in the black-and-white mini-dress and white boots looking so coolly professional you would have never guessed her inner anguish for a second, the first of our guests arrived. Then another and another, until the shop was crowded with people, flashbulbs going off, reporters sticking their notepads under my and Jackie's noses, Lenny taking care of everybody like a perfect peacock butler.

Jenny twirled around the floor striking poses for the cameras, while the till started to ring. Fashion editors, pop stars, glamorous teenagers, actors and actresses talked, bought and ate their way through the cake. It was all we could do to keep the sounds coming from the record player we had rigged up, help Jenny with her costume changes, give interviews and ring up the till.

Toby arrived while I was getting Jenny into another outfit. She had been such a trooper, not once complaining about anything and being charming to all the guests. I watched her step out from the fitting room and saw the eyes of the room zoom in to where Toby and Pat were making their own entrance through the front door.

Toby had really made an effort. These days, he just about lived in his scruffiest jeans, oldest jumpers and most paint-splattered shirts, but today he was wearing a blue tonic suit I had never seen before, which perfectly complemented his hair and his eyes. I wondered if Pat, whipcord thin in a green three-piece suit and candy-striped orange shirt, had been advising him on sartorial matters.

They were surrounded by women by the time I got across the crowded shop floor, but none of them were standing quite so close as Lenny, who was offering Pat what must have been the last slice of our cake.

'Thought you might like to put that in your gallery,' he was saying. 'It might not look like much now, but that was a work of art at the start of the day.'

'Hello darling.' I reached up to kiss my husband. He had a glass in his hand, but there was already an underlying scent of eau de alcohol on his breath. I guessed he and Pat had had one of their 'lunches' already.

'Darling,' said Toby, the colour of his irises intensified by his suit, and also the red lines threading through the whites around them, 'it looks wonderful.'

'Mrs Reade.' Pat turned from Lenny to take my hand in his perfectly cool, smooth palm, raised it up to his lips and kissed my knuckles. 'It really is very impressive. The Op Art direction came from you, did it? Toby was just telling me you made those jigsaw pieces yourself.'

He was smoothness personified, even his voice sounded like a purring cat.

'Yes,' I said, 'when I was at college. They came in pretty useful here, I think.'

'They should be in my gallery,' he said. 'Have you got any more like that at home?'

The way his eyes danced as he spoke, I couldn't tell if he was joking or not.

Toby cleared his throat. 'Well,' he said gruffly, 'we do have a few of Stella's old canvases knocking about, if you want to take a look at them.'

He didn't look very happy at the prospect though.

'Good.' Pat sounded most amused. 'When shall we say? Wednesday, perhaps, I don't think I have anything else on that night. Would that be all right with you, Stella?'

I looked at Toby, awkwardly shuffling from one foot to the other, a frown creasing his brow. 'I think so,' I said. 'Darling?'

'Excellent,' said Pat, slapping his hand down on Lenny's shoulder. 'Then I think we should also invite Mr Jacobson here, make it a foursome.'

Lenny almost jumped out of his skin, while Toby suddenly burst into uproarious laughter.

'Of course,' he said. 'Damned good idea.'

He looked round at me and smiled, his eyes full of mischief.

'Don't you think so darling?'

I shook my head, understanding now what they were up to. 'You're outrageous is what I think.' I smiled at Lenny, who had gone a shade of red that threatened to clash with his suit. 'Wednesday it is then. Now I'd better change the music,' I said. 'This record's about to come to an end.'

The next couple of hours passed in a blur of talking, smiling, taking orders, cashing up purchases and wrapping them in tissue paper to go in our white, black and red carrier bags. When it looked as if there wasn't going to be anything left to sell, Jenny came sashaying towards me with a glass of champagne in each hand.

'Here,' she said, 'didn't I say, ages ago, at Dil's bloody big-top art show that there would be real champagne when we opened our shop? Well it's come true, hasn't it?'

A broad grin stretched across her face.

'It has,' I said, taking my glass and clinking it with hers, watched her take a sip of the alcohol she normally studiously avoided and look around the room with such an intense look of satisfaction on her face that I realised this was as much of a personal triumph for her as it had been for Jackie, Lenny and me.

'Now,' she said, 'will you help get me out of this dress?'

She was almost back into her beatnik fatigues when we heard a loud voice outside the fitting-room door.

'…thought he was quite charming,' it was saying in those nasal tones that turned my stomach every time I heard them. 'He took me to a party once. At *Eaton Square*. Friend of his father's, you know.'

A snort of laughter met this comment. The colour drained out of Jenny's face.

'You know how *she* likes to put on her entertainments?' Bernard Baring went on. 'Well I saw the most extraordinary thing there. We were all arranged around a minstrel's gallery, the lights turned down really low and some sort of curtain stretched across the ceiling. Hadn't a clue what was about to happen, but the old devil assured me I was going to like it, it was a *specialité de la maison*.'

The laughter of his companion got louder.

Jenny stood up slowly, like an automaton, her eyes completely blank.

'Anyway,' Baring said, 'we're all standing around, quivering with anticipation, and then all of a sudden, the lights go on and the curtain drops and there underneath us is this tart, lying on a bed, getting fucked by a gorilla! I mean, it was only a man in a suit, but really, it was *quite* hysterical. Bet she got that from the BBC costume department...'

Jenny pulled back the curtain and Baring almost spilt the contents of his glass all over himself and Pat Innes, who he had been telling his revolting story to.

'You should learn to be more careful,' she said, her face and voice like ice.

Baring recovered his composure quickly. 'I knew I'd met you somewhere before,' he started to say, a nasty grin spreading across his face. 'You're...'

With a crack like a starting pistol, Jenny slapped him across the face.

'You don't know me,' she said. 'If you did, you wouldn't dare even open your mouth.'

'You bitch!' Baring recoiled, pulling his right arm back, his hand balled into a fist. Swiftly, Pat caught hold of it, pulling him away, saying, 'Dreadfully sorry, my dear, and I believe Mr Baring is too. He's quite forgotten his manners. Would you like me to show him the door?'

'Don't trouble yourself,' said Jenny, 'I was just leaving.'

She turned back to me. 'Sorry Stella,' she said, her voice rising an octave, 'but I think your husband needs to start choosing his friends more carefully.'

Then she flounced towards the door, pushed her way out into the street. I just stood there, my mouth open, watching heads turn and curious eyes follow in Jenny's wake.

'Pull yourself together, man,' Pat said, as Baring shook himself out of his grasp.

Baring's creepy grey eyes were pinpoints of rage, his top lip twitching, a vivid impression of Jenny's hand blooming red across his cheek. He looked like he wanted to say quite a lot more, but the look on Pat's face stopped him. He put his head down, muttering curses.

'Is everything all right?' Jackie was coming towards us. 'I thought Jenny was staying for a drink, what's she gone off like that for?'

'Everything's under control,' said Pat. He put his arm round Baring's shoulder. 'I just don't think our friend here has ever worked out how to speak to a lady. I'll make sure he doesn't bother any of your other guests.'

'What the...' Jackie looked at me incredulously as Pat steered Baring away.

'I don't exactly know,' I said, 'but you just missed seeing Jenny doing something I've been wanting to do for years.'

19

Distant Drums

The green hump of cliff rolled away into a forest of pine trees and a curve of sand dunes stretching as far as the eye could see. To the left, an expanse of golden sand meeting the deep blue of the Wash, still and calm and glittering in the morning sun. The scent of pine was carried in the air, along with the distant humming of bees floating through the clover and wildflowers that threaded through the grass beneath their feet. Gulls and terns wheeled graceful arcs through the sky above.

'By heck.' Pete put his arm around Joan, pulled her close as his eyes travelled across the shimmering vista. 'That has to be the best view I've ever seen in my life.'

'Told you,' said Joan, placing her head contentedly on his shoulder.

Pete had forgotten how it felt to be carefree, to feel the sun on his skin and fresh air in his nostrils, to hear no sounds other than the gentle lapping of waves on the shore, the songs of the insects and birds. So long had he been in the dark world of West End Central, he'd almost forgotten how much the countryside could move him. But standing by the lighthouse on Hunstanton cliffs he drank in each tiny detail, committed it to memory so that if he ever felt as bad again as he had during the previous months in Soho, he could come back to this place in his mind and find peace here.

Bell's late night visit had marked the end of it, just as Harold Wesker had brought his own doom down on himself that day of the riot. Giles Somerset had managed to hire a clever solicitor from the Civil Liberties people who had his clothes taken in for forensics at an independent lab. As Somerset had been in the cells all night until he made bail, his suit had never been off his back, so it was easy to prove there were no traces of brick dust in his pockets. Somerset was duly acquitted.

The three men he and Bream had arrested had not been so fortunate, swiftly dealt with at Marylebone before Somerset's hearing. Fairchild and Dixon were fined, but red agitator Kirk copped a two-year sentence, just as Wesker had predicted.

As it was Pete who Kirk attempted to assault, he should by rights have appeared that day. But by then, he was shuttling between Beak Street and Hendon, training for his detective sergeant's exams, Bell's promise to him fulfilled.

Things got steadily worse for the rest of the Bastard Squad as more of the events of the 11th of July unfolded. While Pete and Bream had been dealing with Fairchild, Dixon and Kirk, Grigson had gone back up to Claridge's, where he had arrested four juveniles, taken them back to West End Central and given all of them a piece of brick to carry too. But Grigson had inadvertently nabbed two sons of a local councillor. Questions were asked in Parliament causing the first casualty of the Bastard Squad – Grigson was fired, the case against the boys dismissed.

Then the Civil Rights people began their barrage against Wesker, appealing against a list of sentences going right up to the Togneri gang. The first was scheduled for the 23rd of August but Wesker didn't show. Instead, the judge read a statement from the Director of Public Prosecutions that Detective Sergeant, Second-Class, Harold Wesker had suffered a nervous breakdown and had been committed to Netherne Mental Hospital in Surrey for an indefinite period for observation. There he still languished, pronounced insane by four different doctors.

That wasn't enough to assuage the public outcry though, so a token sacrifice was made. Two of Wesker's young aids were sent down for two years apiece for complicity, men who Pete had never even met. The Togneri racket gang won their appeal. Then, one by one, all the other charges on Pete's report to Bell were quietly dropped.

But the brick cases and Wesker's 'apparent madness', as the Civil Liberties' solicitor had put it, overshadowed the deeper undertow of the Bastard Squad's activities in that long, hot summer. Other things that hadn't caught the popular attention still niggled with Pete's nerves. All the connections to Teddy's, to Marks. The only person he could have talked about it with was wise monkey Bream, the last man standing at West End Central.

But Bell had been insistent that Pete put as much space between himself and the Bastard Squad as possible and Pete had gone along with it. He'd done what he was best at, got his head down and worked, taken his exams and passed with flying colours. After this holiday, so long overdue, he would be back at Notting Hill with two stripes on his arm.

He leant his head to kiss his wife, breathe in the lemony scent of her perfume and feel the softness of her cheek. Hunstanton had been Joan's idea. She had been born in the Fens and came here on holiday every summer until she moved to London.

'Pete.' Joan's blue eyes sparkled like the waters below. 'Can we live here one day?'

'Aye.' Pete stroked her hair, drank in all her loveliness, so thankful he had had her to stand by him through all those long days and never-ending nights. Never complaining, just getting on with it. Just like his own ma in so many ways, how she had made the best of her life and bringing up himself and his sisters after

Dad had gone. He would give Joan anything. 'We shall. I promise you that, love. I could stand here with you forever.'

'Daft ha'porth.' Her laughter lines deepened and she nudged him in the ribs. 'Come on, let's get down to the beach. And you can buy me an ice cream on the way.'

Laughing, they walked towards the little blue van on the crest of the cliff, followed the path down to the sea.

There was more laughter to come, when, a month later, back in Oxford Gardens one night Pete came home to find the table laid with candles and flowers, and Joan put his hand on her belly and told him she was expecting. Pete knew the child had come from that blue and gold week they had spent in Hunstanton.

Delighted with themselves, they began turning their spare bedroom into a nursery. Pete would come home to find her running up red curtains printed with little Scottie dogs, crocheting blankets for the cot, knitting bootees and matinee jackets in soft white wool on thin grey needles. All the spare moments he had he spent in the garage, crafting a wooden cot and a high chair, remembering how Dad had shown him how to use the hammer and the lathe, bringing him back like he was standing over his shoulder smiling, overseeing the arrival of the next generation of Bradleys.

Pete got Joan a dog too, wanting her to have someone there when he wasn't. Fritz was a good-natured old Alsatian, a retired police dog, and it made Pete feel happier having him in the house with them. He had always felt there was a kind of invisible thread connecting his heart to Joan's and now that thread was stronger but its pull on his heart more acute too. The beaten housewives and the little latchkey kids that sat outside the pubs of the Grove affected him like never before.

He started doing something he had not done for a long time, not since Dad died. When he passed St Mary of the Angels church, he sometimes stopped and went inside. Lit a candle for Dad and said a prayer of thanks for everything he had, for Joan and the baby to be kept safe. Thanked God that he was far away from West End Central. Stopped thinking about Wesker, Grigson, Sampson and Bream, locked them in a room in the back of his mind.

Until the morning of Tuesday the 29th of October when a face on the front of the paper brought all the spectres back in black and white.

'Look at this Pete,' said Joan, coming from the front door to the breakfast table with the first edition in her hand. 'That nice singer you got me the autograph from – he's gone and killed himself.' She handed the paper across and sat down, shaking her head. 'What would he do a thing like that for?'

The picture under the headline announcing 'DRUGS KILL TV'S SIMON FITZGERALD' was of him and Teddy, the boxer's arm around the singer's shoulder, both of them smiling as if they were on top of the world. It was taken at the club, five hours before Fitzgerald was rushed to Croydon General hospital with a stomach full of sleeping pills.

'*He came to the club at about 1.30,*' Teddy was reported as saying. '*He'd missed the main show but I got him to go up on stage and do a song, his favourite old Bing Crosby number "I Can't Believe That You're In Love With Me". He was joking around, doing his Jimmy Cagney impersonation. He seemed happy enough. But when I told him to come back tomorrow night he looked me in the eye and said: "There won't be a tomorrow night."*'

Fitzgerald had already sent his estranged wife a suicide note. Pete picked up on that before he replied.

'His wife left him, it says here,' he said, thinking, and no wonder, remembering Fitzgerald's hand on the showgirl's arse, Bream's account of his extra-curricular activities.

Joan raised her eyebrows. 'Well,' she said, 'that's no reason. He had children.'

Pete put the paper down and looked across at her. She was furious.

'I must admit,' he told her, 'I didn't like the look of him when I met him. Thought there was something wrong with him.'

Pete made a bonfire and Joan put the autograph on it, took her Fitzgerald records to the church for jumble. Having spent all her working life trying to save people from illness she couldn't tolerate the idea of suicide. Pete tried not to dwell on it, was as happy as she was to reduce Fitzgerald's memory to ash.

But the autumn chill was settling in. Three days after Guy Fawkes night, Pete got an unexpected call from Dai Jones.

'Something that might interest you,' he said. 'Just over the river from where you found Roberta Clarke, they've just dug up another one. Found her in a field where they'd been having a bonfire, ground they were clearing for a building site.'

'I beg your pardon?' Pete heard Dai but for a moment he couldn't make sense of what he was saying.

'Another dead girl,' said Dai, 'over in Mortlake, just behind The Ship. Not a stitch on her but her stockings. Reckon she's been down there a few months. Made me think of that old case of yours and a few others have been thinking that way too. They got an expert pathologist in to examine her, not much to go on but bones, you see, but they managed to get a match off a fragment of skin to the fingerprint of a missing person and it's another good-time girl. Not that she had much of one in the end.'

'So they got a name?' Pete felt the chills coming.

'Four names actually, any of these mean anything to you? Bronwyn Evans, Bronwyn Jones, Gladys Small, Lena Smart — must be a Valleys girl and she was a little one as well, just like the last one, only five foot of her...'

'Gladys Small,' said Pete, seeing Sampson Marks in Teddy's car park, thinking but not daring to say it, dreading what his words had led to.

And I killed her.

20

In Dreams

The record was still on the turntable when I came down that November morning, still whirling around under the uplifted arm, where Toby had forgotten to switch it off. Cold and hungover, I shivered as I lifted it up and put it back in its sleeve, a Technicolor depiction of the singer in a costume he'd first worn as the ringmaster of an art exhibition, but now accessorised with an ugly-looking cut-throat razor.

If I didn't know Dave, I would be afraid of him, leering at the camera like that, bright red fake blood splattered all over him. It was James's idea, he had explained to us the night before, when he'd turned up to the final night party of Toby's latest show, at Pat's place in Duke Street. James was still doing his séances apparently, and though Dave had never actually taken part in one, he had joined his producer on some mad late night rambles into churchyards and ruined houses that were supposed to be haunted.

Lenny had drifted away at the point in the conversation when Dave had started to describe a talking cat they'd encountered in a graveyard in Essex, while Toby had long since been distracted by one of his patrons. For a moment I had found myself alone in Pat's kitchen with pop's answer to Sweeney Todd, and it was then his demeanour suddenly changed.

'Stella,' he said, lowering his voice. 'Have you seen Jenny?'

I hadn't seen her in months. She had called me the day after the party, to apologise for the way she'd stormed out, hoping that it hadn't caused us any problems. Put it down to the pressures she'd been under that week, Baring's horrible story had just made her snap. I'd told her what I'd said to Jackie, that I thought he had got exactly what he deserved and I was proud of her for doing it. Though there had been some mention of a fracas in one of the gossip columns that wrote up our opening day, it only served to bring more curious customers through our door.

Jenny had done me a favour – Baring's behaviour seemed to have got him barred from my world. Pat was furious with him and Toby was aghast when I told him about that flying fist.

Since then, as far as I knew, Jenny had been back in Italy. The last time I'd heard from her she'd called me from Rome to say she'd landed herself a role in a British production that was shooting out there, with a director she seemed fairly enamoured of, though I'd never heard of him. That was in August, after Giles's case had been dropped and the papers had been full of the rogue Detective Sergeant Wesker and his pieces of brick.

'I was hoping she'd be here, tell you the truth, that's why I crashed the party,' Dave said, drumming his fingers on the top of the table. 'D'you know if she's OK?'

I told him about the movie she was making, how well she had seemed. But Dave shook his head, dragging hard on his fat cigarette, the smell of hashish filling the air.

'Thing is,' he said, 'I've been out on the road for months. I only just seen Chris yesterday, found out what happened with that liability of a brother of hers.'

That gave me a jolt. 'What, you mean Giles?' I said. 'He really is her brother?'

Dave winced and his eyes darted around the room. 'Yeah,' he said. 'Only keep that shtum, she don't like anyone to know, it's one of her family's many dirty secrets. That's why I'm worried about her.'

'But I thought Chris had sorted that all out? The case was dropped...'

'Yeah,' Dave whispered, 'but it don't end there with her old man. That's why she ran off in the first place, thought she could get away from him that way. And that's how he gets his revenge, hanging Giles out to dry, Jenny's Achilles heel that bleedin' moron is.' He crushed the joint in an ashtray, pulled a strand of hair out of his eyes. 'Chris done a good job for him,' he said, 'but believe me, Minton won't leave it at that. You know the copper what did him got shipped off to the funny farm? That's their way of protecting their own. Minton's got the Old Bill in his back pocket, they'll do anything he wants, whenever he wants. If it didn't work with Giles, fuck knows what he'll do to her next.' He shook his curly head. 'Rome, eh?'

I nodded dumbly, wondering how much of this could be true, whether Dave's grief over losing Jenny had unhinged him, or if it was that stuff he was smoking making him paranoid.

'It ain't far enough,' he said.

'Oi Del, there you are,' a big Teddy boy came barrelling up to us, holding a bottle of champagne by the neck. 'Class gaff, this. Shame we can't stay, only we got that gig in Wardour Street to get to, ain't we, mate? Mind you,' he looked me up and down, gave me a lascivious grin, 'I can see why you got distracted...'

'Yeah, all right, Fredo.' Dave snapped back into his usual persona. 'Keep your filthy thoughts to yourself, this is an old friend of mine and she's married.' He swiped hold of the bottle. 'To the bloke what's responsible for all this hospitality you're enjoying.'

Fredo belched. 'Whoops,' he said, 'sorry love. Didn't mean no offence.'

'Come on then.' Dave handed me the bottle and pushed his friend towards the door. 'Let's split.'

He leaned down and kissed my cheek, whispered in my ear: 'I know she makes out she don't want to know me no more, but please, Stella, next time you talk to Jenny, just tell her I'm still here. I ain't going anywhere. Tell her that, won't you, love?'

I could still see the pain in his eyes. Whether it was true or not about Jenny's dad, he obviously believed it.

Dave must have given Toby the copy of his latest single that he started waving about in the taxi home. I wondered whether to tell him about our mad conversation, but Toby had reached that jolly stage of drunkenness that meant nothing would have gone in anyway, and I didn't really want to spoil his night.

When we got in, he insisted on spinning the disc. It began with a woman's scream and a man's laugh, went into a weird kind of carnival organ with a stomping backbeat, Dave cackling murderously over the top of it.

'Oh please,' I said, a dark memory tapping at the corner of my mind. 'Turn it off.'

Toby had laughed but when he'd seen my face he'd lifted the needle up. We'd gone straight to bed then, but however close I had cuddled up to my husband, I couldn't seem to shake the chills that record had put in my bones. At least I had managed to drop off before I remembered where I had heard it before.

All I knew now was that I needed something in my stomach, and a strong cup of coffee to wash it down. Pulling my dressing gown tighter around me, I stepped out of the living room and into the hall. Saw the newspaper lying on the mat, picked it up and tucked it under my arm, dropping it down on the table while I put the kettle on.

When I had made my plate of scrambled eggs and the coffee had brewed, I sat down and tucked in. After a while, I started to feel better, started to wonder again about Dave.

What was it that Jenny had said, the day of Giles's arrest?

'*Daddy dearest does have a certain amount of influence in high places…The trouble is, since I went to Italy, I haven't had any contact with my parents at all…I just can't go back to them now. I've come too far…*'

Jenny's father had been in the news recently. As well as putting up the new council estate just across the train tracks in Westbourne Park, he had just won a contract to build a new flyover, along the side of those tracks, joining the suburbs of west London to a new motorway.

I flashed back to the expression on her face when Baring had been boasting to Pat about the bizarre party he had been to. That look of blankness, like the very first time I met her, when I caught her in our bedroom, rifling through my things.

I heard a woman's scream and a man's laugh, the beginning of Dave's single starting up again in my head. Picking up the paper to distract myself, I unfolded it on the table in front of me, looked down and felt my heart drop through the floor.

Two faces stared back at me in grim black and white, under a headline that screamed: '*MORTLAKE MURDER LINK TO '59 CALL GIRL CRIME?*'

Two faces I had seen before, been before, in my dreams.

My eyes dragged downwards, into the newsprint.

'*Bronwyn Evans was also known by the names of Bronwyn Jones, Gladys Small and Lena Smart,*' I read. '*She had a string of convictions for prostitution dating back to 1958, when she first arrived in London from her native Barry in South Glamorgan, Wales…*'

I knew who she was. She was the girl in the mustard-coloured dress.

'*Roberta "Bobby" Clarke, aged 21, was last seen on the night of 17 June 1959 by handyman Harvey Webb, who dropped her off by a coffee stand on Holland Park at 1.10 a.m. Despite a nationwide appeal, her killer was never apprehended. However, a police spokesman told* The Courier *that there were sufficient similarities between the circumstances of her death for links to be made to Evans. Detective Inspector Reginald Bell said…'*

The girl in the blue-and-white striped dress.

My hands shook as I turned the page. All the details of their lives dovetailed with the knowledge couched in my somnambulant mind. Somehow I had known that Bronwyn Evans was from Barry, known that Roberta Clarke had a boyfriend called Baby and a sister named Pat. I had known they had both been prostitutes because I had felt what they had been through, seen grotesque shades of their memories, everything they were trying to escape from, Bronwyn down a bottle and Bobby with a man who never came.

I had seen the black car that took them away but not the two men in the front seat.

Why had I seen it, how had I seen it?

'You're one of us, dear,' a memory of a voice came to me. *'You have the gift.'*

Feeling a scream welling up in my throat, I picked the paper up and hurled it across the room. Stuck my hand over my mouth as I ran from the room and into the downstairs toilet, a wave of nausea so intense I felt as if I had been poisoned.

Dave's single jarred through my mind as I said goodbye to breakfast and all of last night's wine. I couldn't seem to blank it out now that I knew where it had come from: the dream about Bronwyn Evans. She had heard it, coming through the walls of the club, coming through the car radio…

I sat panting on the cold tiled floor, waiting for the world to come back into focus. Then gingerly, I got to my feet and wobbled back into the kitchen, stared at the paper lying on the floor. Four dead eyes stared back at me.

I picked them back up, smoothed them out on the table. Toby would want to read this later and I would have to act normally when he did, I couldn't bring myself to tell him. How would he ever believe me?

I poured myself a glass of water, sipped it slowly, wondering what I was going to do. For the first time in years, I was filled with an intense longing to see my ma. But I couldn't just call her out of the blue; there would be too many recriminations to get through before I could ask her advice about this. The one thing she would know how to deal with.

It had happened to me only once before. When I was a little girl, we had been bombed out and were staying at my grandparents' house. There had been an air raid that night, a plane came down in a ball of flames and I had woken to find a man standing at the bottom of my cot, a parachute silk trailing from him, soot and blood all over his face, smoke rising up off his uniform, looking at me with wild eyes and saying: '*Wo bin ich? Wo bin ich?*'

Ma had said it was because I was so young, children were much more Sensitive than adults, and with all the madness and death screaming around us, the veil was much thinner in a time of war. The pilot I had seen, she explained, had gone so quickly he didn't even know he had passed.

For years, I had been terrified of what my family called 'the gift', but nothing like that had ever happened again. Not until James and his bloody ouija board, James and that record he had made with Dave. Somehow he had started all this…

'*You're one of us, dear…*'

Then it came to me, a face to the memory of that voice.

I found it in the wardrobe in the spare bedroom, down amongst the old portfolios and other forgotten things, inside my college satchel, under a wedge of creased postcards and dog-eared notebooks. Where I had always known that it would be.

Mya's card.

PART THREE

Jack The Ripper

1964–65

21

Needles and Pins

The girl stood beside the late-night coffee stand on the Bayswater Road, under the orange glow of the streetlight. Bleached blonde hair and an upturned nose, something about her that was slightly different from the other toms. The cut of her dogtooth coat more stylish, the nails that held the Styrofoam cup polished and neatly manicured. Maybe that was why the other girls that passed were giving her daggers.

Or maybe it was because she was talking to Pete at all.

But there was something else coming off her that was at odds with her veneer. The smell of fear, the chink of vulnerability in her eyes as she motioned him away from the main drag and into a sidestreet, out of the lights and the wandering eyes.

'Yeah,' she said, reaching into her white leather bag for her cigarettes. 'I know Geordie Sue…I mean, I knew…Oh shit.' She dropped her lighter.

Pete stooped to pick it up, lit the cigarette for her, cupping his hand around the flame. Waited for her to calm down and tell him about the girl who had come drifting down the Thames, three months after Bronwyn Evans had been lifted from the earth.

The body had come to rest on a floating pontoon on the Upper Mall, just north of Duke's Meadow, outside the London Corinthian Sailing Club, at the beginning of another bright, sunny day. Another tiny slip of a girl, only five foot two with shoulder-length brown hair. Naked but for the stockings wrapped around her ankles and the remains of her torn brown knickers stuffed halfway down her throat.

The post mortem revealed that she had died by drowning... but not necessarily after she landed in the Thames. There were no bruises, cuts or abrasions on her to suggest she had been assaulted or forced into the river, but there was no logical reason to assume she was a suicide, not with that gag in her mouth. Not with the stockings round her ankles, just like Bronwyn Evans's had been.

They got her name when her death mask, photographed with eyes propped open, was beamed out on the early evening news, nearly giving her father a heart attack. The former miner from Newcastle identified his errant daughter as Susannah Houghton, aged thirty, who he hadn't seen in twelve years, not since she skipped off from her job at the chicken factory one morning and never came home again.

She had made a new name for herself in London, several new names, in fact. The nighthawks who frequented the coffee stand at Charing Cross called her Sybil Smith. The loiterers of King's Cross had her down as Margie Mitchell. In West Norwood, where she had lived for a while in a rented room, she was both Suzy Houghton and Susannah Lee. But ask the streets around Pembridge Villas, Notting Hill, where she had shared her last address with her common-law husband Gary Vine and their young daughter Cheryl, and she came back as just Geordie Sue.

'She was a good mate, was Sue,' the girl said. 'We met on the stand there, way back when. Looked out for each other the last time a girl got killed, remember that one from Holland Park?'

Pete nodded, wondering if he had talked to her then too.

'I used to babysit for her when she got together with Gary,

lovely little girl she's got…I mean…Cheryl, she called her. Pretty little thing…'

She inhaled deeply, shutting her eyes.

'You're all right, love.' Pete tried his best to sound soothing, praying that she wouldn't just crack and give up, that she would know something he could use this time.

For he had been powerless to do anything about Bronwyn Evans except pass on what he knew about her former activities in Soho to Dai, leads that got lost in the tangled web the little Welsh girl had woven around her short, unhappy life.

There had been no verifiable sightings of Bronwyn since the summer of 1963, when she had been living in a basement flat in Battersea with a blonde girl. They only stayed a matter of weeks before there had been an argument with the landlord over a gas bill. The girls had agreed to go, but left without taking any of their belongings. The landlord still had them, neatly folded away into two cardboard boxes. A few tatty dresses and worn-down shoes all that was left of Bronwyn's short time on this earth. That and a reputation that lingered, like the smell of mothballs and gin, over the rags of her existence.

Bronwyn had fled Barry at the age of sixteen, after her ma died and her old man could no longer cope with the effort of controlling her. She had been pretty, her brother told the investigating officers, and the photos of her younger self bore this out – black curly hair that fell over one eye and a crookedly endearing smile. Bronwyn had craved the bright lights, dreamed of being an actress. Ended up in Whitechapel, servicing long distance lorry drivers in groups of three or more, ponced by a woman called Beryl Crudgington – Bream's Big Tits Beryl – who had a way with waifs and strays, putting a roof over their heads and turning their silly dreams into performances of a different kind, flat-back acting that paid the rent on the dismal rooms she was providing.

But despite all Beryl's careful tutelage, her methods of discipline including regular thrashings with a wire coat hanger, and no matter how many years she wore her heels down pounding them, it seemed that Bronwyn could never learn the code of the street.

If the Welsh girl had made an enemy of Sampson Marks, he was far from the only one. Beryl had given up on trying to earn from her when it became apparent Bronwyn was mixing business with favours, turning every trick into a potential new ponce and drinking her wages before she could be relieved of them. She went disastrously freelance, having to flee the East End when one Bethnal Green nightclub owner caught her committing the cardinal sin of entertaining two plain-clothes on his premises without the slightest realisation of who they really were.

Still chasing those bright lights, Bronwyn headed west, dreaming of a new career as a dancer. She was hired and fired by every strip club in Soho, Paddington and Bayswater, congenitally unable to turn up on time, sober or presentable. She went back on the game, got herself beaten up so badly that stripping would never again be an option. She told her last landlord she had been working as a waitress and he believed her. He lived above them and she and the blonde never brought any men back to the flat.

That blonde was another mystery vanished into the ether. Nobody could say who she had been and it was highly unlikely she'd come forward voluntarily. Without an exact time of death, every suspect had an alibi. Without any viable leads or even enough evidence left from her skeleton to prove how she had been killed, Bronwyn's trail had gone as cold as her bones.

Until now. The main incident room for Susannah Houghton was being run out of Shepherd's Bush, but every detective in London was engaged in chasing her killer and for Notting Hill CID it was a point of pride: Sue was a local girl. Maybe now this blonde was about to turn up the heat.

'Why do you think anyone would want to do this to her, love?' Pete asked the question gently, pulling out his own cigarettes when she stamped hers out and offering them over. 'Did she ever get involved with anybody you thought was dangerous?'

'They all are.' The girl's voice went flat as she said it, staring past Pete into the night. But after he had lit her up and she'd spent another speculative minute looking him up and down, measuring him up for trust, she started to talk.

'Sue was a specialist, if you know what I mean. The kinky stuff. Thrashing the arse off old colonels or doing girl shows for house parties, that kind of scene. I mean, you get decent gelt for that graft, but you never know what could be coming with some of them upper crust bastards.'

Her eyes hardened and she moved closer to Pete, lowering her voice. 'One time, Sue told me, she got picked up by this chauffeur in Charing Cross. Said he was working for some old lord, wanted to give his son a 21st birthday present, needed someone *experienced*. She gets driven to a house in Eaton Square, twenty-five quid up front, butler shows her to a room and tells her to go in and strip, lie on the bed and wait for his Lordship. Tells her to be gentle with him 'cos he's very shy,' her voice dripped with scorn, 'turns out the lights as he goes. So Sue's lying there in total darkness, waiting. Hears someone coming towards her, reaches out to touch him and gets a handful of fur.'

Connections snapped through Pete's brain as she spoke: *kinky parties, big houses, Simon Fitzgerald…*

But: 'Fur?' He frowned. This was a new one.

The girl scowled, shook her head. 'All of a sudden the lights came on.' She clicked her fingers. 'Sue's being fucked by a gorilla. Well, a geezer in a gorilla suit. But being as rough with her as an actual gorilla, she said.'

'What the bloody hell…' Pete began.

'But that ain't all.' The girl was in full flow now. 'When she gets over the shock of that, she realises there's a whole balcony full of toffs above her, watching the performance. Lords and ladies all done up to the nines, wearing these little tiny black masks, drinking champagne and laughing at her. You know, she done some funny stuff in her time, did Sue, but that really scared her…'

'What kind of a person thinks that's funny?' Pete spoke as much to himself as to his informer.

'Well you know who lives in Eaton Square don't you? That Baron Whatsisname off the telly, one who's always rabbiting on about art, you know who I mean.' Her eyes darted away from Pete and around the houses, as if she had said too much, as if the walls themselves might be listening in. 'Not that I'm saying it was him, mind, but…'

They can't always be that choosy about what girls they can get to do that kind of thing…' Indeed they couldn't – it was only four months since Harold Macmillan had had to resign over Profumo, when the curtain was finally raised for everyone to see the real workings between Upstairs and Downstairs, a big stage version of what had been going on in Ladbroke Grove for years. Now here was a brass telling Pete that another prominent peer was mixed up in the same kind of dirty business.

'Did she ever mention a fella called Sampson Marks, or The Chopper?' he asked, feeling his pulse quickening, his palms starting to sweat, feeling her slipping away.

The girl dropped her gaze along with her cigarette, stamped it out with the toe of her white plastic boots.

'I tell you what,' she said. 'You wanna go and see a fella called Ernie Tidsall, ask him what he knows about Sue and all them parties.' She hitched her bag back over her shoulder, looked down the street, started to walk. 'He's a smudger, another kind of specialist, you get me?' Her pace quickened as Pete turned to follow her, heels tapping along the pavement, moving back towards the shadows, the dim squares of Bayswater.

A smudger. A photographer. *Gypsy George and his bag of filth…*

'You'll find him down the other end of Queensway,' she said, jabbing a finger in the air ahead of her. 'Westbourne Grove, above a paper shop. Now, if you don't mind, I'd best be off.'

Pete let her go, grateful for as much as she had given him. Watched her walk to the corner, turn underneath the lamp post and look back at him.

'When you find the bastard what did for Sue,' she called, making a punching motion in the air. 'Give him one from me.'

22

Anyone Who Had a Heart

I walked out of Holland Park tube and turned left on to Lansdowne Road. Diagonally across from me rose a high tower like a castle's keep made out of red brick, tiny little windows all the way up it. I stopped, sucked in a breath as I read the sign on the wall: *Lansdowne Studios*.

I was standing on the spot where Bobby Clarke had waited in vain for a boy to come and rescue her, got into a long black car instead. Across the road from the studios where James had been working, making his music late into the night.

Which was, in turn, bang opposite the place I was actually looking for. A modest two-storey detached house that, judging from the grey cast of the stucco, had seen better days. Probably during the twenties, in the aftermath of the First World War, when a grieving nation had been desperate to try and reach their lost boys on the other side, at The Christian-Spiritualist Greater World Association.

It felt to me like I had been living through another season of death. Ever since last November, when President Kennedy was assassinated and then, two days later, we watched his killer gunned down in front of the TV cameras. Shortly after, and much closer to home, a little boy called John Kilbride went missing from his home in Hyde, Manchester. He would not be back for Christmas.

December came with a personal reprieve – Macy's in New York invited me and Jackie to design a range for them, flew us over the Atlantic to meet them. Our week there still felt like a dream, from the excitement of the flight to the first appearance of the spectacular Manhattan skyline and the delights of the city itself – the yellow cabs, the Christmas lights, Central Park in the snow. We had such a good time that I almost forgot my worries about Jenny and Dave, almost chased away the shadows of the dead girls.

But all the time, Mya's card sat in my purse, waiting for me to use it.

Christmas and New Year passed in a blur of clinking glasses and excessive food, the start of the Big Freeze. I got a card from Jenny saying that things had gone so well with the film and its director, Robert Mannings, that they had gone and got married. On Christmas Eve in the Eternal City – I envied her the romance of it all, not to mention the climate. As 1964 dawned in blizzards and ice, Toby started work on a new series of canvases, while Jackie and I found ourselves gracing the cover of *Vogue*, alongside a brace of other young designers, as the people putting London on the style map.

Then, on the first night of February, I fell asleep and into another horrific world. When the papers confirmed what I had seen was not just a nightmare, I reached the card out of my handbag, dialled the number and held my breath.

Mya told me to come over right away.

She answered the door herself, her little round face more lined than the last time I had seen her, her hair a shade greyer, but her eyes still bright and clear.

'Come in, my dear,' she said. 'I'm so glad you found us.'

'Thank you for seeing me at such short notice,' I said.

'Not at all, I was expecting you. Please, come through.'

'How's Cedric?' I asked, as she led me into a room at the front of the house that looked more or less like any normal sitting room would do, but for the framed photographs along the wall of Winifred Moyes, Sir Arthur Conan Doyle and a host of other Spiritualists in black lace or mutton-chop whiskers; the crystal ball on the middle of the dining table.

'He's very well, thank you dear,' she said, ushering me into an armchair by the fireplace. 'Thank you for asking. But let's talk about you first, you have a lot to tell me don't you? A lot of trouble on your mind.'

She sat down opposite me, fixed me with an intent stare. 'Give me your hand a minute.'

The moment our fingers touched, I realised we were not going to 'talk' in the normal way. It was going to be like the time I had first met her, at the AGOG party at Chris and Dave's, when I'd somehow lost half an hour in her company. She was going to read my mind. No wonder, I thought, before my eyelids drooped, she was so good in the circus.

I reach into my handbag for another purple heart, my black patent leather handbag that I have filled with everything I need to take me away from here and into my new life. I have £27 10s in my brown plastic purse, the diary I got from the bookies with all my secret numbers, my powder compact and my tissues, my cigarettes but one thing missing – a picture of her. Her who I left sleeping in her cot: How would you like a new Mammy, bonny lass, this one has never done you any good, after all. A prayer that she will never see what I have seen, never be what I have been. Her who I left sleeping while her Daddy snored next door, while I stole away on the bus down the long avenue, the avenue with all the trees where I knew men and they knew me, took me to their parties and made a fool out of me, stripped me and slapped me and snapped me.

My heart constricts with rage as the speed hits home, tightness in my chest as I remember that big house up in Eaton Square, the man in the gorilla suit fucking me senseless to an audience of the great and the good, staring at me up on a minstrel's gallery with fucking masks on their faces and diamonds in their hair, laughing and laughing as he grinded and grinded, the scream in my throat that wouldn't come out, stuck there, lodged there for all time.

Flit through the trees where everyone's on their knees, to another big house up in Kensington and men dressed as women and women dressed as men, women with harnesses strapped round their waists with big fucking dildos strapped round their waists, fucking me and sucking me and cameras out taking it all down, flash bang wallop! What a picture, what a photograph. Ernie in his studio, that dingy old house in Westbourne Grove, taking yet more for the family album, snapping away until there is nothing of me left, nothing but a shell of a woman taking purple hearts from a big black patent leather handbag, me on my way to Shepherd's Bush market, to the night coffee stand where he said he would meet me, he who will take me away from all of this and make me a proper woman again.

We're going to live in Mortlake, he said, in a big house there, a proper house with a stream running through the back garden, with water to wash all the sins away, all the many sins that stain my thirty years on this earth. My halo a flashbulb and I get off the bus and I walk down Shepherd's Bush Green, my black leather court shoes clacking on the pavement, my best shoes, most demure shoes and I cross the road down the Goldhawk Road, towards the market, towards the night stand where I know he is waiting to take me away from all this, my aching body and my vacant soul.

And I see him leaned up against his car, lighting a cigarette, cupping his hands to shelter the flame, big sheepskin coat against the cold of the night and as I do another car pulls up next to me and a fairground organ starts to play a distorted melody, like it's coming up through water, the water to wash my sins away. I look and see *a long black car and in the back seat there are two women staring at me, but there is something wrong with them, their heads are on at funny angles. But they are staring at me and staring at me, this woman with the blue-and-white striped summer dress, this woman in mustard yellow and their eyes are round and their mouths are round, and I try to look away from them, look at the front of the car instead but the front seat is empty, there is no one there, this car is driving itself and I open my mouth and the long black car pulls away fast leaving me there on the corner of Goldhawk Road.*

Leaving me there with him, him who smiles by the light of the flame that ignites his cigarette, illuminates something moving in the back seat of his car. He who comes walking towards me and an alarm bell starts ringing, screaming Danger! Danger! *And an alarm bell starts ringing, screaming* Danger! Danger!...

It had been the telephone that had pulled me out of the vision the first time. As my eyes opened now, it was the clock chiming the hour. Mya still had hold of my hand, her pupils completely dilated as she stared at me and for a moment I thought I saw her surrounded by the same blue light that was pouring out of them, a feeling of great power radiating through her. Then she let my hand drop and I blinked. She was back to being the little old lady that had let me through the door.

'There is a lot of work for us to do,' she said. 'The murdered women screamed out for help and you picked up their cries.' She made a counting motion with her hands while she spoke, as if the fingers that had touched mine continued to relay her information, but her piercing eyes never left mine. 'It's not just because you are Sensitive, dear. Somehow there is a connection between you and whoever has been taking them. Think really hard and tell me, what do you think the connection could be?'

'Over the road,' I said, fear crawling through me, the last image of something moving in the back of the car, a thick, black shape, death in men's clothing. 'Lansdowne Studios. A man I lived next door to was working there at the time the first one was taken. He was trying to create a new sound, using radios to make strange effects. I heard him playing some of it, the very night I dreamt about the first one – I thought that his music had given me a nightmare. Later on, I found out he had also been playing with tarot cards, using a ouija board, holding amateur séances, all the things I was taught never to do. And he's still doing it, still looking for ghosts in churchyards, talking to black cats at midnight...' I cut myself short, realising how angry I sounded. 'I mean,' I said, 'I don't think he killed anyone, but I do think that all his messing about somehow let something through.'

'How very interesting,' Mya said, nodding to herself as she digested the information. She pointed to one of the framed photographs that hung over the fireplace. 'Do you know this man? Sir Oliver Lodge, his name is.'

A melancholy-looking chap with a balding pate, bushy eyebrows and a beard that pointed upwards, flecked with white streaks that were matched by the wavy hair that ran over his ears. I might have seen him before, in one of Grandpa's books of distinguished Spiritualists, but I couldn't place him.

'The inventor of the wireless,' Mya enlightened me. 'Sir Oliver worked on the theory of what we call the aether, that everything in time and space is operating on its own particular frequency and if we learn how to tune in, we can tap in and out like a radio does. It might help you to understand what you still find so hard about all of this.'

'Of course' – a spark went off in my head – 'that's what it felt like, tuning into them.'

'Everyone has their own wavelength,' said Mya, 'the vibrations that keep us here and keep us whole. But the frequency changes at the moment we pass, as if the dial on the radio had suddenly slipped. Your dial keeps tuning into the last moments of transmission, the SOS signal, if you like.'

'So,' I tried to rationalise what she was telling me, 'you think that these experiments in sound somehow *helped* me to tune into them?'

Mya nodded. 'By accident rather than design. The man who was making the music opened up the channel and you tuned in. Did you know him very well?'

'No,' I said. 'I never actually met him. But the man who used to share the flat with him, I am very close to. Only it's impossible that he could have anything to do with this. He was dead against the séances, he had nothing to do with them.'

Mya's words had turned everything I had thought on its head. I had always assumed that James was the malign influence; it couldn't possibly be Lenny. Then another thought hit me.

'Someone else who knows him.' I snapped my fingers. 'Dave Dilworth, you know, who borrowed the stuffed animals from Cedric. He started a band and this man, James Myers is his name, is producing them. Their records are,' I shivered at the memory, 'very sinister. Like horror movie music. They were the soundtrack to the second vision I had, to Bronwyn Evans. And then this last one too.'

Mya put her fingertips together, closed her eyes. I recalled how fond Cedric had been of Dave, wondered if that was why she frowned.

She sat there like that for some time. As the clock ticked away the minutes, I wondered if she had fallen asleep, if the effort of all this had been too much. Then she suddenly opened her eyes, leaning forwards in her seat.

'Go and see him,' she said. 'He'll tell you something you need to know.'

'I don't know.' I was flustered now. Surely she didn't think Dave…?

'I'm not saying that,' she had read my thoughts again. 'Spirit has shown you many things to guide you, but what we do here on earth is our own responsibility. Now, I have a message from your pa.'

I caught my breath. The only time I had ever wished for the gift was to hear from Pa again. But I never had, not in all these years.

Mya smiled. 'He says for you to take courage. Try not to be afraid, he walks beside you always and protects you with his love. He says,' she gave a soft chuckle, looking to her right as if Pa was actually sitting there, talking to her, 'there are no dead.'

I felt tears spring into my eyes. 'But what can I do?' I asked. 'The police can't seem to solve this case, the first girl died five years ago. You're not telling me that I can?'

'No, I'm not.' Mya's eyes were gentle now. 'But you can help. You might be surprised, but not all policemen are sceptics. I have a very good friend at the Notting Hill police, a detective no less, who would listen to anything you could tell him. Now dear,' she leaned on the arms of the chair, slowly rose to her feet, 'I think we have both done enough for today. Please, think about what I've said and know that my door is always open. Don't keep your troubles to yourself any more. You have seen these things for a reason and now you should act upon your knowledge.'

When I stepped outside on to Lansdowne Road I was almost surprised by the sunshine. I felt like I had been inside the Spiritualist's for days, in a world between light and shade. I stared up at the tower opposite for a moment, thinking about all that Mya had said. Then I crossed the road and walked back towards Ladbroke Grove.

23

All Day and All of the Night

The door creaked open to the shabby house on Westbourne Grove, a rotten door with peeling paintwork, sagging on its hinges like an old itinerant stooped over his bundle of rags. The man who opened it was similarly careworn, small with very pale skin and what was left of his hair combed across his balding dome in greasy strands, a tatty old brown cardigan over a stained yellow shirt and grey trousers shiny with age. He stared through bottle-thick glasses in black National Health frames held together by sticking tape, his top lip twitching, revealing yellowing teeth.

'Hello Ernie,' said Dick Willcox.

'Fucking hell,' said Ernie Tidsall as they pushed past him into the hall.

'Up here, is it?' Dick started running up the stairs, while Pete put a restraining hand on the little man's shoulder. He reeked of sweat and stale cigarette smoke, and something else; a chemical smell that Pete realised must be that of developing fluid and stop lotion. The suspect was a photographer, after all.

'Wh-whaddyou want?' Ernie squirmed under Pete's grasp as Dick's size tens crashed around upstairs. 'I ain't done nothing.'

'Yep,' Dick shouted from above. 'We've come to the right place.'

Pete smiled at the little man. It was not a pleasant smile, as it didn't reach his eyes, which bored into the black pupils behind Ernie's specs with an intimidating intensity.

'Good,' he shouted back, then said to Ernie: 'Would you care to show me around?'

Ernie shrank from under him and his voice went up several octaves.

'Look, what's this all about? I'm telling you, I ain't done nothing.'

'Nobody ever has, have they Ernie?' replied Pete. 'Now I've asked you nicely to show us around, so please,' he took his arm off Ernie's shoulder and pointed it instead in the direction of the stairs, 'be a good lad and don't give us no bother.'

Ernie screwed up his face and balled his fists, stamped his foot in rage. He looked like a petulant mole. 'Bloody bogeys!' he screamed.

Pete continued to point at the stairs.

'Get up there Ernie,' he said. 'I'm not telling you again.'

Ernie's shoulders slumped. Cursing and muttering, he did what he was told.

Dick stood lounged against a doorway on the first floor. In his hand was a black-and-white photograph of a naked woman. A naked woman trussed up with ropes and a gag in her mouth.

'Regular little David Bailey we've got here,' he said to Pete. 'Here's his studio.' He pointed through the doorway to a sparsely furnished room, painted white, with two spotlights and a screen, a camera on a tripod in front of an old brass bed made up with black satin sheets. 'And behind us is his dark room. A very dark room if this one's anything to go by.'

Pete took the picture and studied it hard. He didn't recognise the woman but he recognised the look in her eyes. Bombed out, vacant, gone.

'Look!' Ernie had begun stamping his feet again, dust flying up from the hallway carpet. 'You can't just barge in here and do what you like! You ain't got a warrant!'

'Oh sorry, Ernie,' Dick put his hand inside his jacket and took the document out, 'do you mean this? We just wanted to make sure we had the right place first. Now we know that we have, everything's all official and above board and Scotland Yard are just a phone call away. I'm sure they'd love to see what you've got set up here.'

Ernie's face turned red and then green as he peered at the paperwork.

'But there's no need for us to call them yet,' said Pete, blocking the top of the stairs with his full frame in case Ernie got any ideas about running away. 'We just want a little chat with you, about an old friend of yours. Tell us what we need to know and we might just leave you in peace.'

Ernie took his spectacles off, mopped his sweaty brow with a handkerchief taken from his trouser pocket. Another cloud of chemical vapour hit the air as he did.

'What friend?' he said weakly.

'I think you know,' said Dick. 'You've probably got the negatives of her back there, and we've got plenty of time to check.'

'Susannah,' Ernie said. 'Geordie Sue.'

'That's right,' said Pete. 'Now we're getting there.'

The blonde had been right about Ernie. Most of the girls on the Bayswater, Holland Park beat knew the one-time smudger for the *Kensington Post* who'd found an easier way of acquiring his own studios than the tedious grind of a local rag. A few folk at the *Post* still remembered him, with about as much fondness as his current crop of models. Ernie was the sort of guy who gave everyone the creeps, especially the women. Or so Dick's mate on the sports desk had told them, over a few jars in his local, as he passed across Ernie's old address from the files. It was in Westbourne Grove, confirming the blonde's story.

They'd kept the gaff under obs for a while, watched a couple of women come and go out of the front door, Ernie's silhouette moving behind the blinds and the tell-tale red light of his dark room. It wasn't hard to get the warrant. All leads on Houghton's killer were considered high priority.

'Why don't you have a seat?' said Dick, picking up a black vinyl barstool from beside the bed in his studio and plonking it down in the middle of the spotlights. 'Tell us a bit more about Geordie Sue.'

Ernie had stopped his stamping now, turned very white and started shaking. Sweat was rolling off his forehead faster than he could mop it up with his hankie.

'Sh-she was just a tart,' Ernie said, cowering, his fingers resting on the side of the barstool, not wanting to sit. 'Like all the rest. There weren't nothing special about Sue.'

'Oh aye?' Pete wandered over to one of the spotlights, found the switch and turned it on. Watched Ernie flinch, put up his hand as if he was about to be physically assaulted. 'That's not what we heard. We've been told Susannah was a girl with a lot of special talents, a useful lass for a man like yourself.'

'*Very* special talents, Ernie.' Dick leaned close to the smudger's sweaty face. ''Cos let's face it, she weren't exactly your classic pin-up material, now was she?' He strolled over to the other lamp. 'She weren't no Diana Dors.' There was a fizzling noise then a snap as he turned it on. 'Not even a Christine Keeler. Here Ernie, you never did any shots of her did you? 'Cos now they could be worth a few bob.'

'No!' Ernie screamed. 'I never knew Christine Keeler, I never knew Mandy Rice Davies, or the doctor or any of them! You said this was about Geordie Sue, not about them!'

Dick and Pete exchanged a glance and at the same time both began to walk in a circle around Ernie and between the lights, the Blakeys on their shoes loud on the linoleum floor, their footsteps slow, insistent. Ernie continued to grip the side of the stool without sitting, unsure of where to look now, getting hotter under the spots by the second.

'No need to get touchy, Ernie.' Dick continued to keep his tone light, friendly. 'Tell us about Geordie Sue then, how did you meet her? Were you formally introduced?'

'No.' Ernie continued to mop his brow. 'I met her at the coffee stand, what do you think? Just another scrubber willing to drop her knickers for a few quid, there's enough of them out there, you should know.'

'She did more than just drop her knickers, though, didn't she Ernie?' Pete said. There was a horrible smell in this room, underneath the chemicals and the fag smoke. Of old sweat and dried semen, of spilt booze and cheap perfume, of degradation and disgust. 'Is this how you shoot them, Ernie, under these lights? Gets a bit hot, doesn't it? Not very comfortable, I shouldn't think.'

'What do you care?' Ernie snapped back. 'It's easy enough for them. I don't touch them, I don't hurt them, they get paid and everybody's happy. I do them a favour. It's safer for them than...'

He stopped himself short.

'Getting into a car with a strange man?' Dick finished the sentence for him. 'A strange man who could be a killer?'

Ernie's shoulders heaved. 'I didn't kill her,' he said, his voice wobbling, on the edge of tears. 'I ain't seen her. The last job she did for me was before Christmas, a bit extra to buy some toys for her kid, that's all it was and I ain't seen her since. I swear to God.'

'What kind of pictures?' asked Dick. 'A nice Nativity scene, was it? Susannah as the Virgin Mary?'

Ernie looked at the floor, hands wringing at his sopping hanky.

'I can easily check.' Dick moved towards the door.

'No,' said Ernie, waving a hand like a drowning man. 'It was a group shot. That's what I used her for, mainly. Not many girls are up for that scene, not the young ones anyway. Not the pretty ones. But you can get away with using the older tarts for them ones. No one really looks at their faces.'

'Who are your clients, Ernie?' Pete stopped walking for a second, turned and faced the little man. 'Who do you sell the photos to?'

Ernie shook his head, still looking at the floor. Farted loudly, bowels coming loose with the agitation. Another bad smell to add to the miasma in this room.

'That wasn't,' the smudger whispered, twisting the hanky round and round in his hands, 'that wasn't what you said you wanted to know.'

'Well you haven't told us much yet have you?' Dick bellowed into his earhole.

'I don't think he wants to,' said Pete. 'I don't think he understands the notion of a polite chat. Perhaps we'd better just call Scotland Yard after all.'

'Or take him down the station. I'm sure the boys would love to take a look at Ernie's family album.'

Ernie looked from Pete to Dick and back to Pete again. He was quivering all over, ready to collapse. He fumbled in his pocket and drew out a little brown bottle of prescription pills, shook a couple loose into his hand and swallowed them.

'All right then, arrest me,' the little man said, finding a reserve of courage from his medication. 'At least then I'll be entitled to a solicitor. I ain't telling you nothing more, you bastard bogeys.'

'He's an old hand isn't he?' said Dick, looking mildly amused.

'He might well be,' agreed Pete, looking anything but, 'but it didn't take us long to find him. You should have been a lot more careful, shouldn't you Ernie?'

Ernie held his tongue.

'Better get us a bunch of lads to help us, make sure we don't leave anything behind,' said Dick. 'Looks like there's too much for us to carry in that dark room. Phone was in the hallway, wasn't it, Ernie?'

Pete read Ernie his rights as Dick summoned the radio car. Ernie said nothing, wrapped his arms around himself like a child and stared at the floor.

'Who are you scared of, Ernie?' Pete whispered as the siren sounded down Bayswater Road. 'Who's worse than being arrested?'

Ernie continued to stare at the floor, said nothing.

24

Oh, Pretty Woman

'Is there anybody there?'

Jackie made a knocking motion at the side of my head.

'Sorry,' I said, turning away from the window, through which I had been staring blankly at the wall opposite, and back round towards her. 'I was miles away.'

'That I can see.' Jackie sat herself down on the corner of the table, folded her arms. 'You've been off with the fairies all afternoon. Something troubling you, pet?'

'Well, sort of.' I looked past her to where Lenny was hunched over his desk, tapping away on his little adding machine, a pencil clenched between his teeth.

Jackie raised an eyebrow. 'S'all right,' she said. 'He can't hear you. He's so locked in his world of financial intrigue he wouldn't even notice if a troupe of naked dancing boys came through here doing the can-can. Would you Lenny?'

She raised her voice as she asked the question.

Lenny continued tap-tapping away, eyes locked on his ledger.

'So,' she turned back round to me again, 'come on, let's have it.'

'It's...' Jackie had at least managed to make me smile. But I could tell from her demeanour she wasn't going to let it just lie there. 'Well, it's a bit hard to explain. I mean, it's not that I don't want to tell you, it's just a bit...awkward.'

'Ah.' She nodded. 'Would a drink help you to spit it out?'

'It might do, actually,' I said, thinking about the empty house I would otherwise be going back to. Toby had finished his canvases now and Pat had taken him over to the States with them, to San Francisco, Los Angeles and New York. He would be away for a month this time, our longest ever time apart.

'Good,' she said. 'There's this place I've been meaning to take you.' She winked, slid off the table. 'We can leave him to count his pots of cash.'

Round the corner of the King's Road on Bramerton Street, illuminated by a solitary lamp post, was a green door in a high white wall, a gateway to a secret world.

'This is the place,' said Jackie. 'I've been scoping it out for a while, reckon you'll like it. It's kind of,' she smiled mischievously, 'interesting, shall we say.'

The woman behind the green door looked like Cleopatra, or at least, the way Liz Taylor played her, all thick black eyeliner and thick black hair. She stared at us through the smoke of the black Sobranie that rested on her bottom lip, with glittering eyes to match the décor of the entrance.

'Hello Jacks,' she said in a voice that was as theatrical as her appearance. 'And what do we have here?' She removed the cigarette with fingers that flashed with rings and ended with purple-painted talons, fixing her gaze on me.

'This is Stella Reade,' said Jackie, 'my business partner. Stella, this is Gina, she runs the show here.'

'Just business?' A smile twitched at the corner of the woman's mouth as she offered me her hand. 'Bona. Now, the rules here are simple: Jackie vouches for you and signs you in, you pay me ten shillings for the privilege and if either of you can't handle your shandies like ladies, you'll be out on your ear. We don't like having to entertain Miss Lilly around here. All right, darling?'

'Er.' Her grip was hard and I couldn't understand half of what she was saying. 'Yes,' I said as she finally released me. 'That's fine, thank you.'

I dropped the money into her upturned palm and followed Jackie down the vertiginous steps to the basement bar.

The square cellar room was thick with smoke and bodies. Heads turned as we navigated our way through, nostrils finely tuned to the smell of interloper. Some of them flashed hostile glances, others deliberately pressed themselves against me, smirking as I tried not to notice. The way half of them were built and dressed you would never have guessed that they weren't actually men.

'What you having?' Jackie finally elbowed her way through to the counter, nodding at the stout, cropped-haired blonde at the bar.

'Red wine, please,' I said, smiling at her. Up until now, Jackie had been reticent about actually letting me into her other world. This was her way of showing me she could be trusted with any uncomfortable secrets.

'Red wine and a G & T, please Smithy,' Jackie ordered. 'Right,' she said when they arrived. 'We'll go through here, it's a bit less crowded.'

Behind the bar was another small room, with a pool table and a few chairs arranged around it, a row of pegs for coats along the wall, a bit like a miniature youth club. There were a couple in the middle of a game, but the rest of the seats were empty. We made for the furthest away corner.

'Well,' Jackie said as we settled ourselves down. 'What d'you reckon to my little home from home?'

'It's really…something else,' I said.

She laughed. 'I thought it were about time you saw how us lesbians lived.'

I glanced over at the pool players. One of them looked just like a Teddy boy, complete with long ginger sideburns, green drape jacket and brothel creepers. The other, in a tight-fitting black dress, black bouffant hair and muscular, tattooed arms, was recognisably female, if aggressively so.

'Is everyone here a lesbian?' I whispered.

'Mainly.' Jackie surveyed the room. 'You get some old omis come in, theatrical types, you know, or painters. Ancient old fruits, like most of our tutors at college. A few famous faces passing through, an' all, I've seen that Di Dors down here more than once.' She took a sip of her drink, pointed her little finger back through the bar towards the jukebox, where a gaggle of painted ladies lounged, selecting tracks with bored expressions on their faces. 'Those lot are working girls, taking some time off where no one will bother them. That's what Gina meant by entertaining Miss Lilly – Lilly Law's the police. She don't want them sticking their beak in.'

Her words sent a shiver through me.

'Oh.' Jackie waved her hand. 'You don't need to mind them, they keep themselves to themselves...'

'It's not that,' I said. 'Jackie, remember that day in Lenny's flat?'

She cocked her head. 'I'm hardly likely to forget it,' she said.

'Well, remember what I told you about my family and their funny ways?'

'Yes, love, what about it?' She dropped her jokey tone, became serious, concerned.

'Well, unfortunately, I seem to have inherited something from them after all.'

'What? You've not been seeing ghosts, have you?' She put her hand over her heart.

'Not quite,' I said. 'I've been having dreams…nightmares, really. Only worse.'

I did my best to explain it all, then gave her Mya's interpretation of events.

'She thinks that James's experiments are what made it happen – his musical ones, that is. Though I blame that rubbish we threw in the bin that day myself.'

'Christ,' Jackie said. She had listened to my story in silence, not passing any judgement, just encouraging me on with a few gentle words when I thought I was going to start crying. I knew she would find it all very hard to believe, but to my relief, she didn't act as if she thought I had gone round the bend.

'That bloody James,' she said. 'I don't know if this has got owt to do with it, but he's in a bit of a bad way, now, you know.'

'No, I didn't.'

Jackie scowled. 'He got arrested last November, coming on to Lilly in some khazi on the Holloway Road. Total bloody set-up.' She shook her head. 'Reason I know is, I was at Lenny's when he got the call to bail him out. Lenny were that embarrassed. He didn't want us to know, for obvious reasons. But I've come to realise, whenever James clicks his fingers, Lenny still comes running to sort out his mess for him.'

'Did he then?' I said. 'There was nothing about it in the papers, was there?'

Jackie snorted. 'Well lucky for James, poor old JFK got shot the next day, so no one was really all that bothered about him. It got a couple of lines in the *Standard* or something. Just enough for him to start getting blackmailed.'

'God,' I said, 'I had no idea.'

'Aye, well you wouldn't, he keeps it all to himself, does Lenny. Well, most of time. Until James gets so dizzy on his pep pills that he starts smashing up telephones with his bare hands, then he finds the need to talk about it.'

'I thought we had got him away from all of that,' I said, 'I thought him and Pat…'

Jackie shook her head. 'That's not the same, for either of them,' she said. 'That's just a form of entertainment. Pat likes his rough and Lenny likes his posh, but with James it goes deeper. Like I said to you, all them years ago, they really are like man and wife.' She rolled the ice around the bottom of her glass. 'D'you want another one?'

As she went to the bar, I realised that it wasn't just me who had needed to have this conversation. Jackie was definitely at ease here though, I thought, as I watched her chat to the bartender. Then, as if drawn by magnets, my gaze shifted towards the women by the jukebox. One with her hair done like Dusty Springfield had started to sing along to a track by her idol, swaying her hips along to the languid beat.

'So.' Jackie sat back down, passing my drink across. 'What else did this Mya woman have to say about our beloved Mr Myers?'

'I told her about him working with Dave,' I said, 'and how their horrible record was in one of my dreams before I'd even heard it in real life. She said I should go and see him, that he'd have something important to tell me. But now you've got me thinking. The last time I saw Dave must have only been about two weeks before James got arrested.'

'Oh aye?'

'Yeah, it was at Toby's end-of-show party at Duke Street. We were really pleased to see him; it had been such a long time. Seemed like he was on good form too, telling lots of funny stories about his band. Then Toby wandered off somewhere and Dave started to get a bit weirder. Started going on about these ghost hunts he'd done with James, making out that it was really funny – maybe it is to him. Only now I'm wondering if he was just laying it on thick about James to get rid of Lenny, 'cos as soon as he did, Dave completely changed. Started asking all these questions about Jenny, if I'd seen her, if she was still OK…'

'Really?' said Jackie.

'He'd only just found out from Chris about Giles and the riot,' I said, 'and he was really worried about her. He reckoned' – for some reason I started to whisper, as if I cared that the pool-playing Ted and her moll might hear – 'that Giles really is her brother and her dad had him arrested on purpose, to teach her a lesson for running off to Italy.'

'You what?' Jackie frowned. 'That's mad.'

'That's what I thought,' I said. 'But remember the way she reacted that day? Ranting about not going back to her parents, how scared she was of them? And she did call him her brother, we both heard that.'

'Oh yeah.' Jackie nodded slowly, then went into her Jenny impersonation: 'Daddy could have him released just like that. Well?' She dropped the level of her own voice now, moved her chair closer to mine. 'I suppose if he could, then he must be able to get him arrested in the first place too. Lilly Law.' Her eyes darted around the room. 'More bent than anyone round here.'

'Well that's just it,' I said. 'Chris proved it, didn't he? But what Dave said that sounded even more mad was that Jenny's dad can get them to do whatever he wants. I thought a lot about that too. That policeman Chris exposed never did have to stand trial, did he?'

'No,' said Jackie. 'And that would also explain why our Jenny's just hitched herself to a new sugar daddy.'

We stared at each other in silence for a minute.

'So,' Jackie eventually said. 'Are you going to go and see him?'

'I've tried,' I said. 'But he's never in when I go past his house. He's probably on the road somewhere, he said they do a lot of touring.

And they don't have a phone, so I can't just ring up and ask Chris if he knows when Dave's next around. I suppose I could put a note through his door, but how on earth do I explain it without seeing him face-to-face? I know he's a pretty broad-minded guy, but can you imagine? Oh hi, Dave, I've been having all these psychic transmissions from dead prostitutes caused by your producer and I wondered if you could tell me a bit more about that? Oh and, only three months after you first told me, I am beginning to get worried about Jenny…'

'I take your point,' said Jackie. 'I think I need another drink.'

'So do I.' I nodded. 'Is it OK to stay at yours tonight?' I added, watching the Dusty blonde taking her leave and suddenly feeling afraid of being on my own.

The curtains at the end of our bedroom in Arundel Gardens twitch and out comes Dave, wearing his top hat and a funeral director's black coat. He opens his mouth and there's a sound of a toilet flushing and I find myself on the pavement outside Lansdowne Studios. From the top of the building comes a light like a searchlight, or the sweeping beam of a lighthouse, and a weird organ tune starts up, sounding like it's being played underwater. Consumed with a fear that I have been here before, I try to run, but my footsteps are so slow, as if the pavement is made out of treacle, that though I put my whole body's weight into trying to move forwards, my progress is agonisingly slow.

In my mind, I know I have to find Toby. The first house I come to has a green front door and I can hear laughing and music coming from behind it. It opens up and there's Jackie, framed in an orange glow, wearing a black suit. She smiles at me and says:

'Here you are at last, come in. We've all been waiting for you.'

'Is Toby here?' I ask, looking past her down a long hallway with chandeliers and a curving staircase, hearing voices everywhere.

Jackie chuckles. 'You might find him in here,' she says and raises an eyebrow. 'But I think he's hiding.'

I leave her on the doorstep and walk into the room on the left. There are a lot of men in here, all dressed in black, and I scan them desperately to find Toby. They all turn towards me, their hands over their mouths, whispering to each other. Lenny and Bernard Baring sniggering together, looking at me and then looking away. Pat flashes past, unlike the others he's wearing a blue suit, the same intense shade as his eyes. I grab hold of his arm, ask: 'Where's Toby? You must know, where is he?' But Pat shakes his head, says: 'Let him tell you,' and walks off into the crowd.

I look behind him and see her, the girl in the blue-and-white dress, but the dress is now ripped open and her breasts spilling out, covered in bruises and scratches. No one seems to be paying her any attention, despite her outrageous appearance. She looks at me with dull, dead eyes, tears leaking from each corner. 'My father's house has many rooms,' she says, and turns her head towards the door. I walk through it and find myself at the foot of the stairs, where Chris is walking down, a bulging folder under his left arm. He looks shocked to see me.

'Don't go up there,' he says. 'Please don't, Stella.'

'But I must,' I say. 'Toby's up there,' and I push past him to where the girl with the mustard-coloured dress stands in a doorframe, under a red light, grinning a gap-toothed smile. She raises up a smeared glass to me and I can see the red mark around her neck, the deep incision in her flesh.

'For now we see through a glass darkly,' she says, 'but then face to face: now I know in part; but then shall I know even as also I am known.' I feel another great wave of fear and stumble up the next set of stairs in front of me, into a vast ballroom where people are dancing in full evening dress, but wearing black masks over their eyes. I look around, desperately trying to locate Toby, and another *woman sways in front of me, naked but for a dog collar around her neck with a lead attached to it. Her face looks ancient and her body is battered, she shakes her head and says: 'Though I speak with the tongues of men and of angels, and have not charity, I am become as sounding brass, or a tinkling cymbal.'*

Then a man wearing a gorilla suit yanks the lead and pulls her away as the whole room full of people in evening dress bursts into peals of laughter and I turn and run from that place to another staircase, lit only by a shaft of moonlight coming from a skylight above. I hear Pa's voice coming down that silvery trail, saying: 'And though I have the gift of prophecy, and understand all mysteries, and all knowledge; and though I have all faith, so that I could remove mountains, and have not charity, I am nothing.'

'Pa!' I cry, looking around frantically. But he isn't there, Toby isn't there, it's just me alone in a dark house, all the music and laughter below me has stopped.

There is a door in front of me and I know that I don't want to go through it; I know that I shouldn't, but it opens anyway and I am at the top of the house in a dark attic room and in the middle of the room is Jenny, wearing a long white dress, her skin glowing like the moonlight. On one side of her are three other women, on the other side two. I realise with a jolt that one of them is the Dusty blonde from the club tonight and that she, like all the rest of them, has marks around her neck the same as the women downstairs, the ones who are already dead. I try to close my eyes, knowing that they are the ones yet to come.

'Look at me,' says Jenny, and my eyes are impelled towards her, the silvery glow emanating from her growing brighter and brighter, her face both beautiful and terrifying. She puts her hand on her stomach and I suddenly realise that she is pregnant, that this is what's making her glow.

'This,' she says, 'is how it all begins and where it all ends.'

And I felt the ground disappear from under me as I fell backwards, hitting the bed like I had fallen from the ceiling. My heart was pounding like a jackhammer and I didn't know where I was, all I could see were the shapes of the furniture around me and I thought for a second that I was four years old, in my grandparents' house at the time of the Blitz, when a fireball had come down from the sky.

Then the door opened and Jackie was standing there in her pyjamas, the hallway light spilling into the dark and telling me where I was and when it was.

'Christ, Stella,' said Jackie. 'That must have been a right bloody nightmare. You were screaming so loud I thought someone had got in here.'

I tried to open my mouth to speak but nothing would come out.

25

Fever

Ernie in the interview room, still not talking. Not sweating so much since his brief arrived; the kind of stiff upper lip who could have passed off as one of the Cabinet with his steel grey hair and handmade suit. Dick down there with DI Dennis Fielder; the gaffer scenting a whiff of a headline, wanting to break Ernie down before sending him over to Shepherd's Bush and letting them take all the credit.

Pete was upstairs in the CID room, going through Ernie's prints with a couple of aids and an old DS called Stanley Coulter, a big man with a round face framed with white curls and sorrowful, saucer-shaped blue eyes that lent him the aura of an overgrown choirboy. Pete appreciated Coulter's eyes. Coming towards retirement age, there was not a lot those melancholy lamps hadn't shone over before. Although Ernie may have displayed some of it in a slightly different way.

The negs had gone off to the lab to be printed, surprisingly there weren't that many of them, only the results of Ernie's most recent session, it seemed. But that still left them with boxes of filth, all separated into different categories and catalogued in blue biro, a fussy, fastidious hand. FOXY DOXIES represented the high end of Ernie's business, the best looking girls falling out of frilly French maid outfits and polka-dot bikinis. Pete had seen plenty of this kind of stuff before, it was the sort of thing the Soho shops put out front with the nudist books and incongruous travel guides. Round the back would be the specialist stuff, like FEATHER GIRLS – hard-faced women in steel corsets walking naked men wearing gas masks on collars and leads, brandishing horsewhips over sagging old buttocks. Or FLOPSIE'S MOPSIES, the orgy snaps that Ernie had been so loath to discuss – and no wonder – this was fucking and sucking rendered in forensic close up, along with every spot, bruise and semen-splattered cold sore. But it was HOUSE OF WHACKS that formed the most interesting passage of Ernie's oeuvre.

Men with canes, whips and paddles, their faces always carefully out of shot. The lens instead homing in on the flesh of the women, the welts rising out of their skin, black slashes across round white buttocks, thighs patterned with weals. Women with gags in their mouths, women with their hands tied behind their backs. Sometimes in specialist gear to restrain them, leather and vinyl straps, mostly just trussed up with their own lingerie, silk stockings and the cord from a dressing gown.

Not so big a jump from this to Susannah Houghton with her pants stuffed down her throat and her stockings around her ankles. From Bobby Clarke with her dress torn open to expose her breasts. A killer buzzing on a tableau of degradation and violence, hating women so much he couldn't even leave them dead with any dignity – could his lust have been fuelled by images like these?

'I think I've found her.' Tom Spinks, one of the young aids, held up a print he had been studying for some time. 'This is the one we're looking for ain't it?'

They crowded around him.

'Bleedin' hell.' The other aid, Bob Bates, scratched his chin. 'That's a sight you don't see every day.'

Indeed it wasn't. Geordie Sue in her birthday suit, skinny

arms and bruised legs, breasts laying flat as pancakes across her spotty chest – with a dildo strapped around her waist that she was using to poke a similarly malnourished coloured woman in a wonky beehive wig. The expression on her face was supposed to imply ecstasy, but looked more like she was struggling to remain conscious.

'So that's what having a speciality means,' said Pete, shaking his head. Fear and anger welled up inside him. Fear that if he got too close to Ernie, he would find that too much of Wesker and his methods had rubbed off on him. Fear that the anger would take over.

'There's lots more of her in here.' Spinks rifled through the prints in his box. 'They must have done a whole action sequence. Yeah, look at this, they're spanking each other.' He passed another one round. 'And now out come the whips. Dead into this kinky gear is old Ernie, eh?' Spinks was trying to come across as a man of the world, but his face was flushed, a mixture of embarrassment and shock at what he was seeing.

'Recognise the other girl?' asked Coulter. 'She could be a bit of local colour. Look at this...'

Pete's gaze followed where Coulter's finger pointed, to the trackmarks between the coloured girl's fingers, her motivation clearly delineated. Susannah didn't appear to have any, but she had also been a drug addict. It was Drinamyl that Geordie Sue lived on, big purple pills that were always rattling round her handbag, keeping her rattling on for days. You would need to be on something pretty strong to face doing any of this.

'Another local dish,' said Coulter with a sigh. 'Well, in the darker parts of town anyway. That'll be how she ended up coming to do something like this. Would have been supplying her ponce and all, I don't doubt.'

A name rose from the past to the front of Pete's brain, unfinished business from 1959. Algy 'Baby' Ferrier, ex-boxer, Bobby Clarke's ponce, where was he now?

'Well she's the only spade in here so far,' noted Spinks. 'From what I've seen, anyway.'

'Yeah.' Bates rifled through the pile. He was more worldly-wise than Spinks, found Ernie's snaps amusing, something to talk about down the pub after work. 'It's always the jig on the receiving end of it too.'

'Maybe Oswald Mosley commissioned them,' said Pete, only half joking.

'You know,' said Coulter, turning one of the eight-by-tens at right angles to try and make sense of what he was seeing. 'You could be on to something there. Not Mosley hisself, I mean, but it is always the toffs who want this sort of thing, all this caning and spanking, the feather girls, you know? Your average Joe just wants it simple, straightforward. Tits and arse, in and out, no messing. But it takes a certain kind of mind to appreciate this malarkey, and you'll usually find that it's one that's been forged on the playing fields of Eton. All those beatings and buggery, it scars them for life.'

'Aye.' Pete nodded, a *Tatler & Bystander* photograph flashing through his mind, the clean white teeth and Dean Martin hairstyle of Sir Alex Minton, shaking hands with a Cabinet minister, the caption noting they were both Eton old boys.

Coulter put the picture back in Spinks's box. 'We'll mark these up for evidence,' he said to the aid. 'Get a blow-up of the black bird's face and circulate her, get on to it now, if you don't mind.' Turning to Pete: 'I bet you a tanner she comes from Powis Square.'

'Powis Square.' Pete nodded, watching eager Spinks almost collide with Dick and DI Fielder coming through the door. The gaffer had his pipe clenched between his teeth, a gleam in his eyes suggesting he was riled enough to bite the stem in half. Dick's hair was standing up at haphazard angles where he had been raking his hands through the Brylcreem and his eyes were bloodshot from the smoke of a thousand Woodbines.

'It's bloody impossible,' Fielder announced. 'The man has a snake oil salesman for a solicitor. He's claiming this,' he snatched up a picture from the nearest box, a close-up of a girl holding a spurting penis, eyes screwed shut, as she received a full facial, 'is all in the name of art! That our dirty mac down there, Ernest Tidsall, is engaged in the pursuit of aesthetic excellence following the muse of contemporary photography. Can you bloody believe it?' He stared at the unlovely artefact for a moment. 'I suppose this is the Bayswater Botticelli.' He flung it across the room.

Dick raised one eyebrow. 'Don't suppose you've found any nice landscapes in amongst that lot then?' he said. 'Some pretty sunsets, maybe?'

'Not on your life.' Coulter shook his head. 'But we did find Geordie Sue.'

'Aha.' Fielder turned his gimlet eye over the proffered print. The DI had only arrived at Notting Hill this New Year and had done little to endear himself since. Unlike his predecessor, Wally Palmer, who had worked the district man and boy, Fielder appeared to be a careerist copper who had never worn down a pair of soles in his life. On the contrary, his shoes were always polished and he liked to go about in a Gannex car coat like Harold Wilson, which only added to the general feeling of suspicion about him. But here was a chance for him to change that perception.

'We're getting a blow-up done of her friend here's face to circulate, think she's likely to be local,' Coulter explained. 'See if we can't pick her up and ask her in for a chat.'

'Good,' said Fielder, chewing on the end of his pipe as his mind whirred. 'We're going to need more than we've got here to stop Tidsall making bail. I've got a feeling there's something left behind in that studio. The negatives for instance – how come there weren't more of them? Is he hiding them or destroying them? And if he's such an artist, why would he want to do that?'

'If he's such an artist,' said Pete, 'what does he do for his proper living?'

Fielder snapped his fingers. 'That's it. Go back and see if you can't find his books. If we can't get the bugger for obscenity, maybe we can get him for some kind of tax dodge.' The gaffer's face lit up. 'Like Al Capone.'

Pink streaks of dawn were spreading above the chimney pots by the time Pete and Coulter returned from the flat on Westbourne Grove. They'd found what they were looking for under Ernie's spartan single bed, in the little bedsitter room that adjoined the studio and darkroom. A box of ledgers going back ten years or so. They'd had another search for any more negatives, been through every book on his shelves just in case, but there was nothing to find. Ernie tidied up after himself.

His books, written in that same minuscule hand, revealed only the income and expenditure of a legitimate photographer. Neatly spaced columns showing the bills for rates, utilities, materials, stationery, telephone. Income from the *Kensington Post*, Reuters News Agency, the occasional national newspaper, commissions to take wedding photographs. Brown envelopes stuffed with receipts matched the entries in each column, including letters of thanks from the fathers of several brides.

Outside, the morning shift started taking parade.

'Damn it.' Fielder's enthusiasm dimming into the cold light of morning, standing over a pile of paperwork every bit as unyielding as the prisoner downstairs. 'We can't prove anything from this. We can ask the Yard to look into him, get the Revenue to do a check, but as for now...' He stared with watery eyes at the clock on the wall.

'Willcox, come with me to the Magistrates'. Coulter, Bradley, clear this lot up and have it sent to Scotland Yard.'

He shrugged himself into his Gannex. Dick, who had been nodding off in a corner, made a moaning noise as he got to his feet, stretched and tried to smooth down his crumpled shirt and readjust his tie. He looked sorely disappointed. All of them felt it, like the ash in their mouths and the hollowness in their stomachs. So near and yet so bloody far.

'I'll go to the canteen,' said Coulter, 'get us some tea and a bacon sandwich.'

Pete nodded. A weariness was in his bones but his mind was still racing. Alone in the CID room, he found his fingers tapping out an old jazz rhythm on the tabletop, 'Sing, Sing, Sing' by Louis Prima. His fingers danced across the scarred wood towards one of the ledgers, Ernie's cashbook for the tax year of 1959–60. The dates blinked to him like beacons as he picked up the book.

The song played louder in his head, drums beating a heady tattoo, brass and Benny Goodman's clarinet swirling. His finger ran down the back inside cover of the ledger. Felt a ridge underneath where the paper was glued to the cardboard back of the book. Frowned and flipped the book open, put it down on the table, kneeled down so he could look at it flat, gently touching the surface again.

The two back pages had been glued down over the back cover. Very neatly; if his fingers hadn't told him, he might have missed it just by looking.

He pulled out the drawer underneath the table, rummaged around for a scalpel. Remembered just in time to put on a pair of gloves before slipping the blade underneath the glued pages, carefully guiding it along the edge of the card it was stuck to. Turned the book around and slid it under the next side and the next. Delicately lifted up the pages with the edge of it.

Taped down to the back of the book, neatly folded into a sheet of tracing paper, was a single frame of negative.

Pete held it up to the light. It was a woman stood between two men, he could see that much. Looked to be wearing a party frock, her consorts in suits and ties.

'What have you got there?' Coulter at the door with the breakfast tray.

'One of Ernie's missing negs.' Pete's heart was hammering now, a woozy rush of adrenalin against the sleepless night. He could smell the bacon and his stomach lurched. 'Hidden in the back of this cashbook. Bloody hell.' He grabbed one of the teas off Coulter's tray, gulped down the hot, sweet liquid. 'I've got to get this down the lab.'

He reached for his coat as Coulter squinted at the frame.

'This doesn't look like filth,' he said. 'What would he be hiding this for?'

'Precisely.' Pete took another gulp of the tea and snatched up the bacon sandwich. 'Thanks for this Stan, but I've got to go.'

Out the door and running, running against time.

There it was in black and white. Three faces smiling up at them: two white, one black, all of them dressed in their party finery. Two dead, one still out there in Powis Square, or somewhere very close to it.

'Well I'll be blowed,' said Pete.

'Isn't that the singer chap?' Fielder's brow furrowed as he leaned over the print, stabbing a finger towards the wonky grin of Simon Fitzgerald. 'One who offed himself last year with a load of sleeping pills? Wife was a bit of a fan of his. Can't think why.'

'I know who that is.' Coulter's finger hovered over the black face. 'George "Lucky" Steadman, Jamaican, fairly handy light middleweight, handier still at poncing. Nicked him for that a few times, not to mention stealing, dealing, card-sharping and fighting – and that's just off the top of my head.'

'And I know who she is,' Pete pointed to the girl in the middle of them. 'She is, or was, Roberta "Bobby" Clarke. The first of them.'

'The first of them?' Fielder repeated, not following.

'The first of the Thames-side Murders, sir, June 1959, Duke's Meadow in Chiswick.' Shivers down the backbone. Ernie had been granted bail in the hours between Pete leaving the station and coming back here with the print. 'This is a connection between her and Houghton; this could be the proof that it is the same person. Why else would Ernie be hiding it?'

He was pretty sure he recognised where it had been taken too. Teddy Hills's club.

'Jesus Christ!' Fielder snapped. 'Blasted bloody solicitor. Go back and rearrest him. Better still, I will. Come on, let's go.'

The shabby door on Westbourne Grove was no longer locked. It stood eerily ajar, a paper pushed through the letterbox, mail lying on the mat untouched. Pete pushed it all the way open with his finger, walked over the threshold, feeling the chill, hearing the silence. Knowing that something wasn't right in here.

Fielder pushed past him, the photograph in his hand. 'Mr Tidsall,' he shouted down the empty corridor. 'Mr Tidsall, this is the police.'

He bounded up the stairway ahead of them. Pete and Dick exchanged glances. Shut the front door behind them as they listened to his fruitless search from room to room, slumping now the chase was over into the despondency of what was to come.

Fielder standing on the top of the stairs, fuming.

'Sweet suffering Christ!' he yelled. 'He's gone.'

26

Can't Buy Me Love

'Stella dear, this is Detective Sergeant Stanley Coulter.' Mya came back through the parlour door with a big, slightly crumpled-looking man at her side. He was wearing the sort of saggy brown suit that my pa would have favoured, a trilby hat in his hand and a raincoat over his arm. His head was covered in a thick layer of startling white curls, but it was his eyes that really drew your attention. They were huge, like twin blue moons, as full of sorrow as that spooky old song.

Somehow, he wasn't how I expected a policeman to look – like someone you could trust.

'And Stanley, this is Stella Reade.'

He put his hat down on the table, reached out a big paw of a hand.

'Pleased to meet you, Mrs Reade,' he said, in a voice that rolled with northern vowels and was as surprisingly gentle as his shake. 'Please, call me Stanley.'

'Stella,' I said, smiling despite my reservations. I had been back to see Mya a couple of times before she had convinced me that the only way I could make use of my disturbing visions was to tell someone who had the power to do something about them. Now I was less apprehensive about having let her talk me into it. Stanley

Coulter was not a man you could easily picture planting bricks on people or winking at homosexuals in public toilets.

We all sat down around the table that had been set for tea with the best rosebud china. Mya poured us all a cup, while Stanley passed around the milk jug and the sugar bowl. There was an easy familiarity about the way they smiled at each other that suggested their friendship went back a long way.

Stanley waited until both Mya and I were sipping our teas before he took out his notebook and pen and placed them on the table beside him. Then he lifted his own cup and took a thoughtful taste, nodding his head in approval. Replacing it in its saucer, he turned his big blue eyes on me.

'I'd like to thank you for taking the time to talk to me,' he said. 'It's very good of you and I assure you, anything that passes between us in here will remain confidential. That's for our mutual benefit. There's plenty on the force would think me mad if they knew I'd been coming here.' He gave a sad smile. 'I'm coming up for retirement this year. Thirty years in the game and the only thing I've really learned is that there's more things in heaven and on earth than I'll ever understand. But Mrs Matheson here has helped me to prove things I would have had no other way of knowing. I'm not overstating the case to tell you that the help she's given me has saved lives, brought terrible men to justice.'

'He's one of us, dear.'

Mya didn't say the words out loud, but as he turned to her and patted her hand, I could hear her thinking them.

'Now.' He looked back at me, the smile fading from his eyes. 'This is shaping up to be a very difficult and nasty case. We've no substantial proof that the three women were killed by the same man, it just looks increasingly likely – they were all mixed up in a very dangerous world to begin with. So anything that you can tell me, anything at all, would be very useful.'

'Now dear,' Mya turned to me, 'you just tell Stanley what you saw in Spirit. Try and remember everything you can, dear, you don't know which parts could be the most significant.'

She put her hand over mine and I closed my eyes, gathering up all my thoughts.

I didn't stop talking for another hour.

I heard the clock chime. Stanley Coulter stopped, his pen poised in mid-air over his notebook. 'Go back to the first one again,' he said. 'You said she was thinking about a man she called Baby?'

I nodded. Far from fragmenting, as I had feared it might when I started talking, the memory of Bobby standing on the pavement just outside this room remained crystal clear. 'He was her boyfriend but she was fed up with him, I think he had beaten her up a few times. While I was with her, her whole body ached.'

'Did you see what Baby looked like?'

'I think he was a black man. And so was the man she was waiting out here for. The one who didn't come.'

Coutler nodded. 'I think I know who this Baby is. If I remember right, he had an alibi at the time, but it won't hurt to go back and talk to him. I've a feeling I also know who the other fella might be. You say you didn't get a name?'

'No.' Bobby's last thoughts went through my mind as if I was watching a film. 'But he had a big round face and a gap between his front teeth. Quite a sweet face, really.'

Stanley smiled as he wrote down this detail.

'Now the second one, Bronwyn,' he said, 'she was at a nightclub when she encountered a man that she already knew, a man she called The Chopper...'

'Yes.' I shuddered at the thought of that hatchet face, those cruel lips. 'He looked horrible, like Mr Punch. He didn't kill her, but he gave her to the men who did.'

Stanley tapped the end of his pen against his pad. 'The nightclub is an interesting detail. Ties in with some new evidence.' He jotted down a few more of his thoughts. 'But it doesn't appear with the third one, Susannah Houghton.'

'No, she was definitely running away. The man she was going to meet had promised her a new life, a house in Mortlake...'

'Mortlake,' Stanley said. 'Where Bronwyn Evans was buried.'

As we stared at each other, I felt a sickening lurch of fear.

'He tricked her.' My voice came out as a whisper. 'There was someone else in the back of his car...'

That dread black shape squirmed through my memory and my cup, which had been sitting innocently beside me on the table, suddenly toppled out of its saucer and over the edge of the table, rolling across the floor until it smashed against the fire grate.

'It's all right, Stella.' Mya was immediately at my side, holding my hand, while Stanley leapt up to clear up the mess, his face as white as chalk. As Mya's fingers closed around mine, the vision began to recede and fragment. I no longer felt I was standing in a Shepherd's Bush midnight coming face-to-face with death, but was looking instead at the shafts of pale April sunshine slanting through the blinds in the parlour of the Christian-Spiritualist Greater World Association.

'Sorry,' I said, feeling the beginnings of a migraine start to pluck at my temples.

'Shhh now, you've nothing to be sorry for.' Mya put her hand on my forehead.

'Stanley,' she said, 'can you take the cup through to the kitchen, put it in the sink and pour cold water over it. Then come back in here, please.' Her voice was quite commanding and he did as he was told. My breath was coming in short gasps, as if I had been running, but while Mya's hand remained on my head, the pain that was threatening subsided, along with the nausea that normally came straight behind.

Stanley came back and sat down in his chair next to mine.

'Are you all right?' he asked.

I nodded, wondering the same thing about him.

'Let's all join hands for a moment,' said Mya. 'I'll say a blessing to clear the air.'

We all bowed our heads. 'Now may the Lord bless us and keep us.' Her voice was strong and clear. 'May He give us light to guide us, courage to support us and love to unite us. This day and forever more, amen.'

'Amen,' we repeated and sat for a moment with our eyes closed. I opened mine before the detective did and saw a lone tear trickle down his cheek, which he brushed away on the back of his hand as he stood up.

'Well thank you again, Mrs Reade.' His voice was as sombre as his face. 'I can see how hard this is for you and I'm sorry for it, I really am.'

'Well, Stanley,' Mya said, 'let's all pray that what Stella has seen can help you catch this monster. She has been given the gift for a reason.'

Stanley put his hat on his head, picked up his coat from the back of his chair. 'Aye, well,' he said, 'I'd best take my leave of you now, there's a lot for me to follow up on here. Thank you again, Mrs Reade, you've been more than helpful. I hope we get to meet again in happier circumstances.'

We shook hands once more and then Mya threaded her arm through his and walked him back to the front door, murmuring something that I couldn't quite catch. A single tear of my own rolled down under my chin as I watched them.

I dreamt about the next one that night.

•

My white boots crack sharply along the pavement as I walk under the tall trees and smile to myself, thinking about all the money in my white leather handbag, all the easy money me and Ron clipped down the tennis club tonight. A couple of arty types, easy marks, working their way down a bottle of Bell's while Ron works away at the tables. Let 'em build up a big pile of chips and then take 'em out on the courts and blow what's left of their brains out through their dicks while my clever fingers work inside their wallets. Send 'em back in and let Ron cash in the rest.

Daft buggers still didn't know what hit them when they staggered out two hours later and a ton lighter. Best graft I ever done since I hooked up with Ron, no more flophouse tricks for me. No more Ernie and his flash, bang wallop, to hell with him, I hope the bogeys closed him down. I've got a new daddy now and the silly old berk thinks he got an even split, don't realise what I do with 'em once I get 'em outside. Still, what he don't know won't hurt him and it keeps me safe and all, keeps me out of the life that did for Sue.

Soon have enough to get out of the Smoke for good, go back up to Lincoln or Stamford, Peterborough or Cambridge, somewhere where no one ever has to know what I been doing these past five years. I'll be showin' soon and that ain't good for trade.

I put my hand on my stomach as I walk up the steps to my front door. 'All for you, babe,' I whisper. 'All for you.'

'Tut tut tut, Maggie. Someone's been talking out of line.'

The voice comes from behind me and I almost jump out of my skin, out of my best dogtooth check coat, my keys dropping out of my hands and on to my doorstep.

I turn and he's standing there, at the bottom of the steps, under the plane tree, out of the glow of the streetlamp. Never even saw him as I walked past. A tall, broad man in a sheepskin coat, his hat pulled down low so I can't see his face but his voice so familiar it *slices through my nerves like a long sharp dagger to the pit of my stomach, my stomach that is budding with life.*

'Don't know what you're on about.' I try to bluff him out, stoop to pick up my keys, knowing I have to get inside, get away from him. But fear makes me scrabble and miss, my fingers not so clever as he comes bounding up the steps. For one second I think I have them and then he snatches my hand up, yanks my arm behind my back so hard it takes my breath away, sends sparks shooting before my eyes and my keys flying into the dark. I open my mouth to scream but his hand closes over it, his hand in a leather glove that smells of damp and death.

'I told you not to be so bloody stupid. I said I'd come for you if you didn't keep it shtum. That bogey pay you to tell him about Ernie, did he?'

His eyeballs are dark holes that bore through mine and he smells of stale sweat and cheap aftershave, a smell that takes me back to a room above a shop in Westbourne Grove, a room all painted white with a big black bed in the middle of it, a room with lights that flash for the photographs of me and Sue and Christ knows who all fucking and sucking and moaning together. The room I never wanted to go back to and thought I had got rid of, got out of to protect the life that squirms inside my stomach, the life that isn't soiled by that room of lies and lights that flash too bright.

'You love money so much don't you?' he says as he pins me against the door, one leg in front of the other so that I can't even kick him where it hurts, all my tricks deserting me and just red hot fear replacing thought, the banging of my heart like jackhammers roaring in my ears. 'Yeah? Well now you're gonna pay it all back...'

He marches me back down the steps and towards a big black car, a long black car under the trees with something moving in the passenger seat and a back door that opens by itself as my knees go weak and he pushes me in, slamming the door behind me.

I look up and she is sitting there.

Geordie Sue with her head at a funny angle, her eyes full of tears, a big black handbag on her lap lying open and a photograph of Cheryl fallen out on to the leather between us.

I stare at her and I know that I am done for, a kick inside my stomach and my bladder starts to empty all over the black leather seat. The engine starts up behind the wood partition that stops me from seeing who or what was on the passenger seat and a strange music starts with it, like a fairground organ being played under water, the scream of a cat and the car starts moving off.

Warm on the wet leather seat with my hand on my stomach and now you will never be mine, you will never be at all, all the money in the world can't help us now.

Stick it in the family…

I woke up in a bed that was much too warm, the sheets all tangled around me.

For once I could be glad that Toby was still in America, that he hadn't witnessed me wetting our bed in the fear of that vision, the most terrible one yet.

Outside in Powis Terrace, cats were screaming.

27

She's Not There

Searching for her in Powis Square, along the speakeasies of Westbourne Park Road, up through the back streets of Moorhouse Road and Artesian Road, over Westbourne Grove and into Bayswater. Moving through a warren of mews, each with its own olde worlde pub adorned with hanging baskets, where shiv boys and toms shared their counter space with retired majors and red-faced Norfolk farmers. Stop-checking the cars that cruised past Hyde Park at a less-than-purposeful pace, shining a flashlight into the back seats of parked vehicles. Wearing out leather walking up and down sets of stairs in the flophouses and fleapit hotels that made up the trade of Leinster Square. All the twilight places you would expect to find a working girl.

It had only come to Pete days later, as he walked back home past the construction site for the new flyover behind Ladbroke Grove. They had been so busy searching for Ernie and the coloured lass, his own thoughts so wrapped up in the photograph of Bobby and Simon Fitzgerald, that he had forgotten perhaps the most important thing.

The girl who had led them to Ernie.

When he tried to describe her to the brasses who would talk to him in those dodgy pubs or at the late night coffee stands, they wrinkled their noses and averted their eyes. Receptionists in the grim hotels of Leinster Square, where so many rooms were rented by the hour, were most adamant they had never had anyone of her description staying on their premises. Undercover WPCs got no further eliciting the confidences of a nervous and distrustful community. She had vanished, as completely as Ernie.

They had found no traces of a bank book nor a passport inside the smudger's deserted flat, so it was widely assumed he had left the country, was smart enough to prepare contingency plans should he ever get busted. Fielding brooded on his missed opportunity, used his influence to take out an APB and spent his days haranguing people on the telephone. But there hadn't been any sightings of a man matching Ernie's description taking a boat, train or aeroplane out of the country. His bank account, now being inspected by Her Majesty's Inland Revenue at Fielding's behest, reported no activity in his account either. They kept the flat under obs but it remained defiantly dark, lights out and no one coming in. It was as if all the subterranean trade of Bayswater knew at once that the place had suddenly become radioactive.

Anxious days and haunted nights; and all the while Joan's stomach growing, a glow about her illuminating her face as she had brightened up the house, counting the days she was, only a month to go. Pete tried to shut out the dead girls when he returned home, tried to reach back to that summer's morning on Hunstanton cliffs and savour the joy of impending fatherhood with his wife.

But fear hovered over him, like the tall cranes that massed around Rillington Place, old ghosts to be exorcised and concreted over, a vast gravestone of a motorway to rise over the horror, diverting traffic away.

Day after day, Pete's finger hovered over the dial of his own telephone. Day after day he stopped himself. When he shut his eyes each time he went to bed, a snapshot was burned against his retina: Bobby Clarke and Simon Fitzgerald smiling back at him. Bobby

Clarke and Simon Fitzgerald in front of the bar at Teddy Hills's club. He had to find the blonde again before she joined them.

But no one had seen her on the street.

No one saw her go into the water either.

Thirty-five days after Geordie Sue surfaced on the Upper Mall, the dawn of Tuesday the 8th of April broke over the naked body of a woman, beached among the refuse on the mud flats revealed by high tide at Corney Reach. A police boat caught sight of her first. Patrols had been scouring the banks of the river, going over the old routes by Gobbler's Gulch and Mortlake on land and from the Thames, incessantly for the past month. Searching for something they must have missed, some clue that would let anything about these crimes make sense – but still the killer had managed to laugh in their faces, to deliver a new victim right under their noses.

No one wanted to identify her either. She lay in the morgue for a week without a name to go with her empty face or the tattoo on her right arm, a gravestone in the shape of a cross and the words: *John in Memory* inscribed underneath it. The autopsy revealed she had died from drowning but not whether this had been before or after she was dropped into the Thames. She had been dead for several days and the savage wound on her chest had been caused post-mortem, probably from a passing boat's propeller. She was also four months pregnant.

Which explained why she had looked so much better fed and more bonny. She had been glowing with child too.

Only when the £12 10s rent went uncollected from her landlady in Denbigh Road, did they find a reluctant witness to her identification. The blond was Margaret Rose Stephenson, aged twenty-six, originally from Lincolnshire, from a part of the Fens close to Joan's home village.

'Blow me,' said Joan when she read it in the paper. 'That's not ten miles away from where I was born.' She leant over to study the photograph, one hand protectively over her stomach as if shielding the unborn infant from what was waiting out in the world. 'I don't think I know her though.' Joan's brow furrowed. She was two years younger than Margaret Rose and when you saw the picture the papers had dug out of her, as a hopeful-looking nineteen-year-old, you could see a kind of local resemblance in the roundness of her face and the snub nose, an honest, open, country face. Pete tried to remember if the blonde had had cornflower blue eyes too, but he couldn't. He could only see her in the darkness, half lit by the yellow glow of the coffee stand.

'Poor thing.' Joan's voice softened and she shook her head.

They had kept from the press the detail about the pregnancy. One of Shepherd's Bush's theories was that the girls could have been involved in some kind of illegal abortion ring and they didn't want anyone's feathers ruffled until they could get a proper inside line on it. Pete thought the idea was way off the mark, but he was glad that Joan had been spared that detail.

'Ten miles,' he said, leaning down to kiss her goodbye. 'By heck.'

Joan looked up at him, sadness and worry clouding the cornflower blue. 'Be careful, love,' she said. 'Don't take this too personal because of where she's from. She can't have been very much like me really, can she?'

Pete smiled and shook his head. Joan didn't know that he had met Margaret Rose Stephenson before, nor that he could possibly have prevented her death, but she knew the way his mind worked all right. And she was right. The dead woman wasn't very much like Joan at all. Her life had been neither honest nor open, which explained why the hoteliers of Leinster Square were so reluctant to recall her and why she was anathema to the other working girls.

With their ever-open chequebooks, the press unearthed stories faster than the police could from the tight-lipped toms of W2. It seemed that their informers had learnt something at last from Margaret Rose, who was also known as Sheila Dunn, Janey Reid or Rose Dunhill, and was quite happy to lend her name to others in order to further muddy her true identity.

Their stories told of how high-minded Margaret did not like to perform for her money. Instead she had a neat alternative, hiring rooms by the hour wherever there was a receptionist with a sympathetic ear. The scam went two ways – she either would tell the john to wash himself in the sink before their tryst, or else promise she was going to do something 'different' for him and begin running a bath in the room next door. Whichever trick she used, he would be out of his clothes first, enabling Margaret Rose to grab his wallet and slam the door, locking it behind her as she fled.

If the john was angry enough to complain to the receptionist, who had by then received her cut, then the smiling clerk would inevitably ask if he wanted her to call the police. His rage would at once become as impotent as his hopes of a sneaky leg-over had been.

Thorny Rose was also said to have dabbled in blackmail – possibly indicative of a falling out with Ernie and a subsequent desire to wreak revenge, a subject that kept Fielder up at nights and Pete along with him. If ever she actually did undress for one of her hapless pick-ups, it would only be because she had a photographer waiting in the next room with a loaded camera. Then blushing Rose would pretend to be just as shocked as her prey, and afterwards claim she was being extorted for the money for the negatives too. That way she could charge double for 'her share' of the trouble of getting them back.

She had boasted about it all quite freely and it had made the other girls hate her. Which gave the newspapers something quite different from the previous three mysteries to work with. A girl the whole country could learn to hate too.

A girl who was asking for trouble.

Meanwhile, Shepherd's Bush had been through the contents of her flat. They had found a name in a diary that they were anxious to put a face to. Someone called 'Sexy Ron', no surname, no telephone number. Possibly a boyfriend, possibly, and more interestingly, one of her consorts in blackmail. A timid neighbour had admitted to hearing a row late on the Friday night before her body was discovered, Margaret Rose and a man, telling her not to be 'so bloody stupid'. Maybe he was Sexy Ron. Maybe he was the killer.

Whatever he was, the tedious job of making door-to-door calls to anyone called Ronald who had any previous was something that had been taking up much of Pete and Dick's time recently. Four Rons into their shift and not one of them under fifty, they were taking their time over tea and buns in the canteen, putting off the fifth Ron, an inhabitant of Lancaster Road who had been given a caution for drunken disorder in 1947, as long as they possibly could. It was there that Tom Spinks found them, eking out a final cigarette over the remains of the *Kensington Post*.

'Desk Sergeant asked me to look for you,' he said. 'You don't know where the gaffer is by any chance?'

'No,' said Dick folding down the top of the racing pages and exhaling a stream of smoke towards the ceiling. 'We ain't seen him, not that we've been looking. He's probably out at some top brass lunch in Mayfair.'

'We're only talking to fellers called Ron today anyway,' said Pete, looking up from the boxing. 'Gaffer's orders.'

'Well then, you'd better come,' said Spinks. 'There's a bloke at the front desk called Ronald McSweeney. Wants to confess to the murder of Margaret Rose Stephenson.'

28

A World Without Love

The music is just the way I like it. Loud bebop jazz played by a trio from the States, a big fat spade on the bass, a dark-haired Jew at the keyboard and another hep negro, tall and thin, with shades like Ray Charles and a goatee beard, blowing his guts out through his horn. They're all sweating and shaking under the lights and I'm shaking my arse right along with them, grinding my black leather boots down into the floor, knowing I'm looking good in my tight black sweater and pencil skirt, the figure that rode the flying trapeze in Blackpool still supple and lithe. Here in the smoky basements of Westbourne Park Road I can become myself, all my French blood singing to that wild slapping bass, that hot, hectic trumpet, the voodoo rhythm of the drums. Oh yes, once you get down with the brothers there's no going back to whitey. These boys know how to smile and dance, they have better food, better music, sharper clothes...

I shudder as he hits the top note, an unwelcome thought corkscrewing through my brain, a memory of what life was like before I found my way to Ladbroke Grove. Another thing I like about the spades, they don't go in for any of that kinky shit, just a straight screw does them fine. Even talk to you afterwards, let you share your problems, treat you like a human being, not just a piece of meat to be bought and sold.

The tall Negro on the podium in front of me swoops down into a bow as the applause reverberates through the room, cut through with whoops of approval. I try to catch his eye as he takes out a handkerchief from his breast pocket, wipes his brow. An itch inside me that needs to be scratched, that those long, long fingers could find. But he spins round, gives a nod to the bass player and they start into a new tune, a rhapsody in red for The Blue Parrot Club. I give myself up to it, whirl round in a circle and as I do, I catch the eye of another, weaving his way through the tightly packed bodies towards me.

I frown and look around me, the drums pounding loud in my ears like they're sending me a warning, a prickle down my spine despite the heat of the room. Me, he is looking at me from under the rim of his hat, I know this man and he knows me, put my circus skills to good use when I first came to town. I dance away from him, duck and weave through the bodies, making my way towards the Ladies. Step inside, trip through the women leaning over the sink to put their lipstick on in front of the mirror, and lock myself in the one cubicle that has a catch that works. I pull out a reefer from my black plastic handbag, my fingers shaking as I light it up, lean back against the door.

What's he doing here? What's he want from me?

That bad memory catches the corner of my brain again, a man whose teeth are too bright, whose hair is too slick, whose fingers are too small, a white man in a white house, a blond wig in his hands, a long, blond wig...

The drums pounding through the walls, louder and louder.

Hammering on the toilet door. 'Ain't you finished in there? Come on, I'm bursting, gonna wet myself in a minute, you don't hurry up.'

Take another drag and the room swirls as I lurch forwards, a feeling of nausea not from the smoke but from that memory that I bat away to the back of my mind, unlock the door and let the grumpy *little tart push past me, steady myself on the sink as she slams the cubicle door, still squawking her complaints like a chicken.*

Look at my face in the mirror, my black hair up in a chignon, my straight nose and my dark eyes, my French eyes from my father, a steward in the Free French Navy. Hear the drums beat out a warning: Get out of the room, get out of the room...

Duck my head through the door of the Ladies, can't see the man with the hat, just Shorty lounging against the wall. One of my regulars, sturdy little Bajan in a snap brim hat, swaps sweet times for sweeter smokes, flashes me a smile and I know I can trust him.

'Do me a favour?' I say, thrusting my handbag at him. 'Look after this for me for a minute...'

'Sure t'ing sweet'eart,' he drawls, giving me a quizzical look as he slides it under his arm.

'Just need to step outside for a while.' I tip him a wink and he nods knowingly, puts his finger up to the side of his nose.

Don't want that man to know what's in my handbag. Come back for it later, just get out of the room...

My eyes sweep around as I head for the cloakroom, paranoid now, my blood pumping in time to the voodoo drums. Still can't see him as I put on my brown coat with the black leather collar, feel for the coins I have left in my pocket, a plan starting to form in my head as I run up the steps past the doorman, out on to Westbourne Park Road.

Head for the Globe and find one of the big boys to protect me.

My black leather boots clatter down Powis Terrace, the same beat as the drums that I still hear pounding through my brain, the tall Negro blowing the high note out of his horn...

Reach the corner and stop. The Globe right in front of me but my eyes drawn to the right of it, to where a long black car is parked outside my house, to where my front door is open, an orange glow spilling out from the hallway. All the music suddenly stops as my eyes are drawn up to the window of my flat, another orange glow up there even though I turned the light off and locked the door before I came out tonight, my keys still in my handbag that I left with Shorty.

All thoughts of the Globe and my plan drain out of my mind, replaced by a static hum, and somehow my body is no longer my own as I walk towards my front door, as if compelled by a magnetic force to step through into the hallway and up the stairs ahead, not even shutting the front door behind me.

Another type of music starting up as I climb the steps to my room, a pop record I have heard in a coffee bar and never liked, an echoing guitar and a man's voice swathed in reverb, getting louder and louder as I approach the door to my room...The door to my room that is open and as I stand on the threshold and look inside I see him standing by the kitchenette counter, a cup in his hand, see him with his hat pulled down low and then something else, something in the corner of my vision, a black shape moving...

Feet running, loud up the steps outside, and then the front door slammed and I hit the bed like I had dropped from the ceiling, my eyes open in the brightness of our bedroom, the lights all on and my heart beating like the pounding of drums. For a second I thought that the girl with the black hair had come running back up Powis Terrace and into our house.

The room lurched as I sat up, stars dancing in front of my eyes, a magazine sliding off my chest and on to the floor. I must have fallen asleep reading it, as I was still fully dressed, apart from my shoes that I had kicked off before. The fear pounding through my veins was so sharp I felt like my hair must be standing on end and it was only as my vision cleared, to the sound of pans being clattered around in the kitchen below, that I realised it was only Toby down there, back from a meeting with clients at last.

I looked at the clock. It was 2 a.m. A wave of panic swept through me. The girl with the black hair was just around the corner. I had to do something. I had to help her.

I slid off the bed. My legs felt like lead, my head was thick with sleep and disorientation, as if I was completely drunk.

'Shoes,' I said aloud, trying to locate them. As my head turned, my vision blurred again for a second, streaks of white light across the side of my pupils. Then I made out the errant footwear poking out from under the bed, reached out and picked them up. But I couldn't seem to get them back on, I kept falling backwards on to the mattress every time I tried.

'This is stupid!' I cried out. 'I've got to help her!'

Abandoning the shoes, I moved towards the door, only to find that I couldn't seem to walk in a straight line either, banging my hips against the wall and then the doorframe as I tried to manoeuvre. I made it as far as the top of the stairs and then stood there, swaying against the banister, hideous vertigo rooting me to the spot the moment I looked down.

'Darling?' Toby's face appeared in the hall underneath me, his brow crinkling into a frown as he looked at me swaying there. 'What's wrong?'

'We've got to help her,' I said, tears springing into my eyes as terror prevented my legs from moving. 'But I can't…I can't…' I thought I was going to topple over, pitch headlong down towards him, and Toby must have had the same idea, as he started running up the stairs towards me.

I sank down to my knees. 'I can't…I can't…' was all I could say.

Toby put his arms around me, pulled me away from the stairs and back into the bedroom. His eyes were wide with fright and his breath heavy with alcohol.

'What is it darling, what's wrong? Have you had a bad dream?'

I stared at him. Had he guessed? Did he realise? Would he help me to help her?

'Toby.' My voice was little more than a whisper. 'Please. Go outside, to the end of the street. If there is a big black car parked outside the house on the corner by the Globe, come back and call the police.'

'What?' His expression shifted slightly, from worry into incredulity.

'Please,' it came out louder this time, 'please just do it. Somebody's being murdered at the end of our street, we've got to help her, Toby!'

Now he looked worried again. He stood up, glanced from me to the door, uncertain of what he should really be doing.

'If the car is there you have to call Notting Hill police,' I stumbled on, twisting the counterpane round my fists in frustration, 'ask for Detective Sergeant Stanley Coulter and tell him there's another one happening right now. He knows me, he'll believe me!'

Toby opened his mouth to say something, then thought better of it and instead made for the door. I heard him run downstairs and then out of the front door.

I drew my legs up around me, shivering uncontrollably. I had let it all out now. But I had to, I had to try and help her, to stop this...

Toby's footsteps echoed down the empty road and came to a stop.

I heard him turn and walk back slowly. With every step, the knot in my stomach grew tighter and tighter. He slammed the front door, turning the locks behind him and then came back up the stairs, leant against the doorframe of the bedroom, staring at me aghast.

'Darling,' he said very quietly, in a tone of strained patience you might use on a child. 'There was absolutely nothing there. You must have been having a nightmare, it wasn't real. Have you been drinking?'

'Oh God,' I said, bile rising in my throat. 'I think I'm going to be sick.'

He put a hand up to his forehead as I ran into the bathroom. And all I could think of as I heaved and retched was that look in his eyes.

He didn't believe me.

He thought I was mad.

All my worst fears coming true because I couldn't control myself this time, couldn't close the gap between the worlds fast enough.

He was still standing there like that when I came back.

'Stella,' he eventually said, a quaver in his voice now. 'You're not...'

He dropped his hand down and his eyes were red.

'...pregnant, are you?'

Dimly, I tried to think. Was it possible? The last night before he had gone to the States we had...But no, I'd had my period since then. And since he'd come back, well we hadn't...His jetlag, he said...His drinking more likely...

'No,' I said.

He closed his eyes for a moment – a moment that looked like a sigh of relief.

'Ah,' he said, opening them, blinking. 'Well, I was just thinking,' he moved towards me, patted me on the shoulder, 'you know, being sick, having nightmares...It would have made sense, don't you think?'

I sank down on the bed.

'I'm sorry, Toby,' I said. 'But nothing seems to make very much sense to me at the moment.'

He flinched, ever so slightly.

'Oh well,' he said, 'perhaps you'd better try to get to sleep now.' His mouth twitched upwards into a grim approximation of a smile. 'I'll come and join you in a moment, I was just making some supper. Lots of drinks tonight, but they didn't do much in the way of food, you see, I was pretty much starving when I came in. If you don't mind…'

'Fine,' I said, rolling away from him, my face burning with fear and shame. 'Do what you like.' I stared at his reflection in the dressing-table mirror as he rubbed at his eyes and then turned to walk away.

29

You Really Got Me

She must have had a funny definition of 'sexy' must Margaret Rose. For the little man sitting in the interview room was only about five foot two, his scuffed shoes barely reaching the floor as he swung them backwards and forwards in a state of high agitation. Up close he looked around sixty, a shock of grey hair rising up from a furrowed forehead, dark little eyes moving fretfully underneath bushy white eyebrows, tiny hands ripping a cigarette packet to pieces. Dressed in a bottle-green worsted suit with a brown cardigan buttoned up underneath it, nicotine-stained teeth and wiry grey hair curling out of his nostrils. Bits of dried egg down his front. About as far away from being desirable to a twenty-six-year-old con woman as you could possibly imagine.

But Sexy Ron McSweeney, reeking of a night's sweated-out whisky, couldn't wait to tell them how he was the murderer. He jumped to his feet as they walked through the door. 'At last,' he shouted, 'oh my godfathers, at last. It was me what done her officers, I've got to get it off my conscience, I can't bear thinking about it no more.'

'Steady, Mr McSweeney,' said Pete. 'Let's just take some details off you first.'

Sexy Ron looked at them, bewildered. 'But don't you want to get this over with? I can take you to the spot, to the exact spot where I done her.'

'We just have to confirm that you are who you say you are first,' said Dick. 'If you don't mind sitting back down, this shouldn't take too long.'

McSweeney did as he was told, but hesitantly, perhaps reading from the sceptical expressions behind the two detectives' arched eyebrows and half smiles that they were about to make him sweat some more.

By the time DI Fielder had got back from wherever it was he had been to join them, Pete and Dick had ascertained that Ronald George McSweeney, born 1908 in Preston, former Royal Navy and merchant seaman who had gone ashore for good in the London of 1950, was currently the live-in caretaker at the Holland Park Lawn Tennis Club. But far from upholding the genteel standards expected of his post, McSweeney had been living a double life, opening the bar again after the regular patrons had gone home and ushering in instead an entirely different class of night owl. Gamblers, bookmakers, gangsters and, of course, brasses, formed the core of his illicit clientele and this was how he had come to meet Margaret Rose, who helped to supply him with suitably flush and inebriated marks to play poker with.

He couldn't remember how the argument started, he said. He knew it was because he was under pressure – he had been caught trying to steal a hearing aid in the West End and was due to stand trial for it at Marylebone Magistrates'. He'd been advised that he would probably get away with a fine, it being his first offence and all, but the very idea of going to court had shaken him to his core, triggered a bout of heavy drinking unknown since his landlubber days began. When Margaret Rose started to get unreasonable about her cut of the night's takings, money that he would no doubt be needing himself shortly, if he wasn't going to get sent to jail, he simply lost his temper.

'I made up some old spiel about having to visit a mate in a pub in Chiswick to get some gelt he owed me to pay her off,' McSweeney told them. 'It was just so as I could get her somewhere I knew we couldn't be seen, somewhere I could get rid of her quickly. We was down by the water there and I must have put my hands around her throat or something, 'cos stand on me, I looked down the next minute and there she was, dead. The thing is, they teach you these things in the Forces,' he said, his eyes drifting away, 'I didn't know me own strength.'

Fielder didn't greet their news with much enthusiasm. McSweeney was in the cells by then, still pacing about, desperate to show them to the murder spot.

'Just the Stephenson girl,' Fielder said for the fifth time, 'that was all he copped to. Not Clarke, Adams or Houghton. No mention of any of them.'

'No sir,' said Pete. 'The thing is, he's in such an agitated state I don't think he's thinking properly. He can only focus on telling us about Stephenson, not that he can remember actually killing her. Says one minute she was alive, the next minute she was dead at his feet, so he presumed the worst.'

'Did what any self-respecting strangler would do in his position,' said Dick. 'Stripped her, rolled her in the river, took her clothes home and burned them.'

'He didn't happen to tell you where he spent last night, did he?' Fielder asked wearily.

'Getting pissed in the Princess Alexandra,' said Dick, checking his notebook. 'The landlord sold him another bottle to take to bed and said he was helped away by some mate of his he was drinking with.'

'He couldn't face reading another story about poor Margaret Rose in the newspapers,' added Pete. 'And the drinking couldn't help him to forget.'

'Right,' said Fielder, striking a match and taking it to his pipe. 'Then there's not much chance he was out driving round Brentford with a dead body in the back of his car.'

'I don't think he said he had a car, sir.' Dick was still studying his notebook; it took a beat before the words sank in and he looked up startled. 'What did you just say?'

'The reason I've been gone all morning,' said Fielder. 'Every senior officer with links to any of the Thames-side murders got the summons. There's been another one. Not in the river this time, she was dumped in a cul-de-sac in Brentford in the early hours of this morning; naked as the day she was born. From what we know so far it looks like she was another tart and it looks like she was strangled.'

'Damn,' said Pete.

'Indeed,' said Fielder. 'But as you have just said, a lot of Mr McSweeney's story has already proved to be true. I'm afraid we are going to have to take a little trip with him to Chiswick. Let's hope we can get there before' – he winced at the thought of the latest headlines – 'Jack the Stripper strikes again.'

'I just don't get it.' Dick lifted his pint off the counter of the Edinburgh Castle, across the road from the station. 'He got the time and place exactly right. How could he know that if he didn't kill her?'

Pete shrugged. 'Buggered if I know,' he said.

They had taken McSweeney out in the radio car, let him guide them to the Windmill pub in Chiswick and then retread his route to Corney Steps, where he claimed to have rolled Margaret Rose's body into the Thames. His version of events tied in so tightly with the facts there was nothing they could do but charge him.

'We must have missed something,' Pete added, but he couldn't think what. His brain had all but seized up trying to make sense of the funny little man. If McSweeney had gone to pieces over a stolen hearing aid, how could he be so eager to cop the blame for the blonde, land himself on a murder charge? And what about all that snide money he'd been making at the tennis club? He'd had the wit about him to keep all that from his employers for months on end, but now his nerves were so shot he'd given them all that information on a plate as well. His life was a shambles – but on the subject of Margaret Rose's murder, he was crystal clear.

'And what about this other bird?' Dick said. 'Who was she?'

Pete looked past him to where the pub door was opening, a mess of white curls coming through. 'I don't know that either,' he said, 'but it looks like we might be about to find out.'

Coulter had his notebook in his hand, a purposeful look on his face. 'Pete,' he said, 'Dick. Pick your brains for a minute?'

They settled themselves at a table in the snug.

'The girl they found this morning,' Coulter said, 'was another local. Mathilde Bressant, resident of Talbot Road, the only white woman in a house full of West Indians. Came from Scotland, apparently, but she must have been half French with a name like that.'

'Ooh la la,' said Dick, raising his eyebrows. 'That why she had a taste for the exotic?'

'Hmmm, well.' Coulter flicked open his notebook. 'This is what I want to ask you about. Mathilde, or Tilly as they called her, was last seen leaving The Blue Parrot Club on Westbourne Park Road about ten to two this morning.'

'The Blue Parrot?' Pete felt a tingle down his spine.

Coulter gave him a knowing look. 'That's right. She left her handbag down there with one of the darkies, said she was just stepping out a minute, but she never came back.'

'Isn't that the club where Bobby Clarke's boyfriend was supposed to have been on the night of her murder?' Pete said.

'That's what I'd hoped you'd say,' said Coulter, smiling. 'Algernon "Baby" Ferrier and his mate George Steadman, star of Ernie's photograph. We need to find them. They used to spend a lot of time at The Blue Parrot, the pair of them, but they've not been seen around in recent years. Which makes me think that some fine copper must have done society a favour and put them behind bars. If that's the case, it'll make them easier to interview. Would you mind giving me a hand checking out their records?'

'Course,' said Pete, 'be a welcome distraction from Sexy Ron McSweeney.'

'Ah yes,' Coulter said, raising up his index finger. 'To return the favour, let me give you this. I've had a tip-off about one of the fellows Stephenson was playing cards with on the night she died. An artist, no less.' He flicked backwards through his notebook. 'Let's see. Oh yes. Bernard Baring is his name. Lives on the top floor of number 24 Powis Square. I would have looked him up myself, but with all of this I've not had the time. Maybe he can tell you a little more about what Stephenson and Sexy Ron were up to.'

Pete looked up at the clock.

'They keep bohemian hours, these artists, don't they?' he said.

'Yeah.' Dick picked up the remains of his pint and drained it. 'If we get a move on, we might catch him having breakfast…'

Pete had never seen a place like it. From floor to ceiling, the top floor flat of 24 Powis Square was one great collage of paintings and postcards, pictures ripped from magazines and canvases of what looked to him like children's cartoons. A portrait of General Kitchener pointed his finger towards him, his moustache a forest of flowers with bluebirds flying out of it. Trapeze artists swung off the side of his military cap, a butterfly sat on his nose. JOIN THE CIRCUS was written above his head. It was signed at the bottom: *Bernard Baring.*

'I take it,' Pete squinted at the signature, 'this is one of your own, sir?'

The artist nodded, the peevish expression on his thin face intensifying.

'This what you think of the army, is it?' Pete went on.

'It's satire.' Baring spoke in a condescending public-school accent at odds with his scruffy appearance. 'That's what Pop Art mainly is. An ironic commentary on our times, using the mediums of popular culture and folk art. But I don't think that's what you've come here to ask me about, is it?'

'No it isn't,' agreed Pete, 'I'm just curious as to how good a living you can make out of stuff like this.'

'I do all right.' Baring stared down his pointy nose.

'I quite like this one,' said Dick, staring at a canvas of a racing car with a big target on the side of it. He turned and smiled at the artist. 'How much would it cost me?'

Baring didn't bat an eyelid. 'Five hundred guineas,' he said.

'Bloody hell.' Dick looked across at Pete. 'No wonder he can afford to go throwing it about at the Holland Park Lawn Tennis Club.'

Pete kept his eyes on the artist; saw the expression of shock bloom in his eyes as his long thin fingers flew up to his mouth.

'Holland Park Tennis Club?' Baring tried to keep his tone incredulous. 'Do I look the athletic type to you?'

'Oh, we know you weren't there to actually play tennis,' said Pete, hardening his gaze. 'You were there for the poker. You move in higher circles than we do of course, but surely you realised that was an illegal game?'

'Who said I was playing poker?' Baring's voice went up an octave. 'Someone must be spinning you a line, officer.'

'We've got the dealer in custody down the station,' Pete said. 'He kept his own sort of visitors' book and your name was in it.'

This was a line, but it tripped Baring anyway. 'Oh my,' he said, fingers fluttering up to his lips again.

'The thing is,' Pete continued, 'it's not the gambling we're really interested in. It's the fact that he came into the station this morning claiming to have murdered a prostitute who was running the game with him. The same night that you were there, playing poker with him. Do you recognise her, sir?' He took the mugshot out of his jacket pocket. 'You might have been the last person to see her alive.'

Baring's grey eyes widened as he took her in, fear flickered across his sharp face.

'Do you want to sit down and talk about it sir?' said Dick. 'Or do you want to come down the factory with us, make sure we're telling the truth?'

Baring sank down on to his Victorian chaise longue, looking like he could do with some smelling salts. Pete let him have a minute to collect himself while he pulled up an armchair to face him. Dick stood where he was, leaning against the doorframe.

'All right, I'll admit that I did see her,' the artist said. 'But I was just there to play cards, I don't mess about with common street filth like that. As it was, that horrible little man took me to the cleaners for a hundred pounds.' He shuddered, then dragged his gaze up from the floor to meet Pete's. 'She was still there when I left, which would have been about midnight. And I didn't touch her, I assure you.'

'All right,' said Pete. 'That horrible little man is called Ronald McSweeney. How did you find out about his card game, sir?'

'I don't know.' Baring shook his head dismissively, looked away again. 'I was at a club in Kensington and somebody mentioned it, I can't remember who. I thought I'd just go for a giggle, I was halfway in my cups already. I don't like being taken for a fool' – colour suddenly flushed into his cheeks – 'but I was certainly a mug punter that night, wasn't I? I was hoping to forget all about it.'

'Well,' said Pete, 'maybe if you can help us out, we can forget you were there as well. I just want to know, if you can recall, how was McSweeney behaving that night? Did he seem at all agitated? Drunk or angry, perhaps?'

Baring shook his head slowly. 'Not that I can recall. He seemed perfectly collected to me. Perfectly able to deliver me of a large amount of money with a smile on his face. He couldn't possibly have been drunk.'

The bitterness in his voice was genuine. Pete nodded at Dick, got to his feet.

'If anything else comes back to you,' he said, 'call Notting Hill CID. Remember, this is about a murder, sir, not a game of cards.'

Baring nodded, whispered an insincere 'thank you', but made no effort to show them out.

'Do you believe him?' asked Dick as they clattered back down the stairs.

'Aye,' said Pete. 'He lost his purse all right and he never touched her either, the toffee-nosed sod.'

'How can you be sure?'

Pete stood by the front door, looked back up the stairs. 'You saw all the pictures he had on his walls. Not one of them was of a woman.'

'Ah.' Dick smiled. 'I see. He's *that* kind of bohemian.'

30

It's Over

'He went on treating me like Miss Haversham until it was all in the papers. They printed her address and a quote from one of the investigating officers,' I said. 'Detective Sergeant Stanley Coulter. Toby didn't know what to think of me after that. I tried to explain it to him, like you said I should and you were right, you know. We *have* been married for nearly five years and we *shouldn't* have any secrets from each other. But I don't know if it was because I'd never told him any of this before or if...' My voice caught in my throat. 'If I had always known he wouldn't understand.'

'Oh Stel,' Jackie caught hold of my hand and squeezed it, 'and you've kept this to yourself all this time. Why didn't you say something?'

'I don't know. I guess I was just hoping that once he'd had some time to come to terms with it that he would accept that it's not because I'm mad or turning into an alcoholic.' I gave a bitter laugh at that thought. 'But as I said to you in the first place, most people can't bring themselves to think about death in any way, shape or form. And it's not just that, either...'

'We've just never had a moment, have we?' Jackie said. She was right, this was the first time in nearly two months we had actually managed to be alone together. And that was only because we'd had a rush on and had to work late on some samples. Lenny had left ten minutes ago, and as soon as he had, it had all come pouring out of me. The dead girls, Stanley and Toby, what a mess my life was in. Work had been the only thing keeping me sane since that terrible night.

Jackie took a pin out of the side of her mouth and stuck it into the dummy's head.

'Well,' she said, 'let's call it a night, we're never going to get this right now, we're too tired, the both of us. Why don't we go for a drink, d'you fancy coming down the club again?'

'I don't know,' I said, 'last time we were there, I saw that girl…'

'Oh, don't start thinking like that,' Jackie chided. 'It's not your fault, you didn't make it happen – like I said, prozzers go down there the whole time. You can't start thinking like that, love, otherwise you *will* send yourself round the bend. But, I suppose, it is a bit crowded down there for us to have a decent chat.'

'Would you come back to my place?' I could hear the note of pleading in my voice. Toby was away again, in France this time, and the only thing worse than his empty bottles and withdrawn silences was being alone in that house. Every time I shut my eyes I could hear Mathilde Bressant's footsteps running down the street.

'You could stay the night and then we could come in early in the morning. Maybe we can even puzzle this out,' I put my tape measure round the neck of the dummy wearing the toile that we just couldn't seem to get right, '…after a few drinks.'

Jackie nodded. 'Course I will, pet. We'll get some newspapers out and turn them into patterns on your kitchen table, just like our student days.'

'This is the scariest part. When the police got there the next day, her front door was still open. There were two cups sitting by the kettle with coffee granules in them, like she'd just been making them both a nice drink. And there was a record going round on her turntable. Guess who it was?'

Sitting round the kitchen table with cheese on toast, wine and Ella Fitzgerald on the record player, I had somehow found it easier to tell Jackie about the girls than say any more about Toby. Mathilde Bressant had affected me worse than the others, not just because of the proximity of my house to her abduction, or the way Stanley had described her flat to me. It was more the proximity of her life to my own. When I had seen her photo in the paper, looking over her shoulder as if she had never wanted her image to be captured, she looked so beautiful, like the sort of girl who would come into our shop.

Mya had also been upset to discover that Mathilde had once worked at the circus in Blackpool, on the flying trapeze. Maybe it was her French blood, but she was much more of an adventurer than any of the other girls had been, she had a spirit that hadn't been crushed by the things she had done for money. And for the short time I had been with her, I had shared one thing with her entirely – her taste in music.

'That bastard James?' said Jackie.

I nodded. 'Got it in one. The latest one from that horrible-looking blond boy, HP Sauce or whatever his name is.'

Jackie curled her upper lip. 'James was screwing him and all,' she said. 'Broke Lenny's heart all over again.'

'The thing is, though,' I said, 'she didn't even like that sort of music. She liked jazz.'

Jackie shuddered. 'That *is* scary,' she said, reaching for the bottle of wine just as the telephone started ringing. 'Oh my God.' Jackie withdrew her hand and crossed herself. 'I nearly dropped the damn thing. Who's that calling at this time of night?'

I looked up at the clock. The hands were nudging towards eleven.

'It might be my husband,' I speculated. 'He often doesn't know what time it is. Excuse me a minute.' I went out into the hall to get it, lifted the receiver with a sense of trepidation.

'Oh Stella darling, you *are* in!' Jenny's voice came singing down the line. 'I thought you might be out somewhere glamorous but I had to give you a try. How are you?'

I was so relieved it was her and not Toby phoning up to say he loved me the only way he did now – when he was pissed and full of remorse – that I started to laugh. 'I'm fine, Jenny, how are you?'

'I'm brilliant and you won't believe this, but we're back!'

'Back in London?'

'Right around the corner from you, my dear, we've just rented a house in Elgin Crescent. Bob's got himself a big production up in Elstree, pots of cash and a little role for yours truly. But I said we couldn't live all the way out there, we had to come back and be near our friends. God I've missed you, Stella. This film lark is all right, but there's no one decent to talk to. No one,' she laughed, 'who's ever read anything but a script.'

'I can imagine,' I said, wondering what this Bob would be like, if he was just a sugar daddy like Jackie thought.

'And how's your lovely Toby? And Lenny and Jackie?' Jenny said.

'Toby's away in Paris at the moment,' I said, glad we could leave it at that. 'But Lenny's fine and Jackie's here with me now. We're just scheming round the kitchen table like we did when we were students. We're trying to think of something brilliant but at the moment we're stuck.'

'I wish I could join you.' Jenny lowered her voice to a conspiratorial whisper. 'Maybe I could help to inspire you. What are you working on?'

'Well,' I said, 'we've been looking at all this Italian tailoring the mod boys are wearing and wondering how we can make an equivalent for girls. Only skirt suits somehow look too matronly, too old-fashioned, even in a nice tonic fabric.'

'But that's easy,' said Jenny. 'Don't do it with a skirt. Do trousers instead. You know how Jackie always wears men's suits and they look so good on her. Why not dress all of London up like dykes?'

'You're wicked!' I said. 'But I love it. Let me go and tell her.'

'Oh but before you do, are you doing anything next Saturday? We thought we'd have a housewarming party, but only if you can all come.'

'I'm sure we can,' I said. 'We might even run you up a suit for it.'

'Excellent. Look forward to seeing you then, then.' Jenny rang off.

'What was all that giggling about?' Jackie said as I came back into the kitchen. 'Not Toby, I take it?'

'It was Jenny,' I told her. 'She's moved back to London with her sugar daddy.'

'Well, well, well.' Jackie chuckled. 'I must have magicked her up with my voodoo pin.'

'You bloody did as well,' I said. 'She's just given us the most brilliant idea...'

'So,' I said, standing on the doorstep of Jenny's new house, 'what do you think?'

Both Jackie and I were wearing samples of our new trouser suits. Hers was in black, she could never bring herself to wear much in the way of colour, but mine was done in the tonic fabric I had liked so much, blue shot through with purple.

'Wow!' Jenny herself looked wonderful in a white crochet trapeze dress, her hair falling over her shoulders, her skin the colour of honey. 'You look fab, the pair of you. What brilliant mind could have thought of that?'

'Which colour do you like the best?' I asked her.

She cocked her head to one side. 'The black is classic,' she considered, 'but I love that blue.'

'Just as well, then.' Lenny, who had been standing behind us, took his hands from behind his back and presented her with her own version of the suit I was wearing. 'Here you go ducks. Welcome home.'

'Oh thank you.' Jenny was almost tearful as she looked from one of us to the others then attempted to pull us all into one big hug.

'Now come in, come in,' she said. 'I can't wait to show you around.'

She led the way down a white-painted hallway with a long Persian runner down the middle of the dark floorboards, into a big, open-plan kitchen that looked out on to a rambling garden beyond. The back door was open and most of her guests seemed to be out there amongst the trees and the hollyhocks that were swaying on the breeze of a warm summer evening. Even the weather had turned out for Jenny; it was the start of a summer as long and hot as the winter had been cold and hard.

'Is Toby not with you?' she asked, hooking the suit over a chair and opening the door of the fridge.

'We've come straight from work,' I said. 'So I take it he hasn't arrived yet?' I tried to keep the annoyance from my voice. 'Oh well, he did only come back from Paris last night, he probably hasn't sorted himself out yet.'

'You know what men are like,' said Lenny.

Jenny paused for a moment with a bottle of champagne in her hand. I knew she was trying to discern what I was hiding in my eyes; that Toby hadn't returned until dawn. Somebody must have put him in a cab and helped him through the front door, otherwise I don't believe he would even have remembered the luggage that was left neatly lined up in the hallway. I had found him snoring on the sofa, a virtual mirage of booze fumes around him, and left him a note about Jenny's party. All day long I had been hoping against all real hope that the memory of our student days would somehow make him come back to me, turn him back into the Toby I had known then and not the one who so clearly couldn't stand me any more.

'Well,' she said, 'we're not waiting for him, are we?'

She popped the cork and poured us all a glass and we toasted her return, then she gave us a tour of the house. It must have just been redecorated, as all the walls were dazzling white and all the floorboards polished. There were Persian rugs in nearly every room, apart from a games room downstairs that had its own bar and pool table, where Bob could entertain his film friends, Jenny said. In all the others were pieces of mahogany furniture and great, gilt-framed mirrors, lots of spider plants and cacti all over the place. But strangely, there were no paintings anywhere, no signs of all that art she had told me she was making in Italy. Just lots of framed posters of all Robert Mannings's films, and in his study, a whole shelf full of awards and photographs of him and Jenny with their film-star friends.

'It's only the garden that really needs some work,' she said, leading us back out there. It was overgrown; the hollyhocks, cornflower daisies and violets competed with rampant ground elder, buddleia and long grass. But once it must have been laid out by someone who knew what they were doing, as even in its wild state, it looked beguiling.

Mannings himself was standing talking to a group of people I didn't recognise, underneath a willow tree. He was a tall man with dark brown hair going grey at the temples, wearing cream slacks and a pale yellow open-necked shirt that offset his deep tan, the casual attire of the successful, middle-aged filmmaker. As he turned to face us, I noticed how broad his chest was and how muscular his arms were and wondered if Jenny had, after all, married him for some sort of protection. The house and its contents were proof enough of how much money he must have had, but the smile on his face as he looked at Jenny, which illuminated his dark eyes, Roman nose and the deep laughter lines round his mouth, told me that he had married for love alone. As she leaned over to kiss him, the depth of affection in her own eyes was equally clear to see.

I suddenly felt very alone.

A bumblebee droned past and I followed its course towards a pale pink hollyhock, watched it disappear inside a flower. The sun was setting behind us, casting long shadows across the ragged lawn. I knew that Toby wouldn't be coming.

'Shall I try on the suit, then?' said Jenny, putting her hand on my arm.

I nodded, blinking back the tears that had been forming in my eyes, dragging the corners of my mouth up into a smile.

'Come and help me, then,' she said.

Their bedroom was right at the top of the house, she liked it the best because it had an en-suite bathroom. But what she hadn't shown us the first time was that the wardrobe doors actually opened up into a whole other room, her very own dressing room.

Inside were rails of clothes, carefully colour co-ordinated, with matching shoes and handbags all lined up underneath. But what was even more arresting was the portrait of her that hung on the far wall.

'My God,' I said. 'It's that gingham dress you were wearing the first time I met you.'

'Good, isn't it?' Jenny smiled. 'Dil painted it, back when we were at St Martin's. I'd like to have it up somewhere where everyone can see it, only it makes Bob feel jealous. Silly, isn't it? But then, men are.'

She was waiting for me to say something about Toby, but I

couldn't trust myself. Instead I said: 'I saw Dave a while back, he seemed very worried about you.'

'Really?' she said lightly. 'I can't think why.'

'He told me to tell you that he'd always be there for you, no matter what.'

'God,' said Jenny. 'Was he drunk?'

'I don't think so,' I said and we stared at each other in silence for a moment. It was funny, although he had captured a great likeness of her, Dave's portrait looked somehow faded compared to the real Jenny, the way her hair and skin looked so blooming, so full of light…Suddenly it dawned on me.

'Jenny,' the words just fell out of my mouth, 'you're pregnant, aren't you?'

A huge grin spread across her face. 'Yes I am, that was what I brought you up here to tell you, I wanted you to be the first – well, the second to know. I'm nearly two months gone.' She put her hand over her stomach. 'It's going to be a little girl, I know it is. And do you know what? I can't wait to stop this acting lark and just have her all to myself. So there isn't much time for me to fit into your lovely new suit, I'm afraid.'

'But that's wonderful,' I said, unable to stop the tear that now rolled down my cheek. 'Congratulations, Jenny.'

She opened her arms and I walked into her embrace. When we parted, there was a brightness in her eyes too.

'Now then,' she said, 'come on, let's try it on and then we can go and tell everyone else.'

We must have stayed until about midnight, getting to know Bob and his friends, discussing how the nursery should look. Somehow, in those few hours, I managed to forget about Toby and everything else, to just enjoy the company, the infectiousness of Jenny's good news. Until Jackie started yawning and asked if someone could call her a taxi.

'Come on, ducks,' said Lenny to me. 'I'll walk you home.'

Nobody had mentioned Toby's absence beyond Jenny's initial enquiry. I wondered if they were all feeling sorry for me, had an irrational sensation that they knew something more than I did. I tried to shake it off as we walked back down the meandering curve of Elgin Crescent, across the Portobello past Henekeys, where a new group of art students were all enjoying the decadent nights I had once known in there. Turned down Ledbury and then Talbot Road, past the Globe nightclub and up Powis Terrace to my front door.

I looked up at the house. There were no lights on.

Lenny looked at me worriedly. 'Do you think everything's OK?' he said. 'Do you want me to come in with you?'

The sense of dread that had been bearing down on me since we left Jenny's now felt like a lead weight in my heart. I nodded mutely, my hands shaking as I tried to fit my keys into the front door.

'Here,' said Lenny, 'let me.'

He squeezed my hand before he opened the door and I thought about him and James, how he had been made to feel this way too. His warmth gave me a tiny bit of courage.

We walked into the hallway together, turned on the light.

Toby's luggage was still where he had left it.

I put my head through the sitting-room door. He had obviously managed to rouse himself from the sofa. Remains of a meal, the carcass of a roast chicken and half a loaf of bread left out on the kitchen table suggested that he had managed to feed himself as well. An empty wine bottle there too, I couldn't help but notice.

'He must have just gone to bed,' I said. 'He didn't even make it that far when he got in this morning.'

Lenny shook his head. 'Do you want me to check? I'm not leaving you here on your own if he's being a bastard.' There was a vehemence to his voice I had never heard before. Jackie must have said something to him, I thought, although I had told her little enough. But after tonight it seemed pointless to pretend that there wasn't a problem, Toby's very absence had made that public, after all.

'It's OK,' I said. 'I'll do it. I don't want you to have to see what state he might be in.'

'All right,' said Lenny. 'But I'm staying here, just in case.'

Every step up those stairs my feet seemed to get heavier and heavier and even as my hand rested on the bedroom doorknob I knew that I shouldn't go in there, I knew I wouldn't like what I would see. But something inside me that was stronger than my fear made me open the door anyway.

A shaft of silvery moonlight through the curtains, which hadn't been drawn, illuminated the scene, although at first it was hard to make sense of the tangle of limbs and hair lying in the mess of my marital bed. But once I had managed to decode what I was actually seeing, I was still somehow able to close the door without waking them up, to walk back down the stairs like a zombie to where Lenny was standing in the frame of the kitchen door.

'He's in bed all right,' I told him, 'with your old friend Pat.'

31

Not Fade Away

A little old man blinking in a barrage of flashbulbs. 'I've been a bit silly really,' Ronald McSweeney was telling the man from the BBC, 'and I can only say that I'm grateful that the judge took the same view, that there was no evidence against me, and dismissed the case today.'

Standing on the steps of the Chiswick courthouse, he looked like a man freshly woken from a dream and gave a nervous laugh as the assembled pressmen continued to fire their questions at him.

'I've always wanted a quiet life, and that's what I intend from now on. To leave London and go up to the North, somewhere a bit more peaceful.'

'I'll help you move,' said Dick, throwing a scrunched-up paper ball at the TV screen. 'With my size tens up your jacksie, you silly old sod.'

Pete stared at the screen, wondering for the millionth time what made McSweeney do it. There was still no answer, but he couldn't shake the feeling he had missed something about this sad, shabby little man, the same thing as he had missed with Ernie.

Who's worse than being arrested?

He got to his feet, shift over and eager to get back home. 'Aye,' he said. 'He'd best get himself as far away from here as possible, if he knows what's good for him.'

The assembled detectives continued to throw paper darts and balls towards the cathode news conveyor, along with choice expletives. Two months, eight thousand interviews and four thousand statements since Mathilde Bressant's body had been found, the final elimination of McSweeney from the Stripper inquiry was no cause for them to celebrate.

For a while, Bressant's corpse had offered some hope of a breakthrough, for she had not been clean like the rest of them. She was covered, from head to foot, with metallic paint spray. Black and orange, black and yellow, black and green and more black. In the two days that the coroner estimated that she had lain out of view between her death and her discovery, she must have been close to a point where primary and secondary colours, priming, undercoating and finished paintwork were performed by spray. In other words, a garage.

At last they had a location – if they could find the paint shop where these colours had been used, they could find the murderer. But how many little one-man operations were there in London? And how many amateur enthusiasts who liked to tinker around with motors? Two months, eight thousand interviews and four thousand statements later, they still hadn't found a colour match in any of the places they had been. It had only served to make their search seem even more impossible.

The senior crime reporter from the *News of the World* had been moved to help try and flush out the killer by penning him an open letter in a front-page splash that went on for three pages, conjuring a Dickensian vista of London's lowlife, 'the sprawling, teeming, vice-ridden jungle' that stretched from Shaftesbury Avenue to Queensway. He taunted the killer for always picking little women, none of them over five foot three. But he hadn't known the detail that disturbed Pete the most about Bressant's body. Four of her front teeth had been broken, one of them wedged halfway down her throat. The coroner couldn't work out how the killer had done it – there were no other marks of violence.

The streetwalkers themselves were now running a sweepstake, from the bar of the Warwick Castle on Portobello Road, on which one of them would be next. Trying to laugh at the shadow of death that stalked their tapping feet. Every one offered the same theory. The killer was local, a man who knew them all, knew who was friends with whom. That he was working off a long-held grudge, playing peek-a-boo with their lives.

In between all the madness though, there had been joy. Joan had given birth to a perfect little boy, Pete's most fervent prayer answered. They had christened him James Edward, after Pete's dad, but most of the time they called him Little Jim. It was him Pete was thinking of as he stepped towards the door. He wanted to be able to spend a few hours with the lad before he had to go back out. For the searches he and Coulter had been making on tangential matters had finally begun to bear fruit.

Buried beneath the mountain of official Prostitute Murders paperwork, they had finally found the files on Algernon Ferrier and George Steadman – and what interesting reading they made. The latter was in Wormwood Scrubs, where he had been languishing since being nicked the night of 19 June 1959. The former was just about to gain his release from HMP Strangeways, a three-year stretch for living off immoral earnings. Coulter had predicted where Ferrier would go to celebrate his first night of freedom.

They moved through the smoke and the hot bodies pressed together under coloured light bulbs, stooping their heads in a little basement room, the air charged with perfume and sex and the sound of a wild trumpet coming from the tiny stage at the back, where a tall Negro, his skin slick with sweat, was blowing out his soul.

The Blue Parrot Club.

Coulter stopped, inclined his head to the right. Pete followed the motion to a booth by the side of the makeshift rostrum, another tall, handsome coloured man, in a powder blue, one-button suit, canary yellow shirt open at the neck and a snap brim hat tilted on the back of his head. Flash of gold tooth and white arm, a skinny little vixen in a red cocktail dress wrapped around his shoulders, sticking her tongue into his ear. His hand moving up her thigh as they closed in towards them, rocking together as the drummer powered the tune into delirium.

'Good evening, Algernon.' Coulter's voice breaking the spell. 'Thought I'd find you here. And if it isn't little Minnie Brown, too. Does your ma know you're out, Minnie? On a school night too…'

As if an electric current had passed between them, the couple snapped out of their embrace. Little Minnie's eyes flashed up at the detective standing over her, her mouth dropped open into a perfect 'O', and faster than a fish could shimmy, she was off her boyfriend's lap and out towards the door.

The Negro made a grab for the bottle of rum wobbling on the table in her wake. Looked up, outrage in his eyes like the sudden flare of a match, cooling just as quickly as Coulter got there first, fist closing around the neck.

'A little word in your shell-like, Ferrier,' he said.

He sat in the interview room with his legs splayed and head down, alternately dragging from his cigarette or spitting on the floor.

'Well, will you get a load of Mr Cool.' Coulter sat down opposite him. 'Gets caught breaking his parole within five minutes of coming home and he's not even sweating. Life's been dull without you, Algernon.'

Ferrier's top lip curled upwards into a sneer.

'Ya gonna charge me with that?' he said and spat on the floor again. 'Or we just be talkin' bullshit all night?'

'That depends,' said Coulter, nodding at the folder tucked under Pete's arm, 'on how good your memory is.'

'This should take you back.' Pete put the print of Fitzgerald, Clarke and Steadman down in front of him.

Ferrier ignored it, started whistling between his teeth.

'See, what I've been longing to ask you,' said Coulter, 'is what George Steadman was doing out with your woman. That why they call him "Lucky", is it?'

'What you talking about?' Ferrier eyeballed the picture, an expression of shock that he quickly tried to disguise.

'Well, if you cast your mind back, Algernon, it was not long after this photograph was taken that your old lady was found dead by the side of the river in Chiswick,' Coulter said. 'The first of the Jack the Stripper murders, they're saying now.'

'And if you'll notice,' Pete added, 'the dress she's wearing. It's the same one she was in when she was found. What we've been asking ourselves is, could this have been taken on the same night?'

'Were you present when this photograph was taken?' asked Coulter.

Ferrier narrowed his eyes, dragged hard on his cigarette and exhaled in Coulter's face.

'I don't know nuttin' about it,' he said. 'I ain't never seen it before in my life. What you tryin' to frame me for here?'

'Well it's like this,' said Coulter. 'As my colleague just pointed out, the photograph has only recently come to light as a result of our investigations into the so-called Stripper murders. And while the gentlemen of the press may be keen to make out that these murders are the work of just one man, it's not something we can take for granted, is it? I would say that this picture,' Coulter leaned forwards and tapped his finger on the print, 'might suggest a motive for Miss Clarke's murder that has not been considered before. Like here she is, only hours away from her date with death, out on the town with her boyfriend's best pal. People might reasonably ask, where is her old man? Why wasn't he out with them at Teddy Hills's club in the West End, rubbing shoulders with television star Simon Fitzgerald...'

'God rest his soul,' put in Pete, sitting back on his chair, watching Ferrier's body language subtly change.

'God rest his soul indeed,' nodded Coulter. 'There's a lot of death in this picture, don't you think, Algernon? A lot that isn't explained. So, for instance, as I was postulating earlier, if you were present when the photograph was taken, if it was all friends together, there wouldn't be a jealousy motive, would there?'

Ferrier was trying very hard to keep up his macho front, but he had begun sweating as Coulter had been talking, had taken off his hat and begun rubbing his hands through his hair, stopped his spitting on the floor.

'Jealous?' he said and tried to laugh, tried to look incredulous, but a vein started pumping above his left eye. 'I ain't jealous of shit. That dress? I bought that for her myself, cost me a whole week's bread. I looked after that girl. She didn't have no complaints.'

'So,' said Pete, lighting himself a Player's and offering one to Coulter, deliberately not extending the courtesy to Ferrier. 'You buy her a fancy frock, spend all that money on her, and this is what she does to you.' He caught Ferrier's gaze. 'A night on the tiles with George, eh?' Pete shook his head. 'Not the sort of night she was getting round here with you, was it? She was wearing your dress and yet it was George who was showing her a good time.'

Ferrier blinked first. Dropped his gaze and shook his head.

'No, man,' he started to say.

'Then you found out about it, didn't you?' Pete went on. 'Found out about it and didn't like it. A few hours later, your jealous rage is spent and poor old Bobby's lying dead, that dress you bought for her ripped to bloody pieces. See, I know it is the same dress,' Pete bored into Ferrier with his eyes, shifted his weight forwards as he did, 'because I was the one that found her.'

'No, man.' Ferrier leaned backwards, raised up his palms. 'You bluffin' me. You know I didn't do it.' He looked across at Coulter. 'I had an alibi, man, I proved it at the time.'

'We didn't have this photo then,' said Coulter. 'And not to put too fine a point on it, we know that the coloured community do their best not to co-operate with the police, cooking up alibis for each other when it suits. So I went back over all the notes we had here that pertained to yours.' Coulter pulled out his notebook and flicked it open. 'You were at The Blue Parrot club on Westbourne Park Road, same as you were tonight. Interesting that.' Coulter nodded over to Pete, who, on cue, took out his own notebook.

'Meanwhile,' he said, 'I did some checking up on old Lucky George. Seems he got arrested in Shepherd's Bush only two nights after Miss Clarke's murder, trying to break into a chemist's. Claimed that he was doing it out of desperation since he couldn't afford the drugs he'd been prescribed for injuries recently sustained in a fight. A pretty professional going over he'd had, as well; they've got it all recorded. The doctor reckoned it must have been someone who really knew how to hurt. A boxer, for instance.'

Pete sat back himself now and watched it all go through Ferrier's mind, watched his face twitch and his eyes flicker as he pictured how this would look in court, how neatly it would fit together in the minds of the undoubtedly all-white jury. The coloured man put his head in his hands.

'It doesn't look good, does it Algernon?' said Coulter. 'Now, we've spoken to George and he doesn't want to be dragged back through all of this mess either. So in order to help himself stay out of trouble, he admitted that you beat him up over the girl. On the same night she was murdered.'

'What?' Ferrier's head came up, his eyes shining with outrage. 'Oh no, man, he can't have done. He can't have done that to me.'

'Got it all typed up neatly,' Coulter said. 'He'll appear in court if he has to. See, we've been putting in a lot of extra hours on this one, but I think it's all been worth it.'

Ferrier slammed his fist down on the desk. 'That Judas!' he said, his voice descending an octave. 'He lyin'.' He looked at Coulter. 'Lyin' to save his own sorry arse. You know why he in the can now? He in there 'cos he wanna be, 'cos he too scared to be out inna world on his own, the lyin', thievin', yellow-bellied motherfucker.'

'He is that, aye,' said Coulter. 'But why, Algernon? Why did you beat him up and why did he feel the need to get away so urgently? If he wasn't running from you, then who?'

Ferrier started to say something and then shook his head, stamped his foot. Fear was rising off him like steam, coursing through the room, pumping behind his dilated pupils. He was trapped and he knew it, between the devil of grassing his old mate up or the deep blue sea of a trial for Bobby Clarke's murder.

'He tricked her out,' he eventually mumbled.

'I beg your pardon?' Coulter said. 'Can't quite hear you, Algernon.'

'Bobby,' said Ferrier, eyes level with Coulter's now, the whites all yellow and bloodshot, the pupils black as midnight. 'George tricked her out that night. He was supposed to be meeting her when she came off work to take her home, but instead, he told some fellas he be drinking with they could take her to a party. Took twenty-five pounds off them for the privilege.'

He scowled, still sore at the memory of that lost fortune. Feeling it worse than the loss of Bobby. Icy prickles ran up and down Pete's spine.

'Twenty-five quid?' he said. 'Who could afford to give him that kind of money?'

Ferrier slowly lifted the index finger of his right hand, his punching hand, stabbed it down on the photograph.

Pete and Coulter exchanged glances. 'Let me get this straight,' said Coulter. 'Are you telling me that George sold her to the man in this picture here? To Simon Fitzgerald?'

Ferrier leaned towards them, his voice a hiss. 'Why'n't you ask him? See wha' the big man has to say about it now?'

'All right, Algernon.' Coulter got to his feet, scraping his chair back loudly. 'You're nicked.'

'Wha'?' Ferrier was incredulous. 'But I jus' helped you out, man…'

'No you didn't.' Coulter loomed over him, his face a thundercloud dripping icy words like rain. 'You just made a highly fanciful accusation about a man who can't defend himself in order to try and get yourself off the hook. You're a liar and a ponce, Ferrier, and I don't want you back on the streets turning some silly little schoolgirl into your next Roberta Clarke. Women aren't safe around you and I intend to keep you as far away from them as I possibly can. So I'm arresting you for importuning a minor. That should keep you where I want you until we prepare this case for trial.'

32

Where Did Our Love Go?

'There's someone here to see you.' Jackie put her head round the door of her spare bedroom, where I had been sleeping for the last week. 'He says he wants to explain himself. D'you want me to tell him to sling his hook?'

'Toby?' I stared at her with eyes swollen by seven nights of tears and insomnia.

She nodded, her own eyes glittering with rage.

'No,' I said, picking myself up off the bed where I had been languishing in a spare pair of her pyjamas and an old tartan dressing gown. I knew I looked awful and I wanted him to see it, see what he'd done. 'It's about time. I want to hear what he's got to say.'

'All right,' Jackie said and bit her lip. She was leaning across the doorframe like a shield. 'Shall I show him into the kitchen then?'

'If you don't mind.' I brushed a strand of hair out of my eyes. 'And Jackie,' I said as she made to move away, 'is it OK if I do this alone? I'm sorry that it has to be here.'

She grimaced. 'No, no,' she said. ''S'all right. I'll make myself scarce, pop over the club for a game of pool. But I'll not be long. And you just ring Gina if you need me, the number's on a card by the phone.'

If my own appearance was that of an emaciated scarecrow, Toby's was worse. When I walked into the kitchen he was staring out of the window, over the rooftops of Chelsea. My heart moved painfully in my chest as he turned around, blond hair flopping over red-rimmed eyes, hollow cheeks and skin the colour of ash. So far away from the first time I had seen him, caught in a shaft of sunlight in the life-drawing room at the Royal, so full of determination and purpose, glittering like a god. Now he looked more an itinerant, an old school blazer over an ancient striped shirt and jeans only held together by the paint stains, the expression on his face so acute in its misery that I actually felt sorry for him.

'Stella,' he whispered, a tear dropping off from the edge of his long lashes. 'I'm so, so sorry. I never meant for any of this to happen...' His face crumpled and he began to shake, holding out his arms imploringly. What could I do but walk back into them?

It took a while for both of us to stop. But in the end, I couldn't bear his embrace any more.

'Let's have a cup of tea,' I said. 'Try and talk about it.'

He nodded, wiped his eyes with the heels of his hands, sat down unsteadily on one of Jackie's chairs, which was too small to properly accommodate his lanky frame.

I gathered my thoughts about me as I went through the ritual of lighting the gas, warming the pot, scattering the tealeaves. Thinking of Sunday teatimes back in Bloxwich, Ma reading futures in the bottom of the cups, Pa sat by the fire with his pipe and a paper, the ticking of the clock and the purring of the black and white cat at his feet, those last few bittersweet hours together before Monday morning.

I put a cup down in front of him, took my own across to the chair opposite. It wasn't a very big kitchen, with only a little fold-down table that could fit into the space. But somehow, Jackie and I had managed to spend most of our time here rather than any other room, just as I had spent so many lonely hours at Powis Terrace only feeling comfortable in the kitchen.

Toby took a tentative sip and put his cup down on the table in front of him. His gaze roamed across the room and out of the window, anywhere but meeting mine.

'How long,' I asked, 'has it been going on?'

He winced, his mouth twisting up and down.

'I tried so hard not to,' he said. 'I tried to fight it, really I did, you have to believe me, Stella. I didn't want to give in to it. I wanted to be true to you.' His eyes did flick up to mine then, and he gazed at me imploringly.

'How long, Toby?' The iciness in my voice startled me. That feeling I had had, walking home with Lenny, had actually proved to be correct. The reason he was so angry was because he already suspected something had been going on between Toby and Pat. He knew something about Toby's past that I didn't.

'Only since,' more tears streaked down his face, 'we were in the States. It all seemed different there, like it was just a dream that would fade away when I came back home. I was going to put it behind me, honestly I was. But when I got back and you were acting so strangely, I just couldn't handle it…'

'So you used that as an excuse,' I said, 'to reject me. I told you my deepest, darkest secrets and you just treated me like the madwoman in the attic so you could run to your boyfriend without feeling guilty.'

'No!' His voice rose up an octave. 'It wasn't like that, Stella. I just didn't know what to do, it all seemed so…'

I waved my hand. 'Don't bother,' I said. 'I was always afraid that you wouldn't understand, that's why I never told you anything about it before. Even though I felt so guilty that I had kept a secret from you. Hilarious, isn't it, you were keeping your own from me long enough.'

'Stella.' He reached his hand across the table, tried to take hold of mine, but I pulled it away. 'Please, you've got to believe me. I did, I mean I do, still really love you. You were everything to me, encouraging me, standing by me when we had no money, always keeping everything together, the house looking nice, food on the table for all our friends. And you work so hard yourself, you're so talented, I was so proud of you.'

Now it was me who couldn't look at him.

'Why did you marry me in the first place?' I said, my eyes fixed on the kettle and the steam drifting out of the spout.

'Because I loved you. You were the smartest, funniest, most beautiful girl I had ever met. I didn't even know there could be a girl like you. We were so close, weren't we, I felt almost like we could read each other's minds...'

'Ha.' I turned to face him. 'But I thought you didn't believe in things like that?'

My humiliation was making me cruel, making me want to hurt him.

He flinched, his voice dropping to a whisper. 'I didn't ever say that, Stella.'

'So,' I went on, holding on to the rage so I wouldn't break down, needing to know every painful detail. 'You thought that if you married me, you could stop being homosexual?'

'What?' He looked shocked.

'Lenny told me,' I said, 'about the heart-to-heart you once had with him about the boy who was in bed with your mother. The real reason why you left home, and, I suppose, were so eager to start the *straight* life. I always did wonder how I could have been so lucky, that you would propose to me just like that, just when I needed it. It was because you were still trying to get over him, wasn't it?'

Toby shook his head. 'No,' he said, 'no it wasn't. That was nothing but a stupid schoolboy thing, I had grown out of it a long time before I met you. I never wanted to end up like this, you know. Like my bloody father.' His voice broke and he began to sob.

'Oh,' I said, the full realisation of everything he must have gone through seeping through my consciousness and along with it another wave of pain, of love ruined and hopes dashed. 'So that was it.'

The anger all crumbled into ash, into pity for the man who was still my husband, sitting there crying, his whole life in tatters over something he could no more control than I could cut out my communications with the dead.

'The funny thing is,' I reached my hand across to him, 'Lenny believed that you'd put it behind you too. He thought you really loved me, that's why he was so angry when he started to hear rumours about you.'

'What does it matter now?' Toby gripped my hand tight. 'I'm a bastard and I've ruined everything, just like my father ruined my mother's life. That's why I was so scared, you see, Stella, that night you had the nightmare, or whatever it was. I thought you were turning into a secret alcoholic like Pearl did, and I knew that it was all my fault.'

'That's funny,' I said. 'I thought it was you turning into one.'

'I have been, I admit it,' he said. 'Trying to block it all out. And even in the end I took the coward's way out, letting you find me like that instead of just coming clean.'

'Well,' I said. 'What do we do now?'

'You must come back to the house,' he said. 'I'll move out, I'll find somewhere else.'

'No,' I said, 'I don't think that's right. You need that space to paint in…'

'God, never mind about that,' Toby said. 'It's your home.'

I looked at him, horrified at the thought of it. My home was a haunted house.

'I'm sorry but no,' I said. 'I can't go back there.'

He shut his eyes, his own moment of realisation dawning.

'Of course you can't,' he said, letting go of my hand. 'Oh God, Stella, what a mess.'

I couldn't think of anything else to say. We sat listening to the clock ticking, the sounds of traffic drifting up from outside. Sunday evening coming down.

'Well,' he finally said, 'I suppose you'll be wanting a divorce?'

'I don't know,' I said, his words bringing fresh tears at the thought of the finality of it all. 'I hadn't thought about it.'

'I wouldn't contest it,' he said. 'Only if you were to bring a charge of adultery…If you were to say what happened…If you talked to the press…It would ruin me Stella, I could go to jail, you wouldn't do that to me would you?'

Only now did he start to sound like a child and it turned my blood to ice. Was that the real reason for the grey face, the tears, the offer of the house? Was it all out of self-pity, that he was terrified of the power I could have to destroy his life completely? And did he really think I could do that to him, no matter what he had done to me?

'No I wouldn't,' I said, 'and the fact that you even think that I would just goes to show, for all your fancy words about love, you never really knew me at all. I think you'd better go now, Toby.'

'But Stella, I didn't mean…'

'Just go.' I stood up, cutting him off. 'I'm not going to get you arrested if that's all you're worried about. You can divorce me for desertion, you can do what the bloody hell you want, just leave me alone.'

He tried to say one more thing, as he stood at the door to Jackie's flat, but I had heard enough. I shut the door in his face.

Jackie let me stay at hers until I found a flat I could afford to rent. Lenny helped me pack up and move. He talked to Toby, made sure the house would be empty while we did it. 'You did me a mitzvah,' he told me, 'now I'm doing one for you.'

My new lodgings were in Sutherland Place, a quiet road of tall stucco houses and beautiful linden trees, in a mainly Irish enclave that had formed around the St Mary of the Angels church at the top of the road. The landlord rented to art students, he was pretty tolerant and didn't charge much, which was just as well, as I was determined not to take a penny from Toby. We were making enough money from the shop not to have to slum it completely, although it was back to one big room with a kitchenette, the electric on a meter and a tiny bathroom. But my room faced west, with a huge window letting in plenty of light, and somehow the feeling of the place was perfect, far from the oppressive darkness I had come to associate with Powis Terrace. I felt sure I wouldn't be scared to be alone here.

Once we had unloaded, Lenny went to take the van back and go and bring us supper. I felt a sense of calm I hadn't known for a long time as I slowly unpacked, putting out the kitchen things first so that we could eat in relative comfort, making a space on the little, round Formica-topped table. It was a funny thing, I realised – despite all that had happened in Ladbroke Grove, the idea of moving out of the area completely had never crossed my mind. It was still the only place that had ever felt like home.

Here I was determined to make a fresh start.

Lenny came back with some packages, fish and chips and a bottle of ice-cold white wine. It was the second week of July, another warm day hazing into a golden sunset. We opened the big sash window and positioned our chairs so that we could look out across the rooftops and the trees. We were only five streets east of Powis Terrace, but it was a completely different world.

'Mazel tov,' said Lenny, raising his glass. 'To your new home. I have to say, you've been very brave about all of this. I'm proud of you, girl.'

'Mmm,' I said, the hot, salty chips tasting like the best food in the world. 'Well, that's because of you and Jackie. It would have been a lot harder if I didn't have you.'

'I don't know about that,' he said. 'I can't help thinking that I let you down. I should have warned you about that Pat – once I got to really know him, I realised he was bad news. All that glitter, but underneath…' He shook his head. 'It won't come to a good end, you mark my words.'

'What do you mean?' I said.

'You wouldn't want to know some of the people he's mixed up with,' Lenny said. 'Pat likes his highlife high and his lowlife low, believe me. He's in with some right East End rough and they all love him 'cos he's a minor aristocrat. He's like the devil himself, Pat Innes, he turned your Toby's head.'

'Do you really believe,' I asked again, 'that he wasn't just pretending all the time?'

'I do, dear.' Lenny nodded gravely. 'I mean, look, he was surrounded by omis in the art world. All those old queens like Bernard Baring throwing themselves at him the whole time. But he never so much as batted an eyelid. I would tell you if he did.'

'Baring,' I said, narrowing my eyes, wondering if Stanley had paid him a visit yet. It had startled me to see his face pass through the memory of Margaret Rose Stephenson and her last game of cards, but not entirely surprised me. I only wished I knew the man he was playing cards with, the one she managed to rob. But at least it had given Stanley something to go on.

'Frightful old cow,' said Lenny, leaning over to refill my glass. 'No, let's not talk about them any more. Let's just think about the good things – like them suits flying off the rails, the cover of *Vogue*, like Jenny and her baby and your new home. Let the devil take the rest of them.'

I clinked my glass against the side of his. 'Mazel tov,' I said.

33

The In-Crowd

'Right, well,' said Coulter, coat on and a sheaf of paperwork tucked under his arm. 'That was a good night's work. Very satisfying to finally put at least one villain in his place. See you at the Magistrates' in the morning.'

Leaning against his locker, Pete smiled. He had been more than impressed by how Coulter had turned the tables on Ferrier and all his reasons for doing so. They were both looking forward to paying George Steadman another visit at the Scrubs the next day.

'It certainly was,' he said. 'Good night, Stanley.'

He opened his locker and frowned. There was something in there that hadn't been when he had left the station earlier this evening. A thick, brown envelope.

He picked it up. It was addressed to *Detective Sergeant P Bradley*, with the street and number of the police station below and above, underlined, *By Hand*. The handwriting was all in neat capitals, rendered in black ink.

'Stan?' he said, but Coulter had already gone.

The envelope was bulky but light, a layer of tape securing it shut. As he weighed it up in his palm, Pete had an ominous feeling. Maybe it was better not to open it here. Maybe if he did, he wouldn't make it back home at all.

They had scores of tip-off letters each week, it was probably another nutter or nosy neighbour, he told himself as he walked back down Ladbroke Grove. But even as he thought it, he knew there was something different about this. The elderly, vengeful and insane residents of this parish didn't tend to write *By Hand* on their envelopes. That was the mark of someone a bit higher up the social scale.

Joan was already asleep by the time he got home, her arm around the dog, which lay protectively by her side across their bed. He looked in on Jim, sucking his thumb as he lay in his cot, so tiny and peaceful in his innocence it made Pete's heart contract. He knew that if Joan had given birth to a girl he would have loved her all the same. But the reason he had been lighting so many candles in St Mary's while she was pregnant was to pray that they wouldn't have to bear any of the things that could happen to a little girl in this world.

He dropped a gentle kiss on Jim's forehead, walked into his study. Took out some gloves, a scalpel and an evidence bag from his briefcase. Slid the blade under the tape and opened the package up, tipped it upside down.

A small bundle and a note fell out on to the table. A key, wrapped up in tissue paper, again neatly fastened with tape. And a blank postcard, with the words: *Locker 272 Paddington Station* typed on to it.

'You were on duty, but you never saw anyone hand this in?' Pete dropped his cigarette and stamped it out before it burnt his fingers; he had smoked it almost down to the quick. Bert Dugdale, the last man on front desk the night before, shifted uneasily from one foot to the other, his face the same shade as the contents of an ashtray.

'I must have just nipped to the Gents for a moment, or turned my back to look for something,' he said. 'And when I came back it was just there. Never saw a dickie bird. Sorry Sarge, but you know what it's like…'

'Maybe it was a magician and he disappeared in a puff of smoke,' said Pete. 'Like that fag you were smoking out here. Like you'd better do right now, in fact.'

'Yes sir.' Dugdale retreated.

Pete turned his mind back to the contents of locker 272, hidden inside a brown envelope, exactly the same sort of envelope that the key had come in.

The rest of the photographs from the session that had produced the shot of Bobby Clarke, Lucky George and not-so-fortunate Simon. That particular one was missing and there were no more featuring Bobby and George, but Fitzgerald's outfit, hairstyle and the backdrop of Teddy Hills's club were exactly the same. In the frames, a lot of people he didn't know, a handful he wished he'd never known and a couple of faces he hadn't seen for a very long time. Not since the days when he studied *Tatler & Bystander* each week, in fact.

At various tables, all grinning for the camera, were Harold Wesker, Francis Bream and Big Tits Beryl. Bronwyn Evans and Sampson Marks. Simon and Teddy himself, of course, but more surprising than any of them, the handsome face and Dean Martin hairstyle of the man whose firm was currently erecting the enormous flyover, splitting West London in two with a million tons of concrete. Sir Alex Minton beamed out from behind a magnum of champagne. To his right, looking slightly befuddled, was Lord Douglas Somerset, the man that Gypsy George had been in the process of robbing just a few months after these photos had been taken.

All of them in the same room on the same night.

The night that Bobby Clarke was murdered.

When he studied the pictures a second time, he began to notice more familiar faces from his time at West End Central. Sidney Hillman, the mechanic from Shaftesbury Avenue that Wesker had been so keen to arrest and make for the Togneri racket gang. Nobby Clarke and Iain Woods, the felons with a bomb hidden in their car. Horace Golding, the shopkeeper with the stolen lighters; Wally Green, the deaf-and-dumb man who'd menaced the doorman at the Establishment with his sign language; and Kingsley Puttnam, the cricketer he'd last seen spitting out blood in the cells on the day of the Greek riot. All the people that Wesker had systematically fitted up – was it all in order to shut them up?

No one else at the station knew the connections between all these people. No one in the entire force, but for a senior police officer, now a leading light in the ongoing prostitute murder investigation, now Detective Chief Inspector Bell of the Yard, could possibly realise the significance they would have for Pete. Was it he who had left the envelope? Was it Bell who was saying to him, be an honourable Coldstreamer and join these dots together for me? Who else could know what these photographs were prompting him to ask:

Which one of you is the Stripper?

If it was Bell who had left the envelope, then that would explain how it had magicked its way into his locker without anybody noticing. But it also meant that Pete couldn't tell anyone else what he knew. Not Dick, not Coulter, and especially not Joan. He had gone to Paddington Station on the way back from the Magistrates', where the judge had agreed with Coulter's summation of the case against Ferrier and sent Bobby's old beau to Brixton on remand.

Pete told Coulter he needed to meet with a snout in the pool hall near the train station and would see him back at CID in an hour, en route to their second visit to Steadman. Snouts was always a good one to use with the older man, he was so deathly silent about his own.

On the concourse of Paddington Pete had gone into a cubicle in the Gents to look through the contents of locker 272, the cold chills worsening as print followed print and face followed face.

He wandered back out on to the concourse reeling like a drunkard, like he'd taken a powerful left hook to the temple. Sat himself down on a 15 bus going back to the Grove, at the front, near the wing mirror so he could look behind and see if a black Rover happened to be following him. Got off at Notting Hill and walked the backstreets to the station, expecting to hear the sound of a powerful car gliding up beside him any minute. Stopped on the steps and looked behind him. Ladbroke Road empty, save for a young mother pushing her pram, a Jack Russell terrier following at her heels.

There were no more messages waiting for him inside. In an attempt to calm his nerves, he had gone through yesterday's rosters while he waited for Coulter, found that Dugdale had been on duty when the envelope must have arrived. But now he was still none the wiser.

The questions kept coming, breaking over each other like waves in his mind. Why had Ernie held the Bobby Clarke shot back for himself? He must have realised its significance, so what kind of scam was he playing? Blackmail? Or perhaps some kind of life insurance?

Did the people Ernie had taken these shots for – Marks or Hills he presumed, but maybe even Wesker himself – realise that shot was missing? That it had even been taken?

Pete looked at his watch. Ten thirty. It was time to go back through the door and up the steps to CID and Coulter. To lock the envelope in his desk, put the key in his pocket and try to keep his face open, his smile even, as he struggled to find a way out of the maze in his mind.

34

The House of the Rising Sun

I stood on the cobbles of Vernon Yard, looking up at the shuttered windows. It was seven o'clock on a Saturday evening, the first time I had attempted to get back in touch with Dave since the implosion of my marriage, the first time I had really felt up to it. A clattering of feet on stairs and the grind of a succession of locks being rolled back suggested that this time I had been lucky, dropping by on the off-chance.

But it was Chris, not Dave, who opened the door.

'Stella,' he said, 'this is an unexpected surprise.' His eyebrows rose, but his smile said that it wasn't an unpleasant intrusion.

'Hello Chris,' I said, more pleased to see him than I had anticipated. Or maybe it was just the relief of finding that there was still life in Vernon Yard after all. 'Do you mind if I come in for a minute?'

'Please, do come up,' he said. 'I've just made a pot of tea.'

I followed him up the stairs to the ramshackle kitchen, took in the same enormous wooden table with its assortment of ill-matching chairs, Welsh dresser sagging under the collection of strange carvings and curios, and walls plastered with artwork from floor to ceiling. Only now there were some startling new additions to the range.

Posters of Dave wearing his top hat and pulling a mad face,

printed on white, yellow, red and lime-green backgrounds, with the slogans VOTE LUNATIC; LUNATIC FRINGE PARTY and VOTE DIABLO: BETTER A LOON THAN A CROOK in bold typeface surrounding his gurning visage.

'What are all these?' I said.

Chris laughed. 'Were you not aware of David's political activities?' He reached a couple of Cornishware mugs down from the dresser. 'He will be disappointed. He's trying to get himself elected to Parliament, would you believe? He stood for Profumo's seat in Stratford last year – that's what those BETTER A LOON THAN A CROOK posters are all about. And these,' he gently booted a stack of cardboard boxes by the side of the dresser, 'are all full of leaflets for the General Election. He's hoping to do a bit better this time, so he's releasing a single too. He's going on the radio tonight, to talk about it all.'

'My word,' I said, wondering how these things could have passed me by. All the years that I was so desperate for us to get rid of the Tories and now we were on the verge of booting them out, I had been so wrapped up in my problems, I had hardly even noticed. 'Which station is he on?'

'His own,' said Chris, turning to fish out a bottle of milk from under the sink, 'he's got a friend with a boat and a bit of local knowledge, they managed to get a pirate signal going from an old Napoleonic fort in Kent. He won't actually tell me where it is, he's sworn to secrecy about that, but it works, they've done test transmissions before.'

I felt my knees weakening as I sank down in the nearest chair. Could this be the connection that Mya was talking about? Did she know that Dave had been messing about with radio too? I struggled to make sense of it as my eyes ran up and down the walls.

Chris went chatting on about Dave's accomplishments as he poured out the tea. Only when he set a mug down in front of me did I notice the pile of folders on the table, the opened notepad that he must have been writing in before I'd interrupted him.

'Chris,' I said, 'am I stopping you from working?'

'Not at all,' he closed the pad and pushed it and his files to one side, 'I was just going back over some details, just in case I missed something. I find it gets increasingly hard to stop myself from doing that, especially when David's not here to distract me. You've saved me from myself, that's all, no need to look so worried.'

'You sure?' I said.

'Positive,' he said, but his expression changed as he watched me. 'How's life been treating you then, Stella, it's been a long time since our paths last crossed?'

'Where to start?' I said, lifting my tea. There was something reassuringly sturdy about his choice of blue-and-white striped mug, just like the solid unpretentiousness of Chris himself. For a moment I felt like spilling the beans about everything.

'That was a funny time, last time I saw you,' I said instead. 'Jenny and the riot. Still, I suppose it helped in your case against that crooked policeman.'

'It could have done,' he said, 'if the police hadn't put their wagons in a circle around him, carted him straight off to the loony bin so he never had to face the charges.' He took a sip of his tea. 'It was a very strange situation with Jenny, though. I didn't feel entirely good about it. I mean, her friend Somerset definitely did need our help, and I'm glad that through that, we managed to get the proof of Wesker's crooked ways. All of that was well worth doing.'

He shook his head. 'It was just Jenny herself, the effect she had on David when she left him. I must confess, I never did understand their relationship very well, but he was devastated. Still is, which is what I think this,' he gestured to the posters on the wall, 'is really all about. Trying to get her attention back.'

'I know,' I said. 'I saw him at a party last year for Toby's summer show. He was with his band but he'd come specifically to try and find Jenny. Only she'd already moved to Italy. He was really agitated, told me lots of weird things about her family and how she wasn't safe. He'll probably be even worse now. She's just moved back to Ladbroke Grove with a film director husband and a baby on the way. Perhaps you can break it to him gently.'

'Ah.' Chris stared through the steam rising from his cup. 'I see. That *is* going to be difficult. And where is Toby this evening, by the way?' he said.

'I'm surprised you don't already know,' I said. 'But we've,' I struggled for the most tactful expression, 'separated. He was cheating on me.'

'Oh?' Chris put his cup down. 'I am sorry to hear that. Although maybe not surprised.'

'Really?' I said, startled by this information. 'How come?'

'The crowd that Toby started hanging around,' he said, 'were no good. Hastened my departure from the world of modern art and David's too, I think. Especially when they started stealing all our ideas, it made it a bit difficult for us to stay friends with him. I'm sorry, but I think Toby's head was turned by people who had no real love of art at all. Just of money.'

'That's so strange,' I said. 'They're the very words that Lenny used – that he'd had his head turned. Which people do you mean?'

'Bernard Baring was the worst,' said Chris. 'He copied David's circus trope, only he found a way of prettying up what we thought were radical ideas, made himself a small fortune out of it. There is a kind of art in that, I suppose, taking the threat out of it and just leaving the surface gloss. Toby was luckier because his ideas were more opaque, you could more or less read into it what you wanted. I mean, if you really looked at ours now, the things we did in '58, '59 probably seem very dated. Everything was specific to that time, to those months. Toby's work could come from any time, any place. That's why they adopted him, you know.' He smiled. 'They needed the credibility.'

For a moment I thought he was mocking me, but there was nothing malicious in his face, only something like sympathy, something like regret.

'What about Pat Innes?' I asked. 'What do you know about him?'

'Nothing at all good,' he said, with such a big grin that I started to laugh.

'That's better,' he said. 'Want another cup?' His eyes flicked up to the clock as he rose from his seat and collected the mugs. 'David should be coming on the radio any minute now.' He made his way to the windowsill where their wireless sat. 'He said he left it tuned into the right place...'

Chris flicked the switch and the machine crackled into life, Dave's voice filling the room with a clarity I had not expected. 'It's 7 o'clock and time to rock. Your dial is tuned to 197 longwave, Radio Diablo, don't touch that dial!' he announced, and it was all I could do to stop myself from looking around to see where he was hiding. For a second it really did feel like he and Chris were playing an elaborate joke.

'We're playing the hottest sounds from the underground,' Dave's disembodied voice went on, 'starting with a cat who really knows how to sing, rather than scream, which is what I do. Here's the genius Ray Charles and "What I'd Say"...'

As the sound of the record filled the room, we both began to laugh.

'He's rather good at it, isn't he?' Chris stared admiringly at the wireless. 'All that jive talk of his really comes into its own on the radio.'

We sat entranced as Dave continued to play a mix of resolutely American jazz, rock 'n' roll and R & B tunes, talking nineteen-to-the-dozen in between. It was only when he got near the end of the broadcast that I remembered why I had come here.

'And now,' Dave announced, 'time for a bit of self-promotion. As you may or may not know, I, Del Diablo, am standing for Parliament in the General Election on October the fifteenth, representing the Lunatic Fringe Party. A vote for me is a vote against the crooked cabal who have been running the country for their own personal gain these past unlucky thirteen years; and against shifty Harold Wilson, who promises you a New Britain but can only offer you more of the same old, a con-man dressed up as the common man. Only I can truly claim to represent you, the young, the working class, the hepcats who don't care to fit inside society's moral straitjacket. I am of sound mind and clean criminal record – so why do I call myself a Loon, I hear you cry? Well, my wide-eared friends, it's because compared to the villainous skulduggery we have had to put up with for so long, the policies of an honest man are bound to sound a little mad. You dig? So here's to an end to the class system, an end to sexual repression and the right to dance for all. With that in mind, here's the latest cut from my band of groovy ghouls, Del and the Diaboliks, a tribute to the outgoing Tories, if you like. It's called, "Bring Out Your Dead" and it's produced, as ever, by the Head Honcho of Holloway Road, my main man James Myers.'

There was a loud burst of revved-up engine, thundering tom-toms and a maniacal cackle as the song lurched through the airwaves. I tried to suppress the shivers, to make myself enjoy the mock-horror musical hall theatricality of it, Dave's ridiculous lyrics about zombies and the twanging, propulsive guitar, all wrapped up in James's trademark supernatural echo. Chris was clearly loving it, tapping his foot and a wooden spoon along to the beat on the table's edge, that big grin still on his face.

But I couldn't stop the feeling of dread seeping through me. The five faces peering through the window of my mind, the fingernails tapping on the pane. How could I face Dave, I wondered to myself, how could I talk to him about this? What was I supposed to say, how would I even begin?

'Stella?' Chris's voice seemed to be coming from down the end of a long tunnel. I looked up and it was as if the room had blurred and then slowly come back into focus. The broadcast had come to an end; there was nothing but static coming from the wireless.

'Sorry,' I said, trying to shake the feeling away, 'I must have just drifted off for a minute there.'

'Well that was some feat with that racket going on.' Chris turned the radio off.

I tried to laugh, but the fear was inside me now. I got to my feet in a rush.

'Well,' I said, 'I'd better be on my way now, I've taken up enough of your evening already.'

'Oh really?' he said. 'There's no need.' His brow furrowed. 'I was enjoying myself. I'm sorry if David's silly band put you off.'

'No, it's not that,' I lied, flustered now, imagining that his clear blue eyes were seeing straight into my mind. 'I was enjoying myself too, I just didn't realise time had flown so quickly, and there's something I should get back to...'

He put his hand on my arm. 'Well,' he said, 'then at least let me walk you home?'

'Oh, you don't have to do that,' I said, hearing the fear leaking through my voice.

'I'd feel better if I did,' he said. 'You never know who's out there these days.'

Chris didn't ask any questions as we walked home through the twilight, past the glowing lights and laughing punters spilling out of Finches and the Warwick Castle, the places where the girls plied their trade and a man in a long black car stalked their heels. He just linked his arm through mine and talked about everyday things, the latest books he'd read and films he'd seen, things that friends would talk about.

'Well,' he said, as we reached my doorstep, 'here we are, then.' He let go of my arm, put his hands back in the pockets of his jeans as I took the keys from my bag and opened the front door.

'Thanks Chris,' I said, 'that was really good of you.'

'It was nothing,' he said. 'I really enjoyed seeing you. You must drop by more often.'

I didn't want to say goodbye to him. I wanted to invite him in, to tell him everything that was weighing down my mind. But something else was upon me, a sick feeling in my blood I had come to recognise too well.

'I will,' I said, looking back at him in the lamplight. 'Give my love to Dave as well. We'll all have to get together soon.'

He nodded. 'Will do. Well then, cheerio.'

I shut the door, shut my eyes. It was coming, she was coming, the next one out there just beyond the door, out in Ladbroke Grove, tapping her heels towards her death, walking into Jack's embrace.

My steel-tipped white slingback sandals spark on the pavement as I head towards my front door. Another night's graft over, Wimpy burger and strawberry milkshake sloshing in my stomach from my meal with Wendy before, cold slime of lubricant leaking into my knickers from the bunk-up against the wall after. Ten bob note in my purse for the trouble, should see the wains all right for another few days.

I put my foot on the first step, look up to the flat, hear a voice say: 'Mavis!'

Turn and see him standing under the trees, under the trees where he knew me. Flare of a match as he lights a cigarette, illuminating a sheepskin coat and a trilby hat pulled down low, but not the face between. I know who it belongs to though; know it of old. Sexy Ron, procurer for the rich and famous, leaning against a long black car, the sort he always drives. Knows me by one of my many outlaw names.

'Got a job if you want it,' he says, smoke around his face like a wraith. 'Your speciality.' Gives a little chuckle, knows what Mavis is good at, better money than a drunken fuck round the back of the pub at closing time. 'Shouldn't take more than an hour.'

I look back up the steps at the orange glow from the window where Rita Hayworth's looking after the wains – Rita Hayworth she calls herself, I ask you. Dyed red hair and a chipped front tooth, silly auld bag looks more like Will Hay in drag. She won't mind if I take an hour more, she'll be away with the gin by now.

I open my handbag, drop the doorkeys back in and catch the reassuring glint of cold steel in the sodium glow of the streetlight. That's my protection, Glasgow-style. Nae Jack the Stripper's going to get his hands on me.

I straighten my back as I walk towards him, undo the top button of my grey jacket, a sneer on my red lips. He opens the back door of the car, makes a little bow, says: 'After you madam,' then closes it behind me, soft thud of metal on metal as I slide into the leather seat, the smell of real money warming my nostrils. Madam is right. As I often tell the other girls, I've just about serviced all of Burke's Peerage in my time, and most of it thanks to this one. He sets me up with these queer auld dears who want the arse thrashed offa them, pay handsomely for the privilege. Sometimes I think I could go on thrashing and thrashing and thrashing forever, drown out the noise of the wains screaming for their tea, the noise of my landlord screaming for his rent, the noise of the whole fucking world wanting something offa me.

I watch the arc of his cigarette as he flicks it from his fingers under the trees, under the trees where he sold me, climbs into the driver's seat and starts the engine, a gentle purr as he pulls away, moving through the black night, gliding into a stream of red and white. I lean back and close my eyes, remembering the times in the past, the whips and leads and sagging old arses, white flesh turning red and red faces twisting purple in the agony of ecstasy. Me lying naked on a blasphemous altar while a procession of men dressed in black cloaks queue up to take me, one by one, still with their shoes and socks on as they dump their load, hoity toity bastards all. Then the little kid on a street corner shouting: 'Fourpence for a feel, Mavis!' while all his friends snigger behind their hands. The things I have done, the many lives of my thirty-one years...

I open my eyes, shake the thoughts away and look in my handbag again. My fingers touch the blade, a talisman, then slide over to my powder compact. I check myself in the mirror.

A strange music starts up from the front of the car, the sound of a motorcycle revving up and a heavy drumbeat caught in a spectral echo. Nearly as funny as this face that stares back at me. Doesnae look like mine. Looks much younger, prettier, like a French girl with black hair whose face I have seen somewhere before but can't quite picture where. I blink and I look again; a lassie from Lincolnshire with her hair like Dusty Springfield stares back at me, icy fingers running down my spine. Swallow and blink and look again and a hard-faced scrubber with shoulder-length brown hair, the girl I knew as Geordie Sue, curls her top lip into a sneer and I shut the compact, look out of the window.

Not where I was expecting to be at all.

These are not the white mansions of Belgravia, the shady halls of Kensington, where all this malarkey usually takes place. A patch of wasteland Christ knows where, barbed wire and the squat shapes of unlit industrial buildings, far from the glow of streetlights, close to the dark currents of the Thames. The car stops and my stomach *lurches, this is not what should happen. Fucking bastard better not try to pull a fast one on Mavis, I think, grabbing my knife as the door opens and he leans in towards me, but even as I pull up the blade, hands reach round my face from behind me, someone else there on the back seat, pushing something into my face, something that makes me drop the knife and stops the scream that is forming in my mouth, the scream into this black and unholy place, the scream that will never now be heard by any living soul but goes on and on and on...*

I woke up with her scream in my throat, the world slipping from underneath me, on to the armchair I had passed out on in my darkened room, my hair plastered to my face with ice cold sweat. Dear God no, dear God no, oh God, oh someone out there, help me.

Bring out your dead.

35

(Always) Something There To Remind Me

How George Steadman had ever come to be nicknamed 'Lucky' was a mystery even he could no longer recall. Five years of prison food had softened his once formidable frame into rolls of flab, the barber's clippers had less to curtail each week and half that was frosted over with grey. Steadman had never been handsome like Ferrier to begin with, but his round, jovial face and gap-toothed smile had won over enough ladies back in his day. Including little Bobby Clarke, who had let herself believe that he would come Lucky for her and carry her away from the increasingly violent and demanding Ferrier, from the trees that lined Holland Park Avenue and the back seats of the cars that loitered beneath them.

A sorry story which, if he let himself reflect on it, could still almost bring a tear to Steadman's eye. He was reflecting on it now, as for the second time in only a week these bogeys had come to visit him, to dig around at what he had thought was safely buried long ago. He felt like he was wide awake in the middle of a nightmare.

'I wouldn't never hurt Bobby,' he kept trying to explain to the older policeman, the one he remembered from the prime of his youth. 'I never hit a woman in my life. I ain't like Baby, he the bad one, he the one who hurt her.'

But it was the other bogey who was scaring Steadman, the one with eyes like two blue diamonds, the one that stood leaning against the wall and said nothing, just chilled him to the bone with his stare. *Blue eyes hypnotise*, as Steadman's mother used to say. He had a horrible feeling that he was going to tell this one more than he ever wanted to.

Pete, staring back at him, was thinking exactly the same thing. Steadman wasn't a hard case like Ferrier. He had neither the brains nor the instinct of a predator, which was probably why his boxing career had never amounted to much. Every time Pete tried to lock eyes with him, Steadman's sorrowful browns slid back down towards the floor.

'That's not what he's been saying.' Coulter leaned across the desk. 'He told us that you were very lustful over Miss Clarke, that you'd already had a falling out about it and he'd warned you off her. So what was this, George?' He tapped his finger on the photograph that lay between them. 'Took her out and buttered her up with a taste of the highlife, then drove her down to those Elysian fields of Gobbler's Gulch to claim what you thought was rightfully yours? Then, when she didn't want to play her part of the bargain, you started getting rough with her? Ripped the dress from off her and had your way anyway? I mean.' Coulter shook his head regretfully. 'You are a big man, George, and I daresay a bit punch drunk from your time in the ring. You probably didn't know your own strength.'

'No!' Steadman rubbed his eyes. He didn't want a policeman to see him cry. But he couldn't stop the memories of Bobby, the kisses and caresses they had shared, the way she was so nice to him, like no other girl had ever been. The way he had betrayed her.

'But on the other hand...' Steadman heard the other bogey walk towards the desk, the Blakeys on his shoes harsh against the concrete floor. 'There is this matter of twenty-five quid. Your mate Ferrier is still pretty pissed off about it. I don't think he was making that bit up.'

'But I gave it to him...' Steadman began and then looked up, aghast. He wasn't supposed to have said that.

Pete smiled. 'Ah,' he said. 'But what I want to know is, who gave it to you?'

Fear crawled in Steadman's stomach like the claws of a beast. He felt his sphincter muscles loosening and desperately tried to hold back from breaking wind, from avoiding the hypnotic pull of the blue eyes.

'Was it this man, George?' Coulter tapped the end of a cigarette down on Simon Fitzgerald's face before lighting it. 'That's the daft story Algernon told us. We didn't believe him, of course. What would a man in his position be doing giving that much money to a lad like you? He could have got himself a lot better than that for free.'

Coulter exhaled in Steadman's face, the smell of it turned his already roiling stomach. 'We reckon it was a yarn he was spinning to get himself off the hook,' the older detective went on. 'As you just said yourself, Algernon was the one who was hurting Bobby. He killed her, didn't he? You can tell us, George. Tell us enough to put him away. He won't be able to touch you where he's going.'

Steadman looked from the photo to Coulter and then back down again, at Bobby's smiling face, his own cheerful visage and the man in the middle of them, the little singer she had liked so much, who had been so kind to them that night. Tears rolled down his cheeks unstoppably now as the memories came rushing in.

Bobby telling him to meet her at one, at the coffee stand by Holland Park tube, that this would be her last night on the game before they went away together, forever. The sparkle in her eyes as she kissed him goodbye and headed off for Leicester Square. Then the way he had been drawn into an after-hours game of cards at

Teddy's, the man who put the whisky in his hand and went on filling up the glass, the hand on his shoulder as he leaned towards him and whispered in his ear. The man with a face like a butcher's board…

Him staggering home in the early hours, Bobby all forgotten, twenty-five quid in his pocket instead. Baby screaming with rage, where was she, what had he done with her? Baby hitting him and Steadman letting him, putting up no defence, deserving each blow for what he had done. Then the next day and the report on the news about Bobby, knowing now he had done worse than sell her out and stand her up.

The detective that turned up on their doorstep shortly after.

Steadman had turned over the chemist's ineptly on purpose, wanting to get caught. Fear creating the only solution to his problem he could muster. Got to get off the street, stay off the street until all of this was nothing but a distant memory. He already had two previous convictions. One more would guarantee him five years out of harm's way.

But now these double-talking bogeys were saying that Baby had killed her. That if he just told them it was Baby and not him, then Baby would die, Baby would die too, hanged by the neck for murder.

Baby, who had looked after him in London when he'd first come off the boat. Baby who had got him fights and money and seen him all right. Baby whom he had also betrayed. He couldn't say it, they couldn't make him…

Steadman's eyes rolled towards those two blue diamonds and hung there, mesmerised.

'It was The Chopper,' he heard himself say. Knowing he was doomed as he did so, not caring any more. Whatever else he had given away, they couldn't make him kill Baby.

Pete inhaled sharply, a rush of jubilation and relief coursing through him so fast he almost felt faint.

'What did you say?' said Coulter. 'What do you mean, The Chopper?'

'I know what he means,' Pete said. 'He means Sampson Marks, otherwise known as The Chopper. Owns a strip club in Soho and has shares in Teddy's gaff. A real ladies' man, isn't that right, George?'

There was no lying, no fight left in George Steadman's eyes, only the weariness of utter defeat.

'Uh-huh,' the big man said.

'You know this Marks fella then?' Coulter asked as they took their leave of the Scrubs. 'I've heard of him before, in connection with all this, just trying to remember where...'

'He's what they call a bit of a Soho character.' Pete knew he had to chose his words carefully, had to hide his elation from Coulter. Though it was difficult, he wanted to share his knowledge so much that only the thought of Bell stopped him. 'I used to go to Teddy's club with Joan when we were courting, he was a bit of a boyhood hero of mine and she liked the shows. I got to know a few things, like you do. Marks is Teddy's silent partner. They call him The Chopper because he likes to use an axe on his enemies. Funny thing is, he looks like one too.'

Coulter frowned. 'Well there've not been any axe marks on any of our girls,' he pointed out. 'So how does that fit into the picture?'

'He's a procurer,' said Pete. 'He's into girls, pornography, mixing it with the highlife and the lowlife. And if supplying Jack isn't tantamount to killing them himself, then I don't know what is.'

Coulter stared at him. 'You're right,' he said. 'What should we do next? Pass it on to the gaffer?'

Pete nodded. 'Get him to get one of his pals in West End Central to run The Chopper in. I'm sure Marks doesn't know about that photograph either and I'd love to know what effect it has on him. I wonder what he could tell us about our missing friend Ernie...'

'Well,' said Coulter, 'that should put the smile back on his face.'

But when they walked into CID, the room was in uproar. DI Fielder stood in the middle of the room, surrounded by detectives all talking and shouting. His hair had turned another shade greyer, the sheet of paper in his hand said why.

Dick Willcox was standing closest to the door as they entered. 'You've missed the main event,' he informed them. 'There's been another one. Found at 5.30 this morning outside a garage forecourt in Acton. A garage, yeah – but not the garage we were looking for. Bastard's taunting us, you ask me.'

'The body has been taken for tests,' Fielder was saying, 'to ascertain whether traces of paint residue are a match for those found on the Bressant corpse...'

Coulter looked at Pete, both thinking the same thing, the older man saying it out loud: 'We've not been fast enough.'

36

I Just Don't Know What to Do with Myself

I woke up on Sunday morning with only one thought in my head. I had to go and see Mya, had to tell Stanley what I had seen. My head was full of Mavis's visions, faces looming out at me from her memory. Only, as I stood beneath the shower trying to get myself together, it came back to me that I already had a commitment that day.

I had promised Jenny I would go to her house and help her choose some designs for the nursery. Sunday was the only day she didn't have to be on set, the only time I didn't have to be at work. Bob liked to spend his Sunday morning playing football and then going to the pub, so we'd have some time to ourselves.

I could go and see Mya first, I reasoned, slowly getting into my clothes and styling my hair in the mirror. Only what state would I be in after that? I hardly wanted a repeat of the night of Mathilde and Toby round at Jenny's place. There was nothing for it, I realised, I would just have to see Jenny first, have to try and push everything else to the back of my mind. At least she didn't live very far away from the Spiritualists.

I tried my best to look composed as I arrived on her doorstep, but straightaway something happened to throw me, something I hadn't expected. She wasn't alone.

'Stella,' she said, leading me through to the kitchen, 'there's someone I want you to meet. He's not staying long, only when I told him you were coming he wanted to just say thank you for the huge favour you did him last summer.'

As we walked into the room, he was leaning against the kitchen sink, a shy smile on his face and cup of coffee in his hand. Quite a handsome man from a distance, with blond hair cut into a mod style, a Jermyn Street shirt and narrow-fitting trousers. Only when you got closer did you notice the broken nose and the scar that curved in a semi-circle around his top lip.

It was the scar that did it, that jogged the memory out in the open.

'This is Giles,' said Jenny as he offered me his hand.

'So pleased to meet you,' he said, smiling with eyes identical to Jenny's. 'You really saved my bacon,' he gave a little laugh, 'from those filthy pigs.'

As our hands touched I felt a crackle of static electricity running through me. I was back in the Holland Park Lawn Tennis Club with Margaret Rose Stephenson, Ronald McSweeney, Bernard Baring and him...

Giles Somerset. Jenny's brother. He was the other man playing poker that night.

I dropped my hand as quickly as I could, muttered a vague greeting as I tried to blink the vision away from my eyes. It was no good. The room started to go out of focus.

'Oh,' I said, grabbing hold of a chair. 'I'm sorry, I seem to have come over all faint.'

Jenny gave a little snort of amusement. 'You always have this effect on girls, don't you Giles?' But when she saw my face, her expression turned serious.

She pulled out the chair for me, sat me down. 'Oh, you do look pale,' she said. 'Do you want a glass of water?'

I nodded, looking up at Giles the way Margaret Rose had from her knees, feeling the damp grass underneath me, my hand snaking into his pocket…

'I say,' said Giles, 'you're not up the duff as well, are you? Must be contagious.'

'Giles.' Jenny elbowed him in the ribs. 'Don't be so rude. Stella's just had a bit of a time of it recently, haven't you darling? You still not feeling yourself?'

She put the water down on the table in front of me, concern in her eyes, her identical eyes. Dave had been telling the truth about those two, when you saw them together there was no denying it.

Another face loomed out at me, seemed to hang in the air between them. I knew who he was all right, I had seen his face enough times in the paper. He was their father, in a black robe, still wearing his socks as he put his hands on Mavis…

'Are you sleeping all right?' she asked.

She thought I was upset about Toby, I realised, which was probably half the reason she had wanted me to come here today. We had talked briefly about it on the phone, but it was obvious she wanted to hear more, know all the details. At that moment, it seemed like a blessing – it was a good enough reason, after all, and the only way I could plausibly explain my behaviour.

I took a sip of the drink and closed my eyes for a minute, silently praying for an end to this transmission.

'Not really,' I said, glad that the room was back in focus when I opened them again. 'It's been so hard getting used to it all.'

'I know.' She nodded understandingly, put her hand on my shoulder and gave it a little squeeze. 'I'm sorry, I should have realised.'

Giles cleared his throat. 'Well I'd better leave you ladies to it,' he said, putting his cup down in the sink.

'Yes,' said Jenny, 'you can see yourself out, can't you?'

'Hope to see you again some time,' he said, 'when you're feeling better.'

I smiled as best I could, seeing the vulnerability in his face, the childishness that made Jenny want to protect him, her words coming back to me from the moment she found out about his arrest. *'Giles has a tendency to…Get involved with people he shouldn't…'*

Too right he did.

'Me too,' I lied. 'Sorry about this, it's so embarrassing. I'm sure I'll be all right in a minute.'

'Oh Stella.' Jenny sat herself down on the chair opposite me. 'Has it been really awful for you? I mean, of course it has. I can't believe it myself, not you and Toby. You were always such a good advert for love, before…' She stopped herself mid-sentence.

'Before Toby had his head turned?' I pre-empted her. 'By the devil Pat Innes? That's what everybody keeps telling me.'

I hadn't really wanted to talk about this, but now, in the strange half-state that Giles had unwittingly engendered in me, I found that I couldn't stop.

'Was I so blind that I couldn't see what was happening right under my nose?' I said. 'It's funny, you know. When I think back, I was actually having my doubts about those two on the day of our opening party. Only I stopped myself from thinking about it.'

'Really?' said Jenny. 'I never would have guessed.'

'It was that suit he was wearing,' I said. 'For so long he had been dressing like a slob, doing his painting in his old school shirts and the same filthy pair of jeans. It didn't matter how much money he made. I thought it was quite sweet, really, that he was just reverting to his upper-class type, you know, the way country squires always seem to go around with their trousers held up by bale twine and straw in their hair. But when he met Pat, he started paying more attention. He looked so beautiful that day, in that blue suit, I really thought he'd made the effort for me. Only now I can see it. He even told me that Pat picked it out for him. Oh God.' I felt myself on the verge of tears again, another realisation hitting home. 'And to think I made those suits for us that look almost exactly the same...'

'Oh Stella, sweetheart.' Jenny took hold of my hand as I raised it to brush the tear away. 'Those suits were my idea, remember? But that was a funny old day, wasn't it?' Her eyes clouded as her mind reeled back. 'I said that Toby should choose his friends more carefully, didn't I?'

'I thought you meant Baring,' I dared myself to say.

'I did mean him,' she said, her eyes fixed on some far horizon. 'Bloody little bastard. He went to school with Giles, you know, he was always going on about Artistic Baring, the scholarship social climber. I dreaded ever having to meet him, and when I did I knew he was another one of the many people I had to keep him away from.'

Yes, I thought, I can see why.

'But he was always so transfixed by those kind of people. Spiders. He can never realise what they're really after. Not his friendship, just his money, his title, his father's influence. He's such an easy mark. And Pat Innes is just the same, if not worse.'

Her grip on my hand tightened and I flinched.

'Oh God,' she said, letting go. 'I'm sorry. I'm supposed to be comforting you, but here I am, banging on about myself again. Maybe I should have said more at the time, but I never thought that Toby was the sort that would get taken in, honestly I didn't. I thought he had more guts. More sense.'

'So did I,' I said. 'But it's interesting to find out these things, at least it gives me some sort of reason for it, that it wasn't anything that I did wrong.'

'How could it have been?' she said. 'You were the one who did everything for him.'

'Well,' I said, 'me and Chris and Dave. They got him his first show, all the commissions from Lady Maybury. And how did he repay them? We hardly ever saw them once he'd had a taste of success. He was embarrassed by the way he treated them too. He couldn't look them in the eye. He knew Baring was ripping them off and making a fortune out of it. I always thought he was the worst of my enemies,' I admitted. 'I knew he hated me and he was always putting down everything I did, belittling all my work.'

'He hates women full stop,' said Jenny.

'I thought Pat was doing me a favour that day, throwing him out,' I said. 'But he was only getting him out of the way so he could move in himself.'

Jenny shook her head, stood up and put the kettle back on.

'I always thought I was a pretty good judge of character,' she said, staring out of the window. 'But Toby had us all fooled, didn't he? You're right, though, about him reverting to upper-class type.' There was a slight tremor in her voice. 'They're all a bunch of heartless bastards and they always get what they bloody well want, whatever the cost.'

Her hand went up to her stomach.

Dave hadn't made any of it up, I realised. He was right about everything. Those faces I had seen in Mavis McGruder's mind, that procession of lords and policemen, aldermen and politicians all lining up beside a blasphemous altar to take her, one by one. They were all part of it, part of the reason why Mavis and Mathilde, Margaret Rose and Susannah, Bronwyn and Bobby all had to die.

I suddenly couldn't stay with her any longer. I had to go and see Mya. Revelations were falling through my mind like a line of dominoes and I couldn't control it much longer.

'Listen, Jenny,' I said, getting to my feet. 'Do you mind if we do this another day? Only I think I'm getting a migraine, I'd like to go home and lie down.'

'Oh dear,' she said, but relief was written over her features. She had said things she didn't mean to as well. 'Do you want me to call you a taxi?'

'No,' I said, 'it's not far. Maybe the fresh air will do me good, get the blood circulating again. I'm really sorry I've been such a washout.'

'Don't be,' she said. 'I'm really sorry that you've had to go through all this. You helped me so much getting Chris to sort out Giles, I should have done something for you in return. Are you sure you'll be all right?'

'Positive,' I lied.

I managed to make it up the hill to Mya's, to fall into her parlour and tell her.

'I've got to see Stanley. There's been another one, a woman called Mavis, last night. And she started to show me who it was, how it all connects, where he takes them.'

'My dear girl.' Mya's face went white as she put her hand over my forehead.

'She knew him, the driver,' I said, going into a trance, 'he was Sexy Ron, the real Sexy Ron...'

37

Just One Look

When Pete and Coulter told their story to Fielder, he couldn't get to the West End fast enough. Virtually stood over them as they filled in all their paperwork, Steadman's statement typed up, Ernie's pictorial evidence to go with it. Then, when he had snatched it up and fled, there were all the details of the latest body to catch up with.

She had been discovered in a quiet cul-de-sac in a residential neighbourhood of Acton. A chauffeur living across the street had heard a car driving off quickly at 2.30 a.m. and had thought no more about it, until he got up three hours later and looked out of the window to see what he thought was a tailor's dummy, lying on the garage forecourt opposite.

Her parents had christened her Maureen Easton, but the name on her National Assistance card and Family Allowance book was Patricia Fleming, aged thirty-one, resident of Lancaster Road W11. To most of the Notting Hill bobbies, however, she was Mavis McGruder, a loud-mouthed old hand who liked telling tall stories about being the mistress of lords.

Seemed her fantasy world extended to the flatmate who had made the formal ID. Rita Hayworth, she called herself. For the past four days she had continued to babysit Mavis's children, Gloria, four, and Johnny, six, until the knock came on her door this morning. It wasn't certain what would happen to the children, they would probably be taken into care. Their father had been a squaddie, but he had long since vanished. Rita had never known him at all.

Her statement was chilling.

'*I heard her walking home,*' she had told the investigating officers. '*I knew it was her as she was wearing those sling-backs, make a hell of a noise on the steps. She must have got halfway to the front door when I heard her stop, come back down and walk on up the road. All I can think of is that she must have seen someone she knew, someone she trusted. She always said The Stripper would never get her and she carried this knife in her handbag she'd taken off some fella who tried to use it on her. Mavis was no pushover, believe you me. But this is just terrifying – he was waiting for her right outside our front door. I don't know how I'm ever going to get over it...*'

Pete tried to take it all in, add all the new information to the reams of notes in his book. Day turned into night, a return visit to the Scrubs postponed for the morning, he and Coulter instead attempting to work out a strategy for Steadman. How could they get him to confess to a court, when he was clearly so terrified? Without his testimony, they would have nothing concrete on Marks, it was imperative to make sure he stuck to the story.

Pete couldn't help but think that Steadman's fear was a mirror of McSweeney's fear, a mirror of Ernie's sweaty distress.

Something worse than prison.

The exhilaration he'd felt at the start of the day had long turned into exhaustion by the time Pete turned the corner of Oxford Gardens that night, the folder of photographs in his briefcase now, still weighing up whether to share them with Coulter or not.

Something outside his gate that startled him back into wakefulness.

The black Rover.

Detective Chief Inspector Bell sat in the back seat, a briefcase on his knee, the shadow of a smile flickering underneath his moustache. 'I always thought you had initiative, Bradley,' he said. 'But I must say, you have surpassed even my own expectations.'

'Thank you, sir,' said Pete, feeling himself colour uncomfortably with the praise. 'But I was only following your lead. I have to say, it was something of a relief to make sense of it all.' He stopped himself, not wanting to gabble in front of his senior officer. 'So,' he said. 'Sampson Marks. Have you spoken to him, sir? What's he told you?'

Bell's shrewd gaze ran across Pete's face as he spoke, as if he was weighing up every word. 'Let's take a little drive,' he said, 'and I'll tell you about it. Here.' He fished into his inside jacket pocket and produced two cigars in long silver tubes. 'In the meantime, I think you've earned this.'

They drove down Ladbroke Grove, past the ever-increasing construction of the new flyover, down Holland Park Avenue and along to Shepherd's Bush. Pete thought that they would be heading for the station there, but Bell's driver didn't stop, instead he turned down Brook Green towards Hammersmith. The DCI must have seen Pete frown.

'Nothing to worry about, Bradley. We need to have a chat somewhere private before we proceed, a bit of a debriefing, so to speak. As you will appreciate, now that these two cases of ours have dovetailed somewhat, there are still some sensitive matters pertaining to the Wesker affair that are best left off the record.'

'Of course,' Pete said, remembering the two aids that had gone down as a sacrifice for Wesker's crimes, the magnitude of what he actually knew.

The car pulled into a little side street, right beside Hammersmith Bridge. Bell opened the door. 'Let's take a walk,' he said. 'It's a fine night.'

Pete got out, looked up at the bridge, a fantastical construction of Victorian ironwork with towers like a fairytale castle, painted dark green and gold, illuminated now by the streetlights, the dark river rippling below. He remembered how much he had admired Sir Joseph Bazalgette's construction as a young copper, how he had read up as much as he could of the history of the place. But now, this stretch of the Thames was forever tainted by the stain of murder, the memory of Bobby Clarke's vacant eyes on that sunny morning, five long years ago.

As if reading his mind, Bell said: 'I don't know about you, but when I want to get to grips with a case, I find myself walking back over the territory time and time again. Something always draws you back, the idea that you could have left something behind, forgotten to mark some important detail. That's what impressed me about you so much when we first met,' he led the way down the promenade by the river's edge, 'not so far away from here.'

'I know what you mean, sir.' Pete looked across the river to the curve of woods beyond; how quickly London seemed to fall away from this point. They continued to walk in silence for a while, until they came to the end of the quayside.

'Sampson Marks,' said Bell, stopping to lean on the wall, look down at the depths below them. 'A nasty piece of work all round. And now it seems that it was he who Wesker was protecting, which makes things nastier still.'

'Aye,' said Pete. 'But at least we have the proof now, to connect him not just with Roberta Clarke, but Bronwyn Evans too. We've got Steadman's statement that he procured Clarke for him on the night of the murder. Marks knew where to turn up to get her, the rendezvous she was supposed to be making with Steadman. And Evans in the room at the same time, along with everyone else Wesker fitted up. At least we know why Wesker did it all now. We just have to figure out who he did it for, but surely, you can't be far away from that now, sir?'

Bell frowned, drew deeply on his cigar, turned his face towards Pete's, his eyes running up and down him again, the way they had in the car.

'Wesker's out of bounds to us now,' he said. 'It pains me to say it, but that's the way it is. We can't use him in this.'

'We shouldn't need him,' said Pete. 'If I may say, I think we've got enough to lean on Marks and make him confess. If not for being the murderer, or murderers, then at least for procuring for the guilty party.'

'I see,' said Bell, nodding slowly. 'Do you want to go through it as you see it, step by step? I'm not going to take notes, this is between us. But I need to have it all clear in my mind.'

Pete took a deep breath, tried to get his thoughts in order.

'All right,' he said. 'So we have, in the room on the same night, Marks, Wesker and Francis Bream – we know their connection. Then there's six of the people that we know Wesker fitted up, let's put them all to one side for a moment as I think we can safely say that makes them all innocent.'

Bell nodded. 'An accurate analysis. Go on.'

'Teddy,' said Pete, 'who's going to be there anyway, it's his club, and Simon Fitzgerald, who often performed there. Roberta Clarke and Bronwyn Evans, the first two victims. George Steadman, who confessed to me he had sold the services of Roberta Clarke to Marks while in an intoxicated state towards midnight on that night.

'Then we have Sir Alex Minton and Lord Douglas Somerset, Somerset being of particular interest to me for two reasons. One, that I nicked a burglar coming out of his house way back in the summer of 1959, an investigation that Harold Wesker suddenly came out of his jurisdiction to take over when it was revealed that what he had been stealing was some kind of pornography. Two, that the burglar appeared to be in cahoots with Somerset's youngest son Giles, who was then nicked himself at the Greek riot by none other than Harold Wesker.'

'Good God,' muttered Bell, turning his face towards the river. 'Continue, please, Bradley.'

'There are twelve other people in those photographs who I don't recognise and couldn't tell you of their significance. But we do know that Ernest Tidsall was the photographer, and that he kept one frame from that session hidden away in his ledgers, some kind of insurance policy, I would say. Tidsall also had photographs of the next two victims, Susannah Houghton and Margaret Rose Stephenson, girls that he used as pornographic models. We know that Marks had links to the filth trade and that racket is central to the work of CID at West End Central. Tidsall has been missing since April, since he was questioned in connection with the Houghton murder. No one's touched his bank account since, and it would be my opinion that he is no longer with us. That's why he left the insurance policy.'

Bell turned his face back towards Pete. There were no traces of humour left in it now.

'Go back a minute,' he said. 'To the photographs.'

'Yes sir,' said Pete. 'I'm not going to ask where you got them from, but surely, however you did, that must be the connection you need to lean on Marks. He can't deny it, can he? It's all there in black and white.'

Bell dropped the end of his cigar on to the floor and trod on it, sending sparks up into the air and along the edge of the quay.

'I'm going to have to ask you for them back now,' he said, 'and I think you know what I'm going to say next.'

'That I never saw them.'

'Precisely,' said Bell. 'Honourable Coldstreamer. You never showed them to anyone else, did you?'

'Of course not, sir.'

'Good.' Bell's pace quickened, eager to get back to the car now. 'Where are they now?' he said, opening the door for Pete.

'Here,' Pete lifted them out of his briefcase, handed them across. As the Chief Inspector took the envelope, Pete was pleased to see that the relief in the other man's face mirrored his own.

'Bradley,' Bell said, 'you are an exceptional detective. You'll always have my gratitude, even if no one else ever knows of this.'

'That's enough for me sir,' said Pete. 'Just take care of them. I hope you've got the negatives safe and all.'

Bell looked up at him, his eyes steady and calm. 'It won't be long now,' he said, tapping on the glass to his driver. 'Back to Oxford Gardens, please.'

The next morning, Coulter was standing by Pete's desk, his face like a bowl of grey porridge. 'I've just had a call from the governor at the Scrubs,' he said. 'I'm afraid it's bad news.' He pulled out a chair, sat down wearily. 'George Steadman was found hanged in his cell at six fifteen this morning. It appears he ripped his sheets up to make the noose. Left a note to his mother, saying how sorry he was.'

Something worse than prison.

Coulter put his head in his hands as Pete stared at him, dumbstruck.

'This is worse than I thought,' the old detective said. 'Much worse.'

He looked through his fingers at Pete.

'Just what have we stumbled into here?' he said.

38

Baby Love

'Stella?' Dave stood blinking on his doorstep. It was the middle of the day, but clearly he had just rolled out of bed and pulled an old army greatcoat over the top of his pyjamas, his hair a wild cloud that just about hid the dark rings around his eyes. As I stared at his raggedy scarecrow frame, all the clever opening lines I had rehearsed dissolved into the greyness of a wet autumnal afternoon.

Dave hadn't managed to win a seat at the General Election, just as Stanley still hadn't managed to solve the case. The day of Harold Wilson's slim triumph over the Tories had dawned misty and grey, the end of a three-month long heatwave. Gloomy weather had persisted all week since.

According to Stanley, the atmosphere in Notting Hill nick had also turned much colder, since the discovery of Mavis. He feared that his boss had been given orders to shelve all the evidence Stanley had been amassing on the case, or at least pass it over to his superiors for them to bury. The only way he thought they could bring the killer to justice now was to force something out into the open, something that couldn't be covered up. Seeing Dave was the only thing left I could think of that might help him, even if it had taken all this time to finally pin him down. But now it didn't look like I had caught him at a very opportune moment.

'Sorry,' I said. 'Is this a bad time? I can come back later…'

'No,' he shook his head, 'it's really nice to see you. Please, come in love.'

The kitchen looked like a hurricane had hit it – clothes, newspapers, leaflets and flyers all over the place. I picked my way through the carnage to the table, moved a rucksack off the nearest chair and sat down, while Dave rummaged about, finding the kettle, cups and matches.

''Scuse the state of the place,' he said. 'But I only just got back.'

Lying on the table was a newspaper with him on the front cover, the headline IS THIS REALLY THE FACE OF MODERN BRITAIN? in outraged capitals above it.

'Sorry you didn't win,' I said, staring at it. 'But it looks like you had some success after all.'

He grinned, setting cups down around the general mess. 'Yeah,' he said, 'got right up their noses, didn't I? That's all you can do with these bastards. If you can't beat 'em, take the piss – they can't bloody stand it, can they?'

'No,' I said, taking a sip of the tea and trying not to wince at the industrial strength of it.

'What can I do for you, then, love? I'm sorry I ain't been in touch sooner, Chris did tell me you'd been looking for me, but this politics lark just takes over your life. Oh, and sorry to hear about Toby, too,' he added. 'The arsehole.'

I laughed. 'Don't be,' I said. 'I'm beginning to realise that he did me a favour.'

'Oh yeah?' There was a knowing look in Dave's eye, but I didn't want to go down that road, I had to ask him the important things before the conversation got swept round to more sociable matters.

'Anyway,' I said, 'it's about Jenny.'

His face changed instantly. The laughter lines mutated into a frown.

'Yeah?' he said. 'Chris told me that, an' all, about her getting married, having a baby. Don't worry, I won't be hanging round her new house bothering her and Sonny Jim if that's what she's worried about. Did she ask you to come round and tell me that?'

'No,' I said, 'she didn't. Please don't be offended, Dave, it's not that at all.'

'Sorry.' The anger drained back out of his face as quickly as it had flared. 'I didn't mean to come across so bolshy.' He reached a tobacco tin out of a pair of jeans from the heap beside his chair. 'It's just, it's still a painful subject for me, even after all this time.'

He extracted a rolling paper and made a line of tobacco down the middle of it. 'I tried everything to forget about that girl, you know,' he said. 'Joining a band, running for parliament – every kind of distraction you could think of. Only it all keeps coming back to her in the end.'

He licked the edge of the paper, rolled up a skinny cigarette.

'I met Giles,' I said. 'He is her brother, isn't he? It's so obvious when you see them together, only I never had before. Would you mind me asking, why is it such a secret that they're brother and sister?'

Dave gave a sharp laugh. 'I would have thought that was obvious,' he said. 'But then how could you know? I bet she never once invited you back to her house, did she? Never told you nothing personal in all the years you've known her?'

'No,' I said. 'That was the first time I'd ever met anyone from her family.'

'Well her and Giles is,' he struck a match and inhaled deeply, blew a plume of smoke across the room, 'a case of same dad, different mum. Jenny's old man, Sir Alex,' he pronounced the name with scorn, 'cuckolded Giles's old man – well, the official old man – Lord Somerset. It's one of the ripping wheezes these toffs get up to all the time. Somerset couldn't care less, he already had all his heirs at their posts, dispatched his duty, as it were. Jenny reckoned he was queer anyway.'

I choked on the sip of tea I had taken, thinking about what Toby had said about his father.

'I know.' Dave leant over and patted me on the back. 'It's a bleedin' distasteful matter all round. But you got to understand: they live in a different world to us proles. Minton and Somerset had a good war together, that was all what counted. They're still having a good war now, as it goes. Only instead of plotting which bits of Jerry to drive their tanks through next, they use Somerset's grace and favour to plot which bits of London Minton can roll his bulldozers into instead. It won't surprise you to learn that they don't like the idea of poor people living around here,' he said. 'Let alone darkies, wops, Paddies, spics or any other form of Johnny Foreigner. So they've built a load of horrible concrete boxes to shut them all in, keep them in their place.

'And now there's this motorway – *Connecting the Western suburbs to the heart of the City*, yeah?' he quoted from the banners that fluttered from the construction site. 'Ain't it beautiful. Driving their bulldozers right through people's houses, right past their windows, splitting this manor down the middle and changing it all forever. Like I said, Minton and Somerset have made a fortune from their wars. So what do it matter to them if one of them puts the other one's missus in the club? What do it matter what the resultant offspring think about it either?'

'When did Jenny find out?' I asked, my mind swimming.

'When she was about thirteen.' Dave screwed his cigarette into an old tin ashtray, as if he wished he was boring it into the side of Sir Alex's head. 'Her old man reckoned the two of them were getting a bit too close for comfort. Which was bloody ironic, considering,' he turned his head away, 'what he'd been doing to her.'

'Oh God,' I whispered, suddenly realising what it was that

had always been missing from Jenny. The strange silences, the blankness. The careful way that she always avoided revealing anything too personal about herself and how she had lost that ability the moment someone she really cared about was in danger. The illusion she gave of seeming too knowing for her years, yet too childlike for her pulchritudinous appearance. The way she had put her hand over her stomach to protect her unborn child as she thought about it all that morning in her kitchen. Her own father...

'I think I need a drink.' Dave rummaged around in his coat pocket, extracted a bottle of brandy and slugged a load into his teacup.

'Want some?' he said as an afterthought, offering it over to me.

'I think I do,' I said, grateful for the burn of it down the back of my throat.

'Ugh,' said Dave, knocking back his. 'Do you often take confessional like this, your Grace?' He tried to smile.

'No,' I said, 'and I had no idea. But it makes sense of so many things...'

He nodded. 'She hates him, Jenny does. I didn't realise the extent of it when I first met her, I thought a few pranks would sort him out.'

He poured the rest of the bottle between my cup and his. 'He was building in Kensington then, making a right horrible old pile – civic architecture, he called it. Ugly was more like it. So we started a protest movement, No More Ugly. Had a demo right outside his site, got in all the papers. All them Fleet Street hacks fucking loved it, Minton's glamorous daughter protesting against him. We even knocked Princess Margaret off the *Daily Mail*'s gossip column for a day. Worked a treat in pissing him off, so she told me.

'But then...' Dave took another, smaller sip, put his teacup down. 'She had another bright idea, that we go one further. Old Somerset was getting a bit senile in his dotage, you see. Left his private library unlocked one day and Giles found some interesting things in there.' Dave's stare intensified. 'Incriminating photographs, apparently, and a reel of film, showing the sorts of things him and Minton got up to with all their influential friends. I wish I had actually seen them so I'd know for sure, but I'm pretty sure we're talking the same circles here as Profumo – another part of my largely fruitless mission to carry on this work.'

I started to feel light-headed and not just from the brandy.

'Jenny's idea was to sell them to the press, those same old bastards that had been drooling all over her at the demo.' His scowl deepened. 'She thought she had some influence there, how naïve can you get? The pair of us were. It was only then that I found out how much power the old fucker really has.'

'Why? What did he do?'

Dave's almond eyes burned straight past me into the dark corners of the past. 'There was this geezer I knew from Finches, Gypsy George they called him,' he said. 'Irish fella, bit of a tinker and the best cat burglar in the Smoke, never been collared in his life. I reckoned we couldn't fail if he screwed the drum. How wrong I was. Not only did George get caught red-handed with all the loot, but Sir Alex then had some top copper come down from West End Central to take care of all the evidence. George got sent to Pentonville,' he shook his head, 'where, supposedly, he hanged himself three months later. I might as well have wrung his neck myself.'

'Oh God,' I said, shutting my eyes, seeing a ballroom full of people in tuxedos and tiaras, all laughing at Susannah Houghton, who lay naked on a bed, squirming beneath a man in a gorilla suit. Hearing Bernard Baring bragging about witnessing this spectacle to Pat Innes, the pair of them laughing.

'This copper from the West End,' I said. 'He's not the same one...'

'That Chris was investigating? Yeah,' he said. 'And we all know how that ended. Like a bad joke, ain't it?'

'It's worse than that,' I said, now knowing why Mya had always wanted me to see Dave, now knowing what the final connection was.

Me and Vera at the bar in the Warwick Castle, the usual Friday night larks. 'A tanner says he gets me next.' Vera slams her money down on the bar along with the rest. The landlord sweeps it all up, puts it in the pot. Must be a lot in there; nae more bodies for months now. Auld Jack's been getting slack.

'Hey,' I say, catching his eye as I put my empty glass down. 'Another one in here, eh? And one more for my pal.'

'That's your thirteenth this evening, love,' the landlord comments, raising his hairy old eyebrows like he's giving me a warning.

'So?' I say. 'You think I'm superstitious?'

I know he's thinking what everyone else round here is saying. That Jack got the wrong one last time; he took Mavis thinking she was me. Same Glasgow accent, same name: Patsy Fleming a girl we both pretended to be, me for the bogeys, Mavis for the Social. Cannae remember who thought of her first.

'Cheers.' I clink glasses with Vera, know what she's thinking and all. About the time we stood in court for the doctor, the things we saw and the stories we told to keep it all safe. The big houses in Mayfair and Kensington. The smaller rooms in Bayswater and Paddington, the red lights and the flashlights, the smell of stale sex and cheap perfume. Ernie and Margaret Rose, Mavis and her Lords. The reason Vera sleeps with her doors triple locked and her windows bolted, the reason we are out tonight in our matching outfits, turquoise suits with fox-trim collars, brown suede shoes, very refined. Which one of us d'you think is which tonight then, Jack?

The light slides like a halo off the rim of my glass as I down the amber liquid, the taste of home and a song starting up on the jukebox, that old cowboy song by the fella who played Biggles. A girl singing back-up like she's singing from under the earth, a sound that sends prickles down the back of my neck.

'D'you want another, pet?' says Vera, putting her empty glass down and wobbling on her new shoes, leaning back on the bar for support.

The light swims before me, down the side of my glass and around the optics, swirling around Vera's head, her blonde curls with black roots showing, red lipstick stuck to her front tooth, jacket slightly gaping at the front. She's a big girl, Vera, not like me. I am slight but full of Glasgow courage and now fancying it's time I roped myself a cowboy before the night is out, pay for some more of this good stuff.

'Nah,' I say, 'my purse is empty. Let's go ride the high country, eh, hen?'

Vera cackles and leans against my arm as we walk up Portobello Road in our matching suits and our matching heels, trying to remember the words to Biggles's song as we go, only getting as far as the chorus, two of us bellowing a name: 'Johneee…'

'Ladies,' comes a voice from beside me.

I stop and turn, wondering where I have heard that voice before. A big man in a sheepskin coat, leaning against a long black car, smoking a cigarette. I try to make out his face in the glow of the streetlamp but then another voice joins in from across the road.

'Fancy a ride?' A thinner, smaller man walks across to us, not too much hair on this one.

'Where to, cowboy?' asks Vera, stumbling into him, her hand on his arm, an old shabby mac, not too much brass on him either from the looks of things.

'Not far,' says the big man, moving towards me, his eyes in the dark the only things I can see, two glowing coals in a face of shadows. I touch the cross around my neck, wondering where I know him from, thinking back into a past blurred by too much whisky and too many tall tales to know for sure where everything starts and everything ends...

'We'll travel in convoy,' he says to me, 'to Chiswick. I know the way. He's from out of town.'

Vera whispers in my ear. 'I'll take your number plates, you take mine.' Scared Vera, thinking about the doctor, thinking about Jack.

'Madam.' He beckons me towards the open back door and I slide inside across leather seats, a nice car that smells of money, thinking I got the best deal here, I don't like the look of Vera's, as the car pulls out of Portobello Road and turns left on Ladbroke Grove, underneath the trees where everybody sees, right under the trees of Holland Park Avenue, the spreading plane trees, where I knew a man and he knew me...

'So,' he says, looking at me in the driver's mirror, 'Ernie's been looking for you.'

The words hit me like a punch in the stomach.

I look at his eyes in the mirror and see Ernie staring back, Ernie who they say is now buried under the new flyover, a ton of concrete for his grave. I blink and I swallow and I look again and I see the eyes of Margaret Rose sending me a warning, the second warning of the night I haven't heeded. I look behind me and there is no car behind us, there is no Vera following, only a reflection in the wing mirror, Mavis's eyes all full of sadness, and I hear him laugh as his hand moves towards the dial of the radio, a crackling sound filling the air as I remember who he is.

'No!' I try to speak. 'Don't touch that dial! No.' I open my mouth but no sound comes out. 'Don't touch that dial!' But his fingers close in on the knob and the whole picture dissolves in front of my eyes as he tunes me out for the last time...

'No!' I heard my own voice in my ears, screaming: 'Don't touch that dial!'

I opened my eyes and the room came into focus, the parlour of the Christian-Spiritualist Greater World Association. My right hand was still in the grasp of Stanley's, his big blue eyes wide with shock. My left was held by Mya, her eyes still closed, her own right hand frantically writing out messages on the pad in front of her:

VERA THE DOCTOR AND ME – MAVIS ME AND PATSY – ERNIE IN THE FLYOVER DEAD AND BURIED – MAVIS SAYS THE KING IS IN HIS KASTLE AND RON IS BY THE RIVER! FIND HIM BY THE RIVER!

39

There's a Heartache
Following Me

They sat in the lamplight, in the living room, Joan and the baby sleeping overhead. A bottle of whisky on the table in front of them, piles of their notes surrounding it, connecting mugshots of the departed with their best suspects for the killer, while the grandfather clock counted down the night.

Fielder had returned from his meeting about Steadman not with any news of Sampson Marks's imminent arrest, but instead full of the latest information on Mavis McGruder to share with his men.

The lab reports had come in. Analysis by infra-red and ultra-violet spectro-photometers revealed an exact match for the paint stains on Mathilde Bressant, along with identical traces of sacking, rubber and wood. The rubber was the same kind used for lining a car boot, Fielder explained, and the area of the bodies in contact with it suggested that they had been curled up to fit inside the rear of a vehicle, a station wagon or a big car. It was the reason the killer kept the corpses so long – he had to wait for rigor mortis to pass before he could manipulate them into a convenient position for transportation.

'The laboratory's analysis is that the bodies have not been near an actual paint spray shop, but in or near premises where cars were resprayed during repairs, which narrows down our search somewhat,' he had told the assembled CID. 'If we can find that repair shop, we can find our killer. I want you to continue to visit every mechanic in the district, in pairs, with evidence bags in which to collect your dust samples. One of you will ask to see the manager, keep him detained talking about his paperwork, while the other collects the samples out of sight. We don't want them to know why we're really there, we've already lost too many important witnesses in this case...'

He had let his eyes rest on Pete as he said it, a distinct lack of warmth in them too.

When the hubbub had abated, Coulter tried to have a quiet word with him about Marks, but Fielder's reply was terse, dismissive. Something about The Chopper already being part of an ongoing investigation that couldn't be interrupted, that it was the Flying Squad's call and he could say no more about it.

Pete wondering what this really meant.

July turning into August, tramping round garages as per Fielder's orders, sending the envelopes back to the lab, scanning the papers daily for any mention of a Soho strip club owner getting arrested. August turning into September, the long hot summer as stifling as the unanswered questions between Coulter and Pete that weighed heavier by the day.

October and the General Election: Harold Wilson snatching victory from bumbling old Alec Douglas-Home by a matter of 900 votes. No such reward for the pipe-smoking, Gannex-wearing gaffer of Notting Hill nick: still no samples to match the paintwork on the corpses. Meanwhile, Sampson Marks still at liberty, photographed with the Beatles and the Stones at an art gallery in Mayfair, smiling like a proper Renaissance man.

Pete was just studying this latest affront to public decency when

Coulter came into the canteen, looking more anxious and haggard than Pete had ever seen him.

'Pete, Dick,' he said, sitting down between them. 'A question for you. How far did you get in your search for the Sexy Ron in Stephenson's diary before that fool McSweeney got in the way?'

Pete and Dick exchanged glances.

'I think we did about four of them.' Dick scrunched up his brow. 'Weren't we on the way to Ronald number five when we were so rudely interrupted?'

Pete nodded. 'I can go over my notes but I'm sure you're right. I seem to recall Ronald number five was an ageing drunk from Lancaster Road, seemed pretty pointless to us at the time.'

'Well,' Coulter's fingers tapped on the table-top, 'I've been going over everything in my notes this weekend and I think that's where we've gone astray. What say we go back over the list, discount anyone who looks too long in the tooth to be Sexy Ron and go back to looking for him?'

'Why not?' said Dick, scraping back his chair. 'I for one am sick to death of talking MOT certificates and grovelling round on garage floors.' He started stacking up their empty plates and cups on a tray, got up and took it back to the counter.

'Have you had a tip?' Pete whispered while he was gone.

'Aye,' said Coulter, staring after Dick, 'from one of the girls.' He sat in silence for a moment then turned his eyes towards Pete. 'I've got a bad feeling,' he said, 'that there's going to be another one turn up any minute now.'

'Come over this evening,' Pete offered. 'Joan's making stew and cobblers.' He knew Coulter well enough by now, the older man liked just the sort of food he did. 'There'll be plenty enough to go round, and I know she'd love to see you. Then maybe we can discuss it some more.'

·

They'd been at it for hours now, the clock inching its way towards midnight.

'D'you know,' said Coulter, rubbing his tired eyes, 'I've only ever had one case in my life as bad as this. I can still lose sleep over it now. He was a mad man like this one, killed seven women right under our noses. Seven women and a baby girl.'

'Christie?' Pete stared into Coulter's eyes, melancholy lamps in the dark night.

Coulter nodded. 'Did you know he was a policeman, for a while?'

'No.' Hairs bristling on the back of Pete's neck. 'No, I never did.'

'Well, they keep it pretty quiet these days,' Coulter said, 'but he worked up Harrow Road during the war.'

Pete's hand clenched around his glass. 'Stan,' he said. 'I think I've finally realised what it is that we missed. It's been playing on my mind that me and Dick forgot something when we were checking up on McSweeney.'

'Oh yes?' Coulter blinking himself back from his reverie.

'Now I know it.' Pete's pulse quickened. 'The man McSweeney was having a drink with, the night Bressant was murdered. We asked the landlord if McSweeney was in the Princess Alexandra at the time he said he was and he confirmed it. Said he'd been drinking with a friend. Only I never thought to get a description of the fella he was with. God.' He smacked his palm to his forehead. 'What a fool!'

'What are you saying?' Coulter frowned.

'It wasn't a friend of his helping to drown his sorrows was it?' said Pete. 'It was someone else giving him his orders. Telling him that he had to come down the station and confess to murdering Stephenson, telling him the exact time and place to tell us, so that his story couldn't be argued with. Making us look like fools when the next body turned up. And there's only one person who'd know that, isn't there?'

'The killer,' said Coulter. 'Our Jack.'

'Yes,' said Pete, 'someone so bloody scary that he'd rather give himself up than face the consequences of what might happen if he didn't. I always knew McSweeney's story was balls, he was a bloody con man, running that poker game Christ knows how long without turning a hair. But the fear coming off him that morning, by God. Same as Ernie when we arrested him, and who knows what ever happened to him? Same as bloody Steadman. We need to go back to that landlord, Stan, and pray to God he's got as good a memory for faces as a magistrate…'

'Hold on a minute,' said Coulter. 'Who do you think he's going to tell us it is?'

'Marks,' said Pete, 'I'm sure of it. If he can just give us a good enough description…'

'I don't think so,' said Coulter, shaking his head.

Pete stared at him. 'What?' he said.

'I mean, I think you're right about McSweeney getting his orders from a man in the pub, that makes sense,' said Coulter, 'I'm just not sure it would be Marks coming out in the open, doing something as reckless as that. Why would he, if he's so powerful? Wouldn't he have one of his lackies do his dirty work for him, just in case someone in the pub did have a good memory for faces?'

'Bugger.' Pete, who had been halfway out of his chair, sat right back down. 'You're right. Course he wouldn't. He'd have us chasing round after some minor villain, while he sat back and laughed at us, way he has been all along.'

'Well let's just think about this,' said Coulter, rubbing his hands together, 'think about the kind of villain that could put so much fear into men like Tidsall, McSweeney and Steadman. Now, I knew Steadman pretty well and he wasn't a man to be easily intimidated – stupid he may have been, but cowardly he wasn't, not in the ring nor out of it. That meeting you had with the artist fellow suggested that McSweeney was a fairly consummate professional too. And Tidsall thought he was in the clear the moment he got that fancy lawyer, I wonder who was paying for that?'

'Marks,' Pete scowled, 'has more than enough money to cover that.'

'Ah,' said Coulter, looking at him like a kindly teacher who expects to get the right answer from his star pupil next time, 'but is his empire so great that he can engender the kind of fear that would have McSweeney and Steadman putting themselves away for him for years on end, rather than face his wrath? Are his tentacles that long, that far-reaching?'

Pete suddenly felt his stomach drop from a great height. The photographs. The proof that Wesker had fitted up all those people just to stop any of them from talking about what they might have remembered seeing that night.

'Oh my God,' he said, his mind racing, looking through Coulter and back on to the banks of the Thames and DCI Bell, turning his face away from the light.

'*There are still some sensitive matters pertaining to the Wesker affair that are best left off the record...*'

If Wesker wasn't covering up for Marks, who was he really taking his orders from? Who had that kind of power?

Black-and-white images flashed through his mind, a succession of faces smiling for Ernie's camera. Stopped on Sir Alex Minton and Lord Douglas Somerset.

They were the most powerful men in the room, Pete realised. Powerful enough to have Wesker sent up from West End Central when Gypsy George nicked that bag, that bag of filth, of pictures just like the ones Ernie took, '*on the orders of Scotland Yard's finest, Detective Inspector Reginald Bell*' as he had heard Wesker say with his own ears.

Detective Chief Inspector Reginald Bell to whom he had

handed over every shred of evidence they had, every card he would ever have had to play against an operation more ruthless, corrupt and extreme than he could ever have possibly imagined.

'Oh my good God no,' he said as his whisky glass cracked under his fist, Joan's best crystal splintering into his hand, blood and whisky all over her polished table-top.

Bell and The Bastard. Bell and The Bastard. They had been in it together all along. He hadn't been sent to West End Central to uncover corruption, he realised, but to weave himself into the very web of it, to prove how laughably honest he was, how trusting…

He looked up at Coutler, unable to speak, unable to comprehend the mess he had made of the table, only knowing that now they could never catch Jack, whichever face in the frame he actually was. Now he could never tell Coulter, either. If he opened his mouth he was doomed, done for…

'Steady on, lad,' Coulter said gently, getting to his feet and coming over to Pete, helping him out of the chair and into the kitchen, running cold water over his cut hand and inspecting the lacerations.

'It looks all right,' he said, 'nothing deep enough for stitches I don't think, which is just as well, I don't suppose either of us fancied a visit to St Charles's at this time of night. Where d'you keep your first aid kit?'

Pete motioned with his head to the right cupboard and Coulter found the TCP and the bandages, cleaned him up and dressed his wounds, went back into the lounge and cleaned that up too, started making them both a cup of tea while Pete just stood there, shaking. Thinking about everything he could lose, everything he held dear, everything that slept above him, so peaceful and oblivious to it all.

'Now then.' Coulter steered him back into the lounge, sat him down and put the tea in front of him.

'Drink,' he ordered. 'It'll do you good.'

Pete did as he was told, felt his mind start to focus again as the hot sweetness kicked in.

'So,' said Coulter. 'Christie wasn't the only one, then?'

He said it as if he had known it all along.

Pete clenched his injured hand, shaking his head, looking up at the man sitting opposite, a sudden flicker of hope that the old detective really was the man he thought he was. Not like Wesker. Not like Bell.

Coulter reached across, put his hand over Pete's fist. 'Another one died because of that devious bastard,' he said quietly. 'A man who'd still be walking around today if I had only believed him. Timothy Edwards, poor backwards beggar who swung for him first. Oh, you can say that it wasn't just my fault, that he had a judge and jury trial, twelve good men and true. But I know my part in it and I know what it is you're feeling now, how it'll go on and haunt you for the rest of your days if you let him walk away. I'm not asking you how you know what you know. There are certain things I could never explain to you either. But if you want to get this bastard, this animal, whatever it takes, then I'm with you, all the way.'

Pete felt tears pricking at the back of his eyes, staring at this man who reminded him so much of his father.

'I've been such a fool,' he said.

Coulter shook his head, started to say something reassuring, but Pete cut him off.

'I had the evidence, Stan, more than enough to incriminate Marks and all his well-connected friends. I was left an envelope in my locker, the night we arrested Ferrier. If I'd only opened it a few minutes earlier, before you left, you would have seen it too. A key to a locker on Paddington Station, where there was another envelope. Full of all the other photographs Ernie took that night in Teddy's club. I couldn't even begin to tell you who was on them,

Stan, I wouldn't want you to know, it could kill you.' He rubbed his forehead with his good hand. 'No one saw that envelope delivered, it was Dugdale on shift that night and he was round the back, having a fag, when it miraculously appeared. There was no postmark on it, no stamp. It were that slick I assumed it must have been sent from on high.'

Waves of despair and rage washed over him as he admitted it.

'So I gave them back to the person I thought had left them for me. And now I know he's the one we'll never get past, the reason we'll never be able to bring in Jack, however much we want to. The next day, Steadman was dead and Fielder came back with all that crap about Marks being under the Sweeney's watch. Sent us to look round garages all summer long and gave all the evidence we had, every damn bit of it, to the very people who are going to bury it all. Bury me, too.'

Pete was close to breaking down, the thought of losing Joan and Little Jim…

But Coulter didn't turn a hair. 'Photos,' he said, raising his eyebrows. 'They wouldn't happen to have featured a couple of fellows named Minton and Somerset by any chance, would they?'

'How do you know?' asked Pete, astonished.

'Remember the night you brought Gypsy George in?' the older man said. 'Well I was one of the privileged CID who actually got to see some of the contents of his envelopes. And there was more than just one set of prints in there, a lot more. So tell me, was it just the photographs that were left for you in the locker? No negatives or anything?'

Pete shook his head.

'And it was back in July that you handed them over to this fellow from on high?'

'That's right.'

'Well then, in that case, I would say that you're safe. They've left you alone nearly four months haven't they? Can only mean one thing – they haven't got the negatives either. And they still haven't worked out how you got the prints in the first place.'

Coulter was like a magician, Pete thought, pulling another rabbit out of his hat each time it seemed that all was lost. He felt a smile twitching at the corners of his mouth.

'They think I think they gave them to me,' he realised. 'My ignorance has been keeping me safe all along.'

Coulter nodded. 'So long as you never find out and give the game away,' he said, 'then I doubt anyone will touch either you or your mystery benefactor.'

He leant forwards, patted Pete on the shoulder.

'Sleep easy, Pete,' he said. 'That's what I reckon you should do now. Have a good night's kip and then, when you're up to it, just give some thought to what we've been discussing. If you're willing, we can resume our own private investigations tomorrow. Starting with the landlord of the Princess Alexandra.'

40

Walk Away

'Would you look at this?' Lenny dropped yesterday's paper down disgustedly on my desk. It was open at the arts and entertainments page, just where I anticipated it would be. He had seen it too.

A doe-eyed Beatle and a sharp-faced Stone standing either side of them, Toby was pictured clinking champagne glasses with Pat on the opening night of his latest show at Duke Street. But it was the man standing between them that had nearly made me drop my own edition on the tube floor when I had first seen it. *Club owner and entrepreneur Sampson Marks* the caption had referred to him. But I knew him as someone else, had seen his true profession through the eyes of a murdered girl:

The Chopper.

'Those two bastards,' said Lenny, jabbing two fingers down to cover the faces of the pop stars, 'are responsible for sending poor James round the bend. And this one,' he lifted them up again, pointed his index finger down on to the hatchet face, 'is the reason I moved halfway across London to hide myself in a bank.'

'Really?' I said. I was surprised enough at him mentioning James to me, let alone having prior knowledge of Marks.

'Oh yes,' said Lenny, 'I used to be a bit of a wild one in my youth, but not half as much as him. He used to come round all the clubs, all the pool halls in Bethnal Green, getting his protection money with a bloody great cutlass. Slashed a friend of mine from ear to ear with it. Then he took a shine to me, and that's when I had to get out of the East End.' Lenny shuddered at the memory. 'I didn't want to end up being one of his boys, wearing a Glasgow smile if I said the wrong thing one day. And now they're saying he's got a nightclub in the West End?'

'Doesn't say what kind of nightclub, does it?' I pointed out.

'Not hard to guess, though.' Lenny took his finger off The Chopper's face. 'My godfathers,' he said, 'didn't I tell you that Pat was mixing with the worst kind?'

'What's all the commotion?' Jackie came through the door. She was uncharacteristically late and as I turned my head to greet her, I couldn't help but notice she was looking a bit ruffled, her hair not in its usual immaculate style, her eyes a trifle bleary.

'It's Toby,' said Lenny. 'He's hanging out with gangsters now.'

'You what?' Jackie deposited her bag on the desk and came over, rubbing her brow.

Lenny showed her the offending newspaper item. 'I know him,' he informed her. 'He was the terror of Bethnal Green. Ought to be locked up, by rights. Like I said to Stella, it's all going to come to a bad end for Toby, he gets himself mixed up with this lot.'

'And what were you saying about that other pair?' I wanted to know, tapping my fingers down on the picture. 'About them sending James around the bend?'

'Oh.' Lenny's face went bright red. 'I probably shouldn't have mentioned that. It's not their fault really.' He sat down. 'It's all them pills he's been taking for so long. He thinks the Beatles, the Stones and Phil Spector are spying on his studio and stealing all his ideas. Smashed up half his equipment looking for bugs.'

'Is that where you were last night?' asked Jackie. 'When you were supposed to be down the Gates with me?'

Lenny nodded, shamefaced.

'Don't worry, pet, turns out you did me a favour, standing me up.' There was a definite twinkle in her eye. 'Who'd like to make me a cup of tea and I might just tell you why?'

'I'll do it.' Lenny shot out of his seat.

I raised an eyebrow at Jackie. 'Well, well,' I started to say, but the ringing phone cut me off.

By the time I had finished the call, there was a cup of steaming tea in front of me and two pairs of eyes watching me impatiently, eager for Jackie to get on with her story.

'I'm sorry,' I said, still trying to puzzle out what I had just heard, 'but that was Jenny. For some reason she's been taken into the Royal Marsden Hospital in Chelsea and she wants me to come and visit her, bring her some books, this evening. She said it was just the results of a blood test or something she had to have for the baby, just routine. But isn't the Royal Marsden...'

'The cancer hospital,' said Jackie.

Propped up in her bed on crisp white pillows, her skin glowing clear and her hair fanned around her like a halo, Jenny didn't look like someone who could possibly have a life-threatening disease. It was only when I got close that I saw the lines furrowing her forehead as her eyes worked down the front page of the newspaper she was holding.

It wasn't yesterday's paper that was keeping her captive. Jenny was reading the West End Final edition of the *Evening Post* that proclaimed the discovery of another dead nude with the blunt headline: JACK IS BACK.

'Oh here you are.' She looked up sharply as I opened the door to her private room. 'Did you bring them? Emile Zola and Jean Paul Sartre? At last I'll be able to catch up with all those great minds you were reading years ago. Make a nice change from this.' She tossed the paper on to the bedside table.

'All present and correct,' I said, emptying the contents of my bag out for her. I piled the books next to her flowers and fruit bowl and as I did, I couldn't help but glance at the paper.

They didn't have a name for her yet, nor even a photograph. The picture instead showed a man standing by a pile of branches, a dustbin lid in his hand. 'Not another one,' I said.

'I'm afraid so.' The cheer drained out of Jenny's voice.

'What is this?' I picked up the paper, looked closer at the picture. 'Is this where they found her?'

She nodded. 'In Kensington, this time. By one of the vile buildings Daddy made. The very one I once made a protest against, in fact.'

I looked across at her, over the now very large and perfectly formed bump in her stomach. The cheery façade I had been determined to plaster across my face crumbled at the sight of it. 'Jenny,' I said, 'what's going on? Why are you here?'

She raised her eyebrows. 'It's nothing,' she said, 'honestly. I had one dodgy blood test in my antenatal, which is why I've got to stay in overnight, they want to double check it. I'm sure when the next results come back it'll all have been for nothing.' She moved her hands up to encircle her neck. 'It's a touch of glandular fever, that's all. Nothing so bad as…'

She bit her lip. Glanced towards the door and then back at me.

'What time do you make it?' she asked.

'It's just after seven,' I said, checking my watch.

'Good, then we have a while,' she said, indicating the chair by the side of her bed, 'before Bob gets here.'

I sat down, moved closer to her as she lowered her voice.

'Stella,' she said. 'You know you helped me once when I had no one else to turn to?'

I nodded, holding my breath, wondering whether what she was

about to come out with was the same thing that had been haunting my every waking moment.

'Well, I think I'm going to need to ask you for another favour. And it won't be an easy one either.' Her eyes were as heavy as storm clouds.

'Go on,' I said.

She swallowed. 'I need to go and see my mother,' she said, 'and get back something from that house. She's been trying to offer me an olive branch for years.' Her eyes flicked down to the counterpane, where she began picking at a loose thread. 'But I'm not going to take it,' her gaze flashed back up, 'unless she gives me what I want. I've got a feeling I can make her do it too. I've got a feeling things have not been going so well for Mother lately. Only I need to speak to her, make sure I can get her on her own. And that's where you come in.'

A prickle of fear moistened my palms but I tried not to let it show. Instead I nodded and smiled, encouraging her to continue while I battened it down.

'If I can get to see her, would you come with me?' she asked. 'It's not just because I'm so fat I have to lean on you, it's the moral support I need more. It'll be hard for me to go back to that house, you see.' She dropped her gaze again, resumed tugging at the thread. 'I didn't have a happy childhood, Stella. Money doesn't buy you that. Quite the opposite, in fact.'

'I think I understand,' I said, not wanting to break any confidences, but not wanting her to have to say it out loud. 'It's why Dave was so worried about you, you know, when I saw him that time…'

She gave a brief smile that could have been a grimace. 'Dil,' she said, 'dear old Dil. The only man who never judged. That's why I could talk to him. How much did he tell you?'

'That your father is a dangerous man,' I said, trying not to blink, trying not to give into the fear that coiled around my guts.

She nodded. 'He is. But Stella,' she left the thread, put her hand over mine, reading my obvious discomfort, 'don't think I'm going to let him anywhere near you. If we do go back to my parents' house it will only be on the condition that he isn't there, that no one else sees us. I think Mother will agree to it, it's the only chance she's going to get of seeing her granddaughter, after all. It's just that you might have to see a few things that are,' she paused, her fingers clenching against my hand, 'pretty bloody vile. Do you know anything about sado-masochism, Stella?'

I nodded, trying to pluck courage from thin air.

'I do,' I said. 'I've seen some pretty bloody vile things myself.'

She nodded, as if I was verifying something she had thought all along.

'I knew I could trust you,' she said. She leant back on her pillow, her eyelids fluttering. 'Thank you, Stella.' She squeezed my hand and let it go, closed her eyes.

Silence welled around us, as I stared at her, forcing back the tears. Heard somebody turn the handle of the door and turned to see Robert Mannings, his arms full of flowers.

'Gosh,' Jenny came back round, 'I nearly drifted off then. You don't realise what having a baby does to you, how much they knock you out. Oh Bob.' She looked over my shoulder and smiled. 'Here you are, darling.'

'I should go,' I said, standing up. 'Let you two have some time together.'

'Thanks, Stella.' Jenny smiled dreamily.

Mannings nodded, grunting his assent. The dark rings around his eyes and the way he could barely force a smile told me that he was taking this way worse than Jenny was. Either that, or she was only telling me half the story with her glandular fever line. I could hardly bear to look at him either. All I could see was Jenny standing there, in my dream.

I hadn't realised that it meant her as well.

But everything else had come true.

41

Baby, Let Me Take You Home

The blonde girl sat at a table in the far corner of the Warwick Castle, downing her second glass of whisky as she went over her story again. It was three weeks since her friend had gone missing, three weeks' worth of whisky, but still nothing had blurred the memory of that night.

'We went to Oxford Street, shopping, you know,' she said. 'Ended up buying the same outfit, a turquoise two-piece with fur trim, still got mine in the closet at home, I can show it you, if you want. I haven't worn it since.' She shivered, took another gulp of her drink. 'It was Jeanie's idea of a joke, if we wore the same outfit Jack the Stripper wouldn't know which one of us was which. 'Cos the rumour had been going round that when he took Mavis, he was really after Jeanie. They both came from Glasgow and they both used the same name, Patsy Fleming, a little scam they cooked up to fool you lot.' Her kohl-rimmed eyes looked up for an instant at Coulter's, then back down at her empty glass.

'Why would he be after Jeanie, Vera?' Coulter asked.

She picked the glass up, rolled it round in her fingers.

'Because of the doctor,' she said, eyes following the motion. 'Dr Ward. We both testified for him last year. Twice. Marylebone and the Bailey. I'm sure you've got it all on record. We tried to prove he weren't poncing us, he was just our gentleman friend, which he was. But you know what happened.' Her eyelashes flicked upwards and she stared at Coulter. 'Look, d'you mind if I have another one in here?' She lifted up the glass. 'Only it gives me the willies to keep going back over all this.'

'I'll go.' Pete didn't want to break Coulter's concentration, nor the thread of the blonde girl's story. For according to Vera, the body discovered yesterday morning, Wednesday the 25th of November, on a patch of wasteland behind the car park on Hornton Street, Kensington, was her missing friend Jeanette White. Nobody else had been able to come up with a name for her so far; only they had a decomposed naked body of a five-foot-one-inch woman with short black hair, a tattoo on her right arm of a bunch of flowers with *Jeanette* written on top of it and *Mum and Dad* in a scroll underneath. She had been dead about a month.

But Coulter had sprung into action as soon as the news came through. Headed straight to the Warwick Castle looking for this Vera as if he already knew she would have all the answers for him. Maybe he did. So much of Coulter's information seemed to come from the girls themselves, Pete was sure this must have come from one of the other Portobello toms who had seen them drinking together in this pub, on the night of October 23rd.

That night, Jeanette and Vera had staggered out of here with thirteen whiskies each under their belts and been picked up by a couple of men on the corner of Portobello Road and Elgin Avenue. Each man had his own car and they were supposed to be travelling in convoy to Chiswick, where the girls had been told that the business would take place.

'This for Vera?' asked the landlord, raising bushy, salt-and-pepper eyebrows at Pete. 'On the house.'

All that money in the pot, Vera was the only one to claim it back alive.

'Jeanie's one was definitely local,' the blonde was telling Coulter as Pete came back with her drink, 'I could tell by his accent. My one said he was from out of town, which was why we were supposed to be following Jeanie's car, but he sounded pretty London to me. Anyway, Jeanie's john must have done a shortcut, we lost him round the Bush somewhere. Funny, ain't it?' She snatched up the glass Pete had placed in front of her and took a hefty slug. 'It was a flash motor he was driving, a Zephyr I think, one of them ones with the big grilles at the front. How could you lose one of them? I was going to take the number plates down,' she said and grimaced, 'but my john made me sit in the back seat and I couldn't get a good enough look at them from there.'

'Well,' Coulter shifted in his seat, trying to hide his disappointment at this last comment, 'never mind that, Vera, you've been a great help to us so far, better than anyone else as a matter of fact. Which is why I have to ask you if you wouldn't mind performing one last act of kindness for Jeanie and come with me to the morgue to identify the body. After you've finished your drink, of course.'

The blonde's eyes travelled nervously round the pub. 'All right,' she said. 'I suppose it is the least I could do.'

It didn't take long for Pete and Dick to dig up the records of Jeanette White and Vera Barton, their dalliance with the late osteopath Dr Stephen Ward. Both of them had twice testified that they had only known him socially as part of a West London party scene involving a lot of painters, actors, 'and those even higher up the social scale', as White had put it, 'winking at the judge as if to implicate him too', according to the *Daily Record*. Pretty and vivacious, Jeanette had gone down well with the press at both trials, even if the prosecution had made mincemeat of her claims. But she had never been the star of this particular show and unlike some of her younger, more luminous co-defendants, she hadn't been able to capitalise on that momentum, start herself up a singing career out of it.

Jeanette had gone straight back on the beat.

'Imagine the headlines we're going to get as soon as we release her ID,' Dick said. '*Profumo Girl Is Stripper Victim*? *The Doc, The Tart And The Stripper*? They're going to have a field day with us, send a load more nutters our way too, no doubt.'

'Aye.' Pete stared at the newsprint, a photo of Jeanette outside the court, lighting up a cigarette. Side on, her profile was sharp, her nose too long, not such a looker as Miss Keeler or Miss Rice Davies after all.

'I wonder,' Dick continued, 'how this all fits in with the filth angle in ours – Ernie, Houghton, Stephenson and the rest. What's the betting they were all part of the same circle?'

'Odds-on,' said Pete, a succession of black-and-white snapshots running through his mind, icy fingers running down his spine. 'Something else that's strange,' he realised. 'Why was this one left in Kensington? All the others have been in or near the river. For some reason, I always thought that was the thread, maybe because mad men are so often fixated by water. But this…'

Jeanette's body had been found by a warden working for the civil defence station hidden underneath Hornton Street. He had noticed that one of their dustbins was missing its lid and saw the glint of metal from what looked like a big pile of rubbish and branches, followed the trail and picked it up. Found a dead face staring back at him.

None of the others had been hidden this way.

But more than that, there was something about the location that was nagging at Pete. Hornton Street. Where had he seen that name before? Why was it so significant?

He looked back down at the paper. It was Mandy Rice Davies's grin that reminded him. Reminded him of another blonde with an insouciant smile and hair like Brigitte Bardot, waving a placard saying NO MORE UGLY and standing in front of a building site her father was working on. A building site in Kensington...

'Oh, so you have got a theory, then?' Dick said. 'Well, for what it's worth, here's mine, only keep it to yourself if you don't mind, it's a little bit controversial.'

Pete looked up from his paper. 'What?' he said.

'I reckon he's one of us.' Dick dropped his voice down to a whisper. 'A copper. In on the investigation. 'Cos it seems to me like he's laughing at us. Leaving the last one outside a garage, when we were looking at garages. Then this one, right on top of a civil defence bunker...'

Pete stood up. 'Show it me on the map,' he said. 'Where this one were found. I want to try and make a picture of it in my mind.'

'Do you think I'm on to something then?' said Dick.

'Lads,' a voice came from behind them. Coulter was standing in the doorway, illuminated by the first smile that had passed over his countenance for a very long time. 'There's an outside chance I could retire a happy man,' he said. 'Not only did Vera make the formal ID, but she also took the time to help draw up some identikit photos of the two men she and Jeanette went off with. Take a look at these ugly mugs, see if they ring any bells for you.'

He placed them face up on the desk.

'This is Jeanette's john,' he said.

Pete looked, saw a wide face with thick lips, dark crew-cut hair and a pair of sticking-out ears. A furrowed forehead with thick eyebrows meeting in the middle, cruel little eyes beneath. 'She said he was tall,' Coulter elaborated, 'about five foot eleven, six foot and probably between thirty and thirty-two years of age. Wearing a sheepskin jacket and driving a black Ford Zephyr. Speaks with a

London accent. This one,' he tapped his finger down on the second picture, 'is his accomplice, the one that Vera drew the lucky long straw for.'

Pete looked, saw an older face, a thin face with slightly wavy hair, going thin on top. 'This one is shorter and of a lighter build,' said Coulter. 'About the same age, thirty, thirty-two. Said he was from out of town but Vera didn't buy it, thought the two men knew each other well, acted as if tag-team tart-hunting was a sport they were familiar with.'

Familiar with...

Pete felt the blood hammering through his temples as he looked from one face to the other. Felt the ground shifting under his feet as he stared at Jeanette's john. It was exactly the same face the landlord of the Princess Alexandra had sketched out for them a month or so ago. Now he knew for sure.

Jeanette's john was Ron, Sexy Ron. Not McSweeney, nor any other late-night denizen of Ladbroke Grove, but someone Pete had known all along. He hadn't actually featured in any of Ernie's pictures, but he hailed from West End Central all the same. Wesker's right-hand man, the sacked, disgraced former Detective Constable Ronald Grigson.

And his accomplice, Vera's john, looked like none other than Francis Bream.

42

You've Lost That Loving Feeling

The car pulled up on a quiet side road behind Kensington High Street, on the corner of Holland Park. 'This is it,' said Jenny.

Swathed in a long back coat, hat and mittens, Jenny's body was an uncomfortable bulk compared to the pale thinness of her face. But determination smouldered in her blue eyes as she leant towards the driver.

'We shouldn't be any longer than twenty minutes,' she said.

He nodded, stray wisps of sandy hair bouncing on the crown of his pink, freckled head. 'Right you are, love,' he said, picking up a newspaper from the passenger seat, folded at the sports pages.

'Good.' She turned to me. 'Are you ready, nursey?'

I smiled as best as I could, feeling awkward in my stiff clothes, thick black stockings and sensible shoes. It had taken Jenny just over a month to organise this meeting, during which time she had been discharged from hospital with a clean bill of health, she said. Over Christmas she'd kept a full house, inviting round hordes of people to examine her bump and help put the finishing touches to the nursery. None of them had suspected there was anything wrong with her. Only Mannings's fearful eyes, the times when he excused himself to stand outside smoking, gave anything away to me.

Jenny had put a lot of preparation into this moment. The nurse's outfit and medical bag had come from one of their friends who worked in costume, the perfect way of smuggling me in without making her mother nervous. Her father was finally away on business, out of the country, and she'd made her mother promise to give their staff the afternoon off. I didn't have to do anything, she assured me, but wait for her.

I opened the car door, went round to the other side to help Jenny out. As my feet touched the pavement, a flash of memory, another's memory, buzzed through my mind.

Mathilde Bressant, holding a long blond wig.

I caught my breath, closed my eyes for a second, before taking Jenny's arm and walking with her to the gate of a palatial white mansion, encased by a high brick wall and surrounded on all sides by tall fir trees that bent in the bitter, south-easterly wind, as if to shield it further from prying eyes.

'Don't be scared,' Jenny said, pressing the buzzer on the wall by the gate.

'I'm here,' she told the intercom.

The gate clanged, and with an electronic buzz, began to open. We crossed the threshold, walked up the garden path to the front door, where a woman stood waiting beneath Doric columns, in front of the door.

A small woman in a mauve Chanel twinset and a pale yellow blouse, coiffured blonde hair forming a helmet around her pinched face. Ropes of pearls around her neck and gold bracelets at her wrists made her look weighed down by wealth, like her jewellery could snap her skinny limbs at any minute. There was still a ghostly imprint of former beauty hidden under her heavily made-up face, the shape of her high cheekbones that Jenny had inherited. But she was too skeletal, too artificial and much too nervous.

'Jennifer.' Her voice came out high and reedy and she pitched forwards clumsily, watery eyes taking in her daughter's appearance with painful intensity.

'It's all right, Mother,' Jenny said, catching hold of her arm. 'There's no need to panic, that's why I've brought my nurse along.'

Mrs Minton tried her best to smile, the corners of her mouth twitching like a landed fish. She quickly averted her gaze to me, blinking furiously as she offered me her hand.

'Rosemary Minton,' she said. Her hand was frail but her perfume was overpowering. It almost masked the waves of alcohol fumes coming off her breath, but my nose was sensitive to such things.

'I'm Sister Innes,' I said, the black joke temporarily calming my nerves. 'Patricia. I'm here to make sure that Jenny's OK, but I won't get in your way.'

Jenny nodded encouragingly. 'Pats can just wait in the kitchen,' she said. 'We'll only call her if we need her.' She put her hand over her stomach and I watched her mother's eyes being drawn towards it hypnotically.

'I'll show her the way.' Jenny moved forwards, opening the door, leading us into a hallway that looked just as I had imagined it, right down to the sweeping central staircase with its red carpet, the family portraits adorning the walls and the immense chandelier hanging from the ceiling.

'I'm sorry,' Mrs Minton said to me as she closed the door behind us, 'but I've let my staff have the afternoon off. Will you be able to make yourself comfortable?'

'Of course she will.' Jenny swept me down the corridor, the eyes of her ancestors following us as we went. The eyes of her father, not of her mother.

She winked as she left me in front of a range big enough to cook for an army.

'Hold tight, Pats,' she said. She had no fear at all; on the contrary, Jenny looked thrilled with the way this game was going. But the moment she disappeared to join her mother, the dial in my brain switched on.

I saw Susannah Houghton blinded in the flash of a camera, a weird carnival coming into focus around her, of men dressed as women and women dressed as men, half naked and painted, wearing feathers and dildos and wielding whips, heard the high-pitched noise of artificial laughter echoing around a ballroom.

I took hold of a chair, stumbled down into it, shutting my eyes. Tried to visualise instead a blue light around me, the face of my pa, holding tight to what Mya had told me:

'Take courage. He walks beside you always, keeping you safe with his love.'

It only seemed like five minutes before I heard footsteps behind me and almost jumped out of my skin. Jenny was back in the room, her eyes wide and her face flushed.

'Where's your mother?' I asked, my heart hammering.

'Out cold.' She held up a tiny phial in hand. 'It pays to be a good patient, you know. You get to learn all sorts from nurses, especially what works best with gin. Now come on, we've got to do this fast. Pass me your bag.'

My hands shook as I handed it over, but Jenny moved with such speed she didn't notice, snapping it open and dropping the phial in, producing a large ring of keys from its depths. I had imagined she would need some time to talk her mother round to whatever it was she wanted to get from her, I had never envisioned her doing anything like this.

Not for the first time I felt awed and slightly scared by Jenny.

'This way,' she said, moving towards a different door to the one we'd come in by. 'The servants' entrance gets there faster.'

I found myself running to keep up with her, through the door and down a flight of stairs, down into the bowels of the house. Though I tried to keep a hold on the image of Pa, the dial started to slip again, transmissions flashed before my eyes – Mavis on a blasphemous altar, a line of men in cloaks queuing up to take her. Raising her head to look at me as I stood beside them, mouthing the words that I dreaded to hear:

'The King is in his Kastle. He's the dirty rascal.'

We were running down a long corridor, towards a black door in a wall painted red. Jenny stopped in front of it, thrust the medical bag at me and began counting through the keys on her ring, her hands moving in the same fashion that Mya's fingers had counted my visions back to her.

'This one,' she said, putting it into the lock and turning it. The door opened and she turned to face me, her face glowing with exhilaration and power.

'The bag,' she said, taking it back from me. Her eyes ran me up and down. 'It's all right, Stella,' she said, putting her finger up to touch my forehead. 'You just stay here, it'll be all right. You don't have to come inside. Stay on this side.'

I opened my mouth but she had already turned, gone into the room. I took a step to follow but what I saw made me reel back against the wall, turn my face to it, shutting my eyes, trying to block it out.

I was no longer sure which world I was in. Faces and images raced in front of my eyes on fast forward, and I felt sure that if I turned I would see the room pulsing red, pulsing danger and death. I started to slide towards the floor, trying to focus on the blue light, focus on Pa.

'There are no dead.'

I heard the words as if he had spoken them directly into my ear. But when I opened my eyes, it was Jenny standing over me, putting a cool hand on to my forehead.

'It's done,' she said, 'we can go.'

The black door was closed behind her. She took hold of my hand and led me back down the corridor, up the stairs, into the kitchen, where the pale daylight of the winter afternoon slanting through the windows seemed totally incongruous.

'How long have we been here?' I said, my throat raw and dry as if I had been screaming.

Jenny looked at her watch. 'Twenty minutes, all done. You did brilliantly, Stella, now let's get out of here.'

She punched some numbers into a keypad by the front door and then we ran out, down the garden path, towards the gate that was opening. I could no longer think clearly, only that surely in her condition, Jenny shouldn't be running and why did she say I had done brilliantly when I had done nothing at all?

The driver was standing by the gate as we got there; something about him suddenly struck me as familiar, something about those pale strands of sandy hair, but I couldn't place where I had seen him before. I felt as if I had sunk an ocean of booze.

'Take this,' Jenny handed him the bag, 'and help me get her in the car. She's had a bit of a funny turn.'

As I fell down on the back seat, she gave a laugh, a wild and triumphant sound. Then she turned towards me, her eyes blinding, iridescent. 'Come on nursey,' she said. 'Let's get you home.'

I don't remember getting there, only brief fragments of the driver helping Jenny shoulder me into my room and laying me down on my bed. Jenny leaning over me, planting a kiss on my forehead and whispering: 'Thank you.'

Then the dial slipped and it was night.

•

*I step out of the car and on to the kerb, the clack of steel-tipped
stilettos on pavement, stomach lurching as I stumble, black velvet
and vodka curdling inside. The world spins around me for a
moment, gradually comes back into focus as I watch his tail lights
disappearing under the trees.*

*All I know is that this is not where I'm supposed to be. I put my
hand up to my hair that I've just had waved, the style of an actress
I had admired, a vague memory tapping at the corner of my skull.
Should I not be over in the Bush tonight? Giving Mandy a hand with
the kids? So how in God's name did I land myself here? The old black
velvet had me in its spell. Now what am I supposed to do?*

*I look up for the moon but I can't see it through the branches
of these trees. Maybe they've taken it down. Better try to get my
bearings some other way.*

*There's a tube station, but it's all shut up for the night, and I can't
make out the lettering that moves like an Art Nouveau swirl over
the door, the windows gazing back at me blankly, like whatever else
is going on around here, this is surely none of my business. That's
right. It's time to call it a night.*

*I tighten the belt on my long, wool herringbone coat, try to keep
the chill from my bones as I walk around the corner. Mother of God,
what a horrible place. A high tower like a castle's keep made out of
red brick, little tiny windows all the way up it but just one light on,
one yellow light, right at the top. It's like a lighthouse, sweeping its
beam across a dark and choppy sea. They've taken down the moon
and put this here instead, put a lighthouse here to lure me on to the
rocks. Fear lurches in my belly as I back away from it, stumbling
again in my rush, turning around the corner past the tube station,
on to the lonely avenue.*

*The party's over. A tune comes into my mind, something my da
used to play on the phonograph back home in Watling Street, before*

I came to London and all of this charade. A song that played while I danced too long in that place with the flickering candles. But it seemed so right, the way he held me tight, like a beautiful dream that was never going to end. So much for that now. It's time to call it a night.

This isn't the moon, nor the beam of a lighthouse that's coming towards me now. It's a pair of headlights in a long black car that slows down as it catches me in its rays, slows down and turns around across the road, comes to a halt just where the last one did, just where I came in. Is he a cab, come to take me home? I can't make it out.

He winds the window down and says something to me, but it's lost in a burst of static like a radio being turned on, the dial slipped between stations. I lean in towards him.

'Can you take me to Shepherd's Bush, mister?' I hear myself say, and I see him nod, reach out to take the handle of the rear door...

My fingers touch metal and the dial slips.

A squeal of feedback and a burst of static, a cat screams and a woman laughs. The sound of a guitar like the revving of a motorbike engine, the ominous thump of bass, coming up distorted into the night air, like music being played underwater.

The dial slips...

43

Here Comes The Night

Somewhere out of town.

They had pored over the map, marked with red pins for the bodies. Apart from Jeanette White, every single one of them had been found in or around the Thames west of Hammersmith. That was where to look.

Somewhere that looks like a factory, or an electricity substation, with cooling towers and transformers.

Closing in between Brentford and Acton, last resting places of Mathilde Bressant and Mavis McGruder, areas of industrial sprawl. Looking for factory estates with motor repair shops on them, going through lists of employees, security guards, nightwatchmen. Endless lists that took months to comb through; beyond Coulter's retirement, beyond Christmas and New Year, into the early days of 1965.

Then the name they had been searching for came up. A phone call confirmed it.

On the 13th of January, Pete stood on a railway bridge in Acton, looking across the embankment towards the Swan Factory Estate. A bleak, brown range of low brick and concrete buildings, cooling towers rising out of them, corrugated iron and barbed-wire fencing circling them, crouched and frowning under a grey sky.

There were thirty-five factories employing six thousand people on the Swan Estate, a sports ground and plenty of wasteland in between. Unrestricted public access twenty-four hours a day, which was good. Pete didn't want to have to show his credentials. He had the name of the boss of every operation and a cover story about looking for work as security, a riff on his army and police background that sounded feasible, if anybody stopped him to ask.

Pete walked through the south-westerly wind that brought particles of rain stinging against his face. Walked towards the disused Oldham Aero Engine factory, gone bust last August but still left open and unsecured, the premises belonging to the estate, new tenants not yet found. Followed some employees from neighbouring companies as they took a short cut through the empty hangar to a café on Westfields Road beyond it, taking in the old mattresses, discarded beer cans and used rubbers that lay amongst the dust and the still machinery, signs of Oldham Aero developing a night-time identity to rival Gobbler's Gulch and Ronald McSweeney's tennis club.

Turned east towards the next large building, parallel to Oldham Aero, a big brick construction with its name painted in three-foot high letters along the front and sides. YATES & LISTON MOTOR ENGINEERS & COACH BUILDERS.

Went down the side of it, listening to the hammer and clang of the machines, the whirr of the extractor fans, the hiss and whoosh of the paint sprayers. Crossed the road towards the premises at the rear of it, Eastfields, another aircraft firm specialising in precision casting bodywork.

Between these two factories and Oldham Aero, waste ground studded with low buildings. Pete circled back towards them, found a block of men's toilets, an outbuilding housing transformers, another solitary men's toilet, a locked switch-room and a boiler house.

Abandon hope all ye who enter here chalked on the wall of the boiler house.

Walked through the wind and the stinging rain, following a metal pipeline towards a transformer shed. Walked around it, noticing vents on each side tacked over with wire mesh. Felt a prickling down his spine, his blood starting to hum, like the moment before you got up from your corner and danced to the middle of the ring.

Two sliding locks on the door were all that kept the shed closed.

Pete took his torch from his coat pocket, drew back the locks with his gloved hands. Took one look behind him, saw only the dull humps of buildings through the drizzle. Stepped through and closed the door behind him.

It was freezing inside the shed, the wind coming in through the wire mesh vents on either side of him moaning loudly in his ears. His throat felt dry as he switched the torch on, dry and tight, heart hammering in his ribcage as the circle of light swooped across the pipes and valves, across the brick and brass and then stopped as it fell on something that was not metal nor stone, something that was curved and curled and shrouded in sackcloth.

He stepped towards it, his own breath hanging on the air in a cloud, knelt down and touched the sacking. Pulled it away from the white, nude body of a girl, a girl with black hair waved and cut into a bob, a girl who looked so very much like Bobby Clarke, except that her blank, black staring eyes screamed out above a mouth that had been stoppered, a cry that had been cut off forever by the fruit of the original sin –

A bright, hard, green apple forced between her lips.

He lurched upwards, blood pounding, reeled backwards, into something cold, something hard, something pushing against the back of his neck.

'Bradley?' the voice sounded surprised. 'I weren't expecting you.'

He had come in so silently that Pete hadn't even heard above the noise of the wind, the shock of the sight before him. Or maybe

Grigson had been there all along, skulking in the darkest corner of his lair.

'But then,' he went on, 'I always did make you for a rubber heels bastard. I could smell it on you, like flies round shit. What are you, then? The advance party?'

Pete tried to push down the rush of fear that jumped in his gut, keep his voice level.

'Hello Ron,' he said. 'Who did you think it was going to be?'

The man behind him gave a low chuckle. 'Don't give me that old pony,' he said. 'You know full well who I mean.' He shoved the gun into the side of Pete's face, rubbed the cold metal up and down his cheek. As he moved in closer, Pete could smell the decay on his breath, the grease on his hair. He smelt like a man who'd been sleeping rough, a man who had scarcely been home since November. Grigson's wife said she had last seen her husband on Christmas Day, but he hadn't stopped for long.

'We'll both just have to wait for him, won't we?' he said. 'Should make life interesting.'

Pete stared down at the defiled woman at his feet. 'Who is she?' he asked.

'I dunno,' Grigson said. 'Just some Paddy whore I bumped into. She weren't on the list.'

'She looks just like the first one.'

'D'you know?' Grigson's tone turned incredulous again. 'That's just what I thought. She was in the same place and all, just outside Holland Park tube, seemed like it was meant to be. I mean, all this trouble over that silly little tart. Got me so mad that I couldn't resist it. I did have a funny feeling about her when I saw her though, for a minute I thought she might have come back to haunt me.' He gave a sharp laugh. In his fugitive state, Grigson was beginning to unravel. ''Til she opened her gob, that is. No, I reckon it was fate what put her there,' he went on. 'Brought it on herself, she did. And you got to admit, I did a good job on her. Used all the same methods. You'd never be able to tell her from an original, 'cept he always took the apple out of their mouths before I dumped them. I thought I'd leave it, give you flatfoot bastards something more interesting to go on. Something that might explain the motivation.'

All the time Grigson was speaking, Pete had been calculating the distance between his heel and the other man's knee, the trajectory a bullet would take if the trigger were to be squeezed. The gun rested upwards, towards the ceiling. A discharge might temporarily blind him, his skin would get burned, but he wouldn't get hit.

'You a religious man yourself then, Ron?' he asked.

He didn't wait for the reply, just kicked back hard with his right leg, swivelled round to the left, brought up his fist as hard as he had ever punched. Fist connected to jaw as the gun went off, deafeningly loud, the flare of it illuminating Grigson crumpling, the gun dropping out of his hand.

Adrenalin was pumping so hard, Pete couldn't even work out if he had been hit. As Grigson floundered, Pete kicked the gun as far into the darkness as he could, launched himself on top of the other man. Slowly realised that everything still seemed to be working properly. And that Grigson wasn't putting up a fight. The blow to the jaw had KO'd him. He scrambled for the torch he had dropped on the concrete floor, felt his fingers connect with it just as the door swung open.

Francis Bream standing there.

'Pete!' Bream's eyes rapidly took in the tableau before him. 'You got him?'

Pete looked from him to Grigson, eyes rolled to the back of his head.

'Looks like it,' he said, getting to his feet. 'No thanks to you.'

'Sorry, I was...' Bream started to say, but then his eyes fell on the body of the woman, her flesh luminous in the dim light. A muscle twitched in his cheek.

'Not another one,' he said, walking forwards. 'Who's she?'

Pete stepped aside, brushing filth from his coat. 'I don't know,' he said. 'She wasn't on the list, apparently.'

Bream winced, gaze transfixed on the apple in her mouth. 'So that's how he did it with their teeth. Christ.'

Pete put his hand on Bream's arm, noticed the broken skin on his knuckles. 'What's the list, Frank? Can you explain any of this to me?'

Bream shook his head. 'I'll do my best,' he said, dragging his watery eyes away from the corpse and back towards Pete's. 'Suppose I should start at the beginning, shouldn't I?'

'Bobby Clarke?' said Pete.

'Clarke got killed because Simon Fitzgerald took a fancy to her,' said Bream, 'one night at Teddy's. Badgered Marks to get her to come to this party they were having, the usual swingers stuff. Said he had to have her, a right petulant sod about it he was. But they were making a lot of gelt off Simon in them days, so they indulged him.'

Pete flashed back to their last night at Teddy's, Marks talking to the corpulent manager, a brown envelope passing between their hands.

'The Chopper went out to get her, taking our friend here with him. A couple of hours later they were driving her back to Gobbler's Gulch.'

'It *was* Fitzgerald?' Pete frowned.

'It was an accident,' said Bream, 'a bit of rough stuff gone too far. Marks got Grigson to help him wash her clean and then dump her, made sure his pet copper was tied into it. Must have got someone else down to the murder scene too – remember how you told me that the body had been moved after you found her, that night in the pub with Dai? That's when I realised how bloody difficult this was going to be.'

Pete nodded, slow throbbing pain coming into his knuckles now as the adrenalin receded.

'Anyway, nothing happened for months, so they were beginning to feel safe – until you nicked Gypsy George O'Hanrahan with the Somerset family album. Wesker was impressed by how you took O'Hanrahan down, thought you had balls, which was why I encouraged him to offer you a transfer. He trusted me, The Bastard did; thought I was his eyes and his ears. Grigson was dead against it, he read you right from the off, but Wesker was sure there wouldn't be no trouble once you were all tied up in all their bagwork, bringing in all Ernie's faces. Trouble was, right in the middle of us cleaning up the streets of Soho, there was another party and another dead tart to dispose of.'

'Bronwyn Evans.' Pete tried to keep up with his former colleague. 'Or Gladys Small, as they called her. What happened to her?'

Bream rolled his eyes. 'Simon got ants in his pants again,' he said. 'Asked The Chopper for a girl. Well, remember I told you about Big Tits Beryl? She'd been having a bit of bother with Evans, who was a drunk, loud-mouthed sort of tart, her best years long behind her, if she ever had any in the first place. Marks knew her of old, knew she was a liability. He must have thought that if Fitzgerald went off his rocker again, here was one girl who wouldn't be missed. That time, they tried to dispose of her more carefully, but even so, Marks couldn't resist winding us lot up by burying her opposite the first one, just to see how much of a flap he could get us into. Worked and all, didn't it?'

Pete shook his head. 'My God,' was all he could say.

'So, anyway,' Bream went on, 'you know what comes next. The

riot, the pieces of brick. Grigson gets the sack, Wesker gets carted off to the funny farm – and with all his protection gone, Fitzgerald goes and tops himself, even before the Welsh tart's body is found. That was the end of the first Jack the Stripper. But the second one was a whole lot more sinister.'

The wind shrieked through the air vents, icy fingers caressing their ears, their noses. Pete shifted his weight from one foot to the other. 'Go on,' he said.

'Something else happened on the day of the riot, that wasn't realised until later,' Bream said. 'Wesker had retained some of Gypsy George's stash for safekeeping. Not all of it, just the pictures taken at Teddy's,' he raised his eyebrows, 'and the negatives. The stuff that might incriminate him, should it ever fall into the wrong hands. Only in all the bother that day, they somehow got lost...'

'You,' Pete began, but Bream winked, put his finger to his lips.

Bream with the photos on him, that night at Teddy's. Hiding them in plain sight.

'See Marks,' Bream said, 'was only one little cog in a much bigger wheel.'

Minton, thought Pete, *Somerset*.

Bream nodded, as if reading his mind. 'And the ones much higher up than him decided something must be done. They'd already had one of their mates, a respected MP, taking a hit. Not to mention the unfortunate doctor who had tended them with such care.' Bream glanced down at Grigson, poked at him gingerly with his toe to make sure he was still out cold. 'They didn't want no more call-girl scandals. So one of them had a bright idea. Dim old plod still hadn't twigged Simon Fitzgerald for Clarke and Evans, didn't look like we ever would, and Si weren't in a position to tell any tales. So why not just carry on his work? Resurrect him, turn him into a figure of nightmare who preys upon ladies of the night, kills them in mysterious ways and leaves their bodies in places designed to fool us all? Let the press use their all-too predictable brains to come up with a name for him, something the public would enjoy – leave them nude and it wouldn't take long. And so the second Jack the Stripper was born.'

Pete shook his head, all the pictures falling into place now.

'They made a list of all the girls they reckon posed the worst threat. The regulars at these parties,' Bream continued, 'the ones who worked for Ernie. Then the mastermind behind this fiendish plan volunteered his services to play the part of Jack.'

The throbbing in Pete's knuckles was intensifying, along with the expression in Bream's green eyes.

'He had his reasons, you see. He had this daughter he was rather more fond of than any decent father should be. Only she had rebelled against him and made him look stupid, turned her back on him, slipped out of his grasp. He weren't used to not getting his way and his jealous rage turned him into a monster. He'd been in the army, seen active service; he knew how to be cruel and how to do it without leaving a mark. He took his revenge on these women, and good old Grigson here, now that he weren't any use in an official capacity no more, got to be his bagman.

'See, Grigson was in a unique position – the girls all knew him as a good source of income, they'd go off with him willingly, even the ones who were all tooled up to take on the Stripper.' Bream gave a bitter laugh. 'Trouble is, it took me too long to work this all out. And when I did, it weren't just a matter of finding him. That was easy enough, he hadn't moved house or anything. No, my problem was that I had to persuade him I was still as bent as he thought I was. Still the same old Bream, the clown that they all took me for, just wanting to relive old times, chasing skirt and getting pissed, way we used to do in the old days. Months of talking bollocks and standing rounds it took me. I thought I had him, that night on the 'Bello…'

'That's why he went rogue,' said Pete. 'He thought they'd sent you after him, that the game was over and they were taking care of the loose ends. That's why he left Jeanette White where he did, it was a warning. That's why he did for this poor beggar, that's what he was telling me…'

A long groan rose up from the floored bulk between them. Grigson was coming round.

'Better get him cuffed up,' said a voice from the doorway.

The two men turned at the same time.

A dark shape against the pale light.

'The van's parked just around the corner.' DCI Bell motioned with his head.

For the briefest of moments, Pete and Bream exchanged glances, then bent down to haul Grigson up to his feet, not a phantom any more but a woozy, stinking man in a dirty sheepskin coat. His left eye had closed up where his injury had started to swell, his head lolled down on his chest. They pushed him towards the door and he stumbled like the walking dead.

Bell put his hand on Pete's chest. 'Stay here a minute,' he said. 'You go on, Bream.'

Bell waited until Bream was out of earshot before he crossed the threshold, walked over to where the dead girl lay. No flicker of emotion over the face of this senior detective, this old war hero, as he studied the corpse. Just a regretful shaking of his head. Pete would never know how long the DCI had been standing there, listening to him and Bream talk. Never be able to read what was going on behind those hard grey-green eyes.

'Have you recovered *all* of the missing photographs now, sir?' he said instead.

Bell continued to stare at the corpse.

'Sampson Marks,' he said, 'you will be pleased to know, is enjoying his last moments of liberty. Thanks to the continued efforts of both Bream and yourself, the case against him is now complete. He will be arrested and charged within the hour. You are an exceptional detective, Bradley, as I said to you before.'

'An honourable Coldstreamer,' said Pete.

'But I'm afraid,' Bell said softly, 'old army mottos only stretch so far.'

Pete realised he was staring down the barrels of a neat little pistol, so small it was almost hidden in the cuff of the DCI's coat.

'Then you'll want to make sure the negatives are kept safe,' Pete said, dragging his eyes upwards to meet Bell's, 'out of harm's way. Won't you, sir?'

A second stretched out like an elastic band, as Pete's mind spiralled backwards, seeing Vera Barton's white face in the Warwick Castle, the spooked reflection of Jack in her eyes. Coulter sitting in the lamplight in his living room, closing his hand over Pete's fist. Joan in the hospital holding Jim in her arms. Mavis McGruder's children, their faces pressed against a windowpane in Lancaster Road, waiting for a mammy who was never coming home. A record spinning round on the turntable of Mathilde Bressant's empty flat, coffee granules still in the cups. Margaret Rose Stephenson in the glow of the coffee stand on Bayswater Road. Ernie Tidsall, shaking under his own spotlights. Susannah Houghton, bending over a black girl, already dead in her eyes. Bronwyn Evans taking a last drink as The Chopper put his arm around her. Simon Fitzgerald with his hand on a showgirl's arse, fear and paranoia dancing across his face. Sir Alex Minton and Lord Douglas Somerset, Harold Wesker and George Steadman, laughing in the lights of Teddy's club. Teddy himself at the bar, offering him a drink. And little Bobby Clarke, lying under a willow tree, the summer air all still around her. Dad walking in front of him, walking towards the river, looking back and putting his big paw of a hand, calloused by the years spent digging under the earth, around Pete's tiny fingers singing: '*Willow, weep for me*'…

He heard the click of the safety catch, shut his eyes. The wind howled through the air vents like the screaming of the dead.

'Put it down, sir.'

Opened his eyes again to see Bream standing behind Bell, pressing a pistol behind the DCI's ear. 'Now,' Bream hissed.

'Bream?' Confusion spread across Bell's face as he lowered his arm. 'What's the meaning…'

'I'm not working for you.' Bream snaked his arm around the DCI's shoulder, took the gun from out of his hand. 'I never was.'

He released the safety catch of his own pistol, a smile playing across his face.

'How does it feel, *sir?*' he asked. 'How do you like it?'

Bell stared at Pete, fear in his eyes as well as outrage. 'Bradley,' he said, 'do something. Can't you see what's happening? He's still in league with Grigson…'

'No sir.' The smile vanished from Bream's face. 'I'm working for Detective Chief Inspector Alan Ponting, have been for the past six years. My brief was to discover how it was that Sampson Marks had become untouchable. Who was protecting him and why. DCI Ponting's very much looking forward to hearing your explanation.'

Beads of sweat had broken out across Bell's forehead, but he clenched his jaw, stared straight ahead.

'And I think you owe DS Bradley here an apology before we go,' Bream continued. 'He's a much better detective than you are. He's the only one that didn't take me for a mug.'

The relief that coursed through Pete's veins was so strong he had to stop himself from laughing out loud. He felt giddy, light-headed.

'Go on,' Bream said.

Bell's mouth was working but it was some time before anything came out.

'I'm sorry,' he said. 'I appear to have underestimated the pair of you.'

'That's right,' said Bream. 'You did.' He looked over Bell's shoulder at Pete.

'You'll excuse me for not offering you a lift back, but as you can see, my car's already chock full of villains.'

'What about...' Pete looked down at the woman's corpse.

'I'll see to it,' said Bream. 'You just get out of here.'

'But what about jack?'

Bream grimaced. 'I expect the bigger cogs in this wheel of ours will find a way of keeping him safe. Just as they'll do for DCI Bell here, I'm sure. This is all the justice we get, I'm afraid, Pete. That and the knowledge that we kept our own hands clean.'

Pete nodded. Stooped down to retrieve his torch and as he did, he couldn't stop himself from taking the apple out of the girl's mouth and hurling it into the far corner of this makeshift mausoleum, from closing her eyes and offering up a silent prayer for her soul.

'Stay lucky, Pete,' said Bream.

44

The Carnival is Over

The dial slips…

Another burst of static and Holland Park Avenue dissolves, takes her with it, leaving me standing in a long red corridor, at the bottom of this house, this big white house in Kensington. On the threshold of a room that throbs like a big, beating heart, my fingers on the metal of the door handle, my wrist turning.

'My father's house has many rooms.' Jenny's voice in my mind as the door opens.

My eyes travel around his lair. Take in the rack with all the straps. The hooks for all the whips and paddles, the leather hoods and restraints. The coat-stand draped with a long black cape and long blonde wig and behind it, surrounded by red velvet curtains and candelabras, the blasphemous altar itself.

Strange markings are carved all over it, signs I cannot decipher, rude hieroglyphics spelling out unholy creeds. All the walls painted red and in the centre of all this, a black and dreadful shape that begins to take human form, the form of a man sitting in a black leather chair. A light switches on behind his head and projects a beam out in front of him, a screen above the altar, showing a silent film.

A little boy and a little girl, both with white-blond hair, playing in the garden that surrounds this house, underneath the tall pine trees, the trees that bend in the south-easterly wind, bend to protect the lair beneath.

A little boy and a little girl in bright sunshine, skipping under the trees, turning to laugh at the camera with two pairs of identical eyes. His eyes, not their mothers'.

He sits and he watches. Sits there naked, a man I have seen in the papers so many times, a man remaking London to his own design, now naked, red scores across his shoulders and his hair no longer neat, his teeth no longer clean, tears streaming down his face.

On the black tiled floor beside him, scores and scores of photographs ripped from inside brown envelopes. Every one of them identical. A little boy and a little girl with white-blond hair in the bright sunshine, smiling back at him with his eyes, his eyes…

The picture in the film starts to tear, starts to burn, burn into a black hole and then something else emerges, a flame from within the blackness. Margaret Rose Stephenson in her dogtooth check coat, holding up a candle before her. 'Rejoice not in iniquity,' she says, her voice sounding out loud as she steps from out of the frame and through the red wall to stand in front of him, 'but rejoice in truth.'

He looks at her with wild eyes, his hair falling in sweat-soaked strands across his forehead, veins pulsing at his temples like worms. 'But you're not here!' he screams. Reaches down and picks up one of the photographs from off the floor, holds it up to her candle.

'Whether there be prophecies…' His head cracks round as another voice fills the room. Mathilde Bressant in her black sweater and pencil skirt, standing underneath the coat-stand, playing idly with the strands of the blond wig in her hands. '…they shall fail.'

He bares his teeth, streaked and stained in blood.

'You are not here!' he repeats, throwing the picture towards her.

'Whether there be tongues,' Mavis lounging sideways on the altar in her grey suit, her flick knife snapping open in her hand, winking at him, 'they shall cease.'

He gets to his feet, slips on the black tile floor, falls into the piles of photographs. 'None of you are here!' he rages, picking up handfuls and throwing them into the air.

'Whether there be knowledge,' Jeanette White leaning against the rack in her new turquoise twinset, raising a pint glass full of coins towards him, 'it shall vanish away.' She smiles and turns the glass upside down, pouring the coins over his head.

'For we know in part,' the woman I have just left on Holland Park Avenue now standing behind him in her herringbone coat, holding a small silver bell that she rings above his head, 'and we prophesy in part.'

He staggers to his feet, in the middle of the circle they have made around him, clenches his fists and throws back his head. 'None of you are here!' he bellows and the red walls shake at his fury, the sound of interference, the radio starting to hiss as the women shimmer and then disappear. He begins to laugh, long beads of drool stringing from the corners of his mouth. Reaches down, but as his fingers touch the photographs, there is another loud burst of feedback and a sudden flash of light.

'I am here,' she says, dressed in white, hovering above him with the blue light pouring out of her, enveloping the room. 'Daddy dear.'

He looks up at her, his face contorted with horror and desire. Reaches out his hand to try and touch her but it goes straight through her, her laughter pealing out of her, echoing around the walls, the room beginning to shake again, the sound of a howling wind.

'When I was a child, I spoke as a child, I understood as a child, I thought as a child,' Jenny's voice cutting through the gale, 'but now I have put away childish things.'

He staggers, clutches his chest, and as he does so, Jenny rises to the top of the room, filling the place with a blinding light.

'And now abideth faith, hope, Love,' her voice so loud now that *the walls are starting to crumble, 'these three; but the greatest of these is Love.'*

The walls collapsing and the last thing I see is him falling, screaming, into the void of blackness that opens up beneath him.

'This is where I've been keeping them,' the dapper little old man opened the door and turned on the light. 'I think you'll find they're all in order. Please, come in, have a good look around.'

I walked into the room, my eyes travelling from floor to ceiling. A room full of pictures, collages and canvases, dazzling in their colour and beauty. All the work that Jenny had produced at St Martin's, the pictures she had painted in Italy, she had entrusted to the care of her former tutor Murray Partridge. It was all in the letter she had left for me.

I had been bed-bound for two weeks after our visit to her parents' house, exhausted by the fever that had burned through me that afternoon and into the night that followed. Jenny had called a doctor out for me, then sent someone else to come and look after me, bring me the envelope that contained the letter. There was nothing more she could do herself – her contractions had already started.

My eyes took in sketches of nudes, life-drawings from the late fifties, in pencil and charcoal or sometimes with a colour wash, drawn in a draughtsman's hand that rendered them three-dimensional with deceptively skilful ease. The nudes becoming more Cubist as her style developed, but still recognisably women, generously proportioned, coloured so as to make the skin seem to glow off the canvas.

Montages featuring American car number plates, Coca-Cola bottle tops and a badge proclaiming *I love Elvis*. Icarus falling from the sun, first sketched in charcoal, then painted in oil, bright blue and yellow, the colours like a stained-glass window. An actual pastiche of a stained-glass window, the figure of the Queen of Sheba at its centre.

More collages: Japanese flags and American pulp paperback covers, Edwardian fashion plates, planets hovering over purple skies and enormous pin-up women rising over cathedrals. Jean-Paul Belmondo with a huge red rose on the top of his hat. Marilyn Monroe and Mata Hari. Vivid reds and clashing purples, Surrealism to the untrained eye, but now that I knew her real story, Jenny's singular purpose leapt out at me, her grasp of humour and contradiction wise beyond her years.

Then there was a portrait of Dave, leaning forwards, his chin resting on his knuckles, staring at her with laughter in his eyes. The image was almost as clear and precise as a photograph, with a blue wash for a backdrop and then, on a red curtain above him, four slightly stretched caricatures of her own face laughing back.

Most movingly of all, a self-portrait from 1958. Something slightly askew with it, as there always is with self-portraits, the faces you know best always the hardest to capture. Jenny had been brutal to herself, coarsening her features, her hair pulled back from her face in a rough ponytail, an ungroomed look I had never seen in life. But her eyes so big and full of pain and sorrow, they were the focus of it. Jenny looking deep into her own soul and offering it up to the canvas.

'Isn't she beautiful?' said Mr Partridge, dabbing at his eyes with a handkerchief.

'I never realised,' I said, feeling like an explorer, long in the desert, who had stumbled through a crevice into a fantastical lost world.

If you have opened this letter, she had written, *then it means I am no longer with you. So I am afraid I'm going to have to ask you yet another favour...*

Jenny had safely delivered her daughter, Martha Jane Mannings, that same evening. She had been able to hold the baby, make sure she had all her fingers and toes, before she passed from this world to the next. She didn't have glandular fever. She had a rare and malignant form of leukaemia that her pregnancy precluded her from being treated for. Shortly after giving birth she had begun to haemorrhage and there was nothing they could do to staunch it. It happened so quickly and she was already unconscious, so she wouldn't have suffered, I was told.

Unlike her father, who, shortly after his return home, had suffered a massive stroke and fallen into a coma. He had remained in an intensive care unit ever since, trapped in the limbo between life and death. The best possible place he could be.

Martha has another inheritance, you see, apart from her monetary one. And I wish you to be the guardian of it. Mr Murray Partridge was my tutor at St Martin's. Everything of worth that I have ever drawn or painted is in his keeping and now I would like to pass it on to you, to look after for Martha until she is twenty-one. Don't think me awful, Stella, but you are the only person I can trust not to get too sentimental about it, extract things from it for personal reasons, or try to sell any of it. When you see it all, I believe you will know why it's so important for her to have it.

Now I stood in Mr Partridge's flat in South Kensington, in the room he had kept just for her, understanding everything as the tears rolled down my face.

He took hold of my hand with his long, delicate fingers.

'It seems such a pity,' he said, 'that no one will ever get to see them now.'

'I don't know about that,' I said. 'I think I know a way that they can.'

The body of the eighth girl wasn't found until 16 February 1965. She was an Irishwoman called Coral Sweeney, who left a husband

and two children behind in Shepherd's Bush and further family in Dublin. They never got to see any justice done, never got to know who it was that had snatched away their wife, their mother, their daughter, their sister. Coral was discovered, a month and six days after she failed to come home, on a patch of wasteland on a factory estate in Acton, the place that Mavis had shown me. Strangely, the corpse showed no signs of decomposition – the man who had found her was overcome by how beautiful she looked. According to the coroner, she must have been kept in cold storage for all of that time.

At that point the head of the Stripper enquiry, Detective Constable Reginald Bell, announced his retirement, blaming the strain of the investigation for his decision. In the same newspaper, but much further towards the back, was a short report of a suicide. Former detective Ronald Grigson had left a note for his wife saying that he couldn't go on, before locking himself in the kitchen, fixing a tube to his gas supply and asphyxiating himself. His profession at the time of his death was given as a nightwatchman on the Swan Factory Estate.

DCI Bell was replaced by a man called Alan Ponting, the head of Scotland Yard's murder squad, who had just hit the headlines putting Sampson 'The Chopper' Marks behind bars. Ponting promised a speedy conclusion to the hunt but he would have no such result. The Stripper case was never solved, not officially, anyway.

Jack was gone, the dial stuck on static.

PS, Jenny had written at the end of her letter. *If you look in the Emile Zola book you so kindly lent me in hospital, you will find something that I took from you the very first day that we met. It was silly of me, only I wanted us to be friends so much that I thought if I took something personal of yours, then, like a witch, I could somehow make that happen.*

Inside the book were two pieces of card, which shielded something delicate, wrapped up in tissue paper. It was a poppy that I had found growing through a crack in the paving stones, on a street in Bloxwich that had been reduced by the Luftwaffe to a river of glass. Pa had watched me pick it and shown me how to preserve it.

We held the exhibition in March, when the first buds of spring were showing through. For her friends it was like another wake, but a more hopeful one than the distressing hours after her funeral had been. For once, we were all together – Dave shaking hands cautiously with an equally nervous Mannings, then both of them staring at the bundle in his arms, the bright blue eyes of Martha that were just like her mother's, and slowly beginning to smile, slowly letting their defences down as they took her through the treasures that had been left for her.

Jackie and Maria, the girl she had met in the Gateways Club, now the manageress of Brockett & Reade, now sharing the flat in Chelsea with her too. Lenny doing his usual showman's trick, talking to all the visitors and telling them about Jenny, putting his arm around Giles when it all got too much for him. The oldies hanging back, finding much to discuss between them; Cedric and Mya, Stanley and Mr Partridge.

Chris by my side, where he had been ever since Jenny sent him round to take care of me, repaying the favour I had done for her one hundredfold. Both of us amazed at the way that his gallery had come back to life. Back from the dead.

And Jenny in my mind's eye, white and glowing, like an angel.

This is how it all begins, and where it all ends.

Acknowledgements

This book would not have been possible without these books:

Tanky Challenor SAS & The Met by Harold Challenor and Alfred Draper
The Man Who Would be Bing by Ken Crossland
King's Road by Max Décharné
Straight From the Fridge, Dad by Max Décharné
Give the Anarchist a Cigarette by Mick Farren
London Blues by Anthony Frewin
Trouble in West Two by Kevin Fitzgerald
The Challenor Case by Mary Grigg
Memoir of a Fascist Childhood by Trevor Grundy
Tainted Love by Stewart Home
Absolute Beginners by Colin McInnes
City of Spades by Colin McInnes
Fighters by James Morton
Gangland Soho by James Morton
Stand on Me by Frank Norman
Found Naked and Dead by Brian O'Connell
Journal by Kate Paul
The Profession of Violence by John Pearson
Underworld Nights by Charles Raven

The Legendary Joe Meek by John Repsch
Nick of Notting Hill by Anthony Richardson
Jack of Jumps by David Seabrook
Now You See Her: Pauline Boty First Lady of British Pop by Adam Smith
Who Killed Freddie Mills? by Tony Van Den Bergh
Getting it Straight in Notting Hill Gate by Tom Vague
Groovy Bob by Harriet Vyner
and these films:
Beat Girl (dir: Edmond T Greville)
The Boys (dir: Sidney J Furie)
The Blue Lamp (dir: Basil Deardon)
The Killing of Sister George (dir: Robert Aldrich)
The L-Shaped Room (dir: Bryan Forbes)
Pop Goes The Easel (dir: Ken Russell)
Séance on a Wet Afternoon (dir: Bryan Forbes)
and the music of Joe Meek and Roy Orbison.

On the long, strange trip of writing, the following have been of invaluable assistance and inspiration, whether they know it or not: John Williams, Caroline Montgomery and Pete Ayrton for their faith; David Peace, David Knight and Ruth Bayer, David and Bianca Price, Roland Blaney, Paul Willetts, Pete Woodhead, Joe McNally, Max Décharné and Katja Klier, Ken and Rachel Hollings, Jay Clifton, Dr Theo Koulouris and the Tight Lip Group, Marc Glendening, David Fogharty and the Sohemian Society, Lydia Lunch, Terry Edwards, Gallon Drunk, Barry Adamson, Martyn Waites, Jake Arnott, Harriet Vyner, Michael Dillon, Stewart Home, Roger K. Burton, Charlie Gillett, Paolo Hewitt and James Morton for their wisdom; Matthew, Yvette, Billy and Tommy Unsworth, Ann Scanlon, Richard Newson, Ben Newbery, Emma and Paul Murphy, Lynn Taylor, Cath Meekin, Danny

Meekin, Frances Meekin, Eva Snee, Raphael Abraham, Helen and Richard Cox, Damjana and Predrag Finci, James Hollands and Dr Paddy, Kerry Sutch, Tommy Udo, Damon Wise, Mari Mansfield and Billy Chainsaw for their love and friendship; Chris Simmons, Andrew Clark, Ced Fabre, Suzy Prince and Ian Lowey at Nude, Estelle Chardac, Alan Kelly, Jane Bradley, Andrew Stevens and 3AM for their enthusiasm; Niamh Murray, Anna-Marie Fitzgerald, Rebecca Gray, Margaret Nicholls and Claudia Woodward for their understanding; Julian Ibbotson for my hair; the BCN connection for the nicotine; and finally but most importantly, Michael Meekin for everything.